FICTION

THE
ANGELS'
SHARE

BY J. R. WARD

THE BOURBON KINGS

The Bourbon Kings

THE BLACK DAGGER BROTHERHOOD SERIES

Dark Lover

Lover Eternal

Lover Awakened

Lover Revealed

Lover Unbound

Lover Enshrined

The Black Dagger Brotherhood: An Insider's Guide

Lover Avenged

Lover Mine

Lover Unleashed

Lover Reborn

Lover at Last

The King

The Shadows

The Beast

BLACK DAGGER LEGACY

Blood Kiss

NOVELS OF THE FALLEN ANGELS

Covet

Crave

Envy

Rapture

Possession

Immortal

THE ANGELS' SHARE

A BOURBON KINGS NOVEL

J. R. WARD

 NEW AMERICAN LIBRARY

NEW AMERICAN LIBRARY
Published by New American Library,
an imprint of Penguin Random House LLC
375 Hudson Street, New York, New York 10014

This book is an original publication of New American Library.

First Printing, July 2016

LIBRARY OF CONGRESS CATALOGING-IN-PUBLICATION DATA:

Names: Ward, J. R., 1969– author.
Title: The angels' share/J. R. Ward.
Description: New York: New American Library, [2016] | Series: The Bourbon kings; 2 | Description based on print version record and CIP data provided by publisher; resource not viewed.
Identifiers: LCCN 2016019753 (print) | LCCN 2016013524 (ebook) | ISBN 9780698193048 (ebook) | ISBN 9780451475282 (hardcover)
Subjects: LCSH: Family-owned business enterprises—Fiction. | Families—Kentucky—Fiction. | Upper-class families—Fiction. | Bourbon whiskey—Fiction. | Family secrets—Fiction. | Domestic fiction. | BISAC: FICTION/Romance/Contemporary. | FICTION/Contemporary Women. | FICTION/Sagas.
Classification: LCC PS3623.A73227 (print) | LCC PS3623.A73227 A85 2016 (ebook) | DDC 813/.6—dc23
LC record available at https://lccn.loc.gov/2016019753

Printed in the United States of America
10 9 8 7 6 5 4 3 2 1

Jacket art: photo of car and trees by Car Culture/Getty Images; photo of house by Simon Watson/Getty Images; background texture © djgis/Shutterstock Images; author photo by Andrew Hyslop
Jacket design by Anthony Ramondo

Penguin
Random
House

Dedicated with love to:

LeElla Janine Scott

xxx

NOTE FROM THE AUTHOR

The "angels' share" is a term of art used in the bourbon-making industry. Nascent bourbon is put into charred oak barrels for its aging process, which can last up to twelve years or longer. As the barrels are stored in uninsulated facilities, the natural climate shifts in Kentucky's four glorious seasons cause the wood to expand and contract in the heat and the cold and thus interact with, and further flavor, the bourbon. This dynamic environment, with the additive of time, is the final alchemy that produces the Commonwealth's most distinctive, well-known and well-enjoyed product. It also results in a vital evaporation and absorption. This loss, which can average about two percent per year of the original volume, and which varies depending on the humidity of the environment, temperature swings, and the number of years of aging, among other things, is known as the angels' share.

Although there is a perfectly reasonable explanation for the depletion that occurs, a logical rationale, as it were, I love the romantic notion that there are angels in the warehouses of these venerable Kentucky distilleries, enjoying a tipple as they float above the earth. Perhaps it is a mint julep during Derby when it's warm, and then a bourbon up neat during the cold months of winter. Maybe they're using it to make pecan pie or to spice up their chocolates.

NOTE FROM THE AUTHOR

The functions for a good bourbon, as I am coming to learn, are endless.

I also think the term can apply to the weathering that changes us all over time. As the heat and cold of our experiences, our destinies, expand and contract our emotions, our thoughts, our memories, we are, like fine bourbon, a different product at the end—and there is a sacrifice involved: We are made of the same core elements we were at first constructed of, but we are never the same afterward. We are permanently altered. If we are lucky and we are smart and we are freed at the right time, we are improved. If we are aged too long, we are ruined forever.

Timing, like fate, is everything.

Virginia Elizabeth Bradford Baldwine, also known as Little V.E.:
Widow of William Baldwine, mother of Edward, Max, Lane, and Gin Baldwine, and a direct descendant of Elijah Bradford, the originator of Bradford bourbon. A recluse with a chemical dependency on prescription pills, there are many reasons for her addiction, some of which threaten the very fabric of the family.

William Wyatt Baldwine: Deceased husband of Little V.E. and father, with her, of Edward, Max, Lane, and Gin Baldwine. Also father of a son by the family's now deceased controller, Rosalinda Freeland. Also the father of an unborn child by his son Lane's soon-to-be-ex-wife, Chantal. Chief executive officer of the Bradford Bourbon Company when he was alive. A man of low moral standards, great aspirations, and few scruples, whose body was recently found on the far side of the Falls of the Ohio.

Edward Westfork Bradford Baldwine: Eldest son of Little V.E. and William Baldwine. Formally the heir apparent to the mantle of the Bradford Bourbon Company. Now a shadow of his previous self, the result of a tragic kidnapping and torture engineered by his own father, he has turned his back on his family and retired to the Red & Black Stables.

DRAMATIS PERSONAE

Maxwell Prentiss Baldwine: Second eldest son of Little V.E. and William Baldwine. Black sheep of the family who has been away from Easterly, the historic Bradford estate in Charlemont, Kentucky, for years. Sexy, scandalous, and rebellious, his return to the fold is problematic for a number of people in and outside of the family.

Jonathan Tulane Baldwine, known as "Lane": Youngest son of Little V.E. and William Baldwine. Reformed playboy and consummate poker player in the throes of a divorce from his first wife. With the family's fortunes in turmoil and embezzlement rife at the Bradford Bourbon Company, he is forced into the role of family leader and must rely now more than ever on his one true love, Lizzie King.

Virginia Elizabeth Baldwine, soon-to-be Pford, known as "Gin": Youngest offspring and only daughter of Little V.E. and William Baldwine. A rebellious contrarian who thrives on attention, she has been the bane of her family's existence, especially as she had a child out of wedlock during her college years and barely graduated. She is on the verge of marrying Richard Pford, the heir to a liquor distributing company and fortune.

Amelia Franklin Baldwine: Daughter of Gin and Gin's one true love, Samuel T. Lodge. A student at Hotchkiss School, she is a chip off her mother's block.

Lizzie King: Horticulturist who has worked at Easterly for nearly a decade and has kept its gardens nationally renowned showcases of rare specimen plants and flowers. In love with Lane Baldwine and fully committed to their relationship. Not into the drama of the family, however.

Samuel Theodore Lodge III: Attorney, sexy Southern gentleman, stylish dresser, and pedigreed, privileged bad boy. The only man who has ever gotten through to Gin. Has no idea that Amelia is his daughter.

DRAMATIS PERSONAE

Sutton Endicott Smythe: Newly elected CEO of the Sutton Distillery Corporation, Bradford Bourbon Company's biggest rival in the marketplace. In love with Edward for years, she has excelled professionally, but stagnated in her personal life—in large measure because no one compares to Edward.

Shelby Landis: Daughter of a thoroughbred racing legend whose father, Jeb, mentored Edward when it came to horses. A hardworking, strong woman, she takes care of Edward—even when he doesn't want her to.

Miss Aurora Toms: Easterly's head chef for decades, capable of serving up soul food or Cordon Bleu cooking with a strong hand and a warm heart. Suffering from terminal cancer. Maternal force in Lane's, Edward's, Max's, and Gin's lives and the true moral compass for the children.

Edwin "Mack" MacAllan: Master Distiller of the Bradford Bourbon Company. Cultivating a new strain of yeast, he is racing against time and limited resources to keep the stills running. Hasn't been in love with a woman for a long time, if ever. Married to his job.

Chantal Blair Stowe Baldwine: Lane's soon-to-be-ex-wife. Pregnant with William Baldwine's illegitimate child. A beauty queen with all the depth of a saucer, she is threatening to expose the paternity of her unborn baby as a way to get more money from Lane in the divorce proceedings.

Rosalinda Freeland: Former controller for the Bradford Family Estate. Committed suicide in her office in the mansion by taking hemlock. Mother to Randolph Damion Freeland, eighteen, whose father is William Baldwine.

THE
ANGELS'
SHARE

Charlemont Courier Journal

WILLIAM W. BALDWINE

Mr. William Wyatt Baldwine passed into the loving arms of his Lord and Savior two days prior. A world-renowned businessman, philanthropist and civic leader, he had served as Chief Executive Officer of the Bradford Bourbon Company for thirty-six years. Over the course of his tenure, he ushered in a new era of bourbon appreciation, and took the company to over one billion dollars in annual revenue.

A devoted family man, he is survived by his loyal wife, Virginia Elizabeth Bradford Baldwine, and his beloved children, Edward Westfork Bradford Baldwine, Maxwell Prentiss Baldwine, Jonathon Tulane Baldwine and Virginia Elizabeth Baldwine, and his beloved granddaughter, Amelia Franklin Baldwine.

Visitation and private services are at the convenience of the family. In lieu of flowers, donations may be sent to the University of Charlemont in Mr. Baldwine's name.

ONE

Big Five Bridge
Charlemont, Kentucky

Jonathan Tulane Baldwine leaned out over the rail of the new bridge that connected Charlemont, Kentucky, with its closest Indiana neighbor, New Jefferson. The Ohio River was fifty feet below, the muddy, swollen waters reflecting the multicolored lights that graced each of the span's five arches. As he rose up onto the tips of his loafers, he felt as though he were falling, but that was merely an illusion.

He imagined his father jumping off this very ledge to his death.

William Baldwine's body had been found at the base of the Falls of the Ohio two days ago. And for all of the man's accomplishments in life, for all of his lofty pursuits, he had ended his mortal coil tangled and mangled in a boat slip. Next to an old fishing trawler. That had a resale value of two hundred bucks. Three hundred, tops.

Oh, the ignominy.

What had it been like to fall? There must have been a rushing breeze in the face as William had been fisted by gravity and pulled down to the water. Clothes must have flapped as flags, slapping against body and leg. Eyes must have watered, from gust or perhaps even emotion?

No, it would have been the former.

The impact had to have hurt. And then what? A shocked inhale that had sucked the river's foul waves in? A choking sense of suffocation? Or did a knockout render him blissfully unaware? Or . . . perhaps it had all ended with a heart attack from the adrenaline overload of the descent, a stinging pain in the center of the chest radiating down the left arm, preventing a lifesaving swim stroke. Had he still been conscious when the coal barge hit him, when that propeller had chewed him up? Certainly, by the time he went over the falls, he was dead.

Lane wished he knew for sure that the man had suffered.

To know that there had been pain, tremendous, agonizing pain, and also fear, a ringing, overwhelming fear, would have been a powerful relief, a balm to the swill of emotions that his father's watery death caused him to drown in even while he stood on dry land.

"Over sixty-eight million dollars you stole," Lane said into the uncaring wind, the disinterested drop, the bored current down below. "And the company's in even more debt. What the hell did you do with it? Where did the money go?"

There was no answer coming up at him, of course. And that would have been the same if the man were still alive and Lane were confronting him in person.

"And my wife," he barked. "You fucked my *wife*. Under the roof you shared with my mother—and got Chantal *pregnant*."

Not that Lane's marriage to the former Chantal Blair Stowe had been anything other than a certificate he'd been coerced into putting his name to. But at least he was owning that mistake and taking care of it.

"No wonder Mother is a drug addict. No wonder she hides. She must have known about the other women, must have known who and what you were, you bastard."

As Lane closed his eyes, he saw a dead body—but not his father's swollen, mottled mess of a corpse on that slab from when Lane had gone to the morgue to ID the remains. No, he saw a woman sitting upright in her office at the family's mansion, her sensible, modest skirt and button-down blouse arranged perfectly, her bobbed hair only a little mussed, grass-stained running shoes on her feet instead of the flats she had always worn.

There had been a horrible grimace on her face. The Joker's mad grin. From the hemlock she had taken.

He'd found that body two days before his father had jumped.

"Rosalinda is dead because of you, you sonofabitch. She worked for you in our house for thirty years, and you might as well have killed her yourself."

She was the reason Lane had found out about the missing money. The former controller for the family's household accounts had left a kind of suicide note behind, a USB drive with Excel spreadsheets showing the alarming withdrawals, the transfers to WWB Holdings.

William Wyatt Baldwine Holdings.

There were a good sixty-eight million reasons she had poisoned herself. All because Lane's father had forced her to do unethical things until her sense of decency had snapped her in half.

"And I know what you did to Edward. I know that was your fault, too. You set your own *son* up in South America. They kidnapped him because of you, and you refused to pay the ransom so they'd kill him. Business rival gone while you get to look like the grieving father. Or did you do it because he, too, suspected that you were stealing?"

Edward had survived, except Lane's older brother was now nothing but a ruined shell with an irregular heartbeat, no longer the heir apparent to the business, the throne, the crown.

William Baldwine had done so much evil.

And these things were only what Lane knew about. What else was out there?

Equally important was what to do about it all. What *could* he do?

He felt like he was at the helm of a great ship that had been turned to a rocky shore—right before its rudder snapped off.

With a quick surge of strength, he swung his legs up and over the heavy steel railing, his loafers slapping on the six-inch lip on the far side.

Heart pumping, hands and feet going numb, mouth drying out until he could not swallow, he held on behind his hips with an under-grip and leaned even farther into the abyss.

What had it felt like?

He could jump—or just step off . . . and fall, fall, fall until he knew for certain what his father had been through. Would he end up in the same boathouse slip? Would his body also find the propeller of a barge and be great white'd in the filthy fresh waters of the Ohio?

In his mind, clear as day, he heard his momma say in her deep Southern drawl, *God does not give us more than we can handle.*

Miss Aurora's faith had certainly seen her through more things than most mere mortals could bear. As an African-American growing up in the South in the fifties, she had faced discrimination and injustices he couldn't even imagine, and yet Miss Aurora had more than endured, triumphing in culinary school, running the gourmet kitchen at Easterly not just like a French chef, but better—while also mothering him and his brothers and sister as no one else had, becoming the soul of Easterly, the touchstone for so many.

The beacon that, until he had met his Lizzie, had been the only light on the horizon for him.

Lane wished he believed as his momma did. And oh, God, Miss Aurora even had faith in him, faith that he would turn this all around, save the family, be the man she knew he could be.

Be the man his father was not and never had been, no matter the trappings of his wealth and success.

Jump, he could just jump. And it was over.

Was that what his father had thought? With the lies and the embezzlement being exposed, with Rosalinda's death a harbinger for the dirge of discovery, had William come here because he alone knew the true extent of what he had done and the depth of the hole that had to be dug out? Had he recognized that the game was up, his time was coming, and even with all his financial acumen, he wasn't going to be able to solve the problem he'd created?

Or had he decided to fake his own death—and failed by succeeding?

Was somewhere, out there, perhaps in an offshore account or in a bank vault in Switzerland, under his name or another's, everything that had been siphoned off?

So many questions. And the lack of answers, coupled with the stress of having to fix it all, was the kind of thing that could drive you insane.

Lane refocused on the waters. He could barely see them from this height. In fact . . . he could see nothing but blackness with the merest hint of a shimmer.

There was, he realized, a certain siren call to the coward's way out, a pull, like gravity, to an end that he could control: One hard impact and it was all over and done with, the deaths, the deceit, the debt. Everything wiped clean, the festering infection that was going to hold no longer and was about to be unleashed publicly nothing to worry about anymore.

Had there been sleepless nights for his father? Regrets? When William had stood here, had there been a to-and-fro about should he/ shouldn't he fly for a few moments and be done with the terrible mess he had created? Had the man even once considered the ramifications of his actions, an over two-hundred-year-old fortune wiped out not even in a generation, but in a matter of a year or two?

Wind whistled in Lane's ears, that siren call.

Edward, his older, formerly perfect brother, was not going to clean all this up. Gin, his only sister, was incapable of thinking about anything other than herself. Maxwell, his other brother, had been MIA for three years now.

His mother was bedbound and drug-addled.

So everything was in the hands of a poker-playing, former manwhore with no financial, managerial, or relevant practical experience.

All he had, at long last, was the love of a good woman.

But in this horrible reality . . . even that wasn't going to help him.

*T*oyota trucks were not supposed to go seventy-five miles an hour. Especially when they were ten years old.

At least the driver was wide awake, even though it was four a.m.

Lizzie King had a death grip on the steering wheel, and her foot on the accelerator was actually catching floor as she headed for a rise in the highway.

She had woken up in her bed at her farmhouse alone. Ordinarily, that would have been the status quo, but not anymore, not now that Lane was back in her life. The wealthy playboy and the estate's gardener had finally gotten their act together, love bonding two unlikelies closer and stronger than the molecules of a diamond.

And she was going to stand by him, no matter what the future held.

After all, it was so much easier to give up extraordinary wealth when you had never known it, never aspired to it—and especially when you had seen behind its glittering curtain to the sad, desolate desert on the far side of the glamour and prestige.

God, the stress Lane was under.

And so out of bed she had gotten. Down the creaking stairs she had gone. And all around her little house's first floor she had wandered.

When Lizzie had looked outside, she'd discovered his car was missing, the Porsche he drove and parked beside the maple by her front porch nowhere to be seen. And as she had wondered why he had left without telling her, she had begun to worry.

Just a matter of nights since his father had killed himself, only a matter of days since William Baldwine's body had been found on the far side of the Falls of the Ohio. And ever since then Lane's face had had a faraway look, his mind churning always with the missing money, the divorce papers he had served on the rapacious Chantal, the status of the household bills, the precarious situation at the Bradford Bourbon Company, his brother Edward's terrible physical condition, Miss Aurora's illness.

But he hadn't said a thing about any of it. His insomnia had been the only sign of the pressure, and that was what scared her. Lane always made an effort to be composed around her, asking her about her work in Easterly's gardens, rubbing her bad shoulder, making her dinner, usually badly, but who cared. Ever since they had gotten the air cleared between them and had fully recommitted to their relationship, he had all but moved into her farmhouse—and as much as she loved having him with her, she had been waiting for the implosion to occur.

It would almost have been easier if he had been ranting and raving.

And now she feared that time had come—and some sixth sense made her terrified about where he had gone. Easterly, the Bradford Family Estate, was the first place she thought of. Or maybe the Old Site, where his family's bourbon was still made and stored. Or perhaps Miss Aurora's Baptist church?

Yes, Lizzie had tried him on his phone. And when the thing had rung on the table on his side of the bed, she hadn't waited any longer after that. Clothes on. Keys in hand. Out to the truck.

No one else was on I-64 as she headed for the bridge to get across the river, and she kept the gas on even as she crested the hill and hit the decline to the river's edge on the Indiana side. In response, her old truck picked up even more speed along with a death rattle that shook the wheel and the seat, but the damn Toyota was going to hold it together because she *needed* it to.

"Lane . . . where are you?"

God, all the times she had asked him how he was and he'd said, "Fine." All those opportunities to talk that he hadn't taken her up on. All the glances she'd shot him when he hadn't been looking her way, all the time her monitoring for signs of cracking or strain. And yet there had been little to no emotion after that one moment they'd had together in the garden, that private, sacred moment when she had sought him out under the blooms of the fruit trees and told him that she'd gotten it wrong about him, that she had misjudged him, that she was prepared to make a pledge to him with the only thing she had: the deed to her farmhouse—which was exactly the kind of asset that could be sold to help pay for the lawyers' fees as he fought to save his family.

Lane had held her, and told her he loved her—and refused her gift, explaining he was going to fix everything himself, that he was going to somehow find the stolen money, pay back the enormous debt, right the company, resurrect his family's fortunes.

And she had believed him.

She still did.

But ever since then? He had been both as warm and closed off as a space heater, physically present and completely disengaged at the same time.

Lizzie did not blame him in the slightest.

It was strangely terrifying, however.

Off in the distance, across the river, Charlemont's business district glowed and twinkled, a false, earthbound galaxy that was a lovely lie, and the bridge that connected the two shores was still lit up in spring green and bright pink for Derby, a preppy rainbow to that promised land. The good news was that there was no traffic, so as soon as Lizzie was on the other side, she could take the River Road exit off the highway, shoot north to Easterly's hill, and see if his car was parked in front of the mansion.

Then she didn't know what she was going to do.

The newly constructed bridge had three lanes going in both directions, the concrete median separating east from west tall and broad for safety purposes. There were rows of white lights down the middle, and everything was shiny, not just from the illumination, but a lack of exposure to the elements. Construction had only finished in March, and the first lines of traffic had made the crossing in early April, cutting rush-hour delays down—

Up ahead, parked in what was actually the "slow" lane, was a vehicle that her brain recognized before her eyes properly focused on it.

Lane's Porsche. It was Lane's—

Lizzie nailed the brake pedal harder than she'd been pounding the accelerator, and the truck made the transition from full-force forward to full-on stop with the grace of a sofa falling out a second-story window: Everything shuddered and shook, on the verge of structural disintegration, and worse, there was barely any change in velocity, as if her Toyota had worked too hard to gain the speed and wasn't going to let the momentum go without a fight—

There was a figure on the edge of the bridge. On the very farthest edge of the bridge. On the lip of the bridge over the deadly drop.

"Lane," she screamed. "Lane!"

Her truck went into a spin, pirouetting such that she had to wrench her head around to keep him in her sights. And she jumped out before the Toyota came to a full stop, leaving the gearshift in neutral, the engine running, the door open in her wake.

"Lane! No! *Lane!*"

Lizzie pounded across the pavement and surmounted barriers that seemed flimsy, too flimsy, given the distance down to the river.

Lane jerked his head around—

And lost one hold of the rail behind him.

As his grip slipped, shock registered on his face, a flash of surprise . . . that was immediately replaced by horror.

When he fell off into nothing but air.

Lizzie's mouth could not open wide enough to release her scream.

TWO

Poker.

As Lane found himself with nothing between his feet and the Ohio River, as his body went into a free fall, as a sickening burst of fight or flight blasted, too late, through his veins . . . his mind latched on to a poker game he'd played at the Bellagio in Las Vegas, seven years before.

Good thing his descent had gone into slow motion.

There had been ten sitting around the high-stakes table, the buy-in had been twenty-five thousand, and there had been two smokers, eight bourbon drinkers, three with sunglasses on, one with a beard, two wearing baseball caps, and a so-called preacher in an oddly proportioned white silk suit that Elvis might have worn in the eighties—if the King had put up the peanut butter and banana sandwiches and lived long enough to experience the Me Decade's punk influence.

More importantly, as it turned out, there had been a former Navy officer two seats over from Lane, and soon enough, as people had dropped out, the pair of them had ended up with nobody between them. The former solider had had no tell to speak of, likely the result of being in far more deadly situations for a living than a green felt table and a padded stool. He'd also had strange, pale green eyes and a deceptively unassuming presence.

And it was strange to think that that guy, who Lane had ended up beating with a pair of kings, ace high, would be the last person he thought of.

Well, second to last.

Lizzie. Oh, God, he hadn't expected Lizzie to come and find him out there, and the surprise had caused what was going to be a fatal mistake.

Oh, God, *Lizzie*—

Back to the poker player. The guy had talked about his experiences on an aircraft carrier out in the ocean. How they had been trained to jump off heights of thirty, forty, fifty feet above the water. How, if you wanted a shot at living, there was a specific arrangement you needed to get your body into before you hit the surface.

It was all about the drag coefficient. Which you wanted to get as close to zero as possible.

Feet first was a bene; ankles crossed was a necessary—with the latter being critical so that your legs couldn't get snapped open like the wishbone on a Thanksgiving turkey. After that, you wanted one arm in front of your torso, with the hand grabbing the opposite elbow. The other arm you needed running up the middle of your chest, the palm splayed out over your mouth and nose. Head had to be on a level with the top of your spine or you risked concussion or whiplash.

Go in like a knife.

Otherwise, water, when hit at a great speed, had more in common with cement than anything you could pour into a glass.

Displace as little as possible.

Like a cliff diver.

And pray that your internal organs somehow slowed down at a rate that was compatible with their anchoring holds on your skeleton. Otherwise, the Navy guy had said, your insides were going to be a pepper jack omelet before it hit the pan, rushing to fill the spaces in your rib cage.

Lane locked himself in, using every muscle he had to turn himself into thin, strong steel, like that knife blade. The wind, God, the sound of the wind in his ears was like the roar of a tornado, and there was no flapping, or at least none that he was aware of. In fact, the falling had a strange sandblasting quality to it, like he was being hit by waves of particles.

And time stood still.

He felt like he hung forever in the Neverland between the solid footing he'd had and the watery grave that was going to claim him—just as it had his father.

"I love you!"

At least, that was what he meant to say. What came out of his mouth before he hit? No clue.

The impact was something he felt in his hips, his hips and his knees, as his legs jammed into his torso. And then there was the rush of cold. As pain lit up his motherboard, everything got cold, cold, cold.

The river claimed his chest and his head like a body bag being zipped up over a corpse, the black envelope closing, locking out fresh air, light, sound.

Muffled. So muffled.

Swim, he thought. *Swim.*

His arms failed to obey, but as his momentum slowed, his legs kicked out, and then, yes, his hands clawed at the water, which was soft now. He opened his eyes, or maybe they hadn't been shut—but he felt a sudden stinging there, acid against his pupils.

No breathing. As much as his instincts were to release the overload of sensation with an exhale, he hoarded his precious oxygen.

Kicking. Clawing.

He fought.

For life.

So he could get back to the woman he hadn't wanted to leave the first time—and hadn't meant to leave this time.

So he could prove that he was different from his father.

And so he could change the bankrupted future that he feared was written on his family's gravestone.

. . .

*A*s Lane went off the bridge, Lizzie's first thought was that she was going after him. To the point where she nearly did a pole vault over the rail and leaped for the river herself.

But she stopped because she couldn't help him that way. Hell, she would probably land on him just as he came up for air. Assuming he did— oh, *God*—

Fumbling. Phone. Phone, she needed her—

She barely heard the screech of tires right next to her. And the only reason she looked at whoever had stopped was because her cell popped out of her palm and went flying in that direction.

"Did he jump!" the man shouted. "Did he jump—"

"Fell—" She snatched her phone from out of thin air before it hit the asphalt. "He fell!"

"My brother's a cop—"

"Nine-one-one—"

They both dialed at the same time, and Lizzie turned away to lift up on her toes and peer over the rail. She couldn't see anything down below because of the lights all around her and the tears she was blinking away. Her heart was pounding in fits and starts, and she had some vague idea that her hands and feet were tingling. Hot, her body was hot, as if it were high noon in July, and she felt as though she were sweating buckets.

Three rings. What if no one picked up—?

As she wrenched back around, she and the guy who had rushed over from his car looked at each other—and she had the strange sense that she was going to remember this moment for the rest of her life. Maybe he would, too.

"Hello!" she hollered. "I'm on the bridge, the Big Five Bridge! A man has—"

"Hello!" the man said. "Yeah, we have a jumper—"

"He didn't jump! He fell—what? Who cares about my name! Send someone—not to the bridge! Down below—downstream—"

"—that just went off the new bridge. I know you're on duty—you're under the bridge? Can you get someone—"

"—to pick him up! No, I don't know if he survived!" Then Lizzie paused even in her panic, and repeated the question she'd been posed. "Who was it?"

Even in this moment of crisis, she hesitated in giving out the name. Anything involving the Bradfords was news, not just in Charlemont, but nationally, and this jump—*fall*, damn it—was something she was sure Lane wasn't going to want on broadcast. Assuming he survived—

Screw it. This was life and death.

"His name is Lane Bradford—he's my boyfriend. I came out because . . ."

She babbled at that point and turned back to the drop. And then she was leaning out over the rail again, praying she could see his head breach the surface of the water. God, she couldn't see anything!

Lizzie hung up after she had given her name, her number, and as much as she knew. Meanwhile, the man was off his phone as well and he was talking to her, telling her that his brother, or his cousin, or frickin' Santa Claus was coming. But Lizzie wasn't hearing it. The only thing she knew was that she had to get to Lane, had to—

She focused on her beat-to-crap truck.

And then looked at Lane's 911 Turbo convertible.

Lizzie was behind the wheel of that Porsche a split second later. Fortunately, he'd left the key in the ignition, and the engine came alive as she punched in the clutch and cranked those horses over. Flooring the accelerator was a different deal entirely from her old Toyota, tires skidding out as she doughnuted the sports car and raced off—going in the wrong direction

Fine. Let the cops arrest her. At least she'd bring them down to the water.

A set of headlights coming at her got her to pitch the Porsche to the right, and the other vehicle's horn was like the terror in her head, a screaming distraction that might have derailed her but for her laser focus on getting to Lane.

Lizzie took the exit ramp at eighty miles an hour, and by some miracle, no one happened to be heading up it to get on the highway. At the bottom, she pulled another illegal turn and got herself heading the right way, but more traffic laws got broken as she hopped the curb, tore across a grass verge, and bottomed out on a two-laner that ran down to the river's edge.

Lizzie took the Porsche up to nearly a hundred miles an hour.

And then she slammed on the brakes.

One of the region's favorite ice cream parlors was located on the shore, in a Victorian house with a storied past—and in addition to slinging scoops, they also rented bikes . . . and boats.

She didn't park the 911 so much as dump it at the side of the road on the grass shoulder as cockeyed as a drunk's hat. She left the headlights on and facing across the water as she vaulted a fence and gunned across a shallow lawn for the floating docks. There, she found a variety of Boston Whalers, none of which had keys in them, of course—and one measly, tippy flat-bottom with a pull-start outboard.

Which, blessedly, somebody had not chained to the posts.

Lizzie jumped in, and it took her two yanks to get the engine cooking. Then she ripped off the tethers and headed out into the river, the tin can slapping against the waves and kicking spray into her face. With the dearth of artificial light, she could see a little, but not a lot—and the last thing she wanted was to run him over.

She had gone only a hundred yards or so into the river—which seemed to be the size of an ocean—when she saw the most miraculous thing on the horizon.

A miracle.

It was a miracle.

THREE

The Ohio River was so much colder than Lane could ever have imagined. And the shore was farther away, like he was swimming the English Channel. And his body heavier, as if there were cement blocks tied to his feet. And his lungs weren't working right.

The current was carrying him fast, but that was only good news if he wanted to go over the falls like his father had. And as luck would have it, the relentless draw was pulling him into the center of the channel, away from any kind of land, and he had to fight against it if he hoped to get to—

As a piercing illumination hit him from behind, he thought for a split second that his momma's faith had turned out to be real and her Jesus was coming to take him to the Pearly Gates.

"I got him! I got him!"

Okay, that voice sounded way too ordinary to be anything biblical—and the Southern accent was a telltale that it was probably a mortal and not God.

Spitting water out of his mouth, Lane rolled onto his back and had to put an arm over his eyes as he was blinded by the glare.

"He's alive!"

The boat that pulled up beside him was a good thirty feet long and had a cabin, and its engines were cut as the stern swung around toward him.

He was pulled over thanks to a net grappler, and then he helped himself out of the river and onto the platform over the propellers. Flopping on his back, he looked up at the night. He couldn't see the stars. The city's glow was too bright. Or maybe his eyes were just too clouded.

A man's face appeared in his vision. Gray beard. Shaggy hair. "We saw you jump. Good thing we was coming under—"

"Someone's approaching from starboard."

Lane knew without looking who it was. He just knew it. And sure enough, as the spotlight was manually spun in that direction, he saw his Lizzie in a flatboat coming at them, the flimsy, metal craft clapping against the water, her strong body crouched by the outboard motor, that high-pitched whine of the overworked little engine the perfect sound track to the panic on her face.

"Lane!"

"Lizzie!" He sat up and cupped his dripping hands to yell. "I'm all right! I made it!"

She pulled up like an expert right across the stern, and even though he was in wet clothes and cold to the bone, he jumped at her. Or maybe she jumped at him. It was probably the both of them.

He held her tight against him, and she held him back. And then she jerked away and punched him in the biceps so hard, she nearly knocked him back into the river.

"Ow!"

"What the hell were you doing up there—"

"I wasn't—"

"Are you out of your mind—"

"I didn't—"

"You almost killed yourself!"

"Lizzie, I—"

"I am so pissed off at you right now!"

The fishing boat was tipping back and forth as they stood with feet planted on the gunnels. And he was dimly aware that there were three fishermen popcorn-and-Coke'ing it on the larger vessel.

"I could just slap you!"

"Okay, if it'll make you feel better—"

"It won't!" Lizzie said. "Nothing is going to—I thought you were dead!"

As she began to cry, he cursed. "I'm sorry. I'm so sorry . . ."

He brought her back against him and held her tightly, stroking her spine and murmuring things he wasn't going to remember even if the moment itself was unforgettable.

"I'm so sorry . . . I'm so sorry . . ."

Typical of Lizzie, it wasn't long before she pulled herself together and looked up at him. "I really want to hit you again."

Lane rubbed his biceps. "And I'd still deserve it."

"Y'all okay?" one of the guys said as he tossed a faded towel that smelled like bait over. "Y'all need nine-one-one? Either one of you?"

"It was already called," Lizzie answered.

And yup, sure enough, there were flashing red and blue lights up on the bridge now, as well as ones coming down to the river's shore on the Indiana side, too.

Great, he thought as he wrapped himself up. Just frickin' great.

"We're going to be fine." Lane put out his hand. "Thank you."

The man with the gray beard shook what was offered. "I'm glad no one's hurt. You know, people, they jump from there. Just last week, this guy, he jumped and kilt himself. They found him down on the far side of the falls. In a boathouse."

Yes, that was my father, Lane thought.

"Really?" Lane lied. "There hasn't been anything in the press."

"It was my cousin's boathouse. Guess the guy was important or something. They ain't talking."

"Well, that's a shame. For the man's family, whoever they are."

"Thank you," Lizzie said to the guys. "Thank you so much for getting him out."

There was some conversation at that point, not that Lane paid much attention to it—other than them wanting him to keep the towel and him thanking them for it. And then he was lowering himself onto the bench in the middle and tucking everything he had into his torso to conserve body heat. Meanwhile, Lizzie restarted the outboard motor with a couple of powerful yanks and reversed them away, the sweet smell of gasoline and oil tinting the air and making him think of childhood summers. As they turned around, he glanced back at the bigger vessel.

And then laughed.

"What?" she asked.

"The boat's name." He pointed to the lettering on the stern. "Unbelievable."

Aurora, was spelled out in gold lettering.

Yup, somehow, even when she wasn't around, his momma was protecting him, saving him, supporting him.

"That is eerie," Lizzie said as she hit the gas and they slapped their way back to the shore.

Every time Lane blinked, he saw the abyss below the bridge, relived that moment when he went into a free fall. It was strange to realize that even though he was heading for solid ground with the woman he loved, he felt as though he was back in that no-man's land, all security gone, nothing but careless air between him and a hard, hard impact that he was fairly sure was going to kill him.

Focusing on Lizzie, he measured the strong lines of her face and her sharp eyes, the way her blond hair wisped on the breeze, the fact that she didn't care that he'd gotten her wet when they'd hugged.

"I love you," he said.

"What?"

He just shook his head and smiled to himself. His momma's name on that stern . . . his woman behind this wheel . . .

"Did you steal this boat?" he said more loudly.

"Yes," she hollered back. "I didn't care what it took. I was coming to get you."

As they pulled up to a dock, she maneuvered the boat like a boss, driving the outboard by pushing its handle in the opposite direction from where she wanted the bow to go, then reversing things with such skill that in spite of the current, the metal teacup just kissed the pylons.

Lane anchored the bow with a line, Lizzie took the stern, and then he held his palm out to her to help her onto the dock. She didn't come to him right away. Instead, she shoved her hand into her loose jacket. Taking out something, she tucked it into the gas cap.

As she jumped onto the dock by herself, he said, "What was that?"

"A five-dollar bill. I used some of their gas."

For a moment, Lane simply stood before her, even though he was cold to the bone, and they were trespassers, and he'd just taken a swim in the Ohio.

Oh, and then there were the cops pulling up in front of them.

And that little free fall, am-I-going-to-die thing.

Reaching out, he cupped her beautiful face in the illumination from the headlights. Lizzie was everything his family was not. On so many levels.

It was one of the many reasons he loved her. And it was strange, but he felt an urgency to make things permanent between them.

"What?" she whispered.

He started to sink down on one knee. "Lizzie—"

"Oh, God, are you passing out?" She dragged him back to his feet and rubbed his arms. "You're passing out! Come on, let's get you to an ambulance—"

"Put your hands where we can see them," came the demand. "Now!"

Lane looked into all those lights and cursed. There were times and places to ask your woman to marry you. In the crosshairs of the Charlemont Metro Police, soaked with dirty water, and two minutes after a death spiral into the Ohio?

Not. It.

"Hey," one of the cops said. "I know who that is. That's Lane Bradford—"

"Shut up," somebody hissed.

"They did this article on him—"

"Hicks, shut it."

As Hicks went quiet, Lane lifted both arms and stared into the brilliant illumination. He could see nothing of what was ahead. Kind of apt, really.

"Can they arrest me for taking that boat?" Lizzie whispered as she put her palms up.

"I'll take care of it," Lane said quietly. "Don't worry."

Shit.

FOUR

Easterly, the Bradford Family Estate

"*I* hate you!"

As the youngest of the Bradford family's three living Virginia Elizabeths lunged for a lamp, Gin Baldwine, soon-to-be Pford, did not make it. Probably for the best. The thing was made out of an Imari vase she had always been rather fond of and the silk shade was handmade with her initials embroidered in real gold thread.

It would have been a pity to destroy such beauty—and God knew there would be nothing but shards and shreds left after she was done throwing it.

What stopped her was her fiancé's hand grabbing at her hair, catching hold, and whiplashing her right off her stilettoes. After a brief moment of weightlessness, which was kind of fun, there was a smack down that stung her shoulder blades, clapped her teeth together and reminded her that the coccyx was in fact a very unnecessary body part.

The resulting pain down there also took her back to her father spanking her as a child with one of his alligator skin belts.

Of course, she had resolutely refused to learn anything from those slap-happy sessions or alter her behavior in any way. Just to prove he didn't run her life.

And yes, things had worked out so damned well since then.

Richard Pford's thin, angular face came over the top of her head. "Hate me all you like, but you will *not* disrespect me like this again. Are we clear."

He was still pulling on her hair, forcing her neck and spine to counter his strength or risk her being decapitated.

"What I do or do not do"—she grunted—"will not change anyone's opinion of you. Nothing ever has."

As she glared at him, she also smiled. Behind those rat eyes of his, right now, he had gone on a little trip down memory lane, his low self-esteem running through the script of insults that had been ladled out at him while they had been classmates at Charlemont Country Day. Gin had been among the name-callers, very much a mean girl who had run in a pack. Richard, on the other hand, had been a scrawny, pimply kid with a grating sense of entitlement and a voice like Donald Duck. Not even his family's extraordinary wealth had saved him socially—or gotten him laid.

And indeed, nineties slang had yielded such stellar nomenclature, hadn't it: loser, scrub, tool, dork, fucker.

Richard shook himself back into focus. "I expect my wife to be waiting at home for me when I have a business engagement she is not welcome at." He yanked on her hair. "I do *not* expect her to be on a jet to Chicago—"

"You're living in *my* home—"

Richard snapped his hold on her again, like he was schooling a dog with a choke chain. "*Especially* when I told her she was not permitted to use any of my planes."

"But if I'd taken a Bradford one, how could I have been sure you'd find out about it?"

The look of confusion on his face was worth everything that was happening—and what was going to come next.

Gin tore herself free and got back on her feet. Her Gucci dress was twisted about, and she debated whether to leave it that way or straighten it.

Disheveled, she decided.

"The party was divine," she said. "So were both the pilots. You certainly know what kind of men to hire."

As Richard exploded up from the floor and raised his hand over his shoulder, she laughed. "Be careful with the face. My make-up artist is good, but there are limits to concealers."

In her mind, throughout her body, crazy mania sang like a choir at the altar of madness. And for a split second she thought of her mother, lying in her bed just down the hall, as incapacitated as any homeless addict on the streets.

When a Bradford became hooked on opiates, however, they got them from their private physician and it was Porthault rather than cardboard, private nurse rather than shelter. "Medication" instead of "drugs."

Whatever the vocabulary, one could appreciate how it might be better and easier than dealing with reality.

"You need me," Richard hissed. "And when I buy something, I expect it to function properly. Or I throw it out."

"And anyone who wants to be the governor of the Commonwealth of Kentucky someday should know that beating his wife presents a terrible PR problem."

"You'd be surprised. I'm a Republican, remember."

Over Richard's shoulder, the oval mirror above one of her pair of eighteenth-century Italian Louis XV commodes presented her with a perfectly framed image of the two of them: her with her lipstick smudged like blood on her jaw, her blue dress hiked up to the lace tops of her thigh highs, her brunette hair in messy waves like the halo of the whore she was; him in his old-fashioned nightshirt, his hair eighties Wall Street–side part, his Ichabod Crane body strung like a wire about to get tripped. All around them? Silk drapes like ball gowns next to windows tall as waterfalls, antiques worthy of the Victoria and Albert Museum, a bed as big as a reception hall with a monogrammed duvet.

She and Richard in their dishabille and their disregard for polite discourse were the wrong note in a sonata, the tear through the center of a Vermeer, the flat tire on a Phantom Drophead.

And oh, Gin loved the ruination. Seeing her and Richard together, both trembling on the edge of insanity, scratched the itch that she had been seeking to redress.

They were each right, however. With her family's abrupt reversal of financial fortune and his gubernatorial ambitions, they were the union of a parasite and its host, locked in a precarious relationship based on his decades-old crush on the most popular debutante in Charlemont and her unexpectedly finding herself on the red side of the ledger.

Still, marriages had been built on far lesser bases . . . like the illusion of love, for example, the lie of fidelity, the poisonous Kool-Aid of "fate."

At once, she became tired.

"I am going to bed," she announced as she turned away to her bathroom. "This conversation bores me."

When he grabbed her this time, it was not by the hair. "But I am not done with you."

As he spun her around and pulled her against him, she yawned in his face. "Do be quick, will you. Oh, that's right. You're nothing but fast—it's the only thing I enjoy about having sex with you."

FIVE

Lizzie's Farmhouse
Madisonville, Indiana

"You didn't actually think I was there to jump, did you."

As the man Lizzie loved spoke up from the other end of her sofa, she tried to pull herself together . . . and when she got nowhere with that, she settled for stroking the handmade quilt she'd tugged across her legs. Her little living room was in the front of the farmhouse, and had a big six-paned window that looked out onto her porch and across her front lawn and dirt driveway. The decor was rustic and cozy, her collection of antique farm tools mounted on the walls, her old-fashioned upright piano across the way, the braided throw rugs done in primary colors to bring out the color of the wooden floors.

Typically, her sanctuary never failed to calm her. That was a stretch this dawn, however.

What a night. It had taken about two hours to tell the police what had happened, apologize, get the cars sorted, and head back.

If it hadn't been for Lane's friend, Deputy Sheriff Mitchell Ramsey, they'd still be out at the river's edge by the Victorian ice cream place—or maybe down at the police station. In handcuffs. Getting strip searched.

Mitch Ramsey had a way of taking care of difficult situations.

So, yes, now they were here on her couch, Lane showered and in his favorite U.Va. sweatshirt, her changed into one of his button-down shirts and some leggings. But jeez, even though it was May in the South, she felt cold in her bones. Which was the answer to Lane's question, wasn't it.

"Lizzie? Did you think I was going to jump?"

"Of course not."

God, she was never going to forget the image of him on the far side of the rail, turning to look at her . . . losing his grip . . . plummeting out of sight—

"Lizzie—"

Throwing up her hands, she tried to keep her voice level. Failed. "If you weren't going to jump, what the hell were you doing out there? You were leaning over the drop, Lane. You were going to—"

"I was trying to find out what it was like."

"Because you wanted to kill yourself," she concluded through a tight throat.

"No, because I wanted to understand him."

Lizzie frowned. "Who? Your father . . . ?" But come on, like he was trying to figure out someone else? "Lane, seriously, there are other ways to come to terms with this."

For example, he could go to a shrink and sit on a different couch from this one. Which would decrease his chances of falling to his death down to zero as he tried to get a handle on what was going on in his life.

And as a bonus, she wouldn't have to worry about becoming a nautical felon.

Wonder if that five-dollar bill was still tucked into that gas cap, she thought.

Lane stretched out one of his arms like it was stiff and cursed as his elbow, or maybe shoulder, made a popping sound. "Look, now that Father is dead, I'm never going to have any answers. I'm stuck here, cleaning up his fucking mess, and I'm resentful as hell and I just don't get it. Anyone can say he was a shitty human being, and that is the truth . . . but that isn't an explanation of the details. And I was staring at your ceiling, not sleeping, and I couldn't stand it anymore. I went to the bridge, I went over the rail to stand where he had stood . . . because I wanted to see what he saw when he was there. I wanted to get an idea of what he'd felt. I wanted answers. There's nowhere else to go for them—and no, I was *not* there to kill myself. I swear on Miss Aurora's soul."

After a moment, Lizzie sat forward and took his hand. "I'm sorry. I just thought—well, I saw what I did, and you haven't been talking to me about any of this."

"What is there to say? All I'm doing is going around in circles in my head until I want to scream."

"But at least I'd know where you're at. The silence is scary on my end. Your mind is spinning? Well, so is mine."

"I'm sorry." He shook his head. "But I am going to fight. For my family. For us. And trust me, if I were going to commit suicide, the last way I'd end my life is in the same fashion he did. I don't want anything in common with that man. I'm stuck with the DNA, nothing I can do there. But I'm not going to encourage any further parallels."

Lizzie took a deep breath. "Can I help in some way?"

"If there was something you could do, I'd let you know. I promise. But it's all on me right now. I've got to find the missing money, pay back Prospect Trust, and pray to God I can keep the business going. Bradford Bourbon's been around for over two hundred years—it can't end now. It just can't."

As Lane turned to look out of that big window, she studied his face. He was, as her grandmother would have called it, a real looker. Classically handsome, with blue eyes the color of a clear fall sky, and dark hair that was thick between her fingers, and a body that was guaranteed to catch every eye in any room.

But it had not been love at first sight for her. Far from it. The Bradford family's ne'er-do-well youngest son had had pole marks all over him as far as she was concerned—although the truth was that under her disdain had been a vicious attraction she'd moved heaven and earth to ignore. And then they had gotten together . . . and she had fallen in love with him in typical *Sabrina* fashion.

Well, except in her case, the "staff" was a horticulturalist with a master's in landscape architecture from Cornell.

But then Chantal had gone to the press four weeks later and announced she was engaged to Lane, claiming the child she carried was his. That had ended things for Lizzie, and Lane had married the woman.

Only to disappear up North shortly thereafter.

Horrible. What a horrible time it had been. Following the break-up, Lizzie had done her best to keep working at Easterly and stay focused. But everyone noticed when Chantal suddenly wasn't pregnant anymore.

Come to find out later that the woman hadn't "lost" the baby. She had "taken care" of it at a private clinic up in Cinci.

Unbelievable. And thank God Lane was divorcing her.

Thank God also that Lizzie had seen the light when she had and allowed herself to trust the man, not the reputation. Talk about near misses.

"Sun's coming up," Lane murmured. "It's a new day."

His hand stroked its way up her bare foot and onto her ankle, lingering on her skin in a manner she wasn't sure he was aware of. He did that a lot, touching her absently, as if when his focus shifted away from her, his body was compelled to close the mental distance with physical contact.

"God, I love it out here." He smiled at the golden light that drew long shadows out on her lawn and across the fields that had just been seeded. "It's so quiet."

That was true. Her farmhouse with its tract of land and its distant neighbors was a world away from his family's estate. Out here, the only disturbances were plows off in the distance and the occasional rogue cow.

Easterly was never quiet, even when its rooms were silent. Especially now.

The debt. The deaths. The disorder.

"I just wanted to know what he experienced when he died," Lane said softly. "I want it to have hurt. I want him . . . to have hurt."

Lizzie pointed her toes to stroke his forearm. "Don't feel badly about that. The anger is only natural."

"Miss Aurora would tell me I should pray for him, instead. Pray for his soul."

"That's because your momma is a saint."

"Too right."

Lizzie smiled as she pictured the African-American woman who was more Lane's mother than the woman who had birthed him. Thank God for Miss Aurora's presence in his life. There were so few safe places to go in that huge historic house he'd been raised in, but that kitchen, filled with food both of the soul variety and the French kind, had been a sanctuary.

"I did think you were going to jump," she blurted.

He looked directly at her. "I have too much to live for. I have us."

"I love you, too," she whispered.

God, he seemed so much older than even a week before, when he had arrived on a private jet from his hideaway in Manhattan. He had come back to Easterly to make sure Miss Aurora was okay after she had collapsed. He had stayed home because of everything that had happened in such a short time, the trajectory of his family hitting an iceberg hidden in the currents of fate and destiny, the seemingly impenetrable hull of the Bradfords' two-hundred-year history, of their extraordinary financial and social position, pierced by a reversal of fortune from which a recovery seemed . . . impossible.

"We can leave." Lizzie arched her foot again. "We can sell this place and take the money and live a very nice life far away from all of this."

"Don't think I haven't considered it. And hey, I could support us by playing poker. It's not classy, but I'm learning that bills don't care where the money to cover them comes from." He laughed in a hard burst. "Although my family has been living off of liquor revenue all these years, so how should I ever judge?"

For a moment, her heart sang as she pictured the two of them on another farm in another state, tending a small patch of good, clean earth that yielded corn and carrots and tomatoes and green beans. She would spend her days working for a small city taking care of their municipal plantings. And he would become a teacher at the local high school and maybe coach basketball or football, perhaps both. Together, they would watch each other's faces grow lined from laughter and love, and yes, there would be children. Towheaded, straight-haired children, boys who would bring home tadpoles and girls who would climb trees. There would be driving permits and high school proms and tears when everybody went off to college and then holiday joy when the house would fill back up with chaos.

And when the sun finally set upon them, there would be a porch with a pair of rocking chairs on it, set side by side. When one passed on, the other would soon follow. Real Nicholas Sparks stuff.

No more private jets. No more jewels and oil paintings of so-and-so's great-great-great-grandfather. No more Easterly with its seventy-person staff and its acres of formal gardens and its unrelenting grind. No more parties and balls, Rolls-Royces and Porsches, fancy, soulless people smiling with empty eyes.

No more Bradford Bourbon Company.

Although the product itself had never been the problem.

Maybe he would even take her last name so that no one in their new life would know who he was, who his family was.

He would be as she herself was, an anonymous person living a modest life—and yes, there might not be majesty in her fantasy of the two of them. But she would take the simple graces of mediocrity over the empty grandeur of great money every day of the week. And twice on Sunday.

"You know, I can't believe he killed himself," Lane murmured. "It just doesn't seem like something he would do. He was far too arrogant for it—and hell, if the great William Baldwine *was* going to commit suicide, it would have been more fitting for him to put one of Alexander Hamilton's dueling pistols to his mouth and pull the trigger. But jumping off a bridge he'd considered 'garish'? Into water he wouldn't deign to give to a barn cat? It just doesn't make sense."

Lizzie took a deep breath. And dared to put into words something she herself had been wondering. "Are you . . . thinking maybe someone killed him?"

SIX

Red & Black Stables
Ogden County, Kentucky

Sweet smell of hay.

Oh, the sweet smell of hay and the stomping of hooves . . . and the ice-cold concrete of the aisle that ran between the mahogany-doored stalls.

As Edward Westfork Bradford Baldwine sat outside his thoroughbred stallion's sawdust-floored bedroom, his bony ass was suffering from a frigid recontouring, and he marveled at how, even in May, the stone was so cold. Granted, it was dawn, but the temperature outside was seventy even without the sun's help. One would think that the ambient benevolence of late spring would be more generous with its climatic attentions.

Alas, no.

Fortunately, he was drunk.

Lifting the bottle of—what was it? Ah, vodka. Fair enough—to his lips, he was disappointed to find such a light weight in his hand. There was only an inch left in the bottom and the thing had been three-quarters full when he had limped his way out here. Had he put all those ounces away? And damn it, the rest of his supply was at such a distance— although that was relative, he supposed. The caretaker's cottage where he stayed on the Red & Black thoroughbred breeding farm was no more than a hundred yards off, but it might as well have been miles.

He looked down at his legs. Even hidden under denim, the recon- structed, unreliable mess he had to ambulate upon was nothing more than a painfully thin pair of unhinged pins, his modest, size-eleven boots seeming like blown-up clown shoes in proportion. And then you added the inebriation and the fact that he had been sitting here for how long?

His only chance for more vodka was going to be clawing his way forth, dragging his lower body behind like a wheelbarrow that had fallen off its tire onto its side.

Not all was essentially nonfunctional, however. Tragically, his mind remained sharp enough to constantly spit images at him, the impact of the mental constructs like paintballs shot at his frail body.

He saw his brother Lane standing in front of him, telling him that their father was dead. His beautiful, crazy sister, Gin, wearing the mas- sive diamond of a cruel man upon her elegant hand. His beautiful, crazy mother abed and be-dazed, unaware of all that was transpiring.

His Sutton, who was not, in fact, his, and never would be.

And that was the main loop on his mental replay. After all, things before Edward had been tortured and not ransomed were a bit hazy.

Perhaps that was the solution to his inner demons. Booze didn't go far enough—but eight days in the jungle being beaten, starved, and taunted with his impending death had certainly turned the volume down on recollections that had come before his kidnapping. And as a bonus, he was unlikely to survive a second round of such ministrations—

The sound of a small pair of barn boots coming down at him had him rolling his eyes. When they stopped in front of him, he didn't bother looking up.

"You again," he said.

In reply to his cheerful greeting, Shelby Landis's voice was something out of a children's cartoon—or at least its feminine pitch was. Its intonation, as usual, was more drill sergeant than Cinderella.

"Let's getchup, here now."

"Let's leave me here, forever—and that is an order."

Up above Edward's head, behind the iron bars that kept the stallion from biting off pieces of human anatomy, Nebekanzer let out a whinny that sounded curiously close to a hello. Typically, the enormous black stallion uttered equine murder to anyone other than Edward.

And even his owner was never addressed with any kind of joy.

"We can do this the hard way or the harder way," Shelby maintained.

"A bevy of choices you present me with. How magnanimous of you."

And the contrarian in him wanted to be obstreperous just to find out what "harder" involved. Further, even in his weakened condition, most women of her diminutive height would have struggled to manhandle him, and that could have presented added fun. Shelby, however, had a body that had been honed by a lifetime of hours and hours of backbreaking work in and around thoroughbreds.

She was going to win this one. Whatever it was.

And his pride was all he had left with which to justify his manhood.

Although why he would care about even that, he had no clue.

Pushing himself upright was an exercise in hammer-to-nail, brutal strikes of pain battering him internally even with all the alcohol in his system. The grunting was an embarrassment, especially in front of an employee—who happened to have a good Christian's disdain of blasphemy, no sense of boundaries, and a dead sire to whom Edward owed too much.

Which was why he'd had to hire Shelby when she'd shown up on the cottage's front stoop with nothing but an overheating truck, an honest face, and a solid stare to her name—

A lurch born out of his lack of balance sent Edward on a path back down to the concrete, his body collapsing like a folding table, something bad happening to one of his ankles.

But Shelby caught him before he cracked his head open, her strong arms snapping out and grabbing him, pulling him against her. "Come on."

He wanted to fight with her because he hated so much of himself and his condition. This was not him, this cripple, this drunkard, this miscreant malcontent. In his old life, before his own father had had him kidnapped and then refused to pay the ransom, none of this would be happening.

"I don't know if you should be walking."

As Shelby spoke, he swung his "good" bad leg out because the knee didn't like bending, and then relied on her to carry his weight because the ankle he'd just hurt wouldn't have any of it. "Of course I shouldn't. You've seen me naked. You know how bad off I am."

After all, she'd caught him in the bath . . . when she had barged past a closed door, clearly expecting to find him dead and floating in the tub.

"I'm worried about your ankle."

He gritted his teeth. "Such a Good Samaritan."

"I'm calling the doctor."

"No, you're not."

As they emerged into the sunlight, he blinked, although not because he was hungover. One had to be sober for that. And indeed, compared to the coolness of the stables, the golden morning air felt like cashmere against his prickling skin, and oh, the view. All around, the rolling blue-grass fields with their five-rail fences and solitary maples were a balm to the soul, a promise of succor to the impeccable equine bloodlines that would wander and crop at the segregated meadows as they bore forth future generations of Derby and stakes champions.

Even Triple Crown winners.

The earth and its bounties could be trusted, Edward thought. Trees could be relied upon to provide shade in summer's heat, and thunderheads never failed to give you rain, and brooks might swell in the spring and go dry in the fall, but a man could predict their seasons. Hell, even the fury of tornadoes and snowstorms had rhythms that were not personal and never, ever unscrupulous.

Whatever wrath might come down from the heavens was not directed upon any specific person: Although one might feel targeted, in fact, that was never the case.

The same was true for horses and dogs, barn cats and raccoons, even the lowly, ugly possum and the snakes who ate their young. For certain, his stallion, Neb, was a mean cur, but that animal never pretended to be aught than he was. He didn't smile in your face and then tear into your back as you turned away.

Humans were so much more dangerous than so-called "unpredictable" animals and finger-of-God events.

And yes, that made him bitter.

Then again, he was bitter about most things these days.

By the time he and Shelby came up to the caretaker's cottage, his internal rants were tempered by the pain that had bubbled through his intoxication, as if the overload to his nervous system forced so much electrical impulse to his brain that his synapses had no choice but to downgrade his pessimism.

The old door creaked as Shelby pushed it wide, and the one-room interior was as dark as night, the heavy wool drapes pulled closed, the sole light in the galley kitchen like a coal miner's helmet lamp, dulled and at a loss to cover all its territory. The furniture was sparse, cheap and old, the opposite of the precious things he'd grown up with at Easterly—although he supposed that the shelves of sterling silver racing trophies across the way did hold a certainly commonality.

Breaking free of his human crutch, he shambled over to his armchair, the ratty, Archie Bunker–deep seat cupping his weight like a meatpacker's palm. His head fell back and he breathed through his mouth while attempting not to inflate his ribs any more than he absolutely had to.

A tugging on his right foot had him looking down. "What are you doing?"

Shelby's blond head was angled at his boot, her workman's hands moving so much faster over those laces than his ever could. "I'm taking this off so I can see how bad your ankle is."

Edward opened his mouth, a sarcastic bomb on the tip of his tongue.

But God curbed his crassness as that boot came off with a roar. "Damn it!"

"I think you've broken it."

Bracing his hands against the armchair, his heart jumped rope with his ribs. And when all that passed, he sagged.

"I'll bring my truck around—"

"No!" He puffed through his clenched teeth. "You are doing no such thing."

As Shelby looked up at him from the floor, in the back of his mind, he took note of how rare it was for her to meet his eyes. She was always willing to parry his verbal jabs, but rarely would her stare linger anywhere near his.

Her eyes were . . . rather extraordinary. Rimmed with thick, dark, natural lashes, they had flecks of the dawn light in their sky blue color.

"If you're not gonna go to the hospital, what's the name of your private physician? And do not pretend you don't got one. You're a Bradford."

"Not anymore, darling."

She winced at the sobriquet, as if recognizing that she was not the sort of woman that would ever be called such, especially not by someone with his pedigree. And he was ashamed to admit it, but he'd wanted to hurt her for no good reason.

No, actually, that wasn't true. The lack of a reason, that was.

Shelby had an unerring ability to catch him in vulnerable moments, and the defensive part of him hated her for it.

"How long did you take care of your father?" he demanded.

"All my life."

Jeb Landis had been a terrible drinker, gambler, womanizer . . . He had known horses, though. And had taught Edward all he knew at a time when Edward had never thought of going into the racing business as anything other than a rich man's hobby—and certainly never envisioned himself employing the man's daughter.

Hell, he hadn't even known Jeb had a child.

For some reason, Edward found himself wondering how many sarcastic cuts Shelby had taken over the years, the ego-draining obstacle course presented by her miscreant sire training her well . . . for her going on to care for exactly the kind of man Edward had become.

It was as if Jeb, in sending her here, had been determined that his cruelty survive his grave.

Edward sat forward. Reaching out a trembling hand, he touched Shelby's face. He'd expected her skin to be rough. It was not.

As she recoiled away, he focused on her lips. "I want to kiss you."

*B*ack at Lizzie's farmhouse, Lane stared out at the rising sun as her words hung in the quiet air between them.

Are you thinking maybe someone killed him?

Hard question to answer, especially when, for him, he felt cheated because he hadn't been the one to kill the man. And wasn't that a tough pill to swallow, especially as he watched a fresh day dawn across the flat Indiana landscape.

In the face of so much resplendent beauty, his dark thoughts seemed like f-bombs uttered at an altar.

"Well?" Lizzie prompted. "Are you?"

"I don't know. There are a number of people who have a motive, for sure. Most of whom I'm related to." He frowned as he thought about something Deputy Ramsey had told him down by the river. "You know, the security cameras on the bridge haven't been turned on yet."

"What?"

Lane made arches in the thin air. "There are cameras mounted on the spans, and they were supposed to be recording footage that night. But when the police checked the feeds, they discovered that they hadn't been initiated yet."

"So no one knows what really happened, then?"

"Guess not. But Metro Police do think if he jumped it had to be from there. The other bridge is too hard for someone to get to the open drop—

which is something Mitch said they were going to fix on the Big Five now." Lane shook his head. "As for murder, though? No, I do think he jumped. I believe he killed himself. The debt, the embezzlement—it's all coming crashing down, and my father knew this. How the hell could he have held his head up in this town now? Or anywhere else for that matter?"

"Do you know when they'll release the body?"

"Ramsey told me as soon as the autopsy was finished. So it has to be only a matter of time." He refocused on her. "Actually, there is something you could do to help me."

"Name it. Anything."

"It's about the visiting hours for my father. As soon as the remains are released, we're going to have to have people to Easterly, and I want it . . . I mean, I want everything to be as it should."

Lizzie took his hand and gave it a squeeze. "I'll make sure it's done right. Of course."

"Thank you." He bent down and pressed a kiss to the inside of her wrist. "You know, it's funny . . . I don't care about honoring his memory. It's not for my father. It's for the Bradford family name—and yes, that's superficial, but I kind of feel like not on my watch, you know? Those people who come are going to be looking for signs of scandal and weakness, and I'll be damned if they'll get it. And I'm also concerned that Mother will want to make an appearance for something like that."

Yes, it was true that "young" Virginia Elizabeth Bradford Baldwine, who was now over sixty, hadn't been out of bed in the last three years for anything other than hair tending, but there were some standards even an addict like her was going to recognize, and her husband's visitation was one of them. And people had been calling the house already, asking about what arrangements were being made. Not that that was about his father, either. Charlemont high society was as competitive as the NFL, and an event like a Bradford's visiting hours was the Super Bowl.

Everyone wanted a good seat at the fifty-yard line.

It was all just so fake. And though he'd always known that, it hadn't

been until Lizzie had come into his life that he'd cared about the emptiness of it all.

"I'm going to promise you something," he murmured. "After this is
all done . . . after I've fixed all this? Then you and I will leave. Then we
get out. But I have to stay to clean up this mess. It's the only way I'll ever
be free of this family. Righting the wrongs of my father is the only path
to earning my freedom—earning your love."

"You already have that."

"Come here."

He reached for her and pulled her into his lap, finding her mouth in
the morning light. Getting her naked was the work of a moment, and
then she was straddling him and he was yanking his sweatpants down.

"Oh, my Lizzie," he groaned against her mouth.

Her breasts were full in his palms, and she gasped as he cupped them.
She was always a revelation, always new to him . . . every kiss, each touch
like coming home and going to the moon at the same time.

Perfection.

As she lifted up on her knees, he shifted himself into position, and
then they were together, her moving on top of him, him holding her close.
She took all of him with perfect coordination, and with her eyes closed
tightly, as if she didn't want any distractions from what she was feeling.

He kept his open.

Oh, she was beautiful, the way she arched back, her head falling
away, her breasts lifting, the light bathing across her magnificent nakedness and her blond hair.

This he would remember as well, he told himself. This moment on the
far side of the fall, the near-drowning, the panic . . . this wonderful, vital
moment with the one he loved, where they were both alive and together
and alone, sequestered in a privacy no one else could touch and nobody
could take away, he would recall this along with everything else that had
happened tonight.

Yes, he thought. He needed to recharge his strength, his hope, and
his heart with times and memories like this with his Lizzie.

He had battles to fight, and questions as to whether he was worthy, and worries about what was coming ahead. But she gave him the power to be the warrior he wanted and needed to be.

Forget the money, he thought.

Everything he really had to have in life was right here in his arms.

"I love you," he gasped. "I love you . . ."

SEVEN

*E*dward was surprised when Shelby didn't jump to her feet and strut off in a huff out the door. After all, good Christian women who were told that their employer wanted to kiss them tended to get rightfully offended. But the longer she stayed where she was, staring up at him with his boot in her hands, the more intimidated he became.

It was not supposed to go like this, he thought to himself. He'd banked on her backing away from him, leaving him alone, forgetting about the damn doctor.

"Sometimes the land must accept the storm," Shelby whispered.

"What?"

She just shook her head as she moved up his lower body. "It's not important."

And she was right. Nothing much was important at all as she was the one who kissed him, her lips soft and shy, as if she knew nothing about seduction.

That was not a problem for him.

Edward took things from there, and he found himself being more careful with her than he had been with a woman in . . . well, maybe, ever. He kept his hands light as he circled her torso, urging her in between his legs and up against his chest. Underneath her sweatshirt, her body was as hard as his was, but for a different reason. She was tight from all that physical labor, honed from her health and her efforts, from her work with animals that weighed a thousand pounds more than she did and required gallons of feed and wheelbarrows of sawdust and miles of walking from stall to stall, pasture to pasture.

She wasn't wearing a bra.

He discovered that as he pulled that sweatshirt up and over her head. She wasn't wearing a shirt, either. And her breasts were perfect, as small and tight as the rest of her was. The fact that her nipples were a girly pink was a surprise . . .

And it was right about then that he stopped himself.

Even as a delicious greed clawed into his gut, something far more imperative flared in the back of his head.

"Are you a virgin?" he said.

"No."

"I think you're lying."

"Only one way to find out, ain't that right?"

A strange, unfamiliar hesitation froze him and he looked away, not because he didn't like what he saw—but because he did. Everything about her modesty and her awkwardness made him want to pounce on her and take her, claim her like a man did when he found something no one else had had.

And everything about the way she didn't back down told him she'd let him do that and so much more.

Shifting his eyes away, he took a moment to think about this, in a fashion that was characteristic of the way he'd always been as opposed to what he'd become—and that was when he saw the money.

One thousand dollars.

Ten one-hundred-dollar bills, the bundle folded once, the ends fanning out.

Over on the sideboard by the door.

He'd left the cash there the previous Friday for one of the prostitutes he regularly paid to be with him. And in fact, a woman had shown up that night—except instead of her acting and dressing like the one he'd really wanted . . . the actual female herself had come to him.

His Sutton.

They'd had sex, but only because he'd assumed that the perfect doppelgänger for Sutton Smythe had finally presented itself. His first clue that something was off? After it was over, the female had left the money where it was. His second? The following morning, he'd found a purse on the table by his chair. When he'd opened it, he'd found Sutton's driver's license inside.

Sometimes, he still wasn't sure whether it had actually happened or if it had been a dream. Although the tension when he'd returned the purse to her the follow evening had been nuclear—so yes, it must have occurred.

And yes, he knew precisely why he'd had sex with her. Sutton was a classy, dignified, brilliant businesswoman who he'd been in love with for too many years to count. Why she had allowed him to touch her, kiss her, come inside of her?

Yes, she'd told him she thought she was in love with him, too. But how could that possibly be true?

Edward refocused on Jeb's daughter. Gathering her sweatshirt in his hands, he put it back on her gently, covering her nakedness.

"No doctor," he said remotely. "I don't need one."

"Yes, you do."

It was disconcerting the way she calmly rose and went over to the phone like nothing had happened. And when she picked up the receiver from the old-fashioned, wall-mounted dialer, he frowned and resented her pragmatism.

"Moe gave me the number," she explained as she began making circles with her forefinger. "Dr. Qalbi is the name, right."

"Oh, for fuck's sake, if you knew all that, why did you pester me about it."

"I was giving you a chance to be reasonable. I should have known better."

"Goddamn it."

Turning to him, she put the handset up to her ear. "I told you. Do *not* take the Lord's name in vain in my presence, and no cursing. Not 'round me. And yes, I know you'll never be in love with me. It will always be her."

"What the hell are you talking about?" he shot back.

"You say her name in your sleep. What is it? Sut . . . Sutter?"

Edward let his head fall back as he closed his eyes in frustration. Maybe he was just dreaming this. Yes, perhaps he had simply passed out against Neb's stall, and this was all just a figment of the vodka swill that was currently passing for his bloodstream.

One could certainly hope.

"*M*iss Smythe? More coffee?"

As Sutton jerked to attention, she smiled up at the uniformed older woman with the pot in her hand. Ellyn Isaacs had been working at the family's estate for as long as Sutton could remember, a grandmotherly figure who always made her think of Nancy Drew's Hannah Gruen.

"No, thank you, Mrs. Isaacs. It's time for me to go, much as it pains me."

"Your car is waiting for you."

Sutton blotted her mouth with a monogrammed damask napkin and got to her feet. "I'll just go get Daddy."

Mrs. Isaacs smiled and straightened the pressed white apron that hung over the front of her gray dress. "Your father is in his study. And I'll let Don know you're coming out."

"Thank you."

The family dining room was a charming little fifteen-by-fifteen, window-filled annex between the mansion's main kitchen and the formal dining room. Filled with light, especially in the morning, it looked out over the ivy-covered brick walls and carefully tended beds of roses in the formal garden, and had corresponding old-school Colefax and Fowler botanicals as fabrics. It had been one of her mother's favorite rooms in the house. Back when she had been alive, Sutton and her brother had always had breakfast here before school, the whole family chatting away and sharing things. After her mother had passed, and Winn had gone to U.Va., it had been just her father and her.

And finally, when she had gone off to Harvard, it had been only her father—at which point, Mrs. Isaacs had begun serving him his morning repast at his desk.

It was a habit that he had not broken even after Sutton had come back from business school at the University of Chicago and started to work for the Sutton Distillery Corporation.

As she folded her napkin and placed it beside her hollowed-out grape-fruit half, her muffin-crumbled plate and her vacant hard-boiled egg holder, she wondered why she insisted on sitting down here alone every morning.

The tie to the past, perhaps. A fantasy of a future, maybe.

The massive house that she and her father now inhabited by themselves— except when Winn came to visit—was twenty-five thousand square feet of historic, upkeep-intensive grandeur, all the antiques in it passed down from generation to generation, the art museum-quality, the carpets from Persia except for when they'd been handmade in France. It was a resplendent sanctuary where brass railings and gold-leafed fixtures glowed from countless polishings, and hanging crystal twinkled from the ceilings and on the walls, and wood well-mellowed from time's passage offered warmth sure as a banked fire.

But it was a lonely place.

The sound of her stilettos was muffled as she had been taught how to walk properly, the quiet rhythm of her footsteps echoing in the lovely emptiness as she proceeded to the front of the house, passing by sitting rooms and libraries, parlors and powder rooms. Nothing was out of place, no clutter to be found, everything cleaned with reverent hands, no lint or dust anywhere.

The doors to her father's study were opened, and he looked up from his desk. "There she is."

His hands went to grip his chair arms out of a reflex born from always rising to his feet whenever a woman entered a room or left it. But it was an impotent gesture, his strength no longer there, the sad impulse that he couldn't follow through on something she ignored with determination.

"Are you going in now, then?" he said as he dropped his hands into his lap.

"We're going in." She went around and kissed him on the cheek. "Let's go. Finance Committee starts in forty-five minutes."

Reynolds Winn Wilshire Symthe, IV, nodded at the bound book on the corner of the desk. "I read the materials. Things are doing well."

"We're a little soft in South America. I think we need to—"

"Sutton. Sit down, please."

With a frown, she took a seat across from him, linking her ankles under the chair and arranging her suit. As usual, she was dressed in Armani, the peach color one of her father's favorites on her.

"Is there something wrong?"

"It's time to announce things."

As he said the words she had been dreading, her heart stopped.

Later, she would remember every single thing about where the pair of them sat facing each other in the study . . . and how handsome he was with his full head of white hair and his perfectly pressed, pin-striped suit . . . and how her hands, which were just like his, had knotted together in her lap.

"No," she said flatly. "It is not."

As Reynolds went to extend his arm toward her, his palm flapped across the leather blotter, and for a moment, all Sutton wanted to do was scream. Instead, she swallowed the emotion and met his attempt to connect them halfway, leaning over the great expanse of his desk, messing up the piles of papers.

"My darling." He smiled at her. "How proud am I of you."

"Stop it." She made a show of turning her wrist and looking at her gold watch. "And we have to go now so we can meet with Connor before we start—"

"I've already told Connor, Lakshmi and James. The press release will be issued to the *Times* and the *Wall Street Journal* as soon as your employment contract is amended. Lakshmi's drafting it as we speak. This isn't just something between you and I anymore."

Sutton felt cold fear, the kind that pricked the back of your neck and made you sweat under your arms. "No. It's not legal. It has to be ratified by the board—"

"They did it last night."

She sat back, separating them. And as the hard chair hit her shoulder blades, for some absurd reason she thought about the number of employees they had worldwide. Thousands and thousands. And how much business they did between their bourbon distilling, the wine subsidiary, and then their vodka, gin, and rum lines. Ten billion annually with a gross profit of nearly four billion. She thought of her brother and wondered how he was going to feel about this.

Then again, Winn had been told two years ago this was the way things were going to go. And even he had to know that she was the one with the business head.

Sutton looked at her father—and promptly forgot about the corporation.

As her eyes blurred with tears, she threw out all decorum and regressed back to when her mother had been lost. "I don't want you to die."

"Neither do I. And I have no intention of going anywhere." He laughed ruefully. "And with the way this Parkinson's is progressing, I fear that is more true than I should like it."

"Can I do this?" she whispered.

He nodded. "I'm not giving you the position because you're my daughter. Love has a place in families. It is not welcome in business. You are succeeding me because you're the right person to take us into the future. Everything is so different from when my father gave that corner office over to me. It's all . . . so global, so volatile, so competitive now. And you understand all of it."

"I need another year."

"You don't have that. I'm sorry." He went to move his arm again and then gritted his teeth with frustration—which was the closest he came to ever cursing. "Remember this, though. I didn't spend the last forty years of my life pouring everything I had into an endeavor just to turn it over to somebody who wasn't fit for the job. You can do this. Moreover, you *will* do it. There is no other option than to succeed."

Sutton let her eyes drift down until they settled on his hands. He still wore his simple gold wedding band. Her father had never remarried after her mother had passed. He hadn't even dated. He slept with her picture beside his bed and with her nightgowns still hanging in their closet.

The romantic justification for that was true love. The actual one was probably part loyalty and reverence for his dead wife, and part the disease and its course.

The Parkinson's had proven to be debilitating, depressing and scary. And was a testament to the reality that rich people weren't in a special class when it came to the whims of fate.

In fact, her father had been slowing down markedly these last couple of months, and it was only going to get worse until he was bedridden.

"Oh, Daddy . . ." she choked.

"We've both known this has been coming."

Taking a deep breath, Sutton was aware that this was the only time she could ever let any vulnerability show. This was her one chance to be honest about how terrifying it was to be thirty-eight years old and at the helm of a global corporation upon which her family's fortunes rested—and also stare down the barrel of her father's death.

Brushing away a tear, she looked at the wetness on her fingertip and told herself that there would be no more leaking after she left the house. As soon as she got to headquarters, everyone was going to measure her to see what kind of leader they had. And yes, there would be snakes coming out of the woodwork to undermine her and people who didn't take her seriously because she was a woman and she was family, and her own brother was going to be angry.

Just as importantly, she couldn't show any weakness to her father after this, either. If she did, he was going to worry whether he'd done the right thing and possibly even second-guess himself—and stress did not help people with his condition.

"I'm not going to let you down," she said as she met him right in the eye.

The relief that suffused that handsome face was immediate and made her tear up again. But he was right; she no longer had the luxury of emotion.

Love was for family.

It was not for business.

Getting to her feet, she went around and gave him a quick hug, and when she straightened, she made sure her shoulders were back.

"I expect to continue to use you as a resource," she announced. And it was funny to hear that tone in her voice: It was not a request, and it was not something she said to her father. It was from one CEO to his or her predecessor.

"Always," he murmured as he inclined his head. "It would be an honor."

She nodded and turned away before cracks in her façade showed. She was halfway to the door when he said, "Your mother is smiling right now."

Sutton stopped and nearly wept. Oh, her mother. A firebrand for women's rights back when that hadn't been permitted in the South, in their kind of family.

Oh, she would have loved this, it was true. It was everything she had fought for and demanded and stomped about.

"It's not why I picked you over your brother, though," he added.

"I know." They all knew why Winn wasn't a real candidate. "I'm conferencing you in during Finance meetings even though officially you have no role. I expect you to contribute as you would have done."

Again, not a request.

"Of course."

"You will continue to serve on the board as Trustee Emeritus. I will nominate you myself as my first official duty at the next board meeting. And you will be conferenced in during Executive Committee and all Trustee meetings until you are no longer able to breathe."

She said all of this while staring into the foyer.

The chuckle her father let out held so much fatherly pride and businessman-to-businesswoman respect she started blinking hard again.

"As you wish."

"I shall be home tonight at seven for dinner. We will eat in your room."

Usually by then he was back in bed, his will exhausted from dealing with his body's rebellion.

"And I shall look forward to it."

Sutton made it all the way to the study's door before pausing and looking back. Reynolds seemed so small behind that desk, even though the dimensions of neither the man's form nor the furniture had changed. "I love you."

"And I love you almost as much as I loved your mother."

Sutton smiled at that. And then she was on her way, going over to the console table by the front door and picking up her briefcase, before heading out into the warm May morning.

Her legs were shaking as she walked to the Bentley Mulsanne alone. She had expected her father to be ahead of her, the subtle *whrrrrr* of his motorized wheelchair something she resolutely ignored.

"Good morning, Miss Smythe."

The uniformed driver, Don, had been her father's chauffeur for two decades. And as he opened the rear door, he couldn't quite manage to meet her in the eye—although not out of dislike or mistrust.

He had been told, of course.

She squeezed his arm. "You'll stay on. For as long as you want the job."

The man breathed a sigh of relief. "Anything for you."

"I'm going to make him proud."

Now Don looked at her. His eyes shimmered with tears. "Yes, you will."

With a nod, she got in the back, and jumped as the door was shut with a muffled *thump.* A moment later they were off, smoothing their way out of the courtyard, off the estate.

Usually, she and her father discussed things on the way downtown, and as she stared at the empty seat beside her, it dawned on her that the day before was the last time that the pair of them would ride to headquarters together. The final trip . . . had come and gone without her knowing it at the time.

Wasn't that the way of things.

She had assumed there would be many more ahead of them, countless mentoring, ceaseless drives side by side.

Denial was lovely while you were in it, wasn't it. But when you stepped out of its warm pond of delusion, reality carried a shivering, cold sting. And yes, if the partition separating the front from the back of the car hadn't been down, she probably would have wept as hard as if she were going to her father's funeral.

Instead, she placed her palm on the seat that had been his, and looked out the tinted glass. They were getting on River Road now, joining the line up of traffic that eventually funneled into the surface arteries that ran under the highways and bridges of Charlemont's business district.

There was only one person she could think of to call. One person whose voice she wanted to hear. One person . . . who would understand on a visceral level what she was feeling.

But Edward Baldwine didn't care about the liquor industry anymore. No longer was he her competitor's heir apparent, her counterpart across the aisle, the sarcastic, sexy, infuriating friend she had long coveted.

And even if he had still been the number two at the Bradford Bourbon Company, he certainly had made it clear that he didn't want anything to do with a personal relationship with her.

In spite of that . . . crazy hook-up . . . they'd had at that caretaker's cottage out at the Red & Black.

Which she still couldn't believe had happened.

After all the years of fantasizing, she had finally been with him—

Sutton pulled away from that black hole of going-nowhere by remembering their last meeting. It had been in a farm truck parked outside her house, and they had fought over that mortgage she'd given his father. Right before the man had died.

Hardly the stuff of Hallmark cards.

Yet in spite of all that, Edward was still the one she wanted to talk to, the only person other than her father whose opinion she cared about. And before his kidnapping? She would absolutely have dialed him up, and he would have answered on the first ring, and he would have supported her at the same time he would have put her in her place.

Because he was like that.

The fact that he wasn't there anymore, either?

Just one more of the losses.

One more thing to miss.

One more piece of the mourning.

Letting her head fall back, she stared at the river and wished that things were as they had once and always been.

"Oh, Edward . . ."

EIGHT

*S*amuel Theodore Lodge III drove his vintage Jaguar convertible down River Road at a measly fifteen or sixteen miles an hour. Traffic was no slower or faster than it ever was, but he was less frustrated than usual at the delay because this morning, he didn't have to go all the way in to his law office in Charlemont proper. No, today, he was stopping off first to meet one of his clients.

Although to be fair, Lane was more family than anything else.

The big estates up on the hills were to his left, the muddy waters of the Ohio were to his right, and overhead, the milky blue sky promised another hot, humid May day. And as the balmy breeze ruffled through his hair, thanks to the top being down, he turned the local classical music station up so he could hear Chopin's Nocturne Op. 9, No. 2 better.

On his thigh, he played the left-hand part. On the wheel, he commenced the right.

If he had not been a lawyer, as his father, his uncles, and his grandfather had been or currently were, he would have been a classical pianist. Alas, not his destiny—and not only because of the legal legacy. At best, he was serviceable at the keys, capable of impressing laymen at cocktail parties and at Christmas, but not talented enough to challenge the professionals.

He glanced at the passenger seat, at an old briefcase that had been used by his great-uncle T. Beaumont Lodge, Jr. Like the car, the thing was a classic from an earlier era, its brown hide well worn, even bare in patches on the handle and the flap with the gold embossed initials. But it had been handmade by a fine Kentucky craftsman, built to last and look good as it aged—and as it had been in his uncle's time, its belly was full of briefs, notes, and court filings.

Unlike in T. Beaumont's time, there was also a MacBook Air in there, and a cell phone.

Samuel T. was going to pass the briefcase down to a distant cousin, someday. Perhaps a bit of his love of the piano, as well.

But nothing was going to a child of his own. No, there would be no marriage for him, and no children out of wedlock—not because he was religious, and not because it was something that "Lodges simply don't do," although the latter was certainly true.

It was because he was smart enough to know he was incapable of being a father, and he refused to do anything that he did not excel at.

This lifelong tenet was why he was a great trial lawyer. A fantastic womanizer. A highbrow drunkard of the very finest order.

All of which were a ringing endorsement for dad of the year, weren't they—

"We interrupt this broadcast with breaking news. William Baldwine, sixty-five, the chief executive officer of the Bradford Bourbon Company, is dead of an apparent suicide. Numerous anonymous sources report that the body was found in the Ohio River—"

"Oh . . . *hell*," Samuel T. muttered as he reached forward and turned up the tinny radio even further.

The report had more fluff than substance, but the moving parts were all correct as far as Samuel T. knew. Clearly, their efforts to squash the story until they were ready to come forward had failed.

"—follows an accusation against Jonathan Tulane Baldwine of spousal abuse by his estranged wife, Chantal Baldwine, just days ago. Mrs.

Baldwine was admitted to the Bolton Suburban Hospital emergency room with facial bruises and ligature marks around her throat. Initially, she accused her husband of inflicting the injuries. She recanted her story, however, after police refused to charge Mr. Baldwine due to lack of evidence . . ."

As Samuel T. listened to the rest of the report, he looked up ahead to the tallest hill.

Easterly, the Bradford family's historic home, was a glorious spectacle at the apex of the rise. Overlooking the Ohio, the mansion was a whitewashed grand dame in the Federal style, with a hundred windows bracketed by glossy black shutters, too many chimneys to count, and an entrance so grand that the Bradfords had made it their company's logo. Terraces sprawled out in every direction, as did manicured gardens full of specimen flowers and fruit trees, and great magnolias that had dark green leaves and white blossoms as big as a man's head.

When the mansion had been built, the Bradford money had been new. Now, as with those bank accounts, there was a patina of age to it—but all kings started off as paupers, and all venerable dynasties were nouveau riche once. The term "aristocrat" just measured how far back you had to go to get to the upstarts.

Also depended upon how long you could keep your position going into the future.

At least the Bradfords didn't have to worry about money.

The many-acred Bradford estate had two entrances. A staff one, which bisected the cutting gardens and vegetable fields and went up to the garages and the rear of the mansion, and a formal, gated path of glory for family and proper guests. He took the latter, the one Lodges had been using for a century, and as he ascended, he glanced at himself in the rearview.

It was good that he had sunglasses on. Sometimes one didn't need to see one's own eyes.

Gin would be having breakfast, he thought as he pulled up in front of the house. With her new fiancé.

Getting out, he did a pass-through with a hand to make sure his hair was back where it needed to be and picked up his great-uncle's briefcase. His blue and white seersucker suit reordered itself on his body without any prompting, and there was no reason to worry about his bow tie. He'd done it properly before leaving his bedroom suite.

"Good morning!"

Pivoting on his handmade loafer, he raised a hand to the blond woman coming around the side of the house. Lizzie King was pushing a wheelbarrow full of ivy plants and had a glow about her that was the best recommendation for clean living he'd ever seen.

No wonder Lane was in love with her.

"Good morning to you," Samuel T. said with a slight bow. "I'm here to see your man."

"He should be here shortly."

"Ah . . . do you need help? As a gentleman and a farmer, I feel as though I should offer."

Lizzie laughed him off and jogged the handles. "Greta and I've got this. Thanks."

"And I've got your man," Samuel T. replied as he lifted his briefcase.

"Thank you," she said softly.

"Don't worry. I'm going to make Chantal go away—and I'm going to enjoy doing it."

With another wave, he strode over to the mansion's entrance. Easterly's pale stone steps were shallow and broad, and they brought him up to the Corinthian columns around the glossy black door with its lion's head knocker.

Samuel T. didn't bother with formalities. He opened the way into a foyer so big one could have bowled in it.

"Sir," came a British clip. "Are you expected?"

Newark Harris was the most recent in a long line of butlers, this current incarnation trained at Bagshot Park across the pond, or so Samuel T. had heard. The Englishman was very much out of the David Suchet as Hercule Poirot mold, officious, pressed as a fine pair of slacks, and vaguely disapproving of the Americans he served. In his black suit, white shirt, and black tie, he looked like he could have been in place since the house was built.

Alas, that was only appearances. And the man had things to learn.

"Always." Samuel T. smiled. "I am always expected here. So if you'll excuse me, that is all."

The Englishman's dark brows shot up, but Samuel T. was already pivoting away. The dining room was to the right, and emanating from it, he could smell a familiar perfume.

He told himself to stay away. But as usual, he could not.

When it came to young, young Virginia Elizabeth Baldwine, soon-to-be-Pford, he never had been able to distance himself for very long.

It was his only character flaw.

Or rather, the only character flaw that concerned him.

Striding across the black-and-white marble, he walked into the long, thin room with the same attitude as he had dismissed the butler. "Well, isn't this romantic. The affianced enjoying a morning repast together."

Richard Pford's head snapped up from his eggs and toast. Gin, mean-while, showed no reaction—overtly, that was. But Samuel T. smiled at the way her knuckles went white on her coffee cup—and to make things sting more for her, he almost took the pleasure of informing her that her father's suicide was common knowledge.

She was better at being cruel than he was, however.

And as Richard prattled on about something, all that registered was Gin's long dark hair falling on her flowered silk blouse, and the Hermès scarf around her neck, and the perfect arrangement of her elegant body on the Chippendale chair. The overall effect was as if she had been posed by a great artist. Then again, say what one would about the woman's morals, she always looked classy. It was the bone structure. The Bradford superiority. The beauty.

"—invitation soon," Richard said. "We expect you to attend."

Samuel T. glanced at the broomstick sitting across from her. "Oh, for your wedding? Or are we talking about her father's funeral? I get the two confused."

"Our nuptials."

"Well, I'm so honored to be on a list that no doubt will be as exclusive as Wikipedia."

"You don't have to come," Gin said quietly. "I know you're quite busy."

He looked at that diamond ring on her finger and thought, yes, she had done well for herself. He certainly wouldn't have been able to afford a gem of that size, and he was hardly a pauper. Pford's money was on Bradford levels, though.

So yes, it was a helluva lifeboat she had chosen to jump into. It would have been safer for her to try to swim with the sharks.

"I wouldn't miss it for the world," Samuel T. murmured. "And I'm sure that daughter of yours is thrilled to finally get a father."

As Gin blanched, he refused to feel bad. Like so much of Gin's life, "that daughter," Amelia, was a mistake, the result of one of her random hook-ups after she'd gone off to college, a living, breathing bad decision that, as far as he understood, she had failed to parent and barely acknowledged.

Why couldn't he have just hated her? Samuel T. wondered. God knew there was reason enough.

Hatred had never been the problem, however.

"You know," Samuel T. drawled, "I envy you two so much. Marriage is such a beautiful thing."

"How is Lane's divorce going?" Richard said. "That's why you're here, isn't it."

"Among other things. You know, one in three marriages end in divorce. But that won't be you two. True love is so wonderful to see live and in person. You are beacons to us all."

Richard's brow lifted. "I didn't think you were the settling kind."

"I'm not at the moment. But my dream girl is out there. I just know it."

That was not a lie. Unfortunately, she was marrying this asshole having breakfast with her—and the term that better fit Gin's role in Samuel T.'s life was "nightmare." But he'd meant his RSVP. He would be there when she walked down the aisle with this fool just to remind himself of the reality of their relationship.

As the sound of a powerful car engine percolated through the old-fashioned, single-paned windows, Samuel T. nodded to the happy couple. "My client's arrived. I can tell the purr of a Porsche anywhere. It's like the sound of a woman's orgasm—something you never forget."

Turning away, he paused at the archway. "Something for you to work toward with her, Richard. Good luck with that, and call me if you need any instruction. I gave her her first one."

*L*ane pulled up to Easterly in his 911 and parked next to his attorney's classic maroon Jaguar.

"What a view," he said as he got out.

Lizzie looked up from the ivy bed she was on her knees in front of. Wiping her brow with her forearm, she smiled. "I just started about five minutes ago. Things will look even better in an hour."

He walked onto the cropped grass. Off in the distance, he heard the hum of a lawn mower, the chatter of electronic clippers, a low whir from a leaf blower.

"I wasn't talking about the horticulture." Bending down, he kissed her on the mouth. "Where is—"

"*Guten Morgen.*"

Lane straightened and hid his grimace. "Greta. How are you?"

As Lizzie's partner came around the magnolia tree, he braced himself for the German woman's presence. With her short blond hair, her tortoiseshell glasses, and her no-nonsense attitude, Greta von Schlieber was capable of great feats of gardening—and deep, abiding grudges.

As a string of German came back at him, he was pretty sure she was wishing him a good day in such a way that a piano ended up falling on him.

"I'm going to meet with Samuel T.," he said to Lizzie.

"Good luck." Lizzie kissed him again. "I'm here if you need me."

"I need you—"

Greta's snort was part quarter horse, part mother hen . . . part bazooka pointed at his head, and he took the sound as his cue to leave. As much as this was his family's house, he wasn't about to mess with the German—and he couldn't say that he hadn't earned her disregard.

But it was also time to start setting the record straight.

"It's about the divorce," he muttered to Greta. "My divorce. From Chantal."

Icy blue eyes shot daggers at him. "About time. And you talk vis me ink is dry, *ja?*"

"Greta." Lizzie cursed. "He's—"

"You got it." Lane pointed a finger in the other woman's face. "You just watch."

Heading for Easterly's front entrance, he counted himself lucky he didn't get a trowel in the back of his skull. But he'd meant what he'd said. He was taking care of this bad baggage of his.

As the grand door opened, he was prepared to steam by the butler. "I've got a meeting—"

But Samuel T., not the dreaded Mr. Harris, had done the honors.

His lawyer smiled like the Tom Ford model he could have been. "Timeliness is next to godliness."

"Which explains why I'm always late."

"Personally, it's the only religion I've got."

The two clapped hands and went in for a shoulder slap. "I need a drink, Sam."

"This is why I love representing friends. Particularly ones with liquor businesses."

Lane led the way into the parlor. "Friends? We're almost family."

"No, she's marrying someone else." As he looked back, Samuel T. waved the words away. "Not what I meant."

Bullcrap, Lane thought. But he left his sister Gin's torturous relationship with Samuel T. well enough alone. The pair were Scarlett and Rhett, just take away the mustache and add a couple of cell phones. And hell, with the way the finances were going, maybe Gin would even end up making a dress out of the ball gown drapes in this room. They were pale yellow, a color she liked.

Picking up a bottle of Family Reserve, Lane poured two bourbons into a pair of Waterford rocks glasses and shared one half of the load. Both of them drank the liquor on a single swallow, so the refill was quick.

And Lane took the bottle with him as he collapsed onto a silk-covered sofa. "So what have we got, Samuel T. How bad is it going to get—how much is this going to cost me."

His lawyer sat across from him, on the other side of the marble fire-place. Over the mantel, the second Elijah Bradford, the ancestor who had built Easterly as a way to prove the family's net worth, seemed to glare down at them.

"Have you listened to the radio yet this morning?" Samuel T. asked.

"No."

"It's out." Samuel T. held up his palm. "Your father's suicide. Not Chantal being pregnant. I heard it on the NPR affiliate on the way here. I'm sorry—and I have to imagine that it's going to be in all the papers tomorrow. The Internet has got to be rife with it already."

Lane rubbed his eyes. "Goddamn it. Was it Chantal who leaked the news?"

"I don't know. The sources quoted were 'anonymous.' I'll talk to Deputy Ramsey and see what I can find out."

"It wasn't one of Mitch's boys, I'll tell you that. He'd kill them."

"Agreed. And I don't think it was your ex. If it was Chantal, why'd she keep the pregnancy out of it? If she'd wanted to really screw us, she'd have led with that news flash—although based on her choice of lawyer, it is clear she does not intend to go quietly into any good night."

"Who'd she hire?"

"Rachel Prather."

"Who's that?"

"Think Gloria Allred meets the Hulk—although the latter is not a comment on physical appearance, more what happens if you piss her off. She's out of Atlanta and she called me last night at ten o'clock. I was in my jammies. The woman I was with was not."

Lane could only imagine. "They're not wasting any time with the ask, I see. How much do they want?"

Samuel T. held up his glass. "You know, this actually is the best bourbon I've ever had. So full bodied, and—"

"How much."

Samuel T.'s eyes shot across the low-slung coffee table. "Half. Of everything in your name. Which is about eighty million dollars."

"Is she insane?"

"Yes, but to paraphrase, Chantal has information you don't want getting out in the press." When Lane didn't fill in the silence, Samuel T. pointed out the obvious, "That pregnancy is a problem in this regard— even if, in other situations, I could have used it to reduce alimony."

"Her blessed event is just one issue."

"Is that why your father killed himself?" Samuel T. asked softly.

"I don't know." Lane shrugged, thinking he should be making a damn list. "Regardless, I'm not writing that kind of check to her, Samuel. It's not going to happen."

"Look, my advice to you, especially given . . . her circumstances and your father's passing?" Samuel T. seemed to savor some more of the bourbon. "I think you should pay the money—and I can't believe I'm saying that. I was prepared to fight her for everything but the engagement ring. Your family's reputation needs to be considered, though. And yes, I know it's a hit on your bottom line, but with the way bourbon is selling right now, in three years, maybe less, you'll be whole. This is not the time to take a principled stance, for so many reasons—especially not if you've moved on with your gardener."

"She's a horticulturist," Lane gritted out.

Samuel T. held up a palm. "My apologies. As for Chantal, I'll draft an ironclad, nondisclosure agreement, force her to disavow the parentage and ensure no contact for her or the child with anyone under this roof—"

"Even if Chantal signed something like that, I'm still not writing that check."

"Lane. Don't be an ass. This woman has the kind of lawyer who will rake you and this family through the press like you won't believe. And your mother doesn't know about the pregnancy, does she?" When Lane shook his head, Samuel dropped his voice. "Then let's keep things that way, shall we."

Lane pictured the woman who had borne him, lying in state in that satin bed of hers upstairs. It was tempting to believe that he could keep her insulated from all parts of this, but the nurses who tended her round the clock were all out in the world, reading newspapers, listening to the radio, on their smartphones.

But there was a greater problem, wasn't there.

It seemed ironic to be pouring Family Reserve into his glass as he said, "We don't have the money."

"I know there is a spendthrift clause in your trust. My father put it there. But that kicks in only if you get sued by a third party. At your direction, however, your trust company can set up a payment plan. Buying her silence is likely to be cheaper than the fallout. You have a very picky board of old boys who believe mistresses should be neither seen nor heard and suicide is a criminal weakness—"

"We have larger problems, Samuel T., than that pregnancy. Why do you think Gin is marrying Richard."

"Because she needs a man she can control."

"It's because she needs the money."

Under other circumstances, it would have been amusing to watch light dawn on Marblehead, the comprehension bringing a pall over his old friend's face.

"What are you . . . ? I'm sorry, what?"

"My father jumped for a lot of reasons, and some of them are financial. There's a shitload of money missing from the household accounts, and I fear the Bradford Bourbon Company is running out of cash as well. I, literally, don't have the money to pay Chantal, now or over time."

Samuel T. swirled his bourbon around, then finished it. "You'll have to excuse me, but . . . my brain is having trouble processing that. What about your mother's stock portfolio? What about—"

"We're sixty-eight million in the hole right now. Personally. And I think it's the tip of the iceberg."

Samuel T. blinked. Then he held out his empty glass. "I beg of you, may I have some more?"

Lane refilled the guy and then helped himself again. "I've got a buddy of mine here from New York trying to figure it out. Jeff Stern, you remember him from U.Va."

"Good guy. Couldn't hold his liquor like a Southerner, but other than that, he was okay."

"He's upstairs weeding through the company financials, trying to figure out how bad it all is. It would be a mistake for us to assume that my father hasn't misappropriated almost everything. After all, about a year ago, he had my mother declared incompetent and took over her trusts—God only knows whether there's anything left anywhere."

Samuel T. shook his head for a while. "Do you want me to be sympathetic or tell you what I'm honestly thinking?"

"Honest. Always be honest."

"It's too bad your father wasn't murdered."

"I beg your pardon? Although not that I'm arguing with you—and I wish I'd been the one to do it."

"Under most policies, suicide won't let you collect, but if someone killed him? As long as none of the beneficiaries did it, the money would be yours."

Lane laughed. He couldn't help it. "You know, this is not the first time I've thought fondly of homicide when it came to that man—"

From out front, a horrible scream cut through the morning like a gunshot.

"What the hell is that?" Samuel T. barked as they both jumped to their feet.

NINE

"*Scheisse! Meine Güte, ein Finger! Ein Finger—*"

As Lane bolted out of the house with Samuel T. tight on his heels, bourbon splashed from his rocks glass, and he ended up tossing the stuff into the bushes as he leaped off the stone steps. Over on the right, Lizzie was crouched above a hole that had been dug in the ivy bed, one hand planted in the earth, the other shoving her partner back as Greta continued yelling and pointing in German.

"What's wrong?" Lane said as he came running.

"It's a . . ." Lizzie took off her floppy hat and looked up at him. "Lane . . . we have a problem here."

"What is—"

"It's a finger." Lizzie nodded to the raw patch in the ivy. "I think that's a finger."

Lane shook his head, as if maybe that would help what she'd said make sense. And then both his knees cracked as he got down on his haunches. Leaning in for a closer look into the shallow hole—

Holy . . . *shit*. It was a finger. A human finger.

The skin was marked with dirt, but you could see that the digit was still intact all the way around—and the thing was fat, like it had swollen up since it had been cut off or . . . torn off, or whatever. The nail was even across the top and the same flat white as the flesh, and the base, where it had been severed from its hand, was a clean slice, the meat inside gray, the pale circular dot on the bottom the bone.

But none of that was what really interested him.

The heavy gold ring that was on it was the issue.

"That's my father's signet ring," he said in a flat tone.

"Oh . . . *shit*," Samuel T. whispered. "Ask and ye shall receive."

Lane patted his pocket and took out his phone, but then didn't dial anything.

Instead, he looked up, up, up . . . and saw his mother's bedroom window directly above where the finger had been buried in the dirt. As Lizzie's hand went to his shoulder and squeezed, Lane glanced at her.

Keeping his eyes locked with hers, he addressed his lawyer with the obvious. "We need to call the police, right?"

As Gin and Richard Pford came out into the sunshine, Samuel T. put his palm up. "You two, back in the house."

Gin glared at the man. "What's going on?"

Lane nodded. He didn't care if his sister saw, but this was not anything Pford needed exposure to. He was not to be trusted. "Richard, please take her back inside."

"Lane?" When Gin went to step down, at least her fiancé caught her arm. "Lane, what is it?"

"I'll be right in and I'll explain things." Which would be a stretch—because he had no clue what the hell was going on. "Richard, please."

Pford started to pull her back inside, but Gin broke free and ran across the lawn in her high heels. As she came up and looked in the hole, an expression of horror made ugliness out of her beauty.

"What is *that*," she demanded.

Samuel T. steadied Gin and spoke to her in a quiet voice. Then, as he began leading her back toward the house, he looked over his shoulder. "Do you call or shall I?"

"I will."

As Lane fired up his iPhone with Deputy Ramsey's well-dialed number, he absently noticed that his hands weren't shaking. Guess he was becoming an old pro with nasty surprises, bad news, and the police coming to his family's home.

Oh, hey, Officers, long time no see. And to make you feel more welcome, we've got designated parking for you right here in the front of the house.

One ring. Two rings—

"I was about to call you," the deputy said by way of greeting. "They're going to release your father's body for cremation tomorrow—"

"No, they're not."

"Excuse me?"

Lane focused on that pale slice of flesh that was all smudged with fine Kentucky topsoil. "We found something buried. Right under my mother's window. You and your boys in the homicide department are going to want to come back here."

"What are we talking about."

"It's a piece of my father. As far as I can tell."

There was a heartbeat's worth of pause. "Don't touch anything. I'm on my way. Have you called Metro Police yet?"

"No."

"Call them—"

"So the report is logged."

"—so the report is logged."

Lane laughed in a hard burst. "I know the procedure by now."

As they both hung up, Lane let himself ease back onto the grass so that he, Lizzie, and Greta were all sitting in a semi-circle around the hole in true campfire fashion. No s'mores. But there could be a ghost story coming, he thought.

A moment later, from the mansion's open front door, sounds of an argument boiled out into the pretty morning, Gin's voice the loudest, Samuel T.'s right behind hers in terms of volume.

Too bad he wasn't murdered.

Samuel T.'s hypothetical echoed around Lane's head as he wished he hadn't emptied his glass into the boxwood hedges by the front door.

This could be a game changer, he thought to himself. Whether it was good news . . . or bad, remained to be seen.

"Edward," he whispered. "Edward, what did you do . . ."

*O*ut in Ogden County, Edward sat back in his Archie Bunker chair and refused to greet his visitor properly. "There is no reason for you to be here."

Dr. Michael Qalbi smiled in his gentle way. The guy was thirty-five going on twelve, at least by appearances, his handsome face and jet-black hair belying his half-Iraqi heritage, his miss-nothing brown eyes a warning shot across anyone's bow lest they were fooled into thinking his kindness could ever be manipulated. His intellect was so formidable, he'd Doogie Howser'd his medical school and residency programs, and then stepped in to help with his father's concierge practice here in town.

Edward had been a member of their service for years, but he hadn't paid his dues since he'd come back to Charlemont. Good soul that he was, Qalbi didn't seem to care.

"I truly don't need you," Edward tacked on. "And is that a Scrabble tie you're wearing?"

Dr. Qalbi looked down at the multicolored, multi-lettered silk strip that hung from around his neck. "Yes, it is. And if you don't need me, why don't you get up and show me to the door like the gentleman you are?"

"We live in PC times. I wouldn't want to run the risk of insulting your masculinity. It could lead to a barrage of Internet backlash."

Dr. Qalbi nodded at Shelby, who was hanging back, arms crossed over her chest like an MMA fighter at weigh-in. "She said you took a stumble in the stables."

"Say that five times fast." Edward pointed to the old-fashioned black bag in the doctor's hand. "Is that for real or is it a prop?"

"It was my grandfather's. And it's full of goodies."

"I don't like lollipops."

"You don't like anything from what I've heard."

The doctor came forward and kneeled down in front of Edward's monogrammed slippers, the only thing that would fit on his feet, thanks to the ankle from hell and all its swelling.

"These shoes are fantastic."

"They were my grandfather's. I've heard that men in Kentucky never buy anything new except for wives. Our wardrobes, on the other hand, are loaves and fishes."

"Does this hurt?"

As Edward's broken body jerked back in the chair and he threw out hands to the armrests, he was forced to grit, "Not at all."

"How about now?"

When his ankle was moved in the opposite direction, Edward hissed, "Is this payback for my misogynistic comment?"

"So you admit you're in pain."

"Only if you cop to being a democrat."

"I'll say that with pride."

Edward was of a mind to continue the riffing, but his neurons had become overrun with too much sensory information, none of it good. And as he grunted and cursed, he was very much aware of Shelby standing off to the side, watching the show with a glower.

"Can you flex it for me?" Qalbi asked.

"I thought I was."

After two more hours' worth of torture—okay, it was more like two minutes, tops—Dr. Qalbi sat back on his heels. "I don't think it's broken."

Edward shot a look over at Shelby. "Really. Imagine that."

"It's dislocated."

As Shelby's right eyebrow I-told-you-so'd into her hairline, Edward refocused on the doctor. "So put it back in place."

"You said you did this in the stables? How did you get back here?"

"I walked."

"Not possible."

"I'm drunk."

"Well, there you go. We need to get you in to an orthopedist—"

"I'm not going to any hospital. So either you fix it here, or leave me be."

"That is not a course I'd recommend. You need to be—"

"Dr. Qalbi, you know damn well what I've been through. I've spent my lifetime allotment of days in hospitals already. Rather efficient, really. So, no, I will not be going anywhere in an ambulance."

"It would be better to get—"

"Primum non nocere."

"Which is why I want to take you into town."

"And PS, the customer is always right."

"You're my patient, not a customer. So your satisfaction is not my goal. Appropriate care is."

But Qalbi fell silent, and did the whole steady-eyed regard thing—although it was not clear whether he was making further medical assessments or waiting for his "patient" to come to his senses.

"I can't do it alone," the man concluded.

Edward nodded at Shelby. "She is stronger than you are. And I'm sure she would like to hurt me right about now, wouldn't you, darling."

"Whatcha need, Doctor?" was all she said as she came over.

Qalbi stared straight into Edward's face. "If there is no dorsalis pedis or tibialis posterior pulse after I'm done, you're going to the hospital."

"I don't know what either of those are."

"You're the one who started throwing around Latin. And those are my terms. If you decline them, I will leave, but I will also turn you in to social services as a failure-to-thrive case—and then you can have all kinds of fun dealing with the welfare folks."

"You wouldn't dare."

"Try me," came the calm response.

Baby face, my ass, Edward thought.

"You're a hard negotiator, Doctor."

"Only because you're being ridiculous."

And that was how, a few moments later, Edward ended up with his jeans rolled to scrawny thigh, his mangled leg bent at the knee, and Shelby straddling him with her hands locked on his pathetic hamstrings. Due to injuries to his hip, the straight-leg position wasn't going to work, according to the good doctor.

"I'm going to pull on three."

As Edward braced himself, he looked forward . . . directly into Shelby's rather spectacular backside. But yes, that was the end result when you made your living at physical labor and you were twenty-something.

Across on the kitchen wall, the old-fashioned phone started to ring.

"Three—"

Edward screamed and there was a loud snap. But the pain receded to a dull ache quickly. And as he breathed through it, Dr. Qalbi did some probing.

"Pulses are strong. Looks like you dodged a bullet." The doctor got to his enviably functional feet. "But this incident begs the larger question of where you are in your recovery."

"In this chair," Edward groaned. "I am in this chair, obviously."

"You should have better mobility by now. And you shouldn't be self-medicating with alcohol. And you should—"

"Isn't the word 'should' a modern anathema? I thought there were no more 'shoulds.'"

"Pop psychology doesn't interest me. The fact that you are as weak as you are does."

"So I gather this means that a prescription for painkillers is out of the question. Worried about getting a second member of my family hooked on narcotics?"

"I'm not your mother's treating physician. And I assure you that I wouldn't be handling things as they are if I were." Dr. Qalbi bent down and picked up his bag. "I urge you to consider a short readmission into a rehab facility—"

"Not going to happen—"

"—to build up your strength. I also recommend an alcohol treatment—"

"—because I don't believe in doctors—"

"—program. The last thing you need to do—"

"—and there is nothing wrong—"

"—is add alcohol to this mix."

"—with my drinking."

Dr. Qalbi took a business card out of his back pocket. Offering it to Shelby, he said, "Take this. It has my cell phone on it. If you continue to live with him, you're going to be calling me again, and we might as well cut out the middleman answering service."

"I don't live with him," she said softly. "I work here."

"My apologies for the assumption." Dr. Qalbi glanced at Edward. "You can call me, too. And no—you don't need to bother. I know you'll say you won't."

The cottage door shut and a car drove off a moment later. And in the silence, Edward looked at his foot, which was now in the correct position and not angled out to the side. For some reason, he thought about the trip over here from the stables, him leaning on Shelby, his battered flesh draped over her lithe body like the deadweight he was.

As the phone began to ring again, Shelby glanced at it. "Would you like me to—"

"I'm sorry," he said roughly. "You're catching me at a time in my life when I'm just like your father was."

"You're not asking me to take care of you."

"Then why are you?"

"Someone has to."

"Not really. And you might want to ask yourself if you should leave."

"I need this job—"

He met her eyes, and something in his expression shut her up. "Shelby. I've got to be honest with you. Things . . . are only going to get worse from here. Harder."

"So don't drink as much. Or stop."

"That's not what I'm talking about."

Well, wasn't he a gentleman. Trying to save her life as his went to hell. And damn it, he wished that ringing would stop.

"Edward, you're drunk—"

As the phone finally went silent, all he could do was shake his head. "There are things that have happened with my family. Things . . . that are going to come out. It's not going to get better than it is right now."

A problem with his ankle was going to be the least of the issues.

As a car pulled up outside, he rolled his eyes. "Qalbi must have forgotten his bedside manner."

Shelby went over to the door and opened it. "It's someone else."

"If it's a long black limo with a pink Chanel suit in back, tell them to—"

"It's a man."

Edward smiled coldly. "At least I know it's not my father coming to see me. That little headache has been well taken care of."

When Edward looked over to the open doorway, he frowned as he saw who it was out front. "Shelby. Will you excuse us for a moment? Thank you."

TEN

Out in the sunshine at Easterly, Lane ended the call to Metro Police and looked at Samuel T., who'd come back out the grand front door.

"Okay, Counselor," Lane said. "We've got fifteen, twenty minutes before the homicide team arrives. At this point I'm on a first-name basis with them."

"So we've got enough time to hide evidence in case you did it." As Lizzie and Greta pulled a gasp-and-stare, Samuel T. rolled his eyes. "Relax. It was a joke—"

At that moment, Jeff Stern came pile driving out of the mansion. Lane's old college roommate and U.Va. fraternity brother looked about as relaxed and well slept as anybody who'd been up for too many nights straight, living on coffee and microscoping financial spreadsheets.

An extra from *The Walking Dead* had a better chance with *GQ.*

"We got a problem," Jeff said as he stumbled across the lawn.

Under different circumstances, he was actually a handsome guy, a self-professed anti-WASP with his proud Jewish heritage and New Jersey accent. He'd stood out at U.Va. for a lot of reasons, mostly because of his math skills, and had subsequently gone on to Wall Street to make sick money as an investment banker.

Lane had spent the last two years on the bastard's couch up in the Big Apple. And he'd repaid the favor by begging Jeff to take a "vacation" and figure out what the hell his father had done with all that money.

"Can it wait?" Lane said. "I need to—"

"No." Jeff glanced at Lizzie and Greta. "We need to talk."

"Well, we have fifteen minutes before the police get here."

"So you know? What the hell? Why didn't you tell me—"

"Know what?"

Jeff looked at the two women again, but Lane cut that off. "Anything you have to say to me can be done in front of them."

"You sure about that?" The guy put his palms up and cut off any argument. "Fine. Someone's embezzling from the company, too. It's not just whatever happened to your household accounts. There's a river of money leaving Bradford Bourbon, and if you want to have anything left, you better call the FBI now. There are bank wires all over the place, a lot of RICO shit going on—this needs to be handled by the Feds."

Lane looked at Lizzie, and as she reached out and took his hand, he wondered what the hell he would do without her. "Are you sure?"

His old friend shot him a give-me-a-break stare. "And I haven't even gone through all of it. It's that bad. You need to get senior management to halt all activity, then call the FBI, and lock up that business center behind this house."

Lane pivoted toward the mansion. After his mother had "taken ill," his father had converted what had previously been the stables behind the mansion into a fully functional, state-of-the-art office facility right on site. William had moved senior management in, put locks on all the doors, and turned the company's massive headquarters downtown into a second-fiddle, also-ran repository for vice presidents, directors, and middle managers. Ostensibly, the relocation of the brain trust had been so the man could stay home closer to his wife, but really, who could believe that, given that the pair of them had rarely been in the same room together.

Now Lane was seeing the real reason why. Easier to steal with fewer people around.

"Field trip," he announced.

With that, he released Lizzie's palm and strode off, heading around to the soccer-field-sized rear courtyard where the business center stretched out behind the mansion. In his wake, people were talking to him, but he ignored all that.

"Lane," Samuel T. said as he jumped in front. "What are you doing?"

"Saving electricity."

"I think we should call law enforcement—"

"I just did. Remember the finger?"

The business center's back door was locked with a big fat dead bolt secured by a coded system. Fortunately, when he and Edward had broken in a couple of days ago to get the financials, Lane had memorized the correct sequence of digits.

Punching them in on the pad, the entry unlocked and he walked into the hushed, luxurious interior. Every inch of the nearly twenty-thousand-square-foot, single-story structure was done in maroon-and-gold carpeting that was thick as a mattress. Insulated walls meant that no voices or ringing phones or tapping on keyboards traveled outside of a given space. And there were as many portriats on the walls as most iPhones had selfies.

With private offices for senior management, a gourmet kitchen and a reception area that resembled the Oval Office of the White House, the facility represented everything the Bradford Bourbon Company stood for: the highest standards of excellence, the oldest of traditions and the very best of the best for everything.

Lane didn't head for the higher-ups and their private offices, though. He went to the back, where the storage rooms and the kitchen were.

As well as the utilities.

Pushing through a double door, he entered a hot, window-less enclave full of mechanicals that included blowers for heat and air, and a hot-water heater . . . and the electrical panel.

Overhead lights were motion-activated, and he went directly across the concrete floor to the fuse box. Grabbing hold of a red handle at its side, he pulled the thing down, killing all current to the facility.

Everything went dark, and then low-lit security panels flared.

As he stepped back out into the hall, Samuel T. said dryly, "Well, that's one way to do it—"

Like wasps riled from a nest, executives came running, the three men, one woman, and receptionist clown-car'ing their way into the narrow corridor at the same time. They stopped dead as soon as they saw him.

The CFO, a sixty-year-old, Ivy League–educated know-it-all with manicured hands and shoes spit-shined at his private club, recoiled. "What are *you* doing here?"

"Shutting this place down."

"Excuse me?"

While another suit came skidding into the group, Lane just pointed to the back door he himself had come in through. "Get out. All of you."

The CFO got robin-chested and authori-voiced. "You do not have the right to—"

"The police are on their way." Which was technically true. "It's your choice whether you're leaving with them or in your own Mercedes. Or do you drive a Lexus?"

Lane watched their expressions carefully. And was entirely unsurprised when the CFO went on another you-have-no-right offensive.

"This is private property," Samuel T. said smoothly. "This facility is not on corporate land. You have just been informed by the owner that you are not welcome. You all look smart enough to already know trespassing law in Kentucky, but I am more than happy to provide you with a quick lesson or a refresher as necessary. It will involve a shotgun, however, and a—"

Lane elbowed his lawyer in the liver to shut him up.

Meanwhile, the CFO pulled himself together and ran a hand down his red tie. "There are critical functions managed from this—"

Lane went in face-to-face with the guy, prepared to grab him by the Brooks Brothers and drag him out onto the lawn. "Shut up and start walking."

"Your father would be appalled!"

"He's dead, remember. So he doesn't have an opinion. Now, are you leaving peacefully, or am I getting a gun like my lawyer was talking about."

"Are you threatening me?"

Samuel T. spoke up. "You're trespassing in three . . . two . . . one—"

"I'm going to tell the board chair about this—"

Lane crossed his arms over his chest. "As long as it's not on a phone here, I don't care whether you call the President of the United States or your fairy Godmother."

"Wait," Jeff cut in. "One of us will escort you to your offices for your car keys. You are not authorized to remove any equipment, drives, paperwork, or files from the premises."

"Good one," Lane said to his buddy.

O ut at the Red & Black caretaker's cottage, Edward smiled at his visitor as Shelby took her leave of them both. Ricardo Monteverdi was CEO of Prospect Trust, the largest privately held trust company in the middle of the country, and he looked the part, his trim figure and distinguished presentation in that pinstriped suit making Edward think of a brochure for the Wharton School of Business, ca. 1985. With the wall of silver trophies creating a halo around him, the glow suggested, falsely, that he might be a bearer of good tidings.

One knew better, however.

"Have you come to pay your respects about my father?" Edward drawled. "You needn't bother."

"Oh . . . but of course," the banker said with a brief bow. "I am very sorry about your loss."

"Which makes one of us."

There was a pause, and Edward wasn't sure whether the man was chewing on that quip or gearing up for the reason he'd come unannounced. Probably the latter.

"Is there something else?" Edward prompted.

"This is very awkward for me."

"Clearly."

There was another silence, as if the man would have much preferred Edward get to the point. But that was not going to happen. As Edward had long learned in business, he who opened the meeting in any given negotiation lost.

And yes, he knew why the man had driven out to the farm.

Monteverdi coughed a little. "Well, now. Indeed. With your father's death, certain . . . arrangements . . . that he made need to be attended to, and in my case, with alacrity. Although I know you are in mourning, I'm afraid that there is one situation in particular which cannot be put off and which is imminently due. Accordingly, and in order to protect your family's name and reputation, I am coming to you so that things may be handled discreetly."

"I have no idea what you're talking about." Liar, liar, pants on fire. "So I'm afraid you will have to be more specific."

"Your father came to me several months ago for a private loan. I was happy to take care of what he required, but let us say that I had to get creative with the financing. The monies are due now and they must be repaid before the quarterly Prospect Trust board meeting or—"

"Or you will be in a tight spot?"

Monteverdi's face got hard. "No, I will be forced to put your family in a tight spot."

"I can't help you."

"I don't think you understand. If that money is not repaid, I'm going to have to take legal action, and that will become very public, very quickly."

"So sue us. Call the *New York Times* and tell them we owe your Trust company fifty-three million dollars. Tell them we're deadbeats, liars, thieves. I don't care."

"I thought you said you knew nothing of this."

Goddamn drink was still in his veins. Also, he was out of practice with verbal sparring.

"I think the issue," Edward said with a smile, "is your needing to protect yourself. You're trying to strong-arm me so that you don't have to tell your board that you executed a massive, unsecured loan without their knowledge and admit that you've been skimming the interest from it for yourself. My response is that I don't give a shit. Do whatever you have to. I don't care because it's not my problem."

"Your mother is in a delicate state."

"She's in a coma for all intents and purposes."

"As the eldest son, I would think you'd care about her welfare more than this."

"I moved out here to this incredible luxury"—Edward waved a hand around at the ratty furniture—"to get away from all of that and all of them for a good reason. So sink that big fancy ship up on that hill. Shoot your cannons at my family's mansion until the whole lot of it ends up on the seafloor. It is not going to affect me one way or another."

Monteverdi jabbed a finger across the space. "You are not worthy of calling yourself a son."

"Considering who my parents are, I'm proud of having lasted as long as I did under that roof. And do us both a favor. Don't try to mask your self-interest in the rhetoric of altruism while you're threatening my family. Tell me, how much interest did you pocket? Ten percent? Fifteen? If the loan was for six months, that's at least two and a half million right there for you. Nice work if you can find it, huh."

Monteverdi tugged at his icy white French cuffs. "I regard this as a declaration of war. What happens next is your fault."

"How codependent of you." Edward indicated his body. "But I've been tortured for eight days by people who were going to kill me, and in my case, that is not hyperbole. If you think there is anything that you can do to get my attention, you are delusional."

"Just watch. You may not care about your mother, but I wonder if you feel so cavalier about your siblings. As far as I understand it, you have always been quite the caretaker."

"Were."

"We shall see."

The man turned away and was out the door a moment later. And as the old-fashioned phone started to ring again, Edward stared down at his ruined legs . . . and wondered, not for the first time, what might have been.

What should have been.

Too late for all that now, however.

Cranking his head to the side, he stared at that receiver hanging on the wall by the galley kitchen. The thought of walking over there exhausted him, but mostly, he knew what the call probably was about.

They were going to have to come for him if they wanted him, though.

ELEVEN

*E*dwin MacAllan, Master Distiller for the Bradford Bourbon Company, was getting nowhere. Sitting in his office, which had been his father's command central up until the man had died unexpectely a decade ago, Mack was trying to reach someone, anyone at the business center. Nothing. All he was getting was voice mail, which, considering he was dialing senior management's private lines and not going through the receptionist, was unprecedented.

The CFO, COO, and three senior vice presidents were not picking up.

Lane was also not answering his cell.

As Mack hung up the phone again, he knew damn well that caller ID on the corporate phones meant that people knew who it was. And whereas one or two might not have answered, all five? Yes, their CEO had died, and there was chaos, but the business had to keep running.

"Hey, am I doing this—"

Before Mack could get to the word "right," he shut his mouth and remembered that his executive assistant, who had also been his father's, was not out there anymore. And hadn't been since her brother had had a heart attack the day before yesterday.

As if all the interviews he'd done today hadn't reminded him of the loss?

Clearly, they'd just thrown him into a case of denial.

Putting his elbows on the piles of paperwork, he rubbed his head. Hiring was a lot like dating. HR had sent over a number of candidates, and each one of them had been a swipe left, the executive assistant equivalents of high-maintenance, bobbleheaded beauty queens; neurotic, Glenn Close, bunny-boiling clingers; or sex-less, defensive, hairy-armpitted man-haters.

"Shit."

Getting up, he walked around the battered old desk and took a lingering stroll around, looking at the artifacts that were displayed in glass cases and shadowboxes. There was the first barrel that had been stamped with No. Fifteen, the company's brand of relatively reasonably priced bourbon. A line-up of special bottles celebrating the University of Charlemont basketball program's wins in the NCAA tournament in 1980, 1986, and 2013. Historic revolvers. Maps. Letters from Abraham Lincoln and Andrew Jackson to various Bradfords.

But the wallpaper itself was the true testimony to the company's product, longevity, and pride. Every inch of flat, vertical space was layered with labels from countless bottles, the different fonts and colors and images illustrating an evolution of marketing, value proposition, and price.

Even as the product that was packaged stayed exactly the same.

Bradford Bourbon was made precisely the way it had been since the late 1700s, nothing changing, not the make-up of the grain mash, not the strain of yeast, not the special limestone aquifer-fed water source, not the charred oak of the barrels. And God knew the Kentucky seasons and the number of days in a calendar year hadn't altered.

As he measured the history that had come before him, it seemed inconceivable that over two centuries of tradition could end on his watch.

But the corporate bigwigs had decided, before William Baldwine had died, to freeze the purchasing of corn, which meant there was no more mash, which meant Mack had had to shut production down.

It would be unprecedented. Even during Prohibition, the BBC had continued to make its liquor, albeit after a relocation to Canada for a time.

After fighting with the suits and getting nowhere, Mack had turned whistleblower at Easterly and let Lane in on the shutdown—and then Mack had helped the prodigal son get access to some of the corporate financials. But after that? He hadn't heard anything since.

It was like waiting for biopsy results, and the stress was killing him. If he lost this job, this livelihood? He was losing his father, plain and simple.

And he hadn't liked living through that the first time.

Antsy and frustrated, he went out into the reception area. The barney, empty space was too quiet and too cool, the hot air rising up to the exposed beams of the converted cabin's high peaked roof, the AC'd stuff falling to the floorboards. Like the rest of the Old Site, as this campus was known, the Master Distiller's office was housed in a refurbished original structure, the old mortar and log construction retrofitted with everything from running water to Wi-Fi in as unobtrusive a manner as possible.

Hitting the oversized door, he stepped outside and wandered across the cropped lawn. The Old Site was as much a functioning bourbon producing facility as it was a tourist attraction to teach laymen and aficionados alike exactly what made Bradford the best. Accordingly, there was a Disney World cast to the acreage, in the very best sense, the buildings all quaint and painted black and red with little pathways leading from grain silo to mash house to stills and storage barns. And ordinarily, there would be groups of tourists led by guides, the parking lots full, the gift shop and reception buildings bustling with activity.

Out of respect for the passing of William Baldwine, everything was closed to nonessential personnel for the next week.

Or at least that was what senior management had said. More likely? The cost cutting wasn't just stopping at the grain supply.

Eventually, Mack ended up in front of one of the three storage barns. The seven-floor, uninsulated wooden buildings housed hundreds of aging barrels of bourbon on heavy wooden racking systems, the temperature variants of the seasons setting the stage for the alchemy that happened as the alcohol dated, fell in love, and married the charred fibers of its temporary wooden home.

As he opened a paneled door, the handmade hinges creaked, and the rich, earthy scent that hit him as he stepped inside reminded him of his father. The interior was dark, the beams supporting the rows and rows of barrels rough cut and worn, the thin pathways that cut in between the stacked racks two boards wide and thirty feet long.

The center aisle was much broader and made of concrete, and he put his hands in the pockets of his jeans as he stalked deeper and deeper into the building.

"Lane, what are we doing here," he asked out loud.

Bourbon required time. It wasn't like making vodka, where you could just turn on a spigot and there you had it. If the company wanted something to sell seven years, ten years, twelve years from now? You had to keep the sills running now—

"Um . . . excuse me?"

Mack pivoted. Standing in the open doorway, with light streaming in behind her, a woman with an hourglass shape and long dark hair was like an apparition from some sexual fantasy. God . . . he could even smell her perfume or her soap or whatever it was on the fresh air passing by her body and blowing into the stacks.

She seemed equally surprised as she looked at him.

"I'm so sorry," she said in a low, unaccented voice. "I'm looking for Edwin MacAllan. I have an interview with him, but there's nobody in the office—"

"You found me."

There was a pause. "Oh." She shook her head. "I'm sorry. I just— anyway, my name is Beth. Beth Lewis. Do you, ah, do you want me to come back some other time?"

No, he thought as her hair caught the breeze and curled up off her shoulder.

Actually . . . I don't want you to leave.

"*I* can't reach Edward."

As Lane strode across the business center's reception area and into his father's office, it was like walking into a room full of loaded guns pointed in his direction: His skin pricked in warning and his hands cranked into fists and he just wanted to turn around and beat feet out of there.

Then again, the place was eerie as hell. The dim security lighting from his power cut tinted everything with a grim portent, and the ghost of William Baldwine seemed to lurk in the shadows.

Lane had no clue why he'd come in here. The police were probably pulling up in front of Easterly right now.

He shook his head as he looked at the regal desk and the big carved chair that was like a throne. Everything about the pair was like a stage set from a Humphrey Bogart film: A crystal decanter full of bourbon. A silver tray of cut-crystal glasses. A picture of Little V.E. in a silver frame. A humidor with the Cubans his father had liked on the other corner by the Tiffany lamp. A pack of Dunhill cigarettes and a gold lighter next to a clean Cartier ashtray. No computer. No paperwork. And the phone was a high-tech afterthought, dwarfed by the lifestyle, the objet d'arrogance.

"This is only the second time I've been in this office," he murmured toward Lizzie, who'd stayed by the door. "I never envied Edward."

While she glanced around at the leather-bound books, and the diplomas, and the photographs of William with prominent national and international men, he found himself focusing on her: the way her hair, which had been blonded by the sun; her breasts as they filled out her black polo shirt; her long, muscled legs, which were showed off by those shorts.

Lust clawed into his gut.

"Lizzie—"

Jeff walked into the open doorway. "Okay, they've all left. The place is empty, and your lawyer's gone back to the house to meet the police. Do you know how to change the code on that door? Because I would, if I were you."

Lane blinked to clear the mental image of him shoving everything off the desk and putting Lizzie right up on it naked.

"Ah, I don't, but we'll figure it out." Lane stretched his tight back. "Listen, can you give me a quick idea of exactly what you found at corporate?"

Jeff glanced around and didn't seem particularly impressed by the grandeur. "On the surface, the transfers I flagged look like your garden-variety debt-service payments to various banks. But then there are these huge balloon payments—and that was what got me worried first. Tracing the money transfers, I discovered notations for something called WWB Holdings—which turned out to be William Wyatt Baldwine Holdings. I believe it's a case of off-balance sheet financing that's gone out of control, and if so, I'm confident it qualifies as embezzlement. Now, when I did some Internet searches and called in a favor at UBS, I couldn't find anything anywhere on precisely what WWB Holdings is or where it's located, but I'll let you guess who was in charge of it."

"Sonofabitch," Lane muttered. "That's where the household money went, too. WWB Holdings. So how much are we talking about?"

"Seventy-two million. So far."

As Lizzie gasped, Lane shook his head. *"Damn it."*

Lizzie spoke up. "Wait, what's off-sheet balance—"

"Off-balance sheet financing." Jeff rubbed his eyes like he had the same headache Lane did. "Basically, it's when you leverage the assets of one company to secure debt for another. If the second entity fails, the bank or lender expects the first one to pay up. In this case? I'm willing to bet that the funds lent to WWB Holdings were embezzled and when the loan terms weren't met, the Bradford Bourbon Company's money was used to meet the obligations. It's a way of stealing that's a little less obvious than just writing yourself a corporate check and cashing it."

"Over one hundred and forty million?" Lane crossed his arms over his chest as he was struck by a fury that made him want to trash the office. "That's the total. You've got to be kidding me."

"And that seventy plus million is just transfers from the operations accounts through February. There are going to be more. There's an escalating pattern to it all." Jeff shrugged. "I'm telling you, Lane, it's time to involve the FBI. This is too big for me to keep going—especially because I have to go back to New York. It's been a helluva vacation, though."

Lane's phone started ringing, and when he took it out and saw it was Samuel T., he answered with, "Are they here? I'm coming—"

"What are you doing!"

The woman who rushed into the office was sixty and built like the battleship she was. From her gunmetal-gray suit to the dinner-roll bun of her gray hair, Ms. Petersberg was a tightly wrapped piece of work who had been running William Baldwine's business life for close to twenty years. But gone was the usual composure. Red-faced and wall-eyed, she was trembling, the reading glasses that hung down from her neck on a thin chain bouncing on her flat chest as she panted.

Lane kept his voice even. "Get your things. Get out."

"You have no right to be in this office!"

Hysteria erupted from the woman, and she was surprisingly strong as she came at him, her fingers clawing at his face, her knees and feet kicking at him, shrill curses and condemnations punctuating the attack. Lizzie and Jeff lunged forward to try to peel her off, but Lane shook his head at them. Capturing her hands, he let her keep screaming as he eased her up against the bookcases as gently as he could.

By the time she'd worn herself out, that neat bun was looking like a tossed salad on her head and her breathing was so ragged, it was like she needed an oxygen feed or she was going to pass out.

"You can't save him," Lane said grimly. "It was too late for that some time ago. And I know you know things. The question you have to ask yourself is how much are you willing to pay for your loyalty to a dead man. I'm finding out more and more of what went on here, and I know you were a part of it. Are you willing to go to jail for him? Are you that insane?"

He said this even though he wasn't sure whether he was going to call the Feds or not. Prison was usually a good inducement, however, and he wasn't above using that leverage at the moment.

And besides, he told himself, if the fraud was as large as Jeff said it was? Then those lenders were going to start dropping dimes on their end when further payments were not made—and yes, some would call lawyers, and when the assets dried up even further?

It was going to be debt-mageddon at the BBC.

"He was a good man," Ms. Petersberg spat. "Your father was always good to me."

"That's because you were useful to him. Don't take it personally, and don't ruin your own life over the illusion that you were anything other than something he could manipulate."

"I will *never* understand why you boys hate him so much."

"Then you need to wake up."

When she broke free, he let her go so she could pat her hair down and reorder her clothing.

"Your father only ever had his family's best interests and the interests of the company at heart. He was a . . ."

Lane went out-of-body as the woman proselytized about virtues she ascribed to a man who had none to speak of. All of that was not his problem, however. You couldn't change the mind of an apostolate; you couldn't save someone who didn't want to get in the lifeboat.

So this ever-efficient woman was going to go down with her former boss.

Not his problem.

As his phone started to ring again, she concluded, "He was always there when I needed him."

Lane didn't recognize the number and let whoever it was go into voice mail. "Well, then, I hope you enjoy the fond memories—when you end up in jail."

TWELVE

"Do you have any questions for me?"

As Mack put the inquiry out there, he sat back in his office chair and looked at his interviewee's ring finger again. Still vacant. Suggesting this Beth Lewis was as unmarried as she had been at the start of their meeting.

Yeah, wow. Way to be professional, MacAllan.

"Are you going to need me to stay late frequently?" Beth put her palms out. "I mean, the candidate. Will the candidate have to? And it's not because I'm afraid of working. But I take care of my mother and I'll need to get coverage for her after five. I can arrange it, I just need a little notice."

"I'm so sorry to hear, you know, that anyone is . . ." He wasn't sure about HR policy, but he was certain he couldn't ask too much about her personally. "That your mother . . ."

"She was in a car accident two years ago. She was on life support for months, and she has a lot of cognitive challenges now. I moved into her house to take care of her and, you know, we make it work. But I need a job to support us and—"

"You're hired."

Beth recoiled, her dark brows lifting. Then she laughed in a burst. "What? I mean, wow. I didn't expect—"

"You've got four years of experience at the front desk of a real estate company. You're personable, articulate, and professional. There's nothing else I'm looking for really."

"Don't you want to check my references?"

He looked down at the résumé she'd given him. "Yeah. Of course."

"Wait, that sounds like I'm trying to talk you out of it—but I am *so* excited. Thank you. I won't let you down."

As she got to her feet, he did the same, and he forced his eyes to stay on hers—because left to their own devices, they were liable to go on a walkabout heading south. Man, she was tall—and that was very attractive. And so was that long hair. And those eyes that were—

Crap. He probably liked too much about her to hire her. She was, however, very qualified.

Extending his hand across his desk, he said, "Welcome to the party."

She held on to his palm. "Thank you," she breathed. "You will not regret it."

God, he hoped that was true. He was single, she might be single, they were both adults . . . but yeah, it was probably not a great idea to add "employer/employee sexual relationship" to that mix.

"I'll walk you out." Leading the way over to his office's door and then across the reception area, he opened the exit wide for her. "Can you start—"

"Tomorrow? Yes, I can."

"Good."

The car she'd parked in the little gravel side lot was a Kia that was several years old, but as he escorted her to it, he saw that it was neat inside, clean on the outside, and with no dings or scratches on its silver body.

Just before Beth got behind the wheel, she looked up at him. "Why is it so quiet today? I mean, I've been here as a tourist—last year, in fact. There were so many people walking around even on the weekdays."

"We're in mourning. I'm sure you've heard."

"About?" She shook herself. "Oh, wait, yes, I'm embarrassed. Of course. William Baldwine's death. I'm so sorry."

"As am I. I'll see you tomorrow morning at nine?"

"At nine. And thanks again."

Mack wanted to watch her drive off, but that was a date move, not an I-just-hired-you-and-I'm-not-a-creeper one. Heading back around, he was halfway to goal when he decided more desk time was not what he needed.

Changing direction, he proceeded to an outbuilding that had a high hedge around it, no windows, and siding that was modern steel paneling, not logs and mortar. Taking out a pass card, he swiped the thing in a reader and heard the vapor lock release. Inside, there was an anteroom with some protective gear, but he didn't bother with it. Never had, even though everyone else did.

For godsakes, he'd always thought. When the first Bradfords had been making their bourbon, they hadn't needed "gear." They'd done it in the woods, and everything had worked out just fine.

A second glass door also let out a hiss, and the shallow room beyond was a laboratory like something you'd find at the Centers for Disease Control. But they weren't tracking or trying to cure diseases here.

He was growing things, though. Secret things that no one else could know about.

The crux of the issue was, all ingredients in bourbon were necessary and important, but there was only one element that wasn't truly fungible. Assuming you kept the percentages in the mash the same, corn was corn, barley was barley, and rye was rye. The special limestone-fed water source they used was unique to this part of Kentucky, but its yield remained the same year in and year out, the subterranean rock not changing at all. Even the barrels, made from separate trees, were still constructed out of the same species of oak.

Yeast, however, was a different story.

Although all distillers' yeast came from a species called *Saccharomyces cerevisiae*, there were many different strains in that family, and depending on which one you used to ferment your mash, the flavor of your bourbon could vary tremendously. Yes, ethanol was always a by-product of the metabolic process, but there were countless other compounds released as the sugars in the mash were consumed by the yeast. Call it alchemy, call it magic, call it the touch of angels; depending on what strain you used, your product could range from the good to the spectacular . . . to the downright epic.

The BBC had been using the same strains in its No. Fifteen, Family Reserve, Black Mountain, and Bradford I brands forever.

But sometimes change wasn't a bad thing.

Back when his father had died, Mack had been working on new strains of yeast, peeling molds from nuts and bark and soils from all over the South, growing the precious organisms in this lab, and analyzing their DNA among other things. Isolating the proper species, he had then toyed with small-batch fermentations to test all kinds of end results.

There had been a protracted delay in the project when he'd taken on the Master Distiller's job, but over the last three months, he'd had a breakthrough—finally, after all this time, he had become satisfied with one of the results.

As he looked at all the glass containers with their tinfoil tops, the Petri dishes, the samples, the microscopes and computers, he found it hard to imagine that such beauty could come out of so stark a place. Then again, it was kind of like an IVF lab, where human miracles got a little help from science.

Mack went over to the counter and stood in front of his baby, the one bottle with the first new strain that was going to be introduced into a Bradford bourbon fermentation process in two hundred years. It was that good, that special, yielding an unparalleled smoothness with absolutely no sulfur overtones to the taste. And no one else, no other maker of bourbon, had claimed it yet.

He was going to patent the stuff.

This was the other reason the BBC couldn't fail now.

The damn company had to stay alive long enough to get this on the market.

His little yeast discovery was going to change everything.

"*Y*ou need to eat."

It was past five o'clock by the time the police left, and Lane's first thought, as he walked into Easterly's kitchen, was more that he needed a drink. Miss Aurora, however, had other ideas.

As she set her strong body in his path and her black eyes glared up at him, he regressed in an instant back to being five years old. And it was funny—she looked exactly the same as she always had, her hair braided tight to her head, her U of C red apron tied at the waist around her loose chef's whites, her take charge attitude nothing to trifle with.

Given her illness, the immortality was an illusion, but at the moment, he clung to the fiction.

And when she routed him into the staff hallway, he didn't fight her. Not because he was tired, although he was, and not because he wanted to eat anything, because he didn't, but because he had never been able to deny her anything. She was a law of physics in the world, as undeniable as the gravity that had pulled him off that bridge.

It was hard to believe she was dying.

Unlike the formal family dining and breakfast rooms, the staff break room was nothing but white walls, a pine table that sat twelve, and a wooden floor. It did have a couple of windows that looked out over a dark corner of the garden, although those glass panes were more to preserve the symmetry of the mansion's rear exterior than out of any concern for the viewing pleasure of the people who ate there.

"I'm not really hungry," he said to her back as she left him to seat himself.

A minute later, the plate that landed in front of him had about two thousand calories of soul food on it. And as he breathed deep, he thought . . . huh. Miss Aurora might be right.

Lizzie sat down next to him with her own plate. "This looks amazing, Miss Aurora."

His momma took her place at the head of the table. "There's seconds on my stove."

Fried chicken done in an iron skillet. Collard greens. Real corn bread. Hoppin' John. Okra.

And what do you know. After the first bite, he was starving, and then there was a long period of silence as he hoovered forkloads of the food he'd been raised on into his mouth.

When his phone rang, it was like an electric shock nailing him in the ass. Then again, lately that ringing sound was like a tornado siren going off: nothing but bad news, with the only question being what was in the path of destruction.

As he answered, Deputy Ramsey's ocean-deep drawl came over the connection. "You should have the remains in about forty-eight hours at the latest. Even with what was found, the medical examiner has done what she needs to."

"Thank you. Anything surprising in the preliminary report?"

"They were going to sneak me a copy. As soon as I know anything I'll be in touch."

"Homicide left about a half hour ago. They think someone murdered my father, don't they? The detectives wouldn't give me anything to go on, but I mean, it was my father's fucking ring—"

As Miss Aurora cleared her throat sharply, he winced. "Sorry, ma'am."

"What?" Ramsey said.

"My momma's here." Ramsey let out an "uh-huh," as if he knew exactly what was up with dropping an f-bomb in front of Miss Aurora Toms. "I mean, Detective Merrimack said he was going to be interviewing people. How long until they have an idea of what happened?"

"No telling." There was a pause. "Do you know of anyone who might have killed him?"

Yes. "No."

"Not even any suspicions?"

"You sound like that detective."

"Sorry, occupational hazard. So are you aware of anybody who had a motive?"

"You know what my father was like. He had enemies everywhere."

"It's pretty personal, though, cutting off that ring. Burying it in front of the house."

Under his mother's bedroom window, no less. But Lane wasn't going to go into that.

"There were plenty of businesspeople who hated him, too." God, that sounded defensive. "And he owed people money, Mitch. Big money."

"So why didn't they keep the ring and hock it? Lot of gold."

Lane opened his mouth. Then shut it. "I think we're getting off track."

"I'm not so sure about that."

"What's that supposed to mean?"

"Let's just say that I've protected members of your family before. And nothing is going to change that."

Lane closed his eyes, thinking about Edward. "How am I ever going to repay you?"

"I'm the one paying a debt back. But now's not the time for that. And there's another reason I called. Rosalinda Freeland's remains were picked up today."

Lane pushed his plate away. "By her mother?"

"By her son. He just turned eighteen so it was legal."

"And?"

There was another pause, longer this time. "I was there when he came in. Have you seen him?"

"I'm not sure I was even aware she had a kid."

"His photograph is going to be on the front page tomorrow."

"Why? I mean, other than the fact that his mother committed suicide right before my father's body was found."

"Yeah, I'm going to send you a picture after we hang up. I'll call you later."

As Lane ended the connection, he looked across at Miss Aurora. "You know Mitch Ramsey, don't you?"

"I do, yes. All his life. And if he wants to tell you why, he will. That's his business, not mine."

Lane put the cell phone down on the table and dropped the subject—because like there was another option? Glancing at Lizzie, he said, "Do you think there's any way we can do the visitation here on Thursday?"

"Absolutely." Lizzie nodded. "The gardens and grounds are in great shape from the Derby Brunch. Everything else is easy to do on a short turnaround. What are you thinking?"

"Four to seven p.m. on Thursday night. We can keep the burial private and do it on Friday or Saturday. But I want to get that visitation out of the way."

Miss Aurora leaned across and pushed his plate back in front of him. "Eat."

He didn't get a chance to. Before he could start arguing, Mr. Harris, the butler, opened the door. "Mr. Baldwine, you have a guest in the front parlor. I gather he is not expected, but he is refusing to leave."

"Who is it?"

"Mr. Monteverdi of the Prospect Trust Company."

Lane got to his feet and took his cell phone and his plate with him. "I'm coming right now."

Miss Aurora scooped the plate out of his hands. "And this will be waiting for you when you're finished. You don't eat in that part of the house."

"Yes, ma'am."

Dropping a kiss on Lizzie's mouth, Lane headed out, striding through the stark hallway that led past Mr. Harris's suite of rooms, Rosalinda Freeland's office—where she had killed herself—and one of the mansion's three laundry rooms. He was pushing his way out into the formal public rooms when his phone went off with a text.

As he continued across the black-and-white marble floor of the foyer, he put his password in and was just at the archway into the parlor when the image Mitch Ramsey had sent him came up.

Lane stopped dead.

He couldn't believe what he was looking at.

The son who had claimed Rosalinda's body . . . could have been his own twin.

THIRTEEN

*P*rinted spreadsheets everywhere. Multiple laptops with Excel files around him in a semi-circle. Yellow legal pads covered with black chicken scratchings.

For Jeff Stern, all this was business as usual. As a Wall Street investment banker, he made his bread and butter crunching numbers and finding patterns and holes in corporate financial disclosure documents. He was a master at precisely the kind of obsessive, detail-orientated, mind-numbing work required to create sense and concrete out of the oft-times deliberate obstruction and oily, creative accounting techniques used to value large multi-national companies.

"I'm here to refresh your bathroom."

What he was *not* used to when he was working was a twenty-something blonde in a maid's uniform standing in the doorway of the Four Seasons–worthy bedroom suite that was serving as his office.

Well, at least not a woman that some misogynist a-hole in the cesspool he worked in hadn't ordered up from an escort service.

Oh, and with her heavy Southern accent, all that had come out as "Ahhhhm heeyr to rafrash ya bathrum."

That stack of white towels in her arms was like a summer cloud captured on earth and she smelled amazing, some kind of girlie perfume crossing the distance and offering a caress as if she were stroking him. Her face was the sort that its youth was its most attractive attribute, but her eyes were an amazing cornflower blue—and her body turned that actual uniform into something that could have passed at Halloween for a naughty maid.

"You know where it is," he murmured.

"Yes, I do."

He watched the back view as she sauntered by as if she were naked— and she left the door wide open as she futzed around at his sink . . . then bent down low to search for something in the cabinet. That skirt of hers rode up so much, the lace tops on her thigh highs flashed.

Craning around, she looked at him. "My name's Tiphanii. With a *ph* in the middle and two *i*'s on the end. Are you leaving?"

"What?"

She straightened and leaned back against the marble counter, bracing her hands on either side of her hips so that the top of her uniform stretched open. "Your bags are gettin' all packed?"

Jeff glanced over at the bed. On it, the duffels he'd stuffed full of his things were wide open, clothes spilling out of them like soldiers with knife wounds to the gut. And the stuff was going to stay that way. His OCD stopped at spreadsheets and columns of numbers. He didn't care what condition his shit was in when he got back home to Manhattan. That was what they made dry cleaners for.

Jeff refocused on the maid. "I have to go back to work."

"Is it true you're from Manhattan? New York City?"

"Yes."

"I've never been." She rubbed her legs together as if she had a need she wanted him to know about. "I've always wanted to go there."

And then she just stared at him.

This was not a good idea, Jeff thought as he got up and walked across the Oriental carpet. This was *really* not a good idea.

Stepping into the bathroom, he shut the door behind himself. "I'm Jeff."

"I know. We all know who you are. You're that friend of Lane's."

He put his forefinger on the base of her throat. "Word travels fast."

On a slow trail, he traced her soft skin down into the V that was made by the lapels of the uniform. In response, she started to breathe heavily, her breasts pumping.

"I'm here to take care of you," she whispered.

"Are you."

The uniform was gray with a white collar and white pearlescent buttons—and as he rested his fingertip on the top one, his erection throbbed behind his fly. It had been a brutal seventy-two hours, full of nothing but numbers crunching, headaches, and bad news. This very clear offer was like rain falling on parched earth, as far as he was concerned.

Jeff undid the first button. The second. The third. Her bra was black, just like the thigh highs.

Bending down, he kissed her neck, and as she arched back, he slipped his arm around her waist. Condom. He needed a condom—and knowing Lane's old reputation, there had to be one around here . . .

As he pulled the top of the uniform wide and released the front clasp of her bra, her tight nipples were exposed and oh, yeah, they were perfect. And at the same time, he looked around her and opened the first of the drawers.

Good job, he thought as he found a three-pack of bright blue foiled Trojans.

Next thing he knew, he had the maid naked except for the thigh highs. She was magnificent, all real breasts and good hips, supple thighs and sweet flesh. He stayed clothed, and slipped one of those condoms on without losing a beat.

Tiphanii, with two *i*'s at the end, knew exactly how to wrap her legs around and lock her ankles behind his hips, and oh, yeah, the sound she made in his ear. Planting one palm next to the antique mirror on the wall and holding her waist with the other, he started thrusting. As she grabbed on to his shoulders, he closed his eyes.

It was so damned good. Even though this was anonymous, and obviously the result of his foreigner status making him seem exotic. Sometimes, though, you had to take advantage of what crossed your path.

She found her release before he did. Or at least she put a show on as if she did; he wasn't sure and wasn't bothered if it was an act.

His orgasm was for real, though, powerful and racking, a reminder that, at least for him, flesh and blood was better than the alternative every time.

When he was finished, Tiphanii snuggled up to his chest as he caught his breath.

"Mmm," she whispered into his ear. "That was good."

Yes, it was, he thought as he pulled out.

"Then let's do it again," he groaned as he picked her up and headed for the bed.

*D*ownstairs in the parlor, Lane let Ricardo Monteverdi talk everything out even though Lane knew exactly how much was owed and how much of an emergency it was going to be for Monteverdi if those millions weren't paid back.

A glass of Family Reserve helped pass the time—and cut the retinal burn from that photograph of Rosalinda's son. The hair, the eyes, the shape of the face, the build of the body—

"And your brother was not helpful."

Okay, so the speech was wrapping up. "Edward isn't really involved in the family anymore."

"And he calls himself a son—"

"Watch yourself," Lane bit out. "Any insult against my brother is an offense to me."

"Pride can be an expensive luxury."

"So is professional integrity. Especially if it's built on falsity." Lane toasted the man with his bourbon. "But we digress. I haven't been back here for two years, and there is a lot to wrestle with in light of my father's unfortunate demise."

There was a pause, during which Monteverdi was clearly calibrating his approach. When the man finally spoke again, his voice was both smooth and aggressive at the same time. "You must understand that this loan has to be paid back now."

Funny, there had been two weeks only a week ago. Guess the Prospect Trust board had gotten wind of something, or somebody had caught the trail of the loan.

Lane had wondered how the guy had managed to make the deal without getting caught.

"The will is being probated," Lane said, "and I don't have access to any of the family accounts except for my own as I have no power of attorney for my mother, and my father named his personal attorney, Babcock Jefferson, as his executor. If you're looking to be paid, you should be talking to Mr. Jefferson."

When Monteverdi cleared his throat, Lane thought, Ahhhh, so the man had gone that route already and been shut down.

"I should think, Lane, that you'd prefer to take a more personal interest in this."

"And why is that?"

"You have enough to keep out of the press as it is."

"My father's death is already on the news."

"That is not to which I refer."

Lane smiled and got up, heading back to the bar set-up on its brass cart. "Tell me something, how are you going to release the information that my family is broke and not send yourself up the river?" He glanced over his shoulder. "I mean, let's get it all out in the open, shall we? You're threatening me with some kind of reveal, and even if it's an anonymous tip on your part, how exactly is that going to play out for you when your board learns about this loan you and my father thought up together? We're not a good bet right now, and you must have known that going into the loan. You have access to all the trust information. You knew damn well how much was, and was not, in those accounts of ours."

"Well, I would think you'd want to spare your mother the ignominy of—"

"My mother hasn't been out of bed for almost three years. She's not reading the newspaper, and the only guests she has are her nurses—all of whom will adhere to any gag order I give them or they'll lose their jobs. Tell me, did you try that one out on my brother, too, when you spoke with him? I don't imagine it got you very far at all."

"I did nothing but help out an old friend. Your family, however, will not survive the scandal—and you must know that your mother's trust is severely depleted. Unbeknownst to me, your father made a withdrawal of nearly the entire corpus a day before he died. There is less than six million remaining in it. Your sister's trust is gone. Your brother Max's trust is empty. Edward's assets are at zero. And lest you think this is all our mismanagement, your father became the trustee on all of them as soon as he had your mother declared incompetent. And before you ask me why we allowed him to do what he did, I will remind you that he was acting within his legal rights."

Well. Wasn't all that a lovely little news flash. Sixty-eight million had seemed like a big deal. And then the hundred and forty million. And now . . .

Hundreds of millions were gone.

Lane turned his back to Monteverdi as he lifted his glass. He didn't want the other man to see his hands shake.

The six million in his mother's trust was a fortune to most people. But with Easterly's household expenses alone, that figure would be gone in half a year.

"I would have explained this to your brother," Monteverdi murmured, "but he wasn't inclined to listen."

"You went to him first and then to Babcock."

"Can you blame me?"

"Did Babcock tell you where my father put all the money?" Lane shook his head. "Never mind. If he had, you wouldn't be here."

Lane's brain skipped around, and then he looked at the liquor bottle he'd just had in his palm.

At least he knew where he could get his hands on some cash.

"How much time will ten million buy me?" he heard himself say.

"You don't have that—"

"Shut up and answer the question."

"I can give you another week. But I'll need a wire. By tomorrow afternoon."

"And that will reduce the debt to forty-three million."

"No. That is the price for me risking my reputation for your family. The debt level will remain the same."

Lane shot a glare over his shoulder. "Aren't you a gentleman."

The distinguished man shook his head. "This is not personal, Mr. Baldwine. It's business. And from a business perspective, I can . . . delay things for a short period of time."

Thanks, you bastard, Lane thought. "You'll get your blood money. Tomorrow."

"That would be much appreciated."

After the man gave him the details of where the funds needed to go, Monteverdi bowed at the waist and showed himself to the exit. In the quiet that followed, Lane took out his phone.

He knew where to get the money. But he was going to need some help.

FOURTEEN

"*I* need you to do this."

As Edward held the receiver to his ear, his brother Lane's voice was grim—and so was the news. Everything gone. Trusts drained dry. Accounts wiped out. Generations of wealth dematerialized.

"Edward? You have to go see her."

For some reason, Edward glanced around into the kitchen proper. Shelby was at the stove, stirring something in a pot that smelled shockingly good.

"Edward." Lane cursed. "Hello?"

Shelby had a strand of hair that had gotten loose from her ponytail, and she shoved it behind her ear like it was irritating her as she stared down into the soup. Stew. Sauce. Whatever it was.

She had changed her jeans, but not her boots, her shirt but not her fleece. She was always covered up, he noted absently, as if she were cold.

When had he started to catch these little things about her?

"Fine," Lane snapped. "I'll go and take care of it—"

"No." Edward shifted his weight and turned away from the kitchen. "I'll go."

"I need the wire by tomorrow. Monteverdi gave me the routing and account numbers. I'll text them to you."

"I don't have a cell phone. I'll let you know where to send the account details."

"Fine. There's another thing, though." There was a pause. "They found something. Of Father's. I tried to call you earlier."

"Oh? A little piece of the man left behind? Does it have a monetary value? We could use any help we can get."

"Why do you say it like that?"

"You just told me that there is no money anywhere, essentially. Fairly reasonable optimism given the cash constraints."

There was another period of quiet. And then Lane explained what had been found in an ivy bed.

When Edward said nothing, his brother muttered, "You don't seem surprised. About any of this, actually."

Edward's eyes went to the drapes that were pulled over the windows.

"Hello?" Lane said. "You knew, didn't you. You knew the money was gone, didn't you."

"I had my suspicions."

"Tell me something. How much life insurance did Father carry?"

"Seventy-five million," Edward heard himself say. "Key man insurance through the company. At least that's what he had when I was there. I'm going to go now. I'll call you."

Edward hung up and took a deep breath. For a moment, the cottage spun around where he stood, but he willed things to rights.

"I need to leave," he said.

Shelby glanced over her shoulder. "Where are you going?"

"It's business."

"The new mare you were talking about to Moe and his son?"

"Yes. Save me dinner?" As her brows lifted, the center of his chest hurt as if he'd been stabbed. "Please."

"You gonna be real late?"

"I don't think so."

Edward was halfway to the door when he remembered he didn't

have a car. His Porsche was gathering dust back in Easterly's bank of garages.

"May I please borrow your truck?" he asked.

"Aren't you going with Moe or Joey?" When he just shrugged, Shelby shook her head. "It's a stick."

"I'll manage. The ankle's already doing better."

"Keys are in it, but I don't think—"

"Thank you."

Limping out of the cottage, he had no cell phone, no wallet, no driver's license and nothing in his belly to sustain him, but he was sober and he knew exactly where he was going.

Shelby's old pickup had a steering wheel that had been worn smooth, a faded dashboard, and carpets in the wells with so little nap that they were all but tile. The tires were new, however, the engine started with no problem and ran like a top, and everything was neat as a pin.

Hooking up with Route 42, he headed into the suburbs. The clutch wasn't all that stiff, but it killed his ankle and knee nonetheless, and he found himself spending a lot of time in third. Overall, though, he was numb as he drove along. Well, emotionally numb.

After many miles, the houses started to get big and the land began to be professionally tended as if it were an interior space, not an exterior one. There were fancy gates, stone walls, and pieces of sculpture on rolling lawns. Long drives and specimen trees. Security cameras. Rolls-Royces and Bentleys on the road.

Sutton Smythe's family estate was up on the left. Its hill was not as tall as the one Easterly had been built on, and the Georgian brick mansion had only been constructed in the early 1900s, but the square footage was well over thirty thousand square feet, making it bigger than Edward's old haunt.

Approaching the gates, he rolled down the window by hand and then stretched out and entered in the pass code on a keypad. As the great iron bars split down the middle, he headed up the winding lane, the mansion unfurling before him, its tremendous footprint sprawling over the cropped grass. Magnolias framed the house, just as they did at

Easterly, and there were other massive trees on the property. A tennis court was off to the side, discreetly hidden behind a hedgerow, and the garages disappeared off into the distance.

The driveway circled in front of the mansion, and there was a black Town Car, a Mercedes C63, a modest Camry, and two SUVs with blacked-out windows parked in a line.

He halted Shelby's four wheels and a bed as close as he could to the front entrance and then hobbled out and over to the mansion's carved door. As he put the brass knocker to use, he remembered all the times he'd come here in black tie and just walked right in. But he and Sutton weren't like that anymore.

The Smythes' butler, Mr. Graham, opened things up. As composed as the man was, his eyes peeled wide and not just at the fact that Edward was in jeans and a work shirt instead of some suit.

"I need to see Sutton."

"I'm sorry, sir, but she is entertaining—"

"It's business."

Mr. Graham inclined his head. "But of course. The drawing room, if you will?"

"I know the way."

Edward gimped his way in, passing through the foyer and by a study, heading in the opposite direction of the cocktail hour that was rolling out in the main reception room. Given that matched set of SUVs, it was likely that the Kentucky governor had come for dinner, and Edward could only imagine what was being discussed. The bourbon business. Maybe it was fundraising. Schools.

Sutton was very connected with just about everything in the state.

Maybe she would run for the big seat someday.

He would certainly vote for her.

As he entered a grand space, he glanced around and reflected that it had been a long time since he'd been in this particular room. When had he last walked in here? He couldn't quite recall . . . and as he measured the lemon yellow silk wallpaper, the spring green damask drapes, the tasseled sofas, and the oil paintings by Sisley and Manet and Morisot, he decided that, like luxury hotels, there was a certain anonymous quality to homes of pedigree: no modern art, everything perfectly harmonious and priceless, no clutter or knickknacks, the few staged family photos set in sterling-silver frames.

"This is a surprise."

Edward hobbled around, and for a moment, he just stayed quiet. Sutton was wearing a red dress and had her brunette hair up in a chignon, and her perfume was *Must de Cartier*, as usual. But more than all that? She had on the rubies he'd bought her.

"I remember those earrings," he said softly. "And that pin."

One of her long hands snatched up to her earlobe. "I still like them."

"They still suit you."

Van Cleef & Arpels, invisible-set Burmese beauties with diamonds. He'd gotten the set for her when she'd been made vice president of the Sutton Distillery Corporation.

"What happened to your ankle?" she asked.

"Going by all the red, you must be talking about UC tonight." The University of Charlemont. Go Eagles. Fuck the Tigers. "Scholarships? Or an expansion to Papa John's Stadium."

"So you don't want to talk about your limp."

"You look . . . beautiful."

Sutton fiddled with her earring again, shifting her weight. That dress was probably by Calvin Klein, from his *maison de haute couture*, not the company's mass-produced sector, its lines so clean, so elegant, that the woman who had it on was the focus, not the silk.

She cleared her throat. "I can't imagine you came to congratulate me."

"On what?" he asked.

"Never mind. Why are you here?"

"I need you to perform on that mortgage."

She arched a brow. "Oh, really. That's a shift in priority. Last time you brought it up, you demanded that I rip the thing to shreds."

"I have the account number for the wire."

"What's changed?"

"Where do you want me to send the account information?"

Sutton crossed her arms and narrowed her eyes. "I heard about your father. On the news today. I didn't know that he'd committed . . . I'm sorry, Edward."

He let that hang where it was. There was no way he was going into the death with anyone, much less her. And in the silence, he measured her body, remembered what it felt like to touch her, imagined himself getting up close to her again and smelling her hair, her skin—only this time, he would know it was really her.

God, he wanted her naked and stretched out before him, nothing but smooth skin and moans as he covered her with himself.

"Edward?"

"Will you perform on the mortgage?" he pressed.

"Sometimes it helps to talk."

"So let's discuss where you can send that ten million."

Footsteps out in the hall brought his head around.

And what do you know, he thought as the governor himself came into the ornate archway.

Governor Dagney Boone was, yes, a descendant of the original Daniel, and he had the kind of face that should be on a twenty-dollar bill. At forty-seven, he had a full head of naturally dark hair, a body honed by hours of tennis, and the casual power of a man who had just won his second term by a landslide. He'd been married for twenty-three years to his high school sweetheart, had three children, and then had lost his wife four years ago to cancer.

He'd been single ever since, as far as the public knew.

As he looked at Sutton, however, it was not as a politician would. That gaze lingered just a little too long, like he were respectfully enjoying the view.

"So this is a date," Edward drawled. "With state troopers as chaperones. How romantic."

Boone looked over—and did a double take, as if he hadn't recognized Edward in the slightest.

Ignoring the jibe and smothering his shock, Boone strode forward with an outstretched palm. "Edward. I didn't know you were back in the Commonwealth. My condolences on your father's passing."

"Only a part of me has returned." Edward shook what was offered only because Sutton was shooting daggers at him. "Congratulations on your November win. Again."

"There's a lot of work to be done." The governor glanced over at Sutton. "I'm sorry to interrupt, but your staff was wondering whether you wanted to hold dinner? Or maybe set another place at the table? I volunteered to find out."

"He's not staying—"

"I'm not staying—"

"In stereo." The governor smiled. "Well. I'll leave you all to it. It was good seeing you, Edward."

Edward nodded, and didn't miss the way the man gave Sutton's hand a little squeeze before leaving.

"New boyfriend?" he drawled when they were alone again.

"None of your business."

"That's not a no."

"Where do you want the money sent—"

"Why don't you answer the question—"

"Because I don't want to."

"So it *is* a date."

The two of them crashed to a halt, the air sparking between them, anger and something altogether erotic charging the particles that separated them—or at least there was a sexual component to it on his side. And he couldn't help himself. His eyes raked down her dress and he stripped her in his mind, seeing her naked in all her glory.

Except she deserved better than that. Better than him. She deserved a stand-up guy like the Shit Dagney with all his stand-up past and his pretty-boy looks and his power base. The governor was the kind of man who would stand at her side at all her functions and would pull her chair out for her and get to his feet when she had to hit the loo to freshen her lipstick. He would tell her what she needed to hear, but also what she wanted him to say. He would help her in her business and also with her father. The pair of them would accomplish great things for the state, too.

And yes . . . the Shit Dagney would no doubt treat her right in ways Edward couldn't bear thinking about.

He closed his lids and took a deep breath. "About the mortgage. Will you perform on the terms? There's no reason for you not to. The interest rate is good and you'll have a primary and sole secured interest on Easterly. You're safe."

"What's changed your mind?"

"Is that a yes?"

She shrugged one of her elegant shoulders. "I made the deal in good faith, and I have the cash right on hand."

"Good."

As he heard himself calmly explain that Lane would text her the details, he thought about how the governor was waiting for her just down the hall, eager for her to return and look good and be tempting not because she was a loose woman, but because with how beautiful and smart she was, it was impossible for a man not to notice, covet, crave.

And what do you know, Edward was struck by the urge to go into that other room and commit capital murder by nailing the governor of the Commonwealth over the head with a tureen. Of course, he'd be shot in the process, rightfully so, but then a lot of problems would be solved, wouldn't they.

"The funds will be there in the morning," she said. "By eleven a.m."

"Thank you."

"Is that all?"

"Ten million is plenty, yes."

Edward started for the exit to the room, but then he rerouted and went to stand in front of Sutton. "Be careful with our fair governor. Politicians are not known for their scruples."

"And you are?"

He reached out and brushed her mouth with his thumb. "Not at all. Tell me something. Is he staying the night?"

Sutton pushed his hand away. "Not that it's any of your business, but no, he is not."

"I think he wants to."

"You're insane. And stop it."

"Because I'm acknowledging that he finds you attractive? How is that an insult?"

"He's the governor of Kentucky."

"As if that makes a difference? He's still a man."

Tilting her chin up, she stared off over his shoulder. "You've gotten what you came for. You know the way out."

As she went to step around him, he said, "When he tries to kiss you at the end of this party, remember that I told you so."

"Oh, I'll be thinking about you. But not like that."

"Then think of me being the one at your mouth."

FIFTEEN

*A*s Lane walked through Easterly's rooms, everything around him was quiet. This was rare. When you had over seventy full- and part-time staff and half a dozen family members under the same roof, usually there was someone coming and going on every level at all times.

Even that English butler was *in absentia*. Although that was less eerie so much as appreciated.

Outside, night was falling, the darkness easing over the land, smudging the edges of Charlemont's extraordinary trees and the Ohio's liquid low point with gray and black pastels.

Checking his phone, he cursed that Edward had yet to call, and to excise his unease, he opened a set of French doors and stepped out onto the terrace that overlooked the garden and the river down below. Walking over to the far edge, his loafers marked the flagstones with a sharp sound that made him think of cursing.

It seemed unbelievable that the grandeur surrounding him, the trimmed flower and ivy beds, the old stone statues, the flowering fruit trees, the pool house, the majesty of the business center . . . was anything other than rock solid. Permanent. Unalterable.

He thought of everything that was inside the house. The Old Masters paintings. The Aubusson and Persian rugs. The Baccarat crystal chandeliers. The Tiffany and Christofle and even Paul Revere sterling. The Meissen and Limoges and Sèvres porcelain. The Royal Crown Derby sets of dishes and countless Waterford glasses. And then there was his mother's jewelry, a collection so vast, it had a walk-in safe as big as some people's clothes closets.

There had to be seventy or eighty million dollars in all those assets. Well over triple that, if you counted the paintings—after all, they had three properly documented Rembrandts, thanks to his grandparents' obsession with the artist.

The problem? None of it was in cash form. And before it turned green, so to speak, there would need to be valuations, estimates, auctions arranged, and all of that would be so very public. Plus you would have to pay a percentage to Christie's or Sotheby's. And maybe there would be faster dispositions with private sales, but those, too, would have to be brokered and would take time.

It was like bringing blocks of ice to a fire. Helpful, but not urgent enough.

"Hey."

He pivoted toward the house. "Lizzie."

As he held his arms out, she came to him readily, and for a moment, the pressure was off. She was a breeze through his hair when it was hot, the sweet relief as he put a load down, the exhale before he closed his eyes for sleep desperately needed.

"Do you want to stay here tonight?" she asked as she stroked his back.

"I don't know."

"We can, if you want. Or I can go and give you some peace."

"No, I want to be with you." And as he ran his hand up and down her waist, he just wanted to get closer. "Come here."

Taking her hand, he led her around the corner and into the garden she had masterminded, the pair of them going past the formal greenhouse and hooking up with the brick path that led to the pool. His body heated up even further as they closed in on the changing house with its awnings and lanai, its loungers, bar, and grill. The pool itself was lit from down below, the aquamarine glow getting stronger as the last of the sun's rays disappeared over the Indiana side of the river.

Crickets sounded, but it was too early in the season for the fireflies to come out. The enchantment of the soft, humid night was everywhere, though, a melody that was as sexual as a naked form even though it was invisible.

Inside the pool house, there were three dressing rooms, each with its own shower and bath, and he picked the first one because it was the largest. Drawing Lizzie into the sitting area, he shut and locked the door.

He left the lights out. With the pool's glimmer coming through the windows, he could see plenty well enough.

"I've been waiting to do this all day long."

As he spoke, he pulled her in to his body, feeling her against his chest, her hips on his, her shoulders under his hands.

Her mouth was soft and sweet, and as he licked his way inside, she whispered his name on a gasp that made him want to go so much further so much faster. But there were things he needed to tell her. Suspicions he feared but had to share. Plans to be made.

"Lizzie . . ."

Her hands went through his hair. "Yes?"

"I know this is the wrong time. On so many levels."

"We can go back to the house to your room."

Lane broke away and started pacing around the cramped space. Which was like someone trying to go for a stroll around the inside of a gym locker. "I wanted this to be perfect."

"So let's go back."

"I wish I had more to offer you. And I will. After all this. I don't know what it will look like—but there will be something in the future." He was aware he was prattling on, talking to himself. "Maybe it's that farm in your daydreams. Or a grease-monkey garage. Or a diner. But I swear, it's not always going to be like this."

And he'll be divorced. Damn it, maybe he should wait?

Except no, he decided. Life felt very precarious at the moment, and he had always regretted the time they had missed. Waiting to do the right thing, to do what you wanted and needed for yourself and the one you loved, was a luxury for the lucky clueless who had not yet had tragedy in their lives.

And also he wanted to start their future away from Easterly and Charlemont right here, right now. He wanted her to know, on a visceral level, that she was a priority to him, too. Even as Rome burned, she was important, and not because she was some kind of plane ticket out of hell for him. But because he loved her and he was more than looking forward to building a life together with her.

In fact, he was desperate for the freedom he was trying to earn during this awful grind.

As he glanced at her, Lizzie just shook her head and smiled at him. "I don't need anything more than you."

"God . . . I love you. And this should be perfect."

As in happening in a different place. With a ring. And champagne and a string quartet—

No, he thought, as he properly focused on his Lizzie. She wasn't Chantal. She wasn't interested in that country club check list of stuff just so she could share it with her friends in the Wedding Olympics.

Sinking down onto one knee, Lane took her hands in his and kissed each one. As her eyes flared, like she suddenly guessed what was coming and couldn't believe it, he found himself smiling.

A pool house. Who knew that this was going to happen in a pool house?

Well, better than in front of half the Charlemont Metro Police Department with their guns drawn.

"Will you marry me?" he said.

SIXTEEN

*E*dward took the long way home, coasting over the rural lanes that wound in and out of Ogden County's famous horse farms, the headlights of Shelby's truck the only illumination anywhere in the rolling landscape, the window all the way down beside him. The air was warm and gentle on his face and he breathed deep a lot . . . but his hands were tight on the wheel, and his gut was rolling.

He kept thinking of Sutton with that politician of hers.

Indeed, from all he'd heard, the Shit Dagney was actually a gentleman. The governor had been faithful to his wife, and unlike a lot of men, after he'd become a widower, he hadn't run off with some twenty-five-year-old rent-a-fantasy. Instead, he'd focused on his kids and the Commonwealth.

And you could actually believe all that was true because if there had been anything to the contrary, the newspapers would have reported it or the man's opponents would have brought it out during the campaigns.

So, yes, a gentleman through and through, it seemed. But that didn't mean he was dead from the neck down. Hell, a man would have to be insane not to recognize Sutton as a full-blooded woman. And the fact that she was worth billions of dollars didn't hurt, either.

Even penniless, though, she would have been a catch beyond measure. She was levelheaded. Fun. Passionate. Silly and sweet and smart. Capable of standing up to a man and calling him on his stupidity, while at the same time making you feel every ounce of testosterone in your body.

But she was wrong about one thing. That man, sitting governor or not, was going to make a move on her tonight.

The shit.

The truly pathetic thing was, however, that the governor's amorous side wasn't what really bothered Edward. It was Sutton's rightful response that, as much as he hated to admit it, was the real reason he was out here, going around in circles.

Bottom line, the Shit Dagney was an amazing man, worthy of her in too many ways to count. And she was going to figure that out.

And there was nothing that Edward could do about it.

Or *should* do about it, for heaven's sake. Come on, what the hell was wrong with him? Why in the good goddamn would he want to cheat her out of a potentially fulfilling, happy, healthy relationship—

Because I want her for myself.

As his inner voice went center stage and bullhorn, the only thing that stopped him from driving into a tree just to shut the thing up was the fact that he had no right to wreck Shelby's truck.

So he settled for banging the steering wheel a couple of times and carpet-bombing the inside of the cab with the f-word.

Many miles and miles later, when Edward finally decided to actually go to the Red & Black instead of drive around like a sixteen-year-old kid whose cheerleader girlfriend was going to the prom with another football player, he discovered that he'd managed to burn through half a tank of Shelby's gas. Pulling into a Shell station, he eased up to one of three vacant pumps and went for his credit card—but nope. No wallet.

Cursing, he got back in and went on to the Red & Black's main entrance. As he turned in between the two stone pillars, he was no closer to feeling at peace, but driving around all night and leaving Shelby on empty wasn't the solution. All that was going to get him was a hitchhike proposition and an embarrassing conversation when she and Moe and/or Joey had to go and bring her truck home.

After parking in front of Barn B, Edward took the keys with him and then doubled back to crank the window up. Limping over to the cottage, he opened the door and expected it to be empty.

Instead, Shelby was asleep in his chair, her legs tucked up to her chest and her head kicked to the side. Looking past her, he saw the kitchen had been cleaned up, and he would have bet the last of his mobility that there was a bowl full of that stew waiting in the refrigerator for him.

He shut the door softly. "Shelby?"

She came awake, jumping from the chair with a lithe surge he envied. Her ponytail had gotten shoved out of place, and she yanked the tie free, her hair tumbling around her shoulders.

It was longer than he'd thought. Blonder, too.

"What time is it?" she said as she regathered the waves, tying them back up again.

"Almost ten o'clock."

"The mare isn't coming in now, is she?"

"No, she is not."

"I left you a bowl in the refrigerator."

"I know." He found himself tracking her movements, everything from the subtle shift of her feet to the way she tucked that stray hair behind her ear. "I know you did. Thank you."

"I'll see you in the morning, then."

As she went by him, he took her arm. "Don't go."

She didn't look at him. Her eyes . . . they stayed on the floorboards beneath their boots. But her breath quickened and he knew what her answer was going to be.

"Stay with me tonight," he heard himself say. "Not for sex. Just . . . stay with me."

Shelby didn't move for the longest time.

But in the end, she took his hand, and he followed her into the dim bedroom. The glow from the security lights on the barns bled through the homemade gingham curtains, casting gentle shadows off the plain bureau and the modest, queen-sized bed that didn't even have a headboard.

He wasn't sure there were sheets under the duvet.

He'd been sleeping in that chair a lot since he'd moved in. Or passing out in the damn thing was more like it.

Edward went into the bathroom and used the facilities before brushing his teeth. When he came out, she had pulled the covers back.

"I washed these yesterday," she said as he approached the other side of the bed. "I wasn't sure whether you slept in here or not."

"You shouldn't take care of me."

"I know."

She got in first, fully clothed, and once again he envied her easy movements, her legs stretching out without cracking, her back reclining with no hitches or gasps. His trip to the horizontal, in contrast, was paved with groans and curses, and he had to catch his breath when he finally got his head on the thin pillow.

Shelby turned to him, and her hand moved across his hollow stomach. He stiffened, even though he had a T-shirt on. And a fleece.

"You're cold," she said.

"Am I?" He cranked his head to the side to look at her. "I think you're right—"

She kissed him, her soft lips brushing his.

Inching back, she whispered, "You don't have to say it."

"What?"

"You owe me nothin' 'cept this job. And I don't need nothin' from you other than it."

He grunted as he lifted his arm so he could run a fingertip over her jaw and down onto her throat. He found that he was glad things were dark.

"I don't have anything to give anyone." Edward took her callused hand and put it on the center of his chest. "And I am cold."

"I know. And I know lots else 'bout you. I've worked 'round animals all my life. I don't expect any horse to be more or less than they are. And there's no reason for people to be any different than they are, either."

It was the strangest thing. Ever since he had been kidnapped out of that hotel in South America, he had been tight all over his body. First out of terror. Later, from the pain as the torture and starvation had ground him down. And then, after the rescue, his body hadn't functioned well on so many levels—and there had also come the fight to keep his mind from cannibalizing itself.

But now, in this quiet darkness, he felt a vital loosening.

"I can feel you staring at me," he said softly.

"That's because I am. And it's okay. Like I said, you don't owe me a thing. I don't expect nothin' from you."

For some reason, he thought of Moe Brown's son, Joey. Handsome, strapping kid, just her age. Great around the horses, as good natured as they came, and no dummy.

She needed to be spending her nighttime hours with somebody like that.

"So why are you doing this?" he murmured.

"That's my decision, ain't it. My choice that I don't need to explain to nobody, includin' you."

Her calm, forthright declaration, coupled with the conception that he was accepted just exactly as he was . . . furthered the strange and miraculous uncoiling in him.

And the longer he lay next to Shelby, the more his body eased. Or perhaps it was his soul. But then Shelby was the only person who didn't compare him to who he had been. She didn't have any past with him to mourn. She wasn't looking for him to triumph over his tragedy, to rejoin the BBC, to helm his family.

He was a horse recovering from an injury, out to pasture, exposed to the elements . . . that she was prepared to feed and care for. Probably because that was the only thing she knew to do when confronted with suffering.

The exhale he released took years off of him. In fact, he had been unaware of the weight he was carrying inside his heart. Or the resentment he had against everybody that had been in his old life. In fact . . . the truth was, he hated them all, hated every one of them who stared at him with pitying eyes and shock and sadness. He wanted to scream at them that he hadn't volunteered for what had happened to him, or what he looked like, or where he had ended up—and that his tragedy was none of their fucking business.

They thought it was upsetting laying their eyes on him? Screw that. He'd had to live through and with it all.

And yes, he even resented Sutton even though she was no more at fault than any of the rest of them.

Shelby, though . . . Shelby was free of all that. She was clean compared to their contamination. She was fresh air in a garbage dump. She was a vista in what was otherwise a cell with no windows.

Edward groaned as he pushed himself onto his shoulder and kissed her back. And beneath his lips, her mouth was as open and honest as she was. He hardened instantly.

But instead of getting under her sweatshirt and into her jeans, he pulled back and tucked her against him.

"Thank you," he whispered.

"For what?"

He just shook his head. And then he closed his eyes.

For the first time in what felt like forever, he drifted off to sleep . . . stone-cold sober.

"*M*arriage, huh."

As Lizzie stood above Lane, she took his face in her hands and smiled so hard her cheeks hurt. God, he was so handsome, so shatteringly attractive, even with the bags under his eyes and his five-o'-clock—make that nine forty-five p.m.—shadow and his hair that was growing out shaggy from its trim.

"You're asking me to marry you?" she heard herself say. And yes, she was a little breathless.

He nodded. "And can I just tell you? Your smile right now is one for the ages."

"You know"—she passed her hands through his hair—"I'm not one of those women who planned their wedding when they were five."

"This is not a surprise."

"I'm not even sure I want to wear a dress, and I'm not doing it in a church."

"I'm an atheist, so that works."

"And the smaller, the better. That last thing I'm interested in is some big society event."

He swept his hands up and down the backs of her legs, kneading, stroking, turning her on. "Got it."

"And your divorce—"

"It's an annulment, really. And Samuel T. is taking care of all that."

"Good—"

As Lane raised his hand like he was in school, she said, "Mmm?"

"Is that a yes?"

Bending down, she pressed her lips to his. "It absolutely is a yes."

Next thing she knew, he took her onto the chaise lounge, his heavy, warm body rolling on top of hers, and then they were kissing deeply and laughing and kissing some more. And then she was naked and so was he.

She gasped his name as he entered her, and oh, God, he was good, penetrating her nice and deep, stretching her, dominating her. She'd never told him how much she liked the feel of him on her, how she craved the times when he took her wrists and held her down, how the sessions where he was greedy and a little rough turned her on.

But he knew.

Then again, Lane knew everything about her, and this proposal was perfect. Nothing showy, or fancy, and no, she didn't want some big diamond from him, either. All she needed was him. All she wanted was the two of them together.

So they were starting this engagement off on the right foot as far as she was concerned.

Yes, Lane was surrounded by chaos. Yes, there was no way of knowing how any of this was going to shake out. And no, most women with half a brain wouldn't sign on for someone with his background—not even the gold diggers, now.

But love had a funny way of giving you faith in the one who loved you back. And nothing was guaranteed in life, neither riches nor health. At the end of the day, you just had to let yourself go . . . and the best place to land was in the arms of a good man.

As pleasure rocketed through her, Lizzie called out his name and felt his head drop into her neck as he cursed and jerked deep inside of her. So beautiful. So perfect. Especially as he hugged her close afterward.

"God, I love you," he said in her ear. "You're the only thing that makes sense right now."

"I'm not scared," she whispered. "You and I are going to figure this out. Somehow. And we're going to be okay. That's all that matters to me."

Inching back, his blue eyes were the stuff of romance novels, reverent, sincere, full of love. "I'm going to get you a ring."

"I don't want one." She stroked his hair again, flattening it where she had messed it up. "I don't like anything on my hands or my wrists. Not with my job."

"So a diamond watch is out?"

"Definitely—"

His phone rang in his pocket and he shook his head. "I don't care who that is. I'm not—"

"You should probably—"

He settled the issue by kissing her, his body starting to move again. And Lizzie went along with it. There were so many worse things in life than making love with your new fiancé on a warm Kentucky night.

The problems would be waiting for them when they were finished. This little slice of heaven? Was only for the two of them.

A party no one else was invited to.

SEVENTEEN

By the time the crème caramel was cleared, Sutton was ready to scream. It wasn't the conversation. Governor Dagney Boone and Thomas Georgetow, the president of the University of Charlemont, were great company, two of the most powerful men in the state bantering back and forth like the old friends they were. The other people around the table were also wonderful: Georgetow's wife, Beryline, was as Southern and lovely as a sweet tea on a hot afternoon, and the Reverend and Mrs. Nyce, the leaders of the largest Baptist community in the state, were as solid as granite and as uplifting as a sunbeam.

Under any other circumstances, she would have enjoyed the evening. Sure, there was an underlying purpose to it, but they were all good people, and the family chef had outdone himself.

Edward, however, had managed to ruin it for her. If that man stayed up nights trying to get under her skin, he couldn't do a better job.

Dagney was *not* interested in her. That was crazy.

"So . . ." The governor eased back in the Queen Anne style chair to Sutton's right. "I think we should all thank Miss Smythe for her hospitality."

As coffee cups were raised, Sutton shook her head. "It's been my pleasure."

"No, it's been ours."

The governor smiled at her, and God help her, all she could hear was Edward's voice in her head. And that led to other things, other memories. Especially of the last time she had gone to see him when they had—

Stop it, she told herself.

"We missed your father tonight," the governor said.

"Yes, how is he?" the Reverend Nyce asked.

Sutton took a deep breath. "Well, actually, you all will hear the details tomorrow, but he's stepping down. And I am replacing him as CEO."

There was a momentary lull, and then Dagney said, "Congratulations and condolences at the same time."

"Thank you." She inclined her head. "It's a complicated time personally, but professionally, I know exactly what I'm doing."

"The Sutton Distillery Corporation could not be in better hands." The governor smiled and toasted her with his decaf. "And I look forward to presenting you with some of our new tax code proposals. You're one of the biggest employers in the state."

It was strange, but she could feel the shift toward her, the people at the table, even the governor, regarding her with a different focus. She'd sensed it first at the finance committee meeting this morning, and then when she'd interacted with senior management throughout the day. Positional power, it was called—and with the torch changing hands, the respect her father had been paid was now hers by virtue of her promotion.

"And this is why I asked you all here," she said.

"I would have come happily for the dessert," the Reverend Nyce said as he gestured to his clean plate. "That was evidence of the good Lord, as far as I'm concerned."

"Amen," Georgetow interjected. "I would ask for seconds—"

"But I would tell his doctor," Beryline finished for him.

"She is my conscience."

Sutton waited for the laughter to die down, and then she found herself fighting back tears. Clearing her throat, she composed herself.

"My father means the world to me." She looked up to the portrait of him that hung on the wall on the opposite end of the room. "And I would like to recognize his contributions to this state and the community of Charlemont in some significant ways. After much thought, I would like to endow a chair at the University of Charlemont in economics in his name. I have a check for five million dollars to that end, and I am prepared to gift that amount tonight."

There was a gasp from the president—and with good reason. She knew damn well gifts that big didn't come in every day to the university, and certainly not without considerable plying and cultivation on their part. Yet here she was, tossing it into his lap. After his favorite dessert.

Georgetow sat back in his chair. "I am . . . I had no idea—thank you. The university thanks you for this, and it will be an honor to have his name further associated with the school."

There would also be a similar endowment set up at Kentucky University, not that she was going to bring that up at this dinner: She and her family were KU fans when it came to basketball—something that, again, wasn't spoken about around Georgetow.

Sutton looked at the Reverend Nyce. "My father is not a religious man, but he respects you unlike any other man of God in the state. I would therefore like to endow a scholarship fund for African-American students in his name to be administered by you. It will cover the tuition and books of any Kentucky state school." She jokingly put her hand up to Georgetow. "And yes, even Kentucky University. We need more skilled workers in the Commonwealth who are committed to establishing and keeping their careers here. Further, my father has long had a commitment to the underserved, particularly in the West End. This will help."

The Reverend Nyce reached over and took her hand. "The sons and daughters of the five-oh-two thank you and your family for this generosity. And I'll make sure this opportunity is shepherded well in your father's name."

She squeezed his palm. "I know you will."

"Steer them our way first," Georgetow joked. "You and your good wife are both alumni, after all."

The reverend lifted his coffee cup. "That goes without saying. I bleed red first and foremost."

"Boys, boys, you're in mixed company here." Sutton pointed to herself and then turned to the governor. "And finally, I would like to make a gift to the state in my father's name."

Dagney smiled. "I will accept anything—"

"I purchased thirty thousand acres in eastern Kentucky this afternoon."

The governor stiffened in his chair. "You . . . you were the one."

"Four mountain ranges. Four beautiful, pristine mountain ranges—"

"That were on the verge of being strip-mined."

"I would like to give them to the Commonwealth in my father's name and endow the acreage as a park that will be forever wild."

Dagney actually looked down at the table for a moment. "This is . . ."

"My father has hunted all his life. Deer. Dove. Duck. His favorite thing was to get out and be in the natural environment. There is meat in my freezer right now that he brought home to his family, and I grew up eating what he provided us. He can't . . . he is not able to do that anymore, but I assure you, his heart is still out in those woods."

Mountaintop removal was an efficient and cost-effective way of accessing the coal so frequently found in the hills in the eastern counties of the Commonwealth. And the coal industry employed many people in areas that were so poor, families starved in the winter and couldn't get good health care. She understood all of that reality; the coal industry was a complicated issue that wasn't as simple as it being environmentally evil. But her father did love the land, and this way she knew at least those four mountains would remain exactly as they had been for millennia.

And actually, she had negotiated with the seven families who owned the land over a period of months—and even with the millions and millions she had given them, it was nothing compared to what the coal companies had offered. But the owners had wanted exactly what she had promised to give them in addition to the cash—and she was making good on it right now.

Forever wild. Forever as the good Lord made 'em, as her father, Reynolds, would say.

"So," she said with a smile, "do you think the state will pay for a plaque if I give you all those acres?"

Dagney leaned over to her and touched her arm. "Yes, I believe that can be arranged."

For a moment, she could have sworn that his eyes lingered on her lips—but then she thought, no, she had imagined it.

Damn you, Edward.

The party broke up shortly after that, with Georgetow leaving with a five-million-dollar check in his pocket and the reverend with an appointment with her lawyers.

Dagney stayed behind as the others went down the front walkway, got into their cars, and drove off.

"So," she said as she turned to him. "It's going to be hard for me to follow this up with any kind of encore."

"Your family has always been so generous, both here in Charlemont and in the Commonwealth at large."

Sutton watched the last set of brake lights fade down the hill. "It's not to be grand. Not in this case with me and my father. I've got all this . . . emotion . . . and I have to do something with it. I can't hold it inside, and there's nothing to really say about the feelings because they're too much to . . ." She touched her sternum. "They're too much here."

"I know exactly how that is." Dagney's face got tight. "I've walked that path myself."

"My father hasn't died yet, but I feel like I'm losing him by inches." She focused on the treetops off in the distance, measuring the curving outline of where the fluffy branches met the velvet darkness of the night sky. "Seeing him diminish further day by day isn't just about the current suffering. It's a reminder of the pain that's coming when he dies, and I hate that . . . and yet every moment counts with him now. He's as good as he's going to be right this moment."

Dagney closed his eyes. "Yes, I remember how that is. I'm so sorry."

"Well." She wished she hadn't been so open. "I didn't mean to go on."

"Talk as long as you like. Sometimes it's the only way you stay in your own skin. Being the one left behind is a special kind of hell."

Sutton glanced at him. "He's all I have."

"You're not alone. Not if you don't want to be."

"Anyway." She smoothed her hair and hoped her laugh didn't sound as awkward as it felt. "Next time you're just getting dinner."

"And when will that be?" he said softly. "I'm happy to be patient, but I hope I won't have to wait for very long."

Sutton felt her brows rise. "Are you . . . asking me out?"

"Yes, ma'am. I do believe I am." As she shifted her eyes away, Dagney laughed. "Too much? I'm sorry."

"No, I, ah . . . no, I just . . ."

"Yes, I'm afraid my intentions were honorable, but not necessarily platonic, as I came here tonight."

Damn you, Edward, she thought again.

And abruptly, she became aware of the three state police officers who were standing at a discreet number of yards away. As well as the fact that she was blushing.

"I didn't mean to complicate things," Dagney said as he took her hand. "And if I've made this difficult, we can forget I ever crossed that line."

"I, ah . . ."

"We're just going to forget this, okay?" the governor concluded without any edge at all. "I'll chalk it up to experience and move on."

"Experience?"

He rubbed his jaw with his thumb. "I haven't asked a lot of women out. Since my Marilyn died, that is. And you know, statistically, this increases my odds of a 'yes' at some point, and since I'm an optimist, I'm taking that positive away from this evening—along with those four mountains."

Sutton laughed. "So other people have told you no? I find that hard to believe."

"Well, actually . . . you're the first one I've asked. But as I said, I've gotten a rejection out of the way and lived to tell the tale." He smiled and reached out to her face. "Your mouth has fallen open."

"I am just surprised." She laughed. "That I'm your first—I mean, oh . . . crap."

The governor laughed back and then grew serious. "It was so hard when I lost Marilyn, and it's been a long time since anyone else registered, to be honest. And even though this will not make me look like a stud in the slightest . . . it's taken me two months to get the courage up to ask you."

"Two *months?*"

"Remember when I saw you at the capitol building in March? That's when I decided I was going to ask you for a date. And then I chickened out. But you invited me here tonight, and I decided to go for it. Do not feel bad, though. I'm a big boy, I can take it—"

"I'm in love with someone," she blurted.

The governor recoiled. And then cursed softly. "Oh, I'm so sorry. I didn't know you were with anyone. I would never have disrespected your relationship—"

"We're not together." She waved her hand. "There's no relationship. It's not anything that makes sense, actually."

"Well . . ." Dagney stared into her eyes. "Edward Baldwine is a fool, then."

Sutton opened her mouth to deny it, but the man in front of her wasn't an idiot. "There's nothing going on between us, and I guess I still need to get that through my head. And also because of my new role, it's not a great time for me."

"At the risk of being forward, I just want to say that in the future, I'm willing to be your rebound." He laughed. "Yes, that is desperate, but I'm way out of practice with all this, and you are a very intelligent, very beautiful woman who deserves a good man."

"I'm sorry."

"Me, too." He put out his palm for a shake. "But at least we're going to see a lot of each other, especially with this new job of yours."

"Yes, we will."

She left his hand where it was and stepped in to embrace him. "And I look forward to it."

He held her briefly and lightly and then eased back. "Boys? Let's go."

The state police escorted the governor over to the two black-on-black SUVs, and a moment later, the motorcade formed, a pair of police motorcyclists falling in line.

Sadness closed in on her from behind, giving a chill to the balmy night air.

"Damn you, Edward," she whispered to the wind.

EIGHTEEN

The following morning, Lane stepped out of his bedroom suite at Easterly in a good mood. But that didn't last as he looked down the hall, and saw luggage outside his grandfather's room.

"Oh, no, you don't."

Stalking over to the stacked bags, he didn't bother knocking on the partially opened door. "Jeff, you are *not* leaving."

His old college roommate looked up from a prodigious pile of papers on the old desk. "I have to get back to New York, buddy—"

"I need you—"

"—but I've made sure I have everything ready for the Feds." The guy indicated various printouts and held up a flash drive. "I've created a summary of—"

"You're miserable on Wall Street, you realize."

"—the withdrawals that I've found. It's all right here. Just give them this drive, actually, and they'll know what to do. They can call me with questions. I'll leave my card and my cell phone number."

"You have to stay."

Jeff cursed and rubbed his eyes. "Lane, I'm not some magic talisman that's going to make this all go away. I'm not even the best man for this kind of thing. I also have no official role at the company and no legal authority."

"I trust you."

"I already have a job."

"That you hate."

"No offense, but my paychecks are huge and they don't bounce."

"You have more money than you need. You may live in a modest Midtown apartment, but you're sitting on a fortune."

"Because I don't do stupid things. Like leave perfectly good work —"

"*Miserable* work."

"—for a forest fire."

"Well, at least you'll be warm. And we can toast marshmallows. Wassup."

Jeff broke out laughing. "Lane."

"Jeff."

His friend crossed his arms over his chest and pushed his metrosexual glasses up higher on his nose. In his white button-down oxford and his black slacks, he looked like he was prepared to go to his office directly from landing at Teterboro, N.J., airport.

"Tell me something," the guy started.

"No, I don't know the square root of anything, I can't do that *pi* thing to the nth degree, and if you ask me why the caged bird sings, at the moment, I'm feeling like it's because the damn thing has a gun to its head."

"Why haven't you called the Feds yet?"

Lane went on a wander, heading over to the bank of windows that overlooked the side gardens and the river. Down below, in the morning sunlight, the Ohio was a gorgeous, shimmering pathway to Charlemont's business district, as if those glass-and-steel buildings were some kind of nirvana.

"There were crimes committed, Lane. Are you protecting your father even though he's dead?"

"Hell no."

"So drop a dime."

"We're a privately held corporation. If there was malfeasance, my family are the ones who were damaged. It's our money that was lost, not that of thousands of shareholders. It's no one else's problem or concern."

"You're kidding me, right." His old roommate stared across at him like there was a horn growing out of his forehead. "Laws were broken because improper disclosures were filed with the state attorney general and the IRS. I found discrepancies in your mandatory annual reports. You could be brought up on federal charges for collusion, Lane. Hell, I could, too, now that I know what I do."

Lane glanced over his shoulder. "Is that why you're going?"

"Maybe."

"What if I said I could protect you?"

Jeff rolled his eyes and went over to a duffel on the bed. As he zipped the thing closed, he shook his head. "You entitled motherfuckers think the world revolves around you. That the rules are different just because you come from a family tree with some money."

"The money's gone, remember."

"Look, either you call in law enforcement, or I'm going to have to. I love you like a brother, but I'm not willing to go to jail for you—"

"Down here things are taken care of."

Jeff straightened and cranked his head around. He opened his mouth. Then shut it. "You sound like a mobster."

Lane shrugged. "It is what it is. But when I say I can protect you, it includes against things like the government."

"You're crazy."

Lane just stared at his old friend. And the longer he met those eyes behind those glasses, the paler Jeff became.

After a moment, Jeff sat down on the bed and braced his hands on his knees. Staring across the elegant room, he said softly, "Shit."

"No, not shit. You stay here, find out everything that happened, and I will deal with it privately. That's the course we're going to take."

"And if I refuse?"

"You're going to stay."

"Is that a threat?"

"Of course not. You're one of my oldest friends."

But they both knew the truth. The man was going nowhere.

"Jesus Christ." Jeff put a hand to his temple like his head was pounding. "If I'd known what kind of rabbit hole this was, I never would have come down here."

"I'm going to take care of you. Even without the money, there are too many people who owe my family. I have plenty of resources."

"Because you're going to coerce them, too?"

"It is what it is."

"Fuck you, Lane—"

"Let's play this out, okay? You finish what you started, maybe it takes you another week, and then you're free to go. No harm, no foul. It's like you were never here. I'll take it from there."

"And if I leave now?"

"I really can't let you do that. I'm sorry."

Jeff shook his head like he wanted to wake up from a bad dream. "The real world doesn't run like this anymore, Lane. This isn't the fifties. You Bradford types can't control things like you used to. You can't bury accountability in the backyard just because it's inconvenient or you think a veil of privacy is more important than the law of the land. And as for me? Don't push me. Don't put me in this position."

"You're not the only one with information, though." Lane walked over to the desk and picked up the flash drive. "Somehow, I don't think your professional reputation up in Manhattan would survive the disclosure of the gambling ring you ran in college. Students at five universities ran hundreds of thousands of dollars through you and your system of bookies, and before you go down the water-under-the-bridge argument, I'll remind you that it was illegal and of such a large scale that you yourself have some RICO stain on you."

"Fuck you."

"It is what it is."

Jeff looked down at the cuffs on his business shirt for a while. Then he shook his head again. "Man, you are just like your father."

"The hell I am—"

"You're blackmailing me! What the fuck!"

"This is about survival! You think I *want* to do this? You think I'm getting off strong-arming one of my best friends to stick in the viper pit with me? My father would have enjoyed this—I hate it! But what else am I supposed to do?"

Jeff got to his feet and hollered right back. "Call the fucking Feds! Be normal instead of some kind of Kentucky Fried Tony Soprano!"

"I can't do that," Lane said grimly. "I'm sorry, but I can't. And I'm sorry . . . but I need you, and I'm in the tragic situation of having to do anything in my power to make you stay."

Jeff jabbed a finger across the tense air. "You're an asshole if you go down this road. And that doesn't change just because you're playing the poor-me card."

"If you were in my situation, you'd do the same."

"No, I wouldn't."

"You don't know that. Trust me. Shit like this changes everything."

"You got that right," Jeff snapped.

Flashbacks of them as college students at U.Va., in the frat house, in class, on vacations that Lane paid for, filtered through his mind. There had been poker games, and practical jokes, women and more women— especially on Lane's part.

He had never once thought the guy wouldn't be in his life. But he was out of time, out of options, and at the end of the rope.

"I'm *not* like my father," Lane said.

"So delusion also runs in your family. Quite a gene pool you people have got, quite a motherfucking gene pool."

"*H*ere's the company directory. There's the phone. Um . . . the computer. This is a desk. And . . . yup, this is a chair."

As Mack ran out of gas, he glanced around the reception area in front of his office at the Old Site. Like maybe someone would jump out from behind the rustic furniture and give him an orientation lifeline.

The Perfect Beth, as he was coming to think of her, just laughed.

"Don't worry. I'll figure it out. Do I have a user name and password to get into the system?" At his blank look, she tapped the directory. "Okaaaaay, so I'm going to call the IT department and get that started. Unless HR is already on it?"

"Ah . . ."

She took her purse off her shoulder and put it under the desk. "Don't worry. I'll take care of everything. Did you even let them know I've been hired?"

"I . . ."

"Right, how about you send them an e-mail? And tell them I'll be calling around various places to get everything up and rolling?"

"I want you to know, in spite of the stunning incompetence I'm currently throwing around here, I am stellar at many things. Making bourbon being chief among them."

As she smiled at him, Mack found himself looking into her eyes for a little too long. In her red blouse and her black skirt and her flat shoes, she was everything that was competent, attractive and smart.

"Well, I'm good at my job, too," Beth said. "This is why you hired me. So you take care of your stuff, I'll take care of mine, and we'll be set—"

The Old Site's cabin door opened, and Lane Baldwine walked in looking like he'd been in a car wreck and left the injuries untreated: his face was drawn, his hair a mess, his movements as coordinated as a jar of spilled marbles.

"We're going for a ride," he said grimly. "Come on."

"Beth Lewis, my new executive assistant, this is Lane Baldwine. Yes, he is who you think he is."

As Beth lifted a hand, Mack studiously ignored how awestruck she seemed to be. Then again, Lane had been one of *People* magazine's most eligible whatevers a couple of times. Also on TV and in magazines and online for dating actresses. And then there had been that *Vanity Fair* article on the family, where he had played the role of the sexy, commitment-phobic playboy.

Talk about method acting.

And good thing the guy was reformed and in a fully committed relationship or Mack would have wanted to throat punch him.

"Hi," she said. "I'm sorry about your father."

Lane nodded, but didn't seem to really notice her. "Welcome aboard. Mack, we're late."

"I didn't know we had a meeting." But apparently, it was time to hit the road. "Oh, crap. Beth, can you send that e-mail for me?"

As Mack gave her his sign-in details, Lane was already out the door and striding over to his Porsche. "And you'll have to excuse him. There's a lot going on."

Beth nodded. "I totally understand. And I'll take care of everything. Don't worry—oh, what's your cell phone? In case something comes up that I can't handle."

Mack picked up a BBC pad and a pen, and scribbled his digits down for her. "I don't have any meetings scheduled for today—but then, I didn't know I had this one, so who the hell knows what's going to happen next."

"I'll call if I need you."

"I don't know how long I'll be. And I don't know where I'm going."

"Be optimistic. Maybe it's Disneyland."

As he turned away laughing, he told himself not to look back. And he almost made it out the door without pulling a glance over the shoulder.

Almost.

Beth had gone around and sat down at the desktop computer, her fingers flying over the keys. With her hair pulled back in a low ponytail, her face was the picture of professional concentration—but also lovely.

"Any chance you're a U of C fan?" he blurted.

Those blue eyes lifted from the screen and she smiled. "Is there another college in the state? I'm pretty sure there isn't one."

Mack smiled and threw her a wave.

But as he walked over to the Porsche and got in, he wasn't laughing anymore. "What the hell, Lane. You don't return my calls, but show up here pissed off I'm late for something I didn't know about—"

"I'm solving your grain problem, that's what I'm doing." The guy put on a pair of Wayfarers. "And you're coming with me because some-one has to tell my solution how much you require. Still mad at me?"

As Lane hit the gas and skidded out of the loose-gravel parking lot, Mack clicked his seat belt into place. "You get me the corn I need, you can slap me across the face with a dead fish if you want."

"I like a man who thinks outside the box. And in my current mood, I'm likely to pull a pescatarian assault like that just on principle."

NINETEEN

The Charlemont International Airport was located south and a little east from the downtown area, and Lane took the Paterson Expressway around the 'burbs instead of fighting with traffic through spaghetti junction. Overhead, the sky was a gorgeous robin's-egg blue and the sun was bright as a theater light, the day presenting itself as if nothing bad could happen to anyone under its auspices.

Of course, appearances could be deceiving.

"You know John Lenghe, right?" Lane said over the breeze as he took the first of the airport exits and entered the ring-a-round.

"Of course I know who he is," Mack shouted back. "Never met him before, though."

"Well, put your Pepsodent on." As he slowed the convertible's velocity, the engine and the wind got quieter. "And get ready to be charming. We have twenty minutes, tops, to persuade him to front us your corn."

"Wait, what? I thought—you mean, we're not buying from him?"

"We can't afford to pay him. So I'm trying to engineer a carry without the cash situation."

Lane took an exit marked RESTRICTED ACCESS and headed over to the airstrip where the private jets landed and took off.

"So no pressure," Mack muttered as they slowed at the check-in kiosk.

"Nope. None at all."

The uniformed guard waved Lane through. "'Mornin', Mr. Baldwine."

"'Morning, Billy. How's Nells?"

"She's good. Thanks."

"Tell her I said hello."

"Always."

Lane proceeded over to the modernist concierge building and kept on going, passing round-topped hangars where hundreds of millions of dollars of aircraft were stabled. The chauffeur entrance to the runways was a motion-activated gate in a twelve-foot-high chain-link fence, and he sped through, the 911 hitting the tarmac like something out of a magazine ad.

John Lenghe's Embraer Legacy 650 was just coming over, and Lane hit the brakes and killed his engine. As they waited, he thought about him and Jeff going at it.

Man, you're just like your father.

Glancing over at Mack, Lane said, "I should have called beforehand and told you what was up. But right now, there's so much going on, I'm scratching my watch and winding my ass."

Mack shrugged. "Like I told you, we got no problems if my silos are full. But explain something to me."

"What?"

"Where the hell is senior management? It's not like I miss the bastards, but I got voice mail on every single one of them yesterday. Did you fire them all? And you could make my day by telling me that they cried like babies."

"Pretty much. Yup."

"Wait—what? That was a joke, Lane—"

"They're not coming back anytime soon. At least not to the business center at Easterly. Now, as for what they're doing down at headquarters?

I haven't a clue—probably looking to throw me off a bridge. But they're next on my fun-filled to-do list today."

As his Master Distiller's jaw dropped open, Lane got out of the convertible and jacked his slacks up. Lenghe's jet was similar to the ones that made up the BBC's fleet of six, and Lane found himself doing the math on selling all that sky-bound steel and glass.

There had to be sixty million right there.

But he was going to need brokers to handle the sales properly. You didn't Craigslist something like an Embraer.

Mack stepped in front of him, the man's big body the kind of thing you couldn't walk through. "So who's running the company?"

"Right now? This moment?" Lane put his finger up to his mouth and cocked his head like Deadpool. "Ah . . . nobody. Yup, if memory serves, there's nobody in charge."

"Lane . . . *shit.*"

"You looking for a desk job? 'Cuz I'm hiring. Qualifications include a high tolerance for power plays, a closet full of tailor-made suits, and a disaffinity for family members. Oh, wait. That was my father and we already got stuck in that rut. So blue jeans and a good mid-court jump shot will work. Tell me, do you still play basketball as well as you used to?"

The jet's portal opened and a set of stairs extended down to the asphalt. The sixty-ish man who emerged had the stocky build of a former football player, a square jaw like an old-school comic book superhero, and was wearing a set of golf shorts and a polo shirt that probably needed safety glasses to be viewed properly.

Neon fireworks against a black background. But somehow, it worked on the guy.

Then again, when you were worth close to three billion dollars, you could wear whatever the fuck you wanted.

John Lenghe was on the phone as he came down to the tarmac. "—landed. Yup. Okay, right—"

The accent was flat as the Midwestern plains the man came from, the words as unhurried as the stride of his easy descent. But it was wise not to be fooled. Lenghe controlled sixty percent of the corn- and wheat-producing farms in the nation—as well as fifty percent of all milking cows. He was, literally, the Grain God, and it was not a surprise that he wouldn't waste even a trip down a set of stairs when he could be doing business.

"—I'll be home later tonight. And tell Roger not to mow my grass. That's my damn job—what? Yes, I know I pay him and that's why I can tell him what not to do. I love you. What? Of course I'll make you the pork chops, honey. All you have to do is ask. 'Bye now."

Okaaaaaay, so that was his wife on the phone.

"Boys," he called out. "Unexpected surprise."

Lane met the man halfway, putting out his palm. "Thanks for seeing us."

"I'm sorry about your dad." Lenghe shook his head. "I lost mine two years ago and I'm still not over it."

"You know Mack, our Master Distiller?"

"First time in person." Lenghe smiled and clapped the Master Distiller on the shoulder. "I have enjoyed both you and your dad's bourbon forever."

Mack said a bunch of right things. And then there was a pause.

"So," Lenghe jogged his Independence Day shorts a little higher—"about half an hour ago I got a call from your board chair, son. You want to talk about this in private?"

"Yeah, I really do. I need this all to be kept confidential."

"Understood, and consider this in the vault. But I don't have long. Gotta be home for dinner in Kansas, and I've got two stops to make before I get there. Let's use my little paper airplane as a conference room?"

"Sounds good to me, sir."

The inside of Lenghe's jet wasn't at all like what the BBC's planes looked like. Instead of cream leather and burl ash, the Grain God had personalized his to be cozy and welcoming, from the handmade braided blankets to the University of Kansas throw pillows. Buckets of popcorn, not caviar, had been put out, and there were soft drinks instead of anything alcoholic. No stewardess. And if there had been one, she no doubt would have been his wife, not any kind of pneumatic bimbo.

When Lenghe offered them Cokes, he was clearly prepared to serve them himself.

"We're good, thanks," Lane said as he took a seat at a small conference table.

Mack sat next to him and Lenghe took the seat across the way, linking his thick-fingered hands and leaning in, his pale blue eyes shrewd in his tanned face.

"I hear senior management is not happy with you," Lenghe said.

"No, they're not."

"Your board chair told me you locked 'em all out of their offices and shut the corporate server down."

"I did."

"Any reason why?"

"Not anything I'm proud of, I'm afraid. I'm trying to get to the bottom of everything now, but I have reason to believe someone's been stealing from the company. And I'm worried some or all of those suits are in on it. I don't know enough to say anything more than that, however."

Liar, liar, Loudmouth Golf on fire.

"So you haven't talked to your board chair?"

"Before I have the full story? No. Besides, I don't owe him any explanation."

"Well, son, I think he's got a different opinion on that."

"I'll see him as soon as I'm ready to. When you have evidence of theft, on the scale I'm talking about, you can't trust anyone."

Lenghe pulled over a bucket of popcorn. "I'm addicted to this stuff, you know. But it's better than cigarettes."

"And a number of other things."

"You know, you're dancing around the issue pretty good, son, so I'm just going to come out and say it. Have you finally found out about your father's mines?"

Lane sat forward in his seat. "I'm sorry . . . what?"

"I told William to cut the shit with those diamond mines in Africa. Dumbest idea on the planet. Do you know, I went there with the wife last year—I'll bet your dad didn't tell you that I checked them out, did he? No? They're not even holes in the ground. Either he got swindled or—well, the other option doesn't bear thinking about."

"Diamond mines?"

"And that isn't all of it. WWB Holdings had a lot of different businesses under its umbrella. He said there were oil wells in Texas, and of course, now you can't give crude away. A railway or two. Restaurants in Palm Beach, Naples, and Del Ray. And then some tech start-up that I don't think ever went anywhere. Something about an app? I don't get why the hell people waste their time with that shit—pardon my French. There were also a couple of hotels in Singapore and Hong Kong, a fashion house in New York City. I think he even invested in a motion picture or two."

Lane was very aware of having to keep his voice level. "How did you hear about all this?"

"When you've got eighteen holes to get through on a golf course, things come up. I always told him, stick to the core business. All these bright ideas can be tempting, but more than likely, they're just black holes, especially when you don't know the given industry. I'm a farmer, plain and simple. I know the ins and outs of the seasons, the land, the crops and a single kind of cow. I think your father . . . well, I don't want to disparage the dead."

"Rip his memory to shreds, I don't care. I've got to know, and anything you can tell me will help."

Lenghe was silent for a time. "He always took me to Augusta. You want to know why?" When Lane nodded, the man said, "'Cuz those boys would never let a dirty-fingernail type like me in as a member. And while we were going around the course, he would talk about all these investments he was making. He had to compete about everything—and that's not a criticism. I like to win, too. The difference between us, though, is that I know exactly where I come from and I'm not ashamed of it. Your father was really aware that all he had was not his own. The truth is, without him marrying your mom, Augusta wouldn't have had him as a member, either."

"I think that's right."

"And you know, I'd always wondered where he got the money to put into those ventures. Guess you're just finding out now that he's gone."

Lane took a handful of popcorn on a reflex and chewed the stuff down even though he didn't taste anything of it. "You know," he muttered, "I always got the sense he resented my mother."

"I think that's why he was so determined to find these other opportunities. I mean, I get proposals all the time, from friends, associates, financial planners. And I throw them in the trash. Your father was looking for something that was his, always in search of a grounding. Me? I was only at Augusta because I like the course and I love golf." Lenghe's powerful shoulders shrugged, the seams of his polo struggling to hold in all that muscle. "Life is a lot more fun if you mow your own grass. I'm just saying."

Lane fell silent for a time, looking out the oval window at the brown and gold UPS planes that were taking off one after the other in a distant part of the airport. Charlemont was smack-dab in the middle of the country, and that meant it was a perfect shipping hub. Like the BBC and the Sutton Distillery Corporation, UPS was one of the largest employers in the city and state.

It was almost unimaginable to think his family's enterprise could fail. God, there were so many people who depended on it for their paychecks.

He'd never even thought of that before.

"Do you have any information on these businesses?" he said. "Any names? Places? I've got a buddy of mine going through the corporate accounts and he's found the disbursements, but when he searched for anything under the name of WWB Holdings, he came up with nothing."

"Your dad was pretty vague, but he did tell me some things. I can think on it and e-mail you what I know."

"That'd be great."

"So . . . what can I do for you boys? I'm very sure you didn't come here for information you were unaware of my having."

Lane cleared his throat. "Well, as you can guess . . . with senior management shut out and this internal investigation I'm conducting, the business is entering a period of transition that—"

"How much grain do you two need on account?"

Mack spoke up. "Six months would be great."

Lenghe whistled. "That's a lot."

"We'll give you excellent terms," Lane said. "A big interest rate and you can take a security in an entire warehouse worth of bourbon barrels. And bear in mind, no matter what happens internally, our product is selling well and bourbon is hot right now. Cash flow over time is not going to be a problem."

Lenghe made a humming noise, and you could practically smell the wood burning as he thought things over.

"You and I have a shared acquaintance," he said. "Bob Greenblatt?"

"The investment banker?" Lane nodded. "I know him."

"He says you're quite the poker player."

"I've thrown some cards with him."

"You've taken him for some money, you mean." Lenghe sat back and smiled as he wiped his fingers on a paper napkin. "I don't know if you're aware of this, but I'm a bit of a gambler. My wife's a good Christian. She doesn't really approve—she turns a blind eye, though, you know."

Lane narrowed his eyes. "What exactly do you have in mind?"

"Well, I got an invitation to your father's visiting hours. From your butler guy. E-mail was a surprise, but sure saves on postage money, so I liked that. Anyway, I'll be coming into town for it, and what if you and I were to have a little friendly wager on some Texas Hold 'em. We could play for grain. Here's the thing. Your family's account was the first big one I ever had." Lenghe nodded at Mack. "And your daddy's the reason I got it. I took a bus all the way across three states because I didn't have the money for a car, and Big Mack, as we called him, met with me and we hit it off. He gave me a quarter order. Then a half. Within three years, I was the sole corn provider and later, I put in the barley."

"My dad always respected you," Mack said.

"Feeling was mutual. Anyway"—the man refocused on Lane—"I think we should play for it."

"I'm still not really following."

Which wasn't exactly true. He wasn't on the front lines of making bourbon, but he wasn't a total noob, either. Six months of grain was a lot to ante up for. And given that his stock portfolio was ninety-nine percent BBC and the company was about as healthy as an asthmatic in a hayfield . . . he had no idea how he could get enough cash together to buy into the game.

Lenghe shrugged again. "I'll supply you with six months of corn, rye, and barley for free if you win."

"And if I lose?"

"Then you gotta pay me for it over time."

Lane frowned. "Look, I don't mean to talk you out of a deal that's favorable to me, but how is that fair? You're just getting what I would have offered you anyway."

"One, I love a challenge. Two, my instinct tells me you've got a really, really deep financial hole to get out of. You don't have to confirm or deny it, but I don't think you can afford to pay me right now or in the near future. And even if I take a secured interest in a thousand barrels? You're going to need the sale of them to keep the Bradford Bourbon Company going through all this, because without cash from operations, you've got no income to make payroll or your accounts payable to your vendors. That's why I'm doing it. Well, and there's one more reason."

"What's that?"

Lenghe shrugged. "Your family does, in fact, make the best bourbon on the planet. My net worth is well north of a billion dollars—so I can afford to help out the company that supplies my favorite drink to me." The man leaned in again and smiled. "And the ability to do that? It's so much more valuable than getting into a country club. Trust me."

*G*in walked into Easterly's formal Amdega Machin conservatory and smelled sweet hyacinths and lovely lilies in the dense, humid air. Across the lofty, glassed-in space, among the beds of cultivating flowers and the placid faces of specimen orchids, her future sister-in-law had her hands in a pile of dirt and a smudge of same on the ass of her khaki shorts. Lizzie also had no make-up on and her hair pulled back with what looked like a rubber band.

As in a band. That was made of rubber.

Indeed, this gardener was going to be a relation soon. Lane was going to marry the woman, and Gin supposed, considering how unctuous his first wife, Chantal, was, anything short of a farm animal would be an improvement.

"You are certainly being industrious."

Lizzie glanced over her shoulder as she kept her hands where they were over the pot. "Oh, hello."

"Yes." Gin cleared her throat. "I mean, hello."

"Do you need something?"

"As a matter of fact, I do. I need you to do the flowers for my wedding and reception. We're waiting until after the visiting hours, so we'll be doing the event on Saturday after I get married at the courthouse on Friday. I realize this is short notice, but you can put a rush on the order, surely."

Lizzie brushed her palms against each other, getting only the loose dirt off before turning to face across the way. "Have you spoken to Lane about this?"

"Why would I? This is my house. My reception. He's not my father."

"I just thought with all the financial challenges—"

"Ivory and peach for the color scheme. And before you talk to me about cost cutting, I'm keeping the reception small, only four hundred. So we'll have forty tables at the most in the garden. Oh, speaking of which, can you please take care of ordering the tables and chairs, too? Also a tent and the silverware and glassware. I don't really trust Mr. Harris. And I'll let Miss Aurora handle the food-related orders."

"Who's paying for this?"

"I'm sorry?"

"That's a seventy-five thousand dollar event right there. Because, in addition to all that, you're going to need waitstaff. Parkers and buses. And Miss Aurora will have to have help in the kitchen. Who's going to pay for it?"

Gin opened her mouth. And then remembered that Rosalinda was dead. So there was no sense throwing the controller's name out there.

"*We* are going to pay for it." She lifted her chin up. "That's how it will be covered."

"I think you better talk with Lane." Lizzie held up her dirty palms. "And that's all I'm going to say. If he thinks he can afford all that right now, I'll be happy to do whatever it takes to make it happen."

Gin fanned out her hand and inspected her manicure. No chips. Perfectly filed. Red as blood and shiny as a new dime.

"You may be sleeping with my brother, darling, but let's not get ahead of ourselves, shall we? You are still staff, and as such, this is none of your business, is it?"

Yes, there were . . . issues . . . but surely one small gathering wasn't going to break the bank? And it was a necessary expenditure. She was a Bradford, for godsakes.

Lizzie looked away, her brows lowering. When her eyes shifted back, she spoke in a soft voice. "Just so you and I are clear, yes, I may be staff, but I don't need the wake-up call that's coming your way. I am well aware of the situation this household is in, and if it makes you feel better to play *Downton Abbey* with me, that's fine. But it's not going to change the reality that your 'modest' wedding reception is more than you can afford right now. And I'm not ordering so much as a dandelion head without your brother's permission."

Gin felt the branches of her extensive family tree straighten her spine. "Well, I have never—"

"Hello, Mother."

The sound of that insouciant voice was like the claw of a hammer hitting the back of her neck, and Gin didn't immediately turn around. She focused on the glass panel in front of her, seeing who had come up from behind. The face that was reflected had changed since she'd seen it last in September. The coloring was the same, and the long, thick brunette hair remained just like Gin's own—and yes, the expression was exactly as one remembered. But those cheekbones seemed higher, either because of the maturation process or because Amelia had lost some weight.

Never a bad thing.

Gin pivoted around. Her daughter was wearing skinny jeans that made her legs look like soda straws, a black Chanel blouse with a white collar and cuffs, and a set of Tory Burch flats.

Say what you would about her attitude, she looked straight off the streets of Paris.

"Amelia. What are you doing home?"

"It's good to see you, too."

Glancing over her shoulder, Gin went to tell Lizzie to leave, but the woman had already disappeared out one of the back glass doors into the garden, the exit shutting with a quiet *click*.

For a moment, images of Amelia growing up bombarded Gin's mind, replacing the here and now with the then and gone. The past held no improvement on the current estrangement, however, the distance that bred such present hostility forged in the years of Gin behaving like a sister rather than a mother.

A resentful sister.

Even though it was far more complicated than that for her.

Things had certainly been calmer of late, however. Then again, Amelia had been sent off to Hotchkiss not just as a way to further her education, but to quiet the storm that brewed every time she and Gin were in the same room.

"Well, it's always lovely to have you home—"

"Is it."

"—but this is a surprise. I wasn't aware that summer vacation started this early."

"It doesn't. I got kicked out of school. And before you try to go parental on me, may I remind you that I'm just following the example you set?"

Gin looked to heaven for strength—and what do you know, as she was in the conservatory, the glass ceiling permitted her to see the blue sky and clouds far above.

Indeed, parenting was so much easier if one personally set any kind of standard at all.

Make that any kind of positive standard.

"I'll just get settled up in my room," Amelia announced. "And then I'm meeting friends out for dinner tonight. Don't worry. One of them is twenty-five and has a Ferrari. I'll be perfectly fine."

TWENTY

ollowing the meeting with Lenghe, Lane walked into Easterly and didn't get far. Mr. Harris, the butler, strode out of the
dining room with a tray in his hands. On it were half a dozen sterling-
silver *objets d'art*, including the Cartier candy dish that sat on the curved
tail of an upside-down carp.

But the Englishman wasn't coming on the approach to talk about
his polishing plans.

"Oh, well done, sir. I was just going in search of you. You have a visitor. Deputy Ramsey is in the kitchen."

"Yes, I saw his sheriff's vehicle parked outside."

"Also, the notification for the visiting hours has gone out. The e-mail
was necessary due to our time constraints. I would have preferred proper
mail, of course. The responses have already began streaming in, however, and I believe you will be pleased with the turnout."

Three things went through Lane's mind, one after the other: Hopefully
the guests wouldn't eat or drink much; wonder what people would say if
they did a cash bar; and finally, God, he'd never thought about per-head
costs before.

As he became aware that the butler was looking at him expectantly, Lane said, "I'm sorry, what was that?"

"There has also been a new arrival in the household."

The butler stopped the news flash there, as if he had been offended by Lane's mental recession and was going to force interaction as payback.

"So who is it?" The Grim Reaper? No, wait. Bernie Madoff on a work-release program. Krampus—nope, wrong season.

"Miss Amelia has returned. She arrived by taxi about ten minutes ago with some of her bags. I took the liberty of having them placed in her room."

Lane frowned. "Is it summer vacation already? Where is she?"

"I gather she went to find her mother."

"So the mushroom cloud should be hitting the horizon soon. Thank you, Mr. Harris."

"My pleasure, sir."

For some reason, with the way the man said the words, they always came out sounding like "screw you." Which made one want to take that black tie from around his neck and—

No, enough with the dead bodies, even on the hypothetical.

Lane flushed his brain, walked across the foyer, and entered the stark hall that preceded the entrance to the kitchen. As he came up to Rosalinda Freeland's old office, he paused and traced the police seal that remained on the door.

The fact that he wasn't allowed in there seemed emblematic of what his whole life had become.

Maybe Jeff was right. Maybe he couldn't keep a lid on everything that was falling apart. Maybe the world didn't run like it had back in his grandfather's, and even his father's, day, when families like his had the power to protect themselves.

And honestly, why the hell was he ruining relationships that mattered to him for his father's bullshit?

"Hello, sir."

Lane glanced over. A blond woman in a maid's uniform was coming out of the laundry room, a long, loose swath of fine cotton over her arm.

"It's Tiphanii," she said. "With a *ph* and two *i*'s."

"Yes, of course. How are you?"

"I'm taking good care of your friend Jeff. He's working so hard up there." There was a pause. "Is there anything I can do for you?"

"No, thank you." Clean duvet covers aside, she had nothing he wanted. Or ever would. "But I'm sure my old roommate appreciates the personal service."

"Well, you'll let me know, then."

As she sashayed off, he thought of the first season of *American Horror Story* and the maid who was sometimes old, sometimes young. That one there was definitely the latter. The good news? At least Jeff was no doubt getting a chance to burn off some stress. And Tiphanii wasn't a ghost who would go post-menopausal on the guy at an awkward time.

Man, you're just like your father.

"No, I'm not."

When Lane entered the extensive, professionally appointed kitchen, he smelled hot cross buns and found Miss Aurora and Officer Ramsey sitting side by side on stools at her granite countertop, a pair of coffee mugs and a plate of those sweets between them. The deputy was in his tan, brown, and gold uniform, a gun on his hip, a radio up on his huge shoulder. Miss Aurora was in an apron and loose blue slacks.

She was looking thinner since he'd arrived here, Lane thought grimly.

"'Mornin'," Lane said as he went over and clapped palms with Ramsey.

"You, too."

"There room for a third?"

"Always." Miss Aurora pushed an empty mug to him and got up to snag the coffeepot from its machine. "And I'll be leaving you two."

"Stay," Lane said as he sat down. "Please."

God, he'd forgotten how big Ramsey was. Lane was a healthy six two, six three. But as he took the stool next to the deputy, he felt like a Barbie doll.

"So the autopsy report." Mitch glanced over. "The finger is your father's. Definitely. There were cut marks on the remains that matched the scoring on the bone of what was found in your front yard."

"He was murdered, then." Lane nodded a thanks at the coffee that was poured in front of him. "'Cuz you don't do that to yourself."

"Were you aware that your father was sick?"

"In the head? Yes, very."

"He had lung cancer."

Lane slowly lowered his mug. "I'm sorry?"

"Your father was suffering from an advanced lung cancer that had metastasized to his brain. The coroner said he had another six months at the most—and very soon it was going to affect his balance and motor skills to an extent that he wouldn't have been able to hide it from others."

"Those cigarettes." He looked at Miss Aurora. "All those fucking cigarettes."

"Watch your mouth," she said. "But I always wanted him to stop. I didn't volunteer for my cancer. I don't know why anyone would want this disease."

Glancing over at Ramsey, Lane asked, "Was it possible that he didn't know? And how long might he have had it?"

Not that his father would have dropped a dime to Lane with a health report or anything. Hell, knowing the great William Baldwine, the man might well have believed he could simply will the stuff into remission.

"I asked the coroner that myself." Ramsey shook his head. "He said that your father most likely would have been symptomatic. Shortness of breath. Headaches. Dizziness. His remains did not indicate any surgery had been performed and there wasn't a chest port or anything—but that didn't mean he wasn't on chemo or hadn't had radiation. Tissue samples have been sent off, and a toxicology report ordered—although the results of all that will take some time to come in."

Lane rubbed his head. "So then he really could have killed himself. If he knew he was going to die, and he didn't want to suffer, he could have jumped off that bridge."

Except what about the finger? That ring? The fact that, of all the acres that made up the estate, of all the places hidden and obvious, the thing had been buried right beneath his mother's window?

"Or your father could have been thrown off," the deputy suggested.

"Just because the man was sick doesn't mean someone couldn't have murdered him—and water was found in the lungs, which proves that he was alive and took at least one deep breath after he hit the river." Ramsey glanced at Miss Aurora. "Ma'am, I'm sorry to be speaking about this in such graphic terms."

Lane's momma just shrugged. "It is what it is."

Lane looked at Miss Aurora. "I was up all the time in New York. Did you notice anything . . . different about him?"

Although whatever his condition, he'd still had a sex drive. At least according to Chantal and that baby she was carrying.

His momma shook her head. "I didn't pick up on anything unusual. He was gone a lot the last couple of months, but that was always true. And you know, he kept to himself. He was up and out of this house to the business center first thing in the morning, and a lot of the time, he was late getting home. My rooms face the garages so I'd see his chauffeur finally parking his car at midnight, one in the morning, or catch him walking back here from his office. So I don't know."

Ramsey spoke up. "With your family's money and connections, he could have gone anywhere in the States for treatment."

"What does homicide think?" Lane asked.

Ramsey shook his head back and forth. "They're leaning toward foul play. That finger is the key. It changes everything."

Lane stayed for a little while longer and chatted with them. Then he excused himself of their company, put his mug in the sink, and headed up the staff stairs to the second floor. Miss Aurora and Ramsey had known each other since the deputy had been in diapers, and he often visited her when he was off duty before. So they could be there for a while yet.

Cancer.

So his father had been busy killing himself with tobacco . . . until someone had decided to speed up the process and put PAID on a toe tag.

Unbelievable.

As usual, during the morning hours after the family were up and out of their bedrooms, the staff worked in this part of the house, and he could smell the cleaning supplies for the toilets and the showers and the windows, the artificial citrus and vaguely mint-like scents making his nose itch.

Proceeding down to his father's room, it felt wrong not to knock before Lane opened the door—even though the man was dead. And stepping inside the quiet, dark interior of the masculine room was an all-wrong that made him look over his shoulder for no good reason.

There were few personal effects out on the bureau tops and the bedside tables, everything in the suite a consciously arranged and maintained stage set that announced "A Rich and Powerful Man Lays His Head Here at Night": from the monogrammed bedcovers and monogrammed pillows, to the leather-bound books and the Oriental rugs, to the banks of windows that were currently hidden behind heavy silk curtains, you could have been at the Ritz-Carlton in New York or a country seat in England or a castle in Italy.

The bathroom was floor-to-ceiling old-fashioned marble and molding mixed with new plumbing, the fancy glassed-in shower enclosure taking up half the room. Lane paused as he saw his father's monogrammed robe hanging on a brass hook. And then there was the shaving kit with its gold-handled brush and its straight-edge razor. The strip of leather to hone the silver blade. The sterling cup for water. The toothbrush.

There were two gold sinks separated by a mile of marble countertop, but it wasn't as if his mother had ever used the vacant one. And over the expanse was a mirror with gold sconces set into its reflective panels.

No medicine cabinet there.

Lane bent down and started opening drawers. The first one had a bunch of condoms in it, and didn't that make him want to smash something for so many reasons. Next up were supplies like soap, Q-tips, regular razors. On the other side were brushes, combs. Under the sinks were toilet paper, Kleenex boxes, bottles of Listerine.

On some level, it seemed strange that his father had ever used such pedestrian things. Like any other person who was getting themselves ready for work or for bed.

In fact, a mystery had always surrounded the man, although not a cozy one. More a Jack the Ripper pall rooted in their lack of communication, lack of a relationship, lack of any warmth.

Lane found the medications in the tall thin closet by the window seat.

There were six orange pill bottles, each with varying numbers of pills or capsules in them. He didn't recognize the prescribing doctor or the names of the medicines, but given the number of warnings on the sides about not using heavy machinery or driving while on them, he had to guess they were painkillers or muscle relaxants . . . or very serious compounds that made you sicker than your disease, at least in the short term.

Getting out his phone, he typed in the physician's name.

Well. What do you know.

The doctor was at MD Anderson Cancer Center down in Houston.

His father had known he was sick. And likely that he was dying.

"*Y*ou got kicked out?" Gin demanded across the fragrant air of the conservatory.

"Yes," her daughter answered.

Fantastic, Gin thought.

In the silence that followed, she tried on a couple of versions of parental indignation, imagining herself stamping a high-heeled shoe or perhaps going with an old-school wag of the forefinger. Neither fit. The only thing that really seemed appropriate was getting Edward to handle this. He would know what to do.

But no. That avenue was cut off.

In the end, she went with, "May I ask why you were asked to leave school?"

"Why do you think. I'm your daughter after all."

Gin rolled her eyes. "Drinking? Or did you get caught with a boy?"

As Amelia merely lifted her chin, the math added up to an even greater infraction.

"You *slept* with one of your professors? Are you mad?"

"You did. That's why you took a break from school—"

The door in from the house opened and Lane appeared like a beacon to a sailor at sea.

"Guess who's home from school," Gin said dryly.

"I heard. Come here, Ames. It's been a while."

As the girl went into Lane's arms and their two dark heads drew close together, Gin had to look away.

"She has news," Gin muttered as she wandered around and picked at orchid leaves. "Why don't you tell him?"

"I got kicked out."

"For sleeping with a professor." Gin waved a hand. "Of all the legacies to live up to."

Lane cursed and stepped back. "Amelia."

"Oh, he's using your real name." Gin smiled, thinking that Lane sounded like their father. "He means business. Is there someone we can call at Hotchkiss, Lane? Surely we can talk them out of this."

Lane rubbed his face. "Did someone take advantage of you? Were you hurt?"

"No," the girl said. "It wasn't like that."

Gin spoke up. "There has to be a way to get her back in—"

"Aren't finals coming up?" Lane interrupted. "Are you going to lose your credits? Jesus Christ, Ames, seriously. This is a big deal."

"I'm sorry."

"Yes," Gin muttered, "you look sorry. Would you like a tissue? Would that help you play the part better?"

"That's a nice diamond on your finger," Amelia snapped. "You're getting married, I gather?"

"The day after your grandfather's visitation here."

"Yes, nice of you to call me and let me know, Mother."

"The marriage is not important."

"I agree. I'm talking about the death of my grandfather. My own grandfather died, and I read about it in a newspaper."

Lane's eyes swung around. "You didn't call her, Gin? *Really?*"

"I beg your pardon, but *she* is the one who got kicked out of prep school. And you're looking at me like I did something wrong?"

"I can go to school here in Charlemont," Amelia interjected. "Charlemont Country Day is a good school, and I can live here at home—"

"What makes you think they'll take you now?" Gin asked.

"Our family endowed the expansion five years ago," Amelia countered. "Like they won't? And who are you marrying, Mother? Let me guess. He's rich and spineless—"

"Enough!" Lane snapped. "Gin, she's your daughter. For once in your life, will you act like it? And, Amelia, this is a bigger problem than you realize."

"But it's fixable," the girl said. "Everything is fixable in this family, isn't it."

"Actually, that is not true. And you better pray you don't learn that lesson on this particular screw-up of yours."

As Lane went to leave, Gin thought of her wedding reception and called out, "Wait, you and I have something to discuss."

"I'm not calling Charlemont Country Day. You're going to do that for her. It's time you step up."

Gin crossed her arms over her chest and winced as one of Richard's bruises on her elbow let out a squawk. "Amelia, would you be so kind as to go sulk in your room? Or perhaps out by the pool? I'm sure that with the help of your Twitter account you can spend an enjoyable couple of hours informing your friends of the abominable nature of your return unto the fold."

"My pleasure," Amelia said. "It's certainly better than being in your company."

The girl didn't storm off; she swanned away, leaving a ripple of fragrance in the air along with her disdain.

It was a wonder they didn't get along better.

As the door back into the house eased shut, Gin bitched, "Maybe she should just forget school and go to New York to model. She'll have more luck using her face rather than her mouth if she's looking to get ahead."

"Your mouth hasn't stopped you," Lane said. "But it hasn't done you any good. Look at who you're marrying, for instance."

"Richard is one of the wealthiest men in the state, and he can help our business."

"You hate him."

"So does everyone else. That's hardly a news flash—but this brings me to the issue. Your little darling girl Lizzie said I need your permission in order to have my reception here. I told her it was not going to be a large affair—four hundred, at the most—"

"Wait, what?"

"My wedding reception. The licenses are being issued tomorrow, and we are going to the courthouse on Friday. Father's visiting hours are the day after that. The reception will be here on Saturday—just cocktails in the back garden followed by a dinner—"

"Gin."

"What?"

"Who's going to pay for all that?"

"We are. Why?"

Lane's eyes narrowed. "We don't have the money, Gin. As in checks will bounce. Do you understand what I'm telling you? There is no money right now. I'm trying to fix that, but I don't care if it's four hundred or forty people—we can't write any checks that aren't necessary."

"We're paying for Father's visiting hours."

"And that's it. The parties are over, Gin. The private planes. Hell, taxis are out of the question. There are no more clothes, or balls, or trips. Everything is stopping. You need to understand that."

She frowned as she tracked a rather alarming fluttering of her heart. And then she whispered, "I find it hard to believe that you'll put on the funeral of a man you hated, but not give me the reception I deserve."

Lane stared at her for a moment. "You know, Gin, I'm going to be completely honest here. I've always known you were a self-serving narcissist, but I really never thought you were stupid."

"I beg your pardon?"

"If we don't invite half the world here to pay their respects, there's going to be talk—and it's going to be true. I couldn't give a shit about this family's reputation, but the business is our only chance to get out of this mess. There is nothing but fumes keeping the BBC afloat. I'm worried about paying salaries, for fuck's sake. If anything gets out to the press about the financial reversal, we run the risk of vendors panicking and calling accounts payable or cutting us off. Distributors could balk. The union could get riled. There is so much more to this than just a goddamn party. Visiting hours are a necessary ruse. Your reception is not."

Gin put her hand to her throat and thought of being in the Phantom Drophead at that gas station down on River Road . . . and her credit cards not working. But when that had happened the other day, it had been because her father had cut her off, not because funds were unavailable.

And then she remembered her brother breaking the bad financial news to her after he'd picked her up at the police station.

She shook her head, though. "You said there was fifty or sixty million in debt. Surely there are other funds somewhere—"

"The debt is over triple that. That we've found so far. Times have changed, Gin." He turned away. "You want a party, get your new husband to cut the check. It's chump change for him, and that *is* why you're marrying him, after all."

Gin stayed where she was, watching the glass door ease shut once again.

In the silence, a strange feeling of dislocation overcame her, and it took her a moment to realize it was something she had become familiar with whenever Richard . . .

Oh, God. She felt like she was going to throw up.

"It's going to be fine," she said to the plants. "And Pford might as well start making himself useful now."

TWENTY-ONE

The sweeper kissed along the center aisle of the stable, pushing debris ahead, kicking up a fine mist of hay particles. As
Edward walked behind his broom, the muzzles of the breeding females
came out of open stall half doors, snuffing at his T-shirt, bumping his
elbow, blowing at his hair. Sweat had broken out across his brow and a
line of it descended his spine into the loose waistband of his jeans. From
time to time, he stopped and wiped his forearm over his face. Talked to
Joey, Moe's son, who was mucking stalls. Gave a stroke to a graceful
neck or a smooth to a springy mane.

He could feel the alcohol coming out of his pores, like he'd been mar-
inating in the stuff. And yet even as he was working the booze through
his body, he'd had to nurse a vodka bottle a couple of times, otherwise the
shaking got ahead of him.

"You're working hard," came a voice from the far end.

Edward stopped and tried to look over his shoulder. When his body
wouldn't allow him the leeway, he shuffled around, using the broom
handle for leverage.

Squinting against a ray of sunlight, he said, "Who is it?"

"I'm Detective Merrimack. CMP."

A strident set of footfalls came down the concrete, and when they halted in front of him, a wallet was flipped open, and an ID and a badge were presented for inspection.

"I was wondering if I could ask you a couple of questions," the detective said. "Just as a formality."

Edward shifted focus from the display to the face that matched the laminated photograph. Merrimack was African-American, with short cropped hair, a strong jaw, and big hands that suggested he might have been a ballplayer at one time. He was wearing a bright white polo shirt with the Charlemont Metro Police Department's crest on the pec, a good pair of slacks, and a set of leather shoes with rubber soles that made Edward think that, on occasion, the guy had to chase after somebody.

"How may I help you, Detective?"

Merrimack disappeared his credentials. "Do you want to go somewhere to sit down while we talk privately?"

"Here is good enough for me." Edward limped over to a hay bale and let his weight fall off his legs. "There's no one else in this barn right now. And you can use that bucket if you want to turn it over."

Merrimack shook his head. Smiled. Glanced around. "This is some spread you've got here. Lot of beautiful horses."

"You a betting man at the track?"

"Just small stuff. Nothing like you do, I'm sure."

"I don't bet. Anymore, that is."

"Not even on your own horses?"

"Especially not my own. So what can I do for you?"

The detective walked across to the stall whose top half was shut. "Wow. This is a beauty in here—"

Edward shook his head. "I wouldn't get too close if I were—"

Nebekanzer bared his teeth and lunged at the bars, and Merrimack pinwheeled backward, tap-dancing better than Savion Glover.

As the man caught himself on an opposite stall door, Edward said, "You're not familiar with horses, are you?"

"Ah . . . no." The man straightened and retucked his shirt. "No, I'm not."

"Well, when you walk into a barn full of open stall halves and there's one, and only one, that's fully closed? Chances are that's for a good reason."

Merrimack shook his head at the great stallion, who was stalking back and forth like he wanted out and not to shake hands politely. "Tell me no one rides that thing."

"Only me. And I have nothing to lose."

"You? You can get in a saddle on the back of that horse."

"He's my stallion, not just a horse. And yes, I can. When I set my mind to something, I can make it happen even in this body."

Merrimack refocused. Smiled again. "Can you. Well, that must be helping with your recovery. I read about your . . ."

"Unfortunate vacation? Yes, what I went through is never going to show up on Trivago. But at least I got the frequent-flyer points for the trip down. Nothing coming north, though. They had to airlift what was left of me to an Army base, and then the Air Force got me back to the States."

"I can't imagine what that was like."

"Yes, you can." Edward leaned back on the hay bale and rearranged his legs. "So what can I do for you?"

"Wait, you said the Air Force brought you home?"

"The Ambassador to Colombia is a friend of my family's. He was very helpful. So was a sheriff's deputy friend of mine from here in Charlemont."

"Did your father arrange for the help?"

"No, he did not."

"No?"

Edward tilted his head. "He had other priorities at the time. Did you come all the way out to Ogden County just to ask me about my horses? Or is this about my father?"

Merrimack smiled again, in that way that seemed to indicate he was thinking but didn't want to seem threatening. "It is. Just a few background questions. In situations like this, we like to start with family."

"Ask away."

"Can you describe your relationship with your father?"

Edward moved the broom between his knees and batted the handle back and forth. "It was fractious."

"That's a big word."

"Do you need a definition?"

"No, I don't." Merrimack took out a pad from his back pocket and opened it. "So you weren't close."

"I worked with him for a number of years. But I wouldn't say that the traditional father–son relationship was one we shared."

"You were his heir apparent?"

"I was in a business sense."

"But you are not anymore."

"He's dead. He doesn't have any 'anymore,' does he? And why don't you come out and ask me whether I killed him and cut off his finger?"

Another of those smiles. And what do you know, the guy had nice teeth, everything straight and white, but not in a fake, cosmetically enhanced way. "All right. Maybe you'd like to answer your own question."

"How can I possibly kill anyone? I can barely sweep this aisle."

Merrimack looked down and back. "You just told me it was all about motivation for you."

"You're a homicide detective. You must be well aware of how much effort it takes to murder someone. My father was a healthy man, and in my current condition, he weighed about fifty pounds more than I do. I may not have been terribly fond of him, but that doesn't mean patricide was on my bucket list."

"Can you tell me where you were the night he died?"

"I was here."

"Is there anyone who can corroborate that—"

"I can."

Shelby stepped out from the supply room, as unapologetic and calm as a Buddha. Even though she was lying.

"Hello, miss," the detective said, walking over and extending his palm. "I'm from the Charlemont Metro Police Department. And you are?"

"Shelby Landis." She shook hands and stepped back. "I work here as a stable hand."

"For how long?"

"Not long. A week or so. My dad died and he told me to come here."

Merrimack glanced at Edward. "And that night, the night your father died, the two of you were . . ."

"Just here," Edward said. "Sitting around. That's the extent of things for me."

"Well, I'm sure that's understandable." Smile. "Let me ask you something. What kind of car do you drive?"

Edward shrugged. "I don't, really. My Porsche is back at Easterly. It's a stick shift, so it's not really all that practical anymore."

"When was the last time you were back home?"

"That isn't my home anymore. I live here."

"Fine, when were you last at Easterly?"

Edward thought back to him and Lane getting into the business center so that those financial records could see the light of day. Technically, it hadn't been breaking and entering, but Edward sure as hell wouldn't have been welcomed there. And yes, he had stolen corporate information.

Then he had had that moment with Miss Aurora, the woman wrapping her arms around him and breaking him up on the inside.

Lot of security cameras at Easterly. Outside and inside the house. Inside the business center.

"I was there a couple of days ago. To see my brother Lane."

"And what did you do while you were there?"

"Talked to him." Used a back door into the network to extract information. Watched his father make a deal with Sutton. After the bastard hit on her. "We just caught up."

"Hmm." Smile. "Did you borrow one of the other cars? I mean, your family has a lot of different cars, don't they?"

"No."

"They don't? Because when I was there yesterday, I saw a big bank of garage doors out in back. Right across from the business center where your father worked."

"No, as in I didn't take any of the other cars out."

"The keys to those vehicles are in the garage, right? In a lockbox with a combination."

"I guess so."

"Do you know the combination, Mr. Baldwine?"

"If I did, I've forgotten it."

"That happens. People forget pass codes and passwords all the time, don't they. Tell me something, are you aware of anyone who might have held a grudge against your father? Or wanted to harm him? Maybe had a reason to get revenge against him?"

"It's a long list."

"Is it?"

"My father had a habit of not ingratiating himself to others."

"Can you give me any specific examples?"

"Anyone he's ever dealt with on a personal or professional level. How's that."

"Fractious, indeed. You said your father was healthy, in comparison to yourself. But were you aware of any illnesses he might have had?"

"My father believed real men did not get sick."

"Okay." The pad got shut without the detective having written anything in it. "Well, if you can think of anything that will help us, you can call me here. Either one of you."

Edward accepted the business card that was held out to him. There was a gold seal in the center, the same one that was on the detective's shirt. And Merrimack's name and various numbers and addresses were printed around it as if it were the sun.

At the bottom, there was the phrase "To Protect and Serve" in cursive writing.

"So you think he was murdered?" Edward said.

"Do you?" Merrimack gave a card to Shelby. "What do you think, Mr. Baldwine?"

"I don't have an opinion one way or the other."

He wanted to ask if he was a suspect, but he already knew that answer. And Merrimack was keeping his cards close to his chest.

Smile. "Well. Nice to meet you both. You know where to find me—and I know where to find you."

"The pleasure was all my mine."

Edward watched the detective saunter out into the bright light of the early afternoon. Then he waited a little longer as an unmarked police car proceeded down the main lane and out to the road beyond.

"You weren't with me," Edward murmured.

"Does it matter?"

"Unfortunately . . . it does."

TWENTY-TWO

*A*t least his father's attorney wasn't late.

As Lane checked his Piaget, it was four forty-five on the dot when Mr. Harris brought the venerable Babcock Jefferson into Easterly's main parlor.

"Greetings, Mr. Jefferson," Lane said as he got to his feet. "Good of you to come."

"Lane. My condolences."

William Baldwine's executor was dressed in a navy blue suit with a red and blue bow tie and a crisp white kerchief in his breast pocket. He was a sixty-something, wealthy version of a good ol' boy, his jowls protruding over the collar of his formal shirt, the scent of Cuban cigars and Bay Rum aftershave preceding him as he came across to shake hands.

Samuel T. rose from the other sofa. "Mr. Jefferson. I am here in the capacity of Lane's attorney."

"Samuel T. How's your father?"

"Very well."

"Give him my best. And anyone is welcome here upon the invitation of the family."

"Mr. Jefferson," Lane spoke up. "This is my fiancée, Lizzie King."

Annnnd that pretty much hit pause for everybody in the room: Gin rolled her eyes, Samuel T. smiled, and Mr. Jefferson bowed at the waist.

Lizzie, meanwhile, shot a surprised stare in Lane's direction and then recovered by shaking the executor's hand and offering the guy a smile. "It's a very recent thing."

For a moment, Mr. Jefferson seemed positively smitten with her, his eyes twinkling in a friendly way.

"Well, congratulations!" Mr. Jefferson nodded in Lane's direction and then refocused on her. "I would say that you're an upgrade, but that would be disrespectful to his former Mrs. You are, however, a vast improvement."

Lizzie laughed. "You're a charmer, aren't you?"

"Down to my hunting boots, ma'am." Mr. Jefferson grew serious once more as he looked back at Lane. "Where are your brothers?"

Lane took his seat again beside Lizzie. "I don't know what state Max is in, much less how to reach him, and Edward is—"

"Right here."

Edward materialized in the archway, and even though Lane had seen him a day or so ago, his physical appearance was still the kind of thing you had to adjust to. He was freshly shaved and showered, his dark hair damp and curling in a way it had never been permitted to in previous years. His khakis were nearly falling off his hips, held up from the floor only by an alligator belt. His shirt was plain and blue, a leftover from his business wardrobe. It was so loose, though, it was as if he were a child trying on his father's clothes.

And yet he commanded respect as he limped across and sat in one of the armchairs. "Mr. Jefferson. Good to see you again. Excuse my rudeness, but I must sit down."

"I'll come to you, son."

The executor put his briefcase down on one of the side tables and walked over. "It's good to see you again."

Edward shook the man's hand. "Likewise."

There was no small talk after that. Edward had never been one for it, and Mr. Jefferson appeared to remember that.

"Is there anyone else you have invited?"

Lane's reflex was to wait for Edward to answer, but then he remembered that he himself had been the one to get everybody together.

"No." Lane got up and strode across to the pocket doors that opened into the study. "We're ready."

He shut the two halves and went to do the same at the archway into the foyer. When he turned back around, he hung on to Lizzie's stare. She was sitting on the silk sofa in her shorts and her polo, her blond hair pulled back, her face open.

God, he loved her.

"Let's do this," Lane heard himself say.

*E*dward steepled his hands, putting his elbows on the padded arms of the chair. Across the parlor, on the silk sofa, his little brother was cozy-cozy with the horticulturist, Lizzie, and one had to admit, the ease with which the two of them sat side by side was indicative of a connection not typically found in Bradford marriages: It was in the way he casually draped an arm over her shoulders. How she rested her hand on his knee. The fact that they made eye contact with each other as if both were checking that the other was all right.

He wished Lane well. He truly did.

Gin, on the other hand, was in a more traditional relationship with her future spouse. Richard Pford was nowhere to be found, and that was just as well. He might be marrying into the family, but this was private.

"We are here for the reading of William Wyatt Baldwine's last will and testament," Babcock stated as he took a seat in the other armchair and opened his briefcase upon his lap.

"Should Mother be included?" Edward interjected.

The executor glanced over the top half of his case and said smoothly, "I do not believe it is necessary to disturb her. Your father was primarily interested in providing for his offspring."

"But of course."

Babcock resumed extraction of a rather voluminous document. "The decedent engaged me for the previous ten years as his personal attorney, and during that time period, he executed three wills. This is his final will, executed one year ago. In it, he provides that any debts of a personal nature shall be paid, along with any appropriate taxes and professional fees, firstly. Thereafter, he has created a trust for the bulk of his assets. This trust is to be split equally in favor of Miss Virginia Elizabeth Baldwine, Mr. Jonathan Tulane Baldwine, and Mr. Maxwell Prentiss Baldwine."

Cue the pause.

Edward smiled. "I take it my name was omitted on purpose."

Babcock shook his head gravely. "I'm so sorry, son. I advocated for him to include you, I did."

"Cutting me out of his will is the least onerous burden that man put upon me, I assure you. And, Lane, do stop looking at me like that, will you."

As his little brother shifted his eyes away, Edward got up and limped across to the bar cart. "Family Reserve, anyone?"

"For me," Lane said.

"As well," Samuel T. spoke up.

Gin remained silent, but her eyes, too, watched his every move as the lawyer described particulars relative to the trust that had been established. Samuel T. came over for his glass and Lane's, and then Edward was taking his own back across to the armchair he'd been in.

He could honestly say he felt nothing. No anger. No nostalgia. No burning desire to close distance, reconnect, recon order. Fix something.

The detachment had been hard earned, honed by him long living with the contradictions of the fire of his father's resentment and the freeze of the man's estrangement.

It would not do for others to feel anything, either—at least when it came to him and his disinheritence. His relationship with his father, such as it had been, was the business only of the pair of them. Edward didn't want to nurse the sympathy of others; his brother and sister needed to be as phlegmatic as he was.

A year ago, he thought.

Wonder why the change in the will had been made. Or perhaps he had never been provided for, the earlier incarnations not including him, either.

"—now to the individual bequests." At this point, Babcock cleared his throat. "I would note that there was a significant bequest in the will to Ms. Rosalinda Freeland, who has since deceased. The house that she resided in, at three-oh-seven-two Cerise Circle in Rolling Meadows, was in fact owned outright by Mr. Baldwine, and it was his wish that the property be deeded free and clear over to her. However, in the event she predeceased him, which in fact happened, a further provision was made in this instrument that this residence, along with the sum of ten million dollars, be gifted to her son, Randolph Damion Freeland. Said assets to be placed in a trust to his benefit until he is thirty years of age, with myself or my designee serving as trustee."

Silence.

The cricket kind.

Ah, so this was why you didn't want my mother down here, Edward thought to himself.

Samuel T. crossed his arms over his chest. "Well."

And that fairly much covered it, even as no one else said anything. It was clear, however, that Lane's soon-to-be-ex-wife wasn't the only woman William had impregnated out of wedlock.

Perhaps there were other sons or daughters in the world, too.

Although, truly, the answer to that didn't matter to Edward any more than any kind of inheritance did. He had come here for a different reason than the will. It merely had to look as though he had arrived for the same meeting everyone else had gathered for.

He had a necessary to dispose of, as his grandmother would have said.

TWENTY-THREE

*A*s Mr. Jefferson ran through long paragraphs of legalese, Gin wasn't focused on the will reading or, really, the fact that Edward had been cut out. Her only prevalent thought was that Amelia was home . . . and Samuel T., as he sat over there, on that sofa, representing Lane's interest in a professional capacity . . . was under the same roof as his own daughter.

Neither of them knew it, of course.

And that was on Gin.

She tried not to imagine the pair of them sitting side by side. Tried not to see, as she recalled them both with a specificity that burned her memory, the common features, the similar movements, that narrowing of the eye when they were concentrating. She also especially deflected the fact that two of them hid their formidable intelligence behind a laconic sociability . . . like it was something they didn't want to get too showy about.

"And that concludes the salient provisions." Mr. Jefferson removed his reading glasses. "I would like to take this opportunity to answer any questions. The will is in probate at the moment, and a tallying of assets is beginning."

There was a silence. And then Lane spoke up. "I believe you have said it all. I'll see you out. Samuel T., join us?"

Gin ducked her head and only then let her eyes follow Samuel T. as he got to his feet and went to open the double doors for his client and his client's father's executor. He didn't glance back at her. Hadn't greeted her or stared at her.

But this was business.

One thing you could always count on with Samuel T., no matter how wild and crazy he could be after hours, was that as soon as he put his lawyer hat on, he was unshakable.

She literally didn't exist. Any more than anyone else who did not affect his client's interests did.

And ordinarily, this arguably appropriate compartmentalization irked her and made her want to get in his face and demand notice. Knowing that Amelia was somewhere in the mansion cured her of any such immaturity, however.

With them in such close vicinity, it was impossible to ignore the implications of her lack of disclosure. She was a criminal, stealing them of years that were their due, robbing them of knowledge that was their right. And for the first time, she felt a guilt that was so finely edged, she was sure she was bleeding internally.

But the idea of coming out with it all? That was a mountain insurmountable from where she stood now, the distance, the height, the rocky territory that all those missing days and nights, and events small and large, added up to, too far to travel.

Yes, she thought. This was why she caused the drama, this was the root of her escapades. If one created cymbals crashing directly in front of one's face . . . one could hear nothing of anything else. Especially one's conscience.

Her conscience.

"How are you?"

Jerking to attention, she looked up at her brother Edward, and had to blink through tears to properly see him.

"No, no, none of that," he said stiffly.

Just as well he thought he was the cause. "But of course." She wiped her eyes. "Edward . . . you are . . ."

Not looking well, she thought as she let go of her own problems.

And God, to see him hunched and thin, so different from the head of the family that she had forever pictured him as, was a recalibration she did not wish to make. It was so strange. In the ways that mattered, it was easier to lose her father than the incarnation of her brother that had always been.

"I'm well," he filled in when she failed to complete the sentence. "And you?"

Falling apart, she thought to herself. I am our family's fortunes, crumbling first in private . . . and then for all to see.

"I am well." She batted her hand about. "Listen to us. We sound like our parents."

She rose out of the chair and embraced him, and couldn't hold her wince in as she felt bones and not much else. He gave her an awkward pat before he stepped back.

"I understand there are congratulations in order." He bowed stiffly. "I will try to make the wedding. When is it?"

"Ah . . . Friday. No, Saturday. I . . . don't know. We're getting married at the courthouse on Friday, though. I'm not sure about a reception."

Abruptly, it was the last thing that held any interest for her.

"Friday." He nodded. "Well, best wishes to you and your fiancé."

With that, he hobbled out, and she nearly jumped ahead of him and demanded that he tell her what he really thought: Her true brother Edward would never have been so phlegmatic about Richard. Edward had had to do business with Pford Distributors for years and had never been impressed with the man.

And if the old Edward had known what happened behind closed doors?

He would have been murderous.

But he had evolved into a different place, even as she seemed determined to remain on her path. Neither was an improvement, was it.

Left in the room alone, Gin sat back down and stayed where she was, a strange paralysis overtaking her body. Meanwhile, the various voices and footfalls drifted off. And then outside on the lawn in the sunshine, not far from where that gruesome discovery had been made in the ivy bed, the two lawyers and her brother fell into a clutch of conversation.

She stared at Samuel T. through the bubbly glass of the old-fashioned window. His face never seemed to change. It was as chiseled and perfectly formed as ever, his hair just a little on the long side and brushed straight back. His body, long and lean, carried that handmade suit like a hanger, the folds of fabric, the sleeves, the cuffs on the pant legs, falling exactly as the tailor meant them to.

She thought of him in the wine cellar in the basement, fucking that girl on the table at the Derby Brunch. Gin had been down there crying when he had snuck away and taken the woman in a fashion that had made the bimbo sound like a porn star.

Going by the history of Gin's relationship with Samuel T., it was just one more in a long line of nasty tit for tats . . . that had started at their first kiss when she'd been fourteen and culminated in Amelia.

The problem was, though, when they stopped the fighting, the conflict, the pebble-in-the-shoe, thumb-tack-in-the-heel imitations, he could be . . .

Just the most amazing, incredible, dynamic, alive man she had ever known.

And in the past, she would have said that her marriage wouldn't have stopped them from being together. Theirs had always been a love affair that was like a bad intersection with no traffic light, crashes time and time again, sparks, the scent of gasoline, burned-up, tangled metal and rubber everywhere. They were safety glass busted into a spider's web of cracks, air bags deployed, tires popped and sagged.

But the rush just before the impact? There was nothing like it in the world, especially not to a bored, under-utilized, Southern belle like her—and it had never mattered if one or the other of them had been with anyone else. Girlfriends, boyfriends, serious lovers, booty calls. The constant for both of them had been the other one.

She had seen the look on his face when he'd learned of her engagement, however. He had never looked at her like that before, and that expression was what she saw as she lay awake at night—

"Helluva diamond he got you."

She jerked her head up. Samuel T. was leaning against the archway, arms crossed over his chest, lids low on his eyes, mouth tight as if he resented the fact that she was still in the room.

Gin tucked the ring out of sight and cleared her throat. "Couldn't stay away, Solicitor?"

As taunts went, it was a failure. The flat delivery just killed the dig completely.

"Don't be flattered," he said as he came in and headed for the sofa. "I left my briefcase. I'm not coming to see you."

She braced herself for that old familiar surge of anger—looked forward to it, in fact, if only for its familiarity. The corrosive grind in her gut did not bubble up, however, rather like a dinner guest who rudely failed to show and thusly disappointed their hostess. Samuel T., on the other hand, was playing by their old rules, poking, prodding, with an edge that seemed ever sharper.

"Please don't come to the wedding reception," she said abruptly.

He straightened with that old, inherited case of his great-uncle's in his hand. "Oh, but I'm so looking forward to watching you with your true love. I plan on taking inspiration from your amorous example."

"There's no reason for you to come."

"Oh, we differ on that—"

"What happened? Is it over with?"

Amelia burst into the archway, all sixteen-year-old energy in that body and with that sense of style that were not particularly teenaged-looking anymore . . . and those features that seemed to be more and more those of her father's.

Oh, God, Gin thought with a jolt of pain.

"Oh, hello," Samuel T. said to the girl in a bored tone. "I'll let your mother fill you in on the particulars. She's feeling ever so chatty. Looking forward to seeing you in a few days, Gin. In your white dress."

When he just sauntered away, without giving Amelia much of a glance or any thought at all, Gin got to her feet and started marching after him before she could stop herself.

"Mother," the girl demanded as she passed by. "What happened?"

"It's none of your business. You are not a beneficiary. Now, if you'll excuse me."

Amelia said something disrespectful, but Gin was focused on getting to Samuel T. before he sped off in that Jaguar.

"Samuel T.," Gin hissed as her heels clipped over the foyer's marble floor. "Samuel!"

She followed him out the front door just in time to see her father's executor drive off in a big black Mercedes and Lane walk around the back of the house.

"*Samuel!*"

"Yes," he said without stopping or looking back.

"You don't have to be rude."

At his convertible, Samuel T. got behind the wheel, put his briefcase in the empty seat and stared up at her. "*This* coming from *you?*"

"She's a child—"

"Wait, this is about Amelia?"

"Of course it is! You walked by her as if she didn't exist."

Samuel T. shook his head like something was rattling in his skull. "Let me get this straight. You are upset because I failed to acknowledge the kid you had with another man?"

Oh. God. "She's innocent in all this."

"Innocent? FYI, that was the reading of her grandfather's will in there, not a criminal proceeding. Guilt or the relative lack thereof is not relevant."

"You ignored her."

"You know . . ." He tapped his forefinger in her direction. "From what I understand, you're the last person who should be accusing anyone of ignoring that girl."

"How *dare* you."

Samuel T. stared out over the long, undulating hood of the Jaguar. "Gin, I don't have time for this. I have to go talk to your brother's wife's attorney right now—and that, unlike your little stamping display of—"

"You just can't stand anyone telling you you're not God."

"No, I think I can't stand you, actually. The God thing is a side issue."

He didn't wait for any further commentary from her. He started the engine, pumped the gas a couple of times to make sure it caught, and then he was off, following the path the executor had forged down the hill, away from Easterly.

Gin watched him go. Inside of herself, she was screaming.

About Amelia. About Samuel T. About Richard.

Mostly . . . about herself and all of the mistakes she had made. And the sadness that came with knowing that at the ripe old age of thirty-three, there was not enough time left in her life to right the wrongs she had wrought.

*L*ane went around to the back, hoping to catch Edward before he took off. Undoubtedly, his brother had come up the staff way because there had been news crews parked at the front gate since the suicide story had broken. And also, undoubtedly, Edward was in a hurry to leave considering what the will had read.

There were no words adequate for what their father had done: Cutting his firstborn out of an inheritance was at once totally in character for William, and yet a cruel surprise as well.

A final fuck you that could not be countered, the dead carrying a trump card into their grave.

So Lane wanted to . . . say something . . . or check in or . . . he had no idea. What he was clear on was that Edward would no doubt not be interested in anything he had to say, but on occasion, you just had to try—in the hopes that the other person, in a quiet moment of reflection, might remember that you had made the effort even if it was awkward.

There was no Red & Black truck in the short line up of cars by the business center, but Lane did find an old Toyota parked next to the red Mercedes he'd given Miss Aurora. Had to be what Edward had come in, but his brother wasn't behind the wheel, wasn't limping in its direction. Wasn't anywhere to be found, actually.

Ducking in the rear door to the kitchen, Lane found Miss Aurora at the stove. "Have you seen Edward?"

"Is he here?" she asked as she turned around from her pot. "You tell him to come see me if he's here."

"I don't know where he is."

Lane made a quick survey around the first floor and then paused at the stairs. There was no reason for his brother to bother with the effort of going up to the bedrooms.

"Where are you?" he said to himself.

Heading out into the gardens, he went across to the business center. All of the French doors were locked on the side that faced the flowers, and he had to go further around to the rear entrance with its coded lock.

As soon as he was inside, he knew he'd found Edward: There were overhead lights on again—so his brother must have turned the electricity back on.

"Edward?"

Lane walked down the carpeted hall, glancing into empty offices. His phone had been blowing up with calls from the board chair, each one of the pissed-off senior vice presidents, and even the corporate lawyer. But not one of them had dared come to Easterly, and that told him he had something on them. And even if that bunch of suits was busy disappearing evidence from downtown headquarters? It didn't matter. Jeff might dislike him at the moment, but that anal retentive numbers cruncher had saved files of everything that had been in the network before the whistle had gotten blown.

So any changes were just as incriminating as the malfeasance that had required a cover-up.

As Lane proceeded to his father's office, he was aware his heart was pounding and that his mind had retreated behind a wall of brace-yourself.

Rather as someone who was ready for a bomb to go off might take cover behind cement.

"Edward?"

He slowed as he got to the anteroom before his father's office. "Edward . . . ?"

William Baldwine's door was shut, and Lane couldn't remember whether he had been the one to close it when they'd done the evac the day before. As he reached for the knob, he had no idea what he was going to find on the other side.

And he wasn't sure he wanted to see it.

He pushed the panels wide. "Edward—"

The office was dark, and when he hit the light switch on the wall, no one was there. "Where the hell are—"

When he turned around, Edward was right behind him. "Looking for me?"

Lane barked out a curse and grabbed the front of his own chest. "What are you doing here?"

"Visiting my old haunts."

Lane looked for things in his brother's hands, pockets, behind Edward's back. "Seriously. What are you doing?"

"Where is senior management?"

"Down at HQ in smaller offices."

"You fired them?"

"I told them just to get out first." He measured his brother's face. "Or they were going to jail."

Edward smiled. "Are you going to run the company yourself?"

"No."

There was a pause. "What's your plan, then?"

"All I wanted to do was get them out of here."

"And you think that's going to stop the financial bleed?"

"Father is dead. I think that's what will stop it. But until I know that for sure, I'm not taking chances."

Edward nodded. "Well, you're not wrong. Not at all. But you may want to think about who is going to be in charge now that he's dead."

"Any chance you're looking for a job?"

"I have one. I'm an alcoholic now."

Lane stared over his brother's shoulder, out into the empty reception area. "Edward. I have to know something, and it's just you and me here, okay?"

"Actually, this entire place is bugged. Cameras hidden, microphones tucked away. There is nothing secret under this roof, so be careful what you ask."

Lane found himself wanting another drink.

And after a tense moment, he merely muttered, "Are you coming to the visitation?"

"I don't know why I would. I'm not in mourning and I have no intention of paying any respects. No offense."

"None taken and I can understand all that. But Mother will probably come down for it."

"You think so?"

Lane nodded, and waited for his brother to say something further. The man didn't, though. "Listen, Edward . . . I'm really sorry about—"

"Nothing. You're sorry for nothing because none of it, none of this, was your fault. You can only apologize for your own wrongs. Is that all, little brother?"

When Lane couldn't think of anything else, Edward nodded. "That's all, then. Take care, and don't call me if you need something. I'm not the kind of resource you want."

TWENTY-FOUR

The Porsche got a lot of attention as Lane drove through the Rolling Meadows neighborhood, but not because he was going fast. Just the sight of the convertible and sound of the engine were enough to bring out the double takes of the dog walkers, the kids playing in the driveways, the moms pushing strollers. The houses were packed in tight, but they were of good size, most of them brick with cupolas or bay windows on the first floor and dormers or shallow porches on the second to distinguish them—rather like siblings who shared the same coloring but had different facial features. There were Volvos or Infinitis or Acuras parked in short driveways, basketball hoops above garage doors, decks with grills out in back.

With the late-afternoon sun shining down over postcard-worthy trees, and all the lawns glowing green, and all those kids running in packs, it was a throwback to before the iChildhood generation.

With quiet insistence, the GPS on the 911 navigated him through the rabbit warren of streets that were arranged by types of trees, flowers and, finally, fruits.

Cerise Circle was no different from any of the other lanes, roads, and ways in the development. And when he came up to the home he was in search of, there was nothing to distinguish it from its larger gene pool.

Lane let the convertible roll to a stop across the street. With the top down, he could hear the rhythmic dribble of a basketball behind its garage, the bounce-bounce-bounce echoing off the house next door.

Killing the engine, he got out and walked over the pavement toward the sound. The kid who was LeBron'ing it was out of sight around the back, and Lane really wanted to just get back in his damn car and drive away.

But that wasn't because he couldn't stand confronting the living, breathing evidence of his father's infidelities, and he wasn't afraid of looking into a face that was so close to his own, either. And no, the fact that some stranger was his blood and was in the will didn't rock his world.

The bottom line truth to his reticence? He was simply too exhausted to take care of anyone else. The problem was, this poor kid, through no fault of his own, was about to get sucked into the Bradford black hole, and how could Lane not at least try to guide the SOB a little bit.

It was a helluva lottery to win. Especially now that the money was gone.

Not a lot of upside.

The driveway was only about thirty feet long, a mere parking space at Easterly. And as Lane proceeded up, the eighteen-year-old with the basketball was revealed gradually.

Tall. Going to be taller. Dark haired. Big shoulders already.

The kid went up for a dunk, and the ball ricocheted off the rim.

Lane caught it on the fly. "Hey."

Randolph Damion Freeland stopped first because he was surprised. And then because he was shocked.

"So you know who I am, then," Lane said softly.

"I've seen your picture, yeah."

"Do you know why I'm here?"

As the kid crossed his arms over his chest, there was a good deal of space between the pecs and the biceps, but that wasn't going to last for much longer. He was going to fill out and be built strong.

God, his eyes were the exact blue of Lane's own.

"He died," the kid mumbled. "I read about it."

"So you know . . ."

"Who my father was? Yeah." That stare lowered. "Are you going to, like . . ."

"Like what?"

"Get me arrested or something?"

"What? Why would I do that?"

"I dunno. You're a Bradford."

Lane closed his eyes briefly. "No, I came to see you about something important. And also to say that I'm sorry your mother passed."

"She killed herself. In your house."

"I know."

"They say you found her body. I read that in the newspaper."

"I did."

"She didn't say good-bye to me. She just left that morning and then she was gone. You know, like, permanently."

Lane shook his head and squeezed the ball between his palms. "I'm really sorry—"

"Don't you dare! Don't you dare!"

An older woman shot out onto the porch with a full head of steam up, her face twisted into the kind of rage that made a handgun unnecessary. "You get away from him! You get away—"

"Granny, stop! He's just talking—"

As the kid got between them, the grandmother was all arms, fighting to get at Lane. "You stay away! How dare you come here—"

"He's an heir. That's why I came."

As the two of them paused in their struggling, Lane nodded. "He got left the house and ten million dollars. I figured you would want to know. The executor is going to be in touch. I don't know how much money there really is, but I want you both to know that I will fight to make sure this house stays in your grandson's name."

After all, there was a scenario whereby it, too, might be liquidated depending on the debt situation. And then where would this kid go?

As the grandmother snapped out of her surprise, she got right back on the hate-train. "Don't ever come here again—"

Lane locked eyes with the boy. "You know where I live. If you have questions, if you want to talk—"

"Never!" the woman screamed. "He will never come to you! You can't take him, too!"

"Babcock Jefferson," Lane said as he put the ball down on the driveway. "That's the attorney's name."

As he turned away, the image of that young kid holding back that old woman was carved into his brain, and God, he hated his father for new reasons in that moment, he really did.

Back at the Porsche, he got behind the wheel and headed off. He wanted to screech out, take the corners hard, hit a couple of parked cars, roll over some bicycles. But he didn't.

He was coming out to the entrance of the development when his phone rang. He didn't recognize the number, but he answered it because even a telemarketer was better than the thoughts in his head.

"Yes?"

"Mr. Baldwine?" a female voice said. "Mr. Lane Baldwine?"

He hit the directional signal to the left. "This is he."

"My name is LaKeesha Locke. I'm the business reporter for the *Charlemont Courier Journal*. I was wondering if you and I can meet somewhere."

"What is this about?"

"I'm doing a story that the Bradford Bourbon Company is in serious debt and facing a possible bankruptcy. It's running tomorrow morning. I thought you might want to comment."

Lane clenched his jaw to keep the curses in. "Now, why would I want to do that?"

"Well, I understand, and it's fairly self-evident, that your family's personal fortune is inextricably tied to the company, is it not?"

"But I'm not involved in the running of the business."

"So you're saying you were unaware of any difficulty?"

Lane kept his voice level. "Where are you? I'll come to you."

. . .

*T*he Bradford Family Estate's groundskeeping shed was less like a shed and more like an airplane hangar. Located down below and in the back of the extensive property, it was next to where the staff parking lot was and beside the line-up of fifties-era cottages that had been used by servants, workers, and retainers for decades.

As Lizzie walked into the dim gas- and oil-smelling cave, her boots were loud over the stained concrete floor. Tractors, industrial mowers, mulchers, and trucks were parked in an orderly fashion, their exteriors clean, their engines maintained to within an inch of their lives.

"Gary? You in there?"

The head groundskeeper's office was in the far corner, and through the dusty glass, a light glowed.

"Gary?"

"Not in there. Or here."

She changed trajectory, walking around a wood chipper and a couple of snowplow attachments that were the size of her old Yaris.

"Oh, God, don't lift that!" she barked.

Lizzie hurried over, only to be ignored as Gary McAdams hefted part of an engine block off the floor and onto one of the worktables. The feat would have been impressive under any circumstances, but considering the guy had thirty years on her? Then again, Gary was built like a bulldog, strong as an ox, and weathered as a Kentucky fence post.

"Your back," she muttered.

"Is just fine," came the Southern drawl. "Whatchu need, Miss Lizzie?"

He didn't look at her, but that didn't mean he didn't like her. In fact, the pair of them worked well together: When she had started here, she had braced herself for a conflict that had never materialized. The self-professed redneck had proven to be a total sweetheart under that gruff exterior.

"So you know about the visitation," she said.

"I do, yup."

Popping herself up on the worktable, she let her feet dangle and watched as his callused hands made sense of the piece of machinery, moving fast and sure over the old metal. He didn't make a big deal of his competence, though, and that was so him. From what Lizzie understood, he had started working in the fields when he was twelve and had been here ever since. Never been married. Never took vacation days. Didn't drink. Lived down in one of the cottages.

Ruled over the thirty or so workers under him with a fair but iron fist.

"You need the wrench?" she asked.

"Yup, I do."

She handed him what he required, took it back when he was finished, got him something else before he had to ask for it.

"Anyway," she continued. "The visitation will be tomorrow, and I just want to make sure we've got a fresh mow up the main entrance the morning of, a trim on the boxwoods down at the road this afternoon if we can make it happen, and a blow all over the front steps and courtyard."

"Yes'um. Anything you need in the back gardens?"

"I think we're in good shape. I'll go through them with Greta, though."

"One of m' boys'll do a mow out there by the pool."

"Good. Socket?"

"Yup."

As they traded tools again, he asked, "It true what they say you found?"

"Greta found it. And yes, it is."

He didn't shift his eyes from his work, those thick-fingered, heavily veined hands of his never missing a beat. "Huh."

"I don't know, Gary. Up until now, I've been thinking, just like everyone else, that he jumped. But not anymore."

"The police come?"

"Yes, a couple of homicide detectives. The same ones who were here for Rosalinda's death. I talked to them for a while this morning. They're probably going to want to interview you and anyone else who was on the grounds around the time he died."

"Sad business."

"Very. Even though I never liked the man."

She thought about the reading of the will. God, that was like something out of an old movie, the heirs gathered in some fancy room, a distinguished lawyer reciting the provisions in a Charlton Heston voice.

"What they ask you? Them detectives?"

"Just how we found it. Where I was the last couple of days. Like I said, they're going to be talking to everyone, I'm sure."

"Yup."

She handed him a pair of pliers. "Staff are invited, too."

"To the visitation?"

"Uh-huh. It's for everyone to pay their respects."

"They don't want no grease monkey like me in that there house."

"You'd be welcomed. I promise. I'm going."

"That's a'cuz it's your man's poppa."

Lizzie felt the blush hit her cheeks. "How did you know about me and Lane?"

"Ain't nothing that happens 'round here that I don't know about, girl."

He stopped what he was doing and picked up an old red rag. As he wiped his hands, he finally looked over, his weathered face gentle.

"Lane better do right by you. Or I got places to put the body."

Lizzie laughed. "I would hug you right now, but you would faint."

"Oh, I don't know 'bout that." Except he was shuffling his weight around like she'd embarrassed him. "But I think he's probably all right—or you wouldn't be with him. Besides, I've see him look at you. The boy's had love in his eyes for years when it come to you."

"You are much more sentimental than you let on, Gary."

"I didn't get schooled, remember. I don't know the meaning of those big words."

"I think you know exactly what they mean." Lizzie punched him lightly in the arm. "And if you do decide to come to the visitation, you can hang out with me and Greta."

"I got work to do. Don't have time for none of that."

"I understand." She hopped down off the worktable. "Well, I'm going to head out. I've got everything ordered, and Miss Aurora's on the food, of course."

"How's that fool butler doing?"

"He's not so bad."

"Depends on what you're using as a comparison."

With a laugh, she lifted her hand over her shoulder as a good-bye and headed for the bright outdoors. But she didn't get far before he spoke up again.

"Miss Lizzie?"

Turning around, she retucked her polo into the waistband of her shorts. "Yes?"

"They doing anything for Little V.E.'s birthday this year? I need to be getting anything done for that?"

"Oh, God. I'd forgotten that was coming up. I don't think we did anything last year, did we?"

"She's turning sixty-five. That's the only reason I asked."

"That is a milestone." Lizzie thought of Lane's birth mother up in that bedroom. "I'll ask. And shoot, I need to freshen her flowers tomorrow."

"There are some early peonies coming in."

"I was thinking the same thing."

"Let me know if you be wanting anything else done."

"Always, Gary. Always."

TWENTY-FIVE

*W*hen Lane finally got back to Easterly, after what had felt like years in the presence of that reporter, he went directly to the second floor, bypassing the dinner that had been served in the formal dining room and ignoring Mr. Harris's fussing about something or another.

At his grandfather's door, he knocked once and opened it wide—

Over on the bed, Tiphanii sat up fast and took the covers with her, hiding that which was very clearly naked.

"Please excuse us," he told her. "He and I have some business."

Jeff nodded at the woman to leave, and God love her, she took her frickin' time, sauntering around with that sheet while Jeff pulled the duvet over himself and sat up.

After a trip into the bathroom, she reemerged in her uniform and disappeared out the door, although Lane was very sure she purposely left her black panties behind on the floor at the foot of the bed.

"It was totally consensual," Jeff muttered. "And I am allowed to come up for air—"

"The local newspaper knows everything. *Everything.*"

As Jeff opened his mouth, Lane barked, "You didn't have to fuck me like that!"

"You think *I* talked to the press?" Jeff threw his head back and laughed. "You actually think I dropped a dime and gave them anything—"

"They have the information you're working from. Page for page. Explain how that happened. I thought I could trust you—"

"I'm sorry, are you accusing me of malfeasance after you black-mailed me into doing this for you? *Really?*"

"You screwed me."

"Okay, first of all, if I were going to fuck you like that I would have gone to the *Wall Street Journal,* not the *Charlemont Herald Post Ledger* or whatever the hell it's called. I can name half a dozen reporters in the Big Apple. I couldn't tell you who to call down here in goddamn Kentucky. And more to the point, after this little nightmare is over, I'm going *back* to Manhattan. You think I couldn't use a couple of favors owed to me? The shit about your family and your little bourbon business is big news, ass-hole. Bigger than some Podunk, *USA Today* wrapper of a daily. So yeah, if I were going to leak anything, I would want some upside for me per-sonally."

Lane breathed hard. "Jesus Christ."

"I also wouldn't call him. But that's because I'm a Jew."

Dropping his head, Lane rubbed his eyes. Then he walked around, going between the bed and the desk. The desk and one of the long-paned windows. The window and the bureau.

He ended up back at the windows. Night had yet to fall, but it was coming soon, the sunset scrumming down at the horizon, making the curve of the earth bleed pink and purple. In his peripheral vision, all of Jeff's work, the notes, the computers, the printouts were like a scream in his ear.

And then there was the fact that his old college roommate was naked across the room, staring at him with a remote expression: Behind all that anger that had just jumped out of Jeff's mouth, there was hurt, real hurt.

"I'm sorry," Lane breathed. "I'm sorry . . . I jumped to the wrong conclusions."

"Thank you."

"I'm also sorry that I'm making you do this. I just . . . I'm losing my damn mind over here. I feel like I'm in a house that's on fire, and every way out is nothing but flames. I'm burning and I'm desperate and I'm sick of this shit."

"Oh, for fuck's sake," his old friend muttered in his New Jersey accent. "See, there you go."

Lane glanced over his shoulder. "What?"

"Being all nice. I hate that about you. You piss me off and drive me crazy, and then you get all honest and it becomes impossible for me to hate your sorry, white-privileged ass. FYI, I was enjoying being furious at you. It was the only exercise I was getting—well, Tiphanii notwithstanding."

Lane smiled a little and then refocused on the view. "Honest, huh. You want honest? As in something I haven't told anybody?"

"Yes. The better I know what's happening here, the more I can help and the less I resent being trapped."

Off in the distance, a hawk soared on invisible currents, riding the sky with sharp corners and fast straightaways, like the gloaming was full of highways and byways that only birds could see.

"I think my brother killed him," Lane heard himself say. "I think Edward was the one who did it."

Man, Jeff had so totally been enjoying the righteous pissed thing. It had been a smooth, but intense ride, the burn in his chest an inexhaustible gas tank that kept him awake throughout the night, focused on the numbers, moving through the data.

But he and Lane the Asshole had hit these corners before during the course of their long relationship, patches of miscommunication or stupidity jarring them apart. Somehow, that Southerner over there always closed the distance, though.

And yup, he'd done it again. Especially with that jarring little news flash of his.

"Shit," Jeff said as he lay back against the pillows. "You serious?"

Dumbass question.

Because that was not the kind of thing anyone said, even in jest, given what was happening in this household. And it was also especially not something Lane would have even thought to himself about his hero older brother unless he had a really good reason.

"Why?" Jeff murmured. "Why would Edward do something like that?"

"He's the one with the real motive. My father was a terrible man and he did a lot of terrible things to a lot of powerful people. But is Monteverdi going to kill him over that debt? No. He's going to want to get his money back. And Rosalinda didn't do it. She was dead before my father went over the falls. Gin has always hated him, but she wouldn't want to get her hands dirty. My mother has always had reason, but never the capacity. Who else could have done it?"

"Your brother isn't in good shape, though. I mean, I was getting something to eat and heading back up here when he came in the house. He was limping like his leg was broken. It didn't seem like he could handle shutting the damn door, much less throwing someone off a bridge."

"He could have had help." Lane looked over his shoulder, and yeah, that handsome face looked like it had been through the washer—and not in a good way. "The people out at the farm are devoted to him. My brother has that way about him, and he knows how to get things done."

"Has he been here? To the house?"

"I don't know."

"There are security cameras, right? Here on the estate."

"Yeah, and he knows that. He put in the goddamn system, and if you erase things, it's going to show. There are log-ins that can be traced."

"Have the detectives asked for the footage?"

"Not yet. But they will."

"Are you going to give it to them?"

Lane cursed. "Do I have a choice? And I don't know . . . I was alone with Edward today. I almost asked him."

"What stopped you? Were you afraid he'd get pissed?"

"Among other things, I was afraid of the answer."

"What's your next move?"

"I wait. The detectives aren't going away. They'll go out to see him at the farm. And if he did it . . . "

"You can't save him."

"No, I can't."

"Why exactly would your brother want your dad dead, though? Lot of trouble to go to just because you got grounded a couple of times as a kid."

"Father tried to have him killed down in South America—"

"*Excuse me?*"

"Yeah, Edward is the way he is now because of what was done to him down there. And there was a lot of bad history between them before that. Hell, even in his will, Father deliberately left him out. Also, you know, my brother is no one you screw with. He's got that way about him."

Dear God, Jeff thought.

In the silence that followed, he considered his brother and sister, both of whom lived up in Manhattan, too. They were married. Multiple children. His parents split their time between Florida and Connecticut, but had a pied-à-terre in SoHo. The whole lot of them got together for all holidays, and there was warmth and conflict and joy and tears and laughter.

Always laughter.

Lane had a nice house. With a lot of nice stuff. Good cars.

There was no comparison, was there.

The guy went over and parked it on the chair at the desk. "Anyway, enough on that. So if you didn't leak it, who did?"

"Senior management. I mean, come on. I got the information from their sources. The spreadsheets I'm doing the analysis on are their work product."

Lane rubbed his head like everything hurt. "Of course."

"Look, buddy, you can't freeze those suits out forever, and clearly, they're not coloring in the lines, which is not a surprise. Now's not a good time for there to be no one at the helm."

"Yeah, I need someone to run the company on an interim basis. The board chair wants to meet with me. He's got to be thinking that, too."

"Well, just in case I didn't put a fine enough point on it—unless you take control, senior management, the very assholes you booted out, are in charge."

"But I'm not qualified. The only thing I'm smart enough to know is that I don't know shit about a business on this scale." Lane threw up his hands. "For crissakes, I can't worry about this right now. I have to get through the visitation tomorrow, and then we'll go from there. Damn it, Edward was the one who was going to take over."

As everything got quiet, Jeff smoothed the duvet over his thighs because he didn't know what the hell else to do. Eventually, he said half-jokingly, "When do I get the maid back? And not to clean the bathroom."

"That's up to you. I'm her employer, not her pimp."

"So you are in charge of this family, huh."

"No one else is volunteering for the job." Lane got to his feet. "Maybe because of what happened to the last guy who gave it a shot."

"You got this, my man. You can do it."

Lane came over and put out his hand. "I am really sorry I've put you in this position. Honestly. And after this is over, I promise, I'll never contact you again for anything."

For a moment, Jeff measured what was offered. Then he clasped the palm. "Yeah, well, I don't forgive you."

"Then why are you shaking my hand?"

"'Cuz I'm one of those people who forgets easily. I know, I know, it's backward. But it's worked for me so far—and it's getting you off the hook, so fuck off with your principles."

TWENTY-SIX

"*N*ow, this is more like it."

As Richard Pford lanked into Easterly's family sitting room at around nine that evening, Gin wanted to roll her eyes and tell him the nineteen fifties wanted its mores back. But the truth was, yes, she had stayed in to speak with him, and yes, as she watched him proceed to the bar as if he were lord of the manor, she was reminded of how much she despised him.

After pouring himself a bourbon, he went over and sat in the oxblood leather chair beside the sofa she had tucked herself into. The room was not a large one, and the oil paintings of prized Bradford thoroughbreds hanging on the paneled walls made things seem even smaller. Adding Pford's physical proximity to the mix? Well, that shrunk things down to the point that the wide-screen TV showing a rerun of *The Real House-wives of Beverly Hills* felt like it was pressed against her face.

"Why are you watching this drivel?" he said.

"Because I like it."

"It's a waste of time." He took the remote and changed the channel to some financial pundit in a red tie and a pale blue shirt. "You should be looking at things of value."

Then allow me to cast my stare away from you, she thought.

"We need to talk about the reception." She narrowed her eyes. "And I must introduce you to Amelia."

"Who?" he said without looking away from the NASDAQ crawl.

"My daughter."

That got his attention and he glanced over, one thin eyebrow lifting. "Where is she? Is she home from school?"

"Yes."

Gin extended a hand to the house phone that was discreetly hidden behind a lamp made from a sterling-silver fillies trophy from the nineteen hundreds. Picking up the receiver, she called the butler's extension.

"Mr. Harris? Do get Amelia and bring her here? Thank you."

When she hung up, she looked at Richard. "I need you to pay for the wedding reception we're having here on Saturday. You can write me the check. It will be about fifty thousand. If it's more, I'll come back to you."

Richard lowered his glass and refocused on her. "Why am I paying for anything?"

"Because we're getting married. The two of us."

"At your home."

"So you're going to make no contribution at all?"

"I already have."

She looked at her ring. "Richard, you're living under this roof, eating our food—"

He laughed and swirled his bourbon around. "You're not actually making that argument, are you?"

"You're going to write that check and that's that."

"I suggest you hold your breath for the ink to be dry, darling." Richard toasted her. "Now, that would be a show worth watching."

"If you don't pay, I'll cancel the party. And don't lie. You are looking forward to the attention."

Trophies, after all, needed a presentation ceremony.

Richard sat forward, the movement of his butt causing the leather to creak in a muffled way. "I know you aren't aware of this, but there are problems at your family's company."

"Oh, really." She played dumb. "Someone lose the key to an office supply closet? Oh, the tragedy."

There was no value in letting him in on their financial reversal, after all. Certainly not before their marriage certificate had been issued.

He smiled, and for the first time, something close to joy truly hit his eyes. "Guess who called me today? A friend of mine at the *Charlemont Courier Journal*. And you want to know what she told me?"

"That they're doing an exposé on penile implants and they want you to be a subject?"

"That's crass."

"True, but I think it might help."

Richard sat back and crossed his legs, his jaw tightening. "First of all, it's a she, not a they. And secondly, she told me that there are very serious issues at your company, Gin. Big financial issues. There's going to be a story first thing in the morning about it all. So don't try to play me with this ruse about needing a check made out to you for the reception so that things are equitable between as. Your father has died, and his will is being probated, your mother's trust is tied up until she passes, and the BBC is struggling so your dividends are down. If you want to hold a fundraiser and expect me to contribute, you better declare yourself a five-oh-one C three so I can get the write-off. Otherwise, I'm not giving you a dime. Darling."

"I don't know what you are talking about."

"You don't? Well, then, read up first thing in the morning and you'll learn something." He indicated the television. "Or better yet, come in here and watch this channel. I'm very sure you're going to be all over the TV tomorrow."

Gin lifted her chin, even as her heart went on a broken field run in her chest. "We have plenty of money here at the house, and I don't feel it is unreasonable for you to pay for something—so if you aren't prepared to share in the cost, then the reception is off."

Richard nursed his bourbon. "A tip on negotiations. If you're going to issue threats, make sure they're backed up by an outcome the other party is compromised by."

"You want to show me off. You want to prove that you got me. Don't pretend I'm not a prize to you."

"But as soon as the ink is dry, you're mine. And that will also be in the newspaper. Everyone will read about it. I don't need a cocktail party to prove it."

Gin shook her head. "You are so shallow."

The laughter that filled the room made her want to throw something at him again—and she eyed the sterling-silver lamp.

"This coming from you?" he said. "My dearest one, the only reason you're marrying me is because of the favorable contracts that I agreed to give your father's company. And I wish I had known about the downturn at corporate. I probably could have gotten you for nothing but that ring, given the financial state of things."

At that point, there was a knock on the door, and then Mr. Harris came in with Amelia.

The girl had changed into a Gucci pantsuit, and her head was buried in her phone, her fingers moving over the screen.

"Miss Amelia, madam," the Englishman intoned. "Will there be anything else?"

"No, thank you," Gin dismissed.

"My pleasure."

As the butler ducked out and the door was shut, the girl did not look up.

"Amelia," Gin said sharply. "This is my fiancé, Richard."

"Yes," the girl said. "I know."

"As you haven't greeted him, I find that hard to believe."

"It was on the net." Shrug. "Anyway, congratulations, both of you. I'm just thrilled."

"Amelia," Gin snapped. "What the hell is so fascinating?"

The girl turned her phone around, flashing a screen that was lit up like an old-fashioned Lite-Brite. "Dymonds."

"I find it hard to argue with that," Gin muttered. "But you're being rude."

"It's a new game."

Gin indicated Richard. "Will you at least say hello properly."

"I can see the resemblance," Richard offered. "You are quite beautiful."

"Am I supposed to be flattered?" Amelia tilted her head. "Oh, thank you so much. I'm in *such* a hurry to have anything in common with her. It's my life's ambition, to be like my mother when I grow up. Now, if you'll excuse me, I'd rather be in a virtual reality with fake diamonds than anywhere near her or anyone who would volunteer to marry her. Good luck to you."

Amelia was out the door a second later, but not because she was running.

Amelia didn't run from anything.

She sauntered places. Just like her father.

"Mission accomplished," Richard said as he got to his feet and headed back to the bar. "The apple has not fallen far from the tree with that one. And allow me to reiterate, I will not be writing you any kind of check. Cancel the reception as you wish and we'll just get married at the courthouse. It matters not to me."

Gin focused on the TV screen, her mind churning. And she was still staring into space when Richard put himself in front of her.

"Just remember one thing," he said. "You have a tendency to become creative when you're quiet like this. May I remind you that I do not curry disrespect—and you may choose to recall the precise consequences of any insults to me."

Oh, but you enjoy it, you sick bastard, Gin thought bitterly. You enjoy every minute of it.

"John, you came through. Atta boy."

As Lizzie heard Lane speak, she looked up from her mostly empty refrigerator. Across her farmhouse's kitchen, he was sitting at her circular table, talking to the laptop that was open in front of him, his brows locked together like two halves of a pocket door pulled tight.

"I'm sorry?" she said as she closed things up.

"John Lenghe. The Grain God. He told me he'd get me as much

information as he had on the companies involved in WWB Holdings. And here they are."

When he pushed the screen around, she bent down and looked at an e-mail that seemed long as a book. "Wow. That's a lot of names."

"Now we've got to find them." Lane sat back and stretched his arms over his head, something cracking loud enough to make her wince. "I swear this is like a never-ending roller-coaster ride, the kind that doesn't stop even after you get nauseous."

Stepping in behind him, she massaged his shoulders. "You talked to that reporter again?"

"Yeah." He slumped. "Oh, God, that feels good."

"You're so tight."

"I know." He exhaled. "But yeah, I just spoke with her. She's running the story. There's nothing I can do to stop it. One of those vice presidents must have talked. She knew so damned much."

"How can she share that information, though? The Bradford Bourbon Company isn't a public company. Isn't it a violation of privacy?"

"There's no HIPAA when it comes to businesses. And as long as she couches things in a certain way, she'll be all right. It'll be like when they put the word 'alleged' in front of almost everything when they report on crimes."

"What will happen next?"

"I don't know, and I'm really past the point of worrying about it. All I have to do is get through the visitation tomorrow, and then the next crisis will be honored with my full attention."

"Well, we're ready. Mr. Harris and I took care of the staffing, Miss Aurora is ready in the kitchen. The grounds are taken care of with a final touch up being done in the morning. How many people do you expect?"

"A thousand, maybe. At least as much as—oh, right there. Yeeeeeeeeeeah." As he let his head fall to the opposite side, she admired the line of his strong neck. "As much as we had for the Derby brunch at least. One thing you can always take to the bank, particularly if you've lost your money? People loooooove to stare at the carcass of greatness. And after that article tomorrow, that's what we're going to look like at the butcher's counter."

Lizzie shook her head. "Remember my fantasy where we leave this all behind?"

Lane twisted around and pulled her into his lap. As he brushed her hair back and looked at her, his smile almost reached his eyes. "Yes, oh, yes. Tell me what it's like again."

She stroked his jaw, his throat, his shoulders. "We live on a farm far away. You spend your days coaching basketball. I plant flowers for the city. Every night, we sit together on our porch and watch the sun go down over the cornstalks. On Saturdays, we go to the flea market. Maybe I sell things there. Maybe you do. We shop at a little grocery store where Ragu is considered a foreign delicacy, and I make a lot of soup in the winter and potato salad in the summer."

As his lids sank down, he nodded. "And apple pie."

She laughed. "Apple pie, too. And we go skinny-dipping—in our pond out back."

"Oh, I like that part."

"I thought you would."

His hands started to wander, circling her waist, moving higher. "Can I confess something?"

"Absolutely."

"It's not going to reflect well on my character." He frowned deeply. "Then again, there isn't a lot doing that at the moment."

"What is it?"

It was a while before he answered. "When you and I were in my father's office, I wanted to push everything off the top of his desk and have sex with you on the damn thing."

"Really?"

"Yeah." He shrugged. "Depraved?"

Lizzie considered the hypothetical with a smile. "Not really. Although I actually can't decide whether that's erotic or just going to create a mess on the floor that it's going to kill me not to clean up."

As he laughed, she got to her feet but stayed straddling him. "But I have an idea."

"Oh?"

Arching her back, she untucked her shirt and slowly pulled it up and over her head. "There's a table right here—and although there's nothing but your laptop on it, and I wouldn't suggest throwing that on the floor, we could still . . . you know."

"Oh, yeaaaaah . . ."

As Lizzie stretched out on her kitchen table, Lane was right on her, leaning over her, his mouth finding hers on a surge of heat.

"By the way," she gasped, "in my fantasy, we do this a lot . . ."

TWENTY-SEVEN

The following morning, Lane slowed down as he approached the Big Five Bridge from the Indiana side, traffic choking up the highway with morning commuters. The Porsche's radio was off. He hadn't checked his phone. And he hadn't cracked his laptop before leaving Lizzie's.

The sun was once again bright in a mostly clear blue sky, a few streaky clouds passing by on the edges. The good weather wasn't supposed to last, though. A low-pressure system was coming in and storms were due.

Seemed fitting.

As he downshifted into third, and then second, he saw up ahead that the delay was more than just rush hour. Up ahead, there was some construction on the span, the merging lines of cars forming a bottleneck that winked in the sunshine and threw off waves of heat. Inching forward, he knew he was going to be late, but he was not going to get worked up over that.

He didn't want this meeting now. But he'd been given no choice.

When he finally got into the single line, things started to move, and he almost laughed when he finally pulled up next to the workers in their orange bibs, hard hats, and blue jeans.

They were installing a chain-link fencing system to keep people away from the drop.

No more jumping. Or at least, if you insisted on trying it, you were going to need to get your climb on first.

Hitting spaghetti junction, he took a tight curve, shot under an overpass, got onto I-91. Two exits later, he was off at Dorn Avenue and going down onto River Road.

The Shell station on the corner was the kind of place that was part drugstore, part supermarket, part liquor store . . . and part newsstand.

And he intended to go by it as he made a right. After all, there was going to be a copy of the *Charlemont Courier Journal* at Easterly.

In the end, though, his hands made the decision for him. Wrenching the wheel to the right, he shot into the service station, bypassed the gas tanks and parked by the double-doored silver freezer that had ICE painted across it along with a picture of a cartoon penguin with a red scarf around its neck.

The baseball cap he pulled down low over his face had the U of C logo on the front.

At the pumps, there were a couple of guys filling up their pick-up trucks. A municipal vehicle. A CG&E cherry picker. A woman in a Civic with a baby she kept checking on in the back.

He felt like they were all staring at him. But he was wrong. If they were looking in his direction, it was because they were checking out his Porsche.

A tinny bell rang as he pushed into the cold space of the store, and there it was. A line-up of *Charlemont Courier Journals,* all with the headline he'd been dreading splashed above the fold in Las Vegas Strip–sized font.

Bradford Bourbon Bankruptcy.

The *New York Post* couldn't have done it better, he thought as he got a dollar bill and a quarter out. Picking up one of the copies, he put the money on the counter and gave a rap of his knuckles. The guy at the cash register looked over from whoever he was helping and nodded.

Back at the Porsche, Lane got behind the wheel and popped the front page flat. Scanning the first set of columns, he opened to the inside to finish the article.

Oh, great. They had reproduced a couple of the documents. And there was a lot of commentary. Even an editorial on corporate greed and the rich's lack of accountability, with a tie-in on karma.

Tossing the thing aside, he reversed out and hit the gas.

When he got to the main gates of the estate, he eased off on the speed, but it was only to count the number of news trucks parked on the grassy shoulder like they were expecting a mushroom cloud to take flight over Easterly at any second. Continuing on, he entered the property at the staff road and shot up the back way, passing by the vegetable fields that Lizzie cultivated for Miss Aurora's kitchen and then the barrel-topped greenhouses and finally the cottages and the groundskeeping shed.

The staff parking lot was full of cars, all kinds of extra help already on site to get things prepared for the visitation hours. The paved lane continued beyond that, mounting the hill parallel to the walkway that workers used to get to the house. At the top, there were the garages, the back of the business center, and the rear entrances to the mansion.

He parked by the maroon Lexus that was in one of the spots reserved for senior management.

As soon as Lane got out, Steadman W. Morgan, chairman of the Bradford Bourbon Company's board of trustees, emerged from his sedan.

The man was dressed in golfing clothes, but not like Lenghe, the Grain God, had been. Steadman was in Charlemont Country Club whites, the crest of the private institution in royal blue and gold on his pectoral, a Princeton Tiger needlepoint belt around his waist. His shoes were the same kind of loafers Lane wore, without socks. Watch was Piaget. Tan was earned on the links, not sprayed on. Vitality was good breeding, careful diet, and the result of the man never having had to wonder where his next meal was coming from.

"Quite an article," Steadman said as they met face-to-face.

"Now do you understand why I kicked them all out of here?"

There was no shake of the hands. No formalities honored or exchanged. But then good ol' Steadman was not used to be anyone's second-highest priority and clearly his Brooks Brothers boxers were in a bunch.

Then again, he had just learned he was sitting at the head of the table at a very bad time in BBC history. And Lane could sure as hell relate to that.

With a sweep of his hand, Lane indicated the way to the back door of the business center and he let the two of them in with the new pass code. Turning lights on as they went, he led the way into the small conference room.

"I'd offer you coffee," Lane said as he took a seat. "But I suck at making it."

"I'm not thirsty."

"And it's a little early for bourbon or I'd be drinking some." Lane linked his hands and leaned in. "So. I'd ask you what's on your mind, but that would be rhetorical."

"It would have been nice if you'd have given me a heads-up on the article. On the issues. On the financial chaos. On why the hell you locked senior management out."

Lane shrugged. "I'm still trying to get to the bottom of it myself. So I don't have a lot to say."

"There was plenty in that damned article."

"Not my fault. I wasn't a source, and my no comment was as bulletproof as Kevlar." Although the reporter had given him quite a bit to go on. "I will say that a friend of mine, who is an investment banker who specializes in evaluating multi-national corporations, is here from New York, and he's figuring it all out."

Steadman seemed to compose himself. Which was a little like a marble statue struggling to keep a straight face: Not a lot of work.

"Lane," the man started off in a tone that made Walter Cronkite seem like Pee-wee Herman, "I need you to understand that the Bradford Bourbon Company may have your family's name on it, but it's not some lemonade stand you can shut down or move at your will just because you're blood. There are corporate procedures, lines of command, ways of—"

"My mother is the single largest shareholder."

"That doesn't give you the right to turn this into a dictatorship. Senior management has an imperative to get back into this facility. We have to convene a search committee to hire a new CEO. An interim leader must be appointed and announced. And above all, a proper internal audit of this financial mess must be—"

"Allow me to be perfectly clear. My ancestor, Elijah Bradford, started this company. And I absolutely will close it down if I have to. If I want to. I *am* in charge, and it will be so much more efficient if you recognize this and get out of my way. Or I'll replace you, too."

The WASP equivalent of murderous rage narrowed Steadman's baby blues. Which, again, was not much of a change. "You don't know who you're dealing with."

"And you have no idea how little I have to lose. I will be the one to appoint a successor to my father, and it will *not* be any of the senior vice presidents who came in here every morning to suck up to him. I *will* find out where the money went, and I *will* singlehandedly keep us in business if I have to go down and run the sills myself." He jabbed a finger into Steadman's flushed face. "You work for me. The board works for me. Every one of the ten thousand employees getting a paycheck works for me—because I'm the sonofabitch who's going to turn everything around."

"And exactly how do you propose to do that? According to that article, there are millions missing."

"Watch me."

Steadman stared across the glossy table for a moment. "The board will—"

"Be getting out of my way. Listen, you each get paid a hundred thousand dollars to sit around and do absolutely nothing. I'll guarantee every one of you a quarter of a million dollars this year. That's a one hundred and fifty percent raise."

The man's chin went up. "Are you attempting to bribe me? Bribe us?"

"Or I can shut the board down. Your choice."

"There are bylaws—"

"You know what my father did to my brother, correct?" Lane leaned in once more. "Do you think I don't have the same contacts my old man did in the States? Do you honestly believe I can't make things very difficult for the lot of you? Most accidents happen in the home, but cars can be tricky, too. Boats. Planes."

Guess his Kentucky Fried Tony was coming out again.

And the truly scary thing was, as he said the words, he wasn't sure whether he was bluffing or not. Sitting here, where his father had sat, Lane found himself feeling perfectly capable of murder.

Abruptly, the memory of falling from the bridge, of watching the water come at him, of being in that hinterland between safety and death, returned to him.

"So what is it going to be?" Lane murmured. "A raise or a grave?"

Steadman took his sweet time, and Lane let the man stare into his eyes for as long as he wanted.

"I'm not sure you can promise either, son."

Lane shrugged. "The question is whether you want to test that theory out on the positive or the negative, isn't it?"

"If that article is true, how are you going to get the money?"

"That's my problem, not yours." Lane sat back. "And I'll let you in on a little secret."

"What's that?"

"My father's ring finger was found buried out in front of the house. It's not been released to the press yet. So don't kid yourself. It wasn't suicide. Someone killed him."

There was a little throat clearing at that point. And then good ol' Steadman said, "When exactly would we be receiving payment?"

Gotcha, Lane thought.

"Now, here's what we're going to do," he said to the man.

*J*eff took his breakfast upstairs in Lane's grandfather's crib, and he was on the phone the entire time. With his father.

When he finally hung up, he sat back in the antique chair and looked out at the grass of the garden. The flowers. The blooming trees. It was like a stage set for the Carringtons back in the eighties. Then he picked up the copy of the *Charlemont Courier Journal* he'd stolen from downstairs in the kitchen and stared at the story.

He'd read it first online.

After that, when he'd gone down to snag some coffee and a Danish, he'd asked Miss Aurora if he could take the physical copy. Lane's momma, as she was called, hadn't looked up from whatever she'd been chopping at the counter. *Get it out of here*, was all she had said.

Jeff had pretty much memorized every word, each number, all the pictures of the documents.

When a knock sounded, he said, "Yes?"

Lane came in with some coffee for himself, and even though he'd shaved, he looked like shit. "So—oh, yup," the guy said. "You've seen it."

"Yeah." Jeff put the goddamn thing down. "It's a hatchet job. The problem is, nothing is misrepresented."

"I'm not going to worry about it."

"You should."

"I just bought the board."

Jeff recoiled. "I'm sorry, what?"

"I need you to find me two point five million dollars."

Putting his palms up to his face and holding in a curse, Jeff just shook his head. "Lane, I don't work for the Bradford Bourbon Company—"

"So I'll pay you."

"With what?"

"Take a painting from downstairs."

"No offense, but I don't like museums and I hate representational art. Everything you have was done before the advent of the camera. It's boring."

"There's value in it." When Jeff didn't give a response, Lane shrugged. "Fine, I'll give you a piece of my mother's jewelry—"

"Lane."

His college roommate didn't budge. "Or take the Phantom Drophead. I'll deed it to you. We own all the cars. How about my Porsche?"

"Are you . . . insane?"

Lane indicated all around them. "There's money here. Everywhere. You want a horse?"

"Jesus Christ, it's like your garage sale'ing—"

"What do you want? It's yours. Then help me find that money. I need two hundred and fifty grand each for ten people."

Jeff started shaking his head. "It doesn't work like that. You can't just divert funds on a whim—"

"There is no whim here, Jeff. It's about survival."

"You need a plan, *Lane*. A comprehensive plan that immediately reduces expenses, consolidates function, and anticipates a possible federal investigation—especially with that article out now."

"Which brings me to my second reason for being here. I need you to prove that my father did it all."

"Lane—what the fuck! Do you think I can just pull this stuff out of my—"

"I'm not naive and you're right. Law enforcement is going to come knocking after that article, and I want to present them with a clear path to my father."

Jeff exhaled. Cracked his knuckles. Wondered what it would feel like if he struck his forehead with the desk. A couple of hundred times. "Well, at least that looks like a no-brainer."

"That's the beauty of all this. It just came to me. My father is dead so it's not like they're going to dig him up and put him behind bars. And after everything he pulled, I'm not concerned with preserving his memory. Let the bastard go down in flames for everything, and then let's move forward with the company." He took a drink from his mug. "Oh, which reminds me. I e-mailed you what Lenghe sent me on the WWB Holdings companies. It's more than we had and yet not nearly enough."

All Jeff could do was stare at the guy. "You know, I can't decide whether you are incredibly entitled or simply so desperate you have lost your damn mind."

"Both. But I can tell you that the latter is more material. It's hard to be entitled when you can't pay for anything. And as for your compensation, as far as I'm concerned I'm in a fire-sale situation here. So back up a truck and load the damn thing to the roof. Whatever you think is fair."

Jeff looked down at the newspaper again. It seemed appropriate that the article was covering all of the work he'd been doing.

"I can't be down here forever, Lane."

But he did have something he had to take care for himself. In addition to Lane's newest laundry list of demands and bright ideas.

"What about senior management?" Jeff asked. "Did you bribe them, too?"

"Not at all. For that bunch of suits, I put them on unpaid administrative leave for the next month. I figured there was enough evidence so that it was justified, and the board is sending them notice. The middle managers will pick up the slack until I find an interim CEO."

"Gonna be hard with this out." Jeff tapped the front page. "Not exactly a good recruiting platform."

As Lane just looked across at him, Jeff felt a splash of figurative cold water hit his head. Putting up both his palms, he started shaking his head again. "No. Absolutely not—"

"You'd be in charge."

"Of a torpedoed ship."

"You could do anything you want."

"Which is like telling me I can redecorate a house that's in the middle of a mudslide?"

"I'll give you equity."

Annnnnd cue the screeching of tires. "What did you just say?"

Lane turned away and went to the door. "You heard me. I'm offering you equity in the oldest and finest liquor company in America. And before you tell me I'm not allowed to, blah, blah, blah, may I remind you that the board's in my back pocket. I can do whatever the hell I want and need to."

"As long as you can find the money to pay them."

"Think about it." The slick bastard looked over his shoulder. "You can own something, Jeff. Not just crunch numbers for an investment bank that's paying you for being a glorified calculator. You can be the first non-family shareholder in the Bradford Bourbon Company, and you can help determine our future."

Jeff went back to staring at the article. "Would you have ever asked me if things were going well?"

"No, but that's because in that case, I wouldn't be involved in the company at all."

"And what happens when all this is over?"

"Depends on what 'over' looks like, doesn't it? This could change your life, Jeff."

"Yeah, there's a recommendation. Look what it's done to you. And P.S., last time you wanted me to stay you threatened me. Now, you're trying to bribe me."

"Is it working?" When he didn't answer, Lane opened the way out. "I didn't like strong-arming you. I really didn't. And you're right. I am thrashing around here like an idiot. But I'm out of options, and there is no savior coming down from heaven to give me a miracle and make this all go away."

"That's because there is no making this go away."

"No shit. But I've got to deal with it. I don't have a choice."

Jeff cursed. "I don't know if I can trust you."

"What do you need from me so you can?"

"After all this? I'm not sure I ever can."

"Then be self-interested. If you own part of what you're saving, if there's a tremendous upside—and there is—then that's all the incentive you need. Think about it. You're a businessman. You know exactly how lucrative this could be. I give you the stock now, and then things turn around? There are Bradford cousins who will be dying to buy the shit back. This represents the single best chance of an eight-digit capitalizing event for you—outside of the fucking lottery."

On that note, because the bastard knew precisely when to pull out, Lane left, closing the door silently.

"Fuck. Me," Jeff muttered to himself.

TWENTY-EIGHT

*L*izzie shucked her khaki shorts and put them on the counter in Lane's bathroom next to her work shirt. As she straightened, the mirror showed her a reflection that was familiar, but also strange: Her hair was fuzzed up from her ponytail, the sunscreen she'd put on earlier in the afternoon made her skin too shiny, and her eyes had bags under them.

All that was normal, though.

Picking up the black dress in front of her, she slipped it over her head and thought, okay, here was the weirdness.

At Easterly's last big party, less than a week ago, she had been firmly in the staff camp. Now, she was this odd hybrid, part family by virtue of being engaged to Lane, but still on the payroll and very much involved in the preparations and staging for the visitation.

Yanking the tie out, she brushed her hair, but it had a kink in it from the rubber band and looked bad down.

Maybe there was time for a—

Nope. As she looked at her phone, the numbers read 3:43. Not enough for even one of her in-and-out showers.

In seventeen minutes, people were going to start arriving, the buses carrying them up from the parking area down on River Road to the top of the hill and Easterly's grand front door.

"You look perfect."

Glancing over to the doorway, she smiled at Lane. "You're biased."

Lane was dressed in a navy blue suit with a pale blue shirt and a coral-colored tie. His hair was still wet from his shower, and he smelled like the cologne he always wore.

Lizzie refocused on herself, smoothing the simple cotton sheath down. God, she felt like she was wearing someone else's clothes, and jeez, she guessed she was. Hadn't she borrowed this dress from her cousin a decade ago—also for a funeral? The thing had been laundered enough to fade out around the seams, but she'd had nothing else in her closet.

"I'd rather just be working this event," she said.

"I know."

"Do you think Chantal will come?"

"She wouldn't dare."

Lizzie wasn't too sure about that. Lane's soon-to-be-ex-wife was an attention grabber, and this was a prime opportunity for the woman to assert her retained relevance even though their marriage was no longer happening.

Lizzie fluffed her hair up and brought it around front. Which did nothing to help the kink.

Screw it, she thought. She was leaving it down.

"Are you ready?" she said as she went over to him. "You look worried. How can I help?"

"No, I'm fine." He offered her his elbow. "Come on. Let's do this."

He led her out of his bedroom and into the corridor. As they came up to his mother's suite of rooms, he slowed. Then stopped.

"Do you want to go in?" she asked. "I'll wait for you downstairs."

"No, I'll leave her be."

As they continued on to the grand staircase and began their descent, she felt like an imposter—until she sensed the tension in his arm and realized he was leaning on her.

"I couldn't do this without you," he whispered when they got to the bottom.

"You won't have to," she said quietly as they stepped off onto the marble floor. "I'm not going to leave your side."

All around, waiters in black ties and jackets stood at the ready with silver trays, prepared to take drink orders. There were two bars set up, one in the dining room to the left, another in the front parlor to the right, with only Bradford Family Reserve, white wine, and soda available. Flowers that she had ordered and arranged were displayed prominently in each room, and there was an antique circular table centered in the entryway with a condolences book and a silver plate for receiving cards.

Gin and Richard were the next of the family to arrive, the pair of them coming down the stairs with the distance of a football field between them.

"Sister," Lane said as he kissed her cheek. "Richard."

The pair of them sauntered off without acknowledging Lizzie, but in her mind, it was a case of sometimes you lucked out. Anything they would say or do was likely to come across as condescending anyway.

"That is not okay," Lane muttered at the slight. "I'm going to have to—"

"Do nothing." Lizzie squeezed his hand to get his attention. "Listen to me when I say this. It doesn't bother me. At all. I know where I stand, and whether your sister approves or disapproves of me? Doesn't change my zip code in the slightest."

"It's disrespectful."

"It's high school mean girls. And I got over that fifteen years ago. Besides, she's like that because she's miserable. You could be standing next to Jesus Christ, son of God, and she'd hate the fact that he was in a robe and sandals."

Lane laughed and kissed her on the temple. "And once again, you remind me of exactly why I'm with you."

"*W*ait. Your tie is crooked."

Mack twisted around. His office came with a shower, sink, and loo set-up, and he hadn't bothered to shut the door when he'd gone in to . . . well, screw up getting this silk noose around his throat.

Beth put some papers on his desk and came over.

The cramped space got even tighter as she stepped in with him, and God, her perfume as she reached up and slid the knot off.

"I don't think this even matches," he said as he tried not to focus on her lips. "The shirt, I mean."

Man, they looked soft.

"It doesn't." She smiled. "But it's okay. You're not judged on your fashion sense."

For a split second, he imagined putting his hands on her waist and pulling her against the front of his hips. Then he would dip his head and find out what she tasted like. Maybe get her up on the lip of the sink and—

"Well?" she prompted as she threw one end of the length over the other at his heart.

"What?"

"Where are you going all dressed up?"

"William Baldwine's visitation at Easterly. I'm late. It starts at four."

The tugging at his throat was erotic, even though it was taking him in the wrong direction: If Beth was messing with his clothes, he wanted her to be taking them off of him.

"Oh. Wow." More tugging. Then she stepped back. "Better."

He leaned to one side and checked himself in the mirror. The damn thing lay straight as a line on a highway, and the knot was right at the collar—and not all wonked one way or the other, either. "Very impressive."

Beth stepped out, and he watched her walk away before he kicked his own ass. By the time he was ready to refocus, she was over at his desk, motioning at things, talking.

She was in red again, and the dress was over the knee, but not too far, and down at the neck, but not too much. Sleeves were short. Stockings? No, he didn't think so—and damn, those were good legs. Flat shoes.

"Well?" she said again.

Okay, he needed to cut the crap before she picked up on this hostile-work-environment vibe he was throwing around.

"I'm sorry?" he asked as he came out of the loo.

"Do you think I could join you? I mean, I didn't work for the man, but I am with the company now."

This was not a date, he told himself as he nodded. Absolutely not.

"Sure." He cleared his throat. "It's an open event. I imagine there'll be a lot of people from the BBC. We should probably go in your car, though. My pick-up truck is not a place for a lady."

Beth smiled. "I'll get my purse. Happy to drive."

Mack stayed behind for a second as she went out to her desk. Forcing himself to look at all the labels on the walls, he reminded his partial erection that she was his executive assistant. And yes, she was beautiful, but there were more important things to worry about than his currently non-existent love life.

Time to go get laid somewhere, he thought. He'd been too damn busy with work lately, and this was what happened: You got a desperate guy around a so much more than halfway decent woman and their dumb handle took over.

"Mack?" she called out.

"Coming—" Stop. It. "No, I mean . . . I'm, ah . . ."

Oh, for godsakes.

TWENTY-NINE

*N*o one showed.

About an hour and twenty minutes into the visitation, when there should have been a line out the front door and a carousel of buses going up and down the mountain, there had been only a few stragglers, all of whom had taken one look at the dearth of a crowd and beaten a hasty exit out Easterly's door.

As if they had worn Halloween costumes to a ball. Or white after Labor Day.

Or been seated at the children's table during some big event.

Guess he'd been wrong about people wanting to see the mighty fallen up close and in person.

Lane passed a lot of the time wandering from room to room, hands in his pockets because he was feeling like drinking and knew that it was a bad idea. Gin and Richard had disappeared somewhere. Amelia had never come down. Edward was MIA.

Lizzie was sticking right with him.

"Excuse me, sir."

Lane pivoted around to the uniformed butler. "Yes?"

"Is there anything I can do?"

Maybe it was the English accent, but Lane could have sworn Mr. Harris was subtly pleased by the ignominy. And didn't that make Lane want to reach over and rub all that Brylcreem'ed hair into a frosting-on-the-cake mess.

"Yes, tell the waiters to pack up the bars and then they can go home." No reason to pay them to stand around. "And let the parkers and the buses go. If anyone wants to come, they can just leave their cars out front."

"Of course, sir."

As Mr. Harris dematerialized, Lane went over to the base of the stairs and sat down. Staring out through the front door to the fading sunshine, he thought back to the meeting with the board chair. The scenes with Jeff. The meeting with John Lenghe.

Who was supposed to show in an hour, but who knew.

Jeff was right. He was using strong-arm tactics, and muscling people and money around. And yes, it was under the guise of helping the family— shit, saving the family. But the idea that he might be turning into his father made his stomach churn.

Funny, when he had gone to that bridge and leaned over that edge, he had wanted some kind of connection with or understanding of the man. But now he was filing that under be-careful-what-you-wish-for. Too many parallels were mounting, thanks to the way he was behaving.

What if he turned into the sonofabitch—

"Hey." Lizzie sat down next to him, tucking her skirt under her thighs. "How're you doing? Or wait, that's a stupid question, isn't it."

He leaned in and kissed her. "I'm all right—"

"Have I missed it?"

At the sound of a familiar voice that he hadn't heard in a very long time, Lane stiffened and twisted around slowly. ". . . Mother?"

Up at the top of the landing, for the first time in years, his mother stood with the support of her nurse. Virginia Elizabeth Bradford Baldwine, or Little V.E. as she was known in the family, was dressed in a long white chiffon gown, and there were diamonds at her ears and pearls around her throat. Her hair was coiffed perfectly on her head and her coloring was lovely, although definitely the result of a good make-up job as opposed to health.

"Mother," he repeated as he got to his feet and took the stairs two at a time.

"Edward, darling, how are you?"

Lane blinked a couple of times. And then took the nurse's place, offering an arm that was readily taken. "Do you want to come downstairs?"

"I think it's appropriate. But oh, I am late. I have missed everyone."

"Yes, they have come and gone. But it is all right, Mother. Let us proceed."

His mother's arm was like that of a bird, so thin under her sleeve, and as she leaned on him, her weight barely registered. They took the descent slowly, and the whole time, he wanted to swing her up and carry her because it seemed as if that might be a safer option.

She took a tumble? He was afraid she was liable to shatter at the bottom of the stairs.

"Your grandfather was a great man," she said as they came down to the foyer's black-and-white marble flooring. "Oh, look, they are removing the drinks."

"It is late."

"I love the sunlight hours in the summer, don't you? They last ever so long."

"Would you like to sit in the parlor?"

"Please, darling, thank you."

His mother didn't so much walk as shuffle across to the archway, and when they finally got to the silk sofas in front of the fireplace, Lane sat her in the one that faced away from the front door.

"Oh, the gardens." She smiled as she looked out of the French doors across the way. "They look so wonderful. You know, Lizzie works so very hard at it all."

Lane hid his surprise by going over and helping himself to a bourbon at the family's cart. It was beyond time that he gave in to his craving. "You know Lizzie?"

"She brings me my flowers—oh, there you are. Lizzie, do you know my son Edward? You must."

Lane looked up in time to see Lizzie do a double take and then cover the reaction well. "Mrs. Bradford, how are you? It's wonderful to see you up and around."

Even though his mother's last name was legally Baldwine, she had always been Mrs. Bradford around the estate. That's just the way things were, and one of the first things his father had learned to hate, no doubt.

"Well, thank you, dear. Now, do you know Edward?"

"Why, yes," Lizzie said gently. "I've met him."

"Tell me, are you helping out with the party, dear?"

"Yes, ma'am."

"I gather I have missed it. They always told me I would be late for my own funeral. It appears as if I've misjudged my father's as well."

When a couple of the waiters came in to start shutting down the bar in the corner, Lane shook his head in their direction and they ducked back out. Off in the distance, he could hear the clanking of glassware and bottles and a patter of talk from the staff as things were dealt with in the dining room—and he hoped her brain interpreted that as the party winding down.

"Your choice of color is always perfect," his mother said to Lizzie. "I love my bouquets. I look forward to the days you change them. Always a new combination of blooms, and never a one out of place."

"Thank you, Mrs. Bradford. Now, if you will excuse me?"

"Of course, dear. There is much to do. I imagine we had a terrible crush of people." His mother waved a hand as gracefully as a feather floating through thin air, her huge pear-shaped diamond flashing like a Christmas light. "Now, tell me, Edward. How are things at the Old Site? I fear I have been out of circulation for a bit of time."

Lizzie gave his arm a squeeze before she left the two of them alone, and God, what he wouldn't have traded to follow her out of the room. Instead, he sat down on the far side of the sofa, that picture of Elijah Bradford seeming to glare down at him from over the fireplace.

"Everything is fine, Mother. Just fine."

"You were always such a wonderful businessman. You take after my father, you know."

"That is quite a compliment."

"It is meant to be."

Her blue eyes were paler than he remembered, although perhaps that was because they didn't really focus. And her Queen Elizabeth–coiffed hair wasn't as thick. And her skin seemed as thin as a sheet of paper and as translucent as fine silk.

She looked eighty-five, not sixty-five.

"Mother?" he said.

"Yes, darling?"

"My father is dead. You know that, right? I told you."

Her brows drew together, but no lines appeared and not because she'd had Botox. On the contrary, she'd been raised in an era when young ladies had been urged not to go in the sun—not because the dangers of skin cancer had been fully known back then, and not because of any worry about the ozone layer being depleted. But rather because both parasols and liesure had been stylish accessories for the daughters of the rich.

The sixties in the wealthy South had been more analogous to the forties everywhere else.

"My husband . . ."

"Yes, Father has died, not Grandfather."

"It is hard for me to . . . time is hard for me now." She smiled in a way that gave him no clue whether she was feeling anything or whether what he was saying was sinking in at all. "But I shall adjust. Bradfords always adjust. Oh, Maxwell, darling, you came."

As she extended her hand and looked up, he wondered who in the hell she thought had arrived.

When he turned around, he nearly spilled his drink. *"Maxwell?"*

"Yes, through there, please. And out to the mudroom."

Lizzie pointed a waiter holding a flat of unused, rented club glasses toward the kitchen. Then she went back to shifting the last of the unopened bottles of white wine into the sleeves of a liquor box on the floor. Thank God there was something to clean up. If she had to stand around all those empty rooms for any longer, she was going to lose her mind.

Lane hadn't seemed to care one way or the other that essentially nobody came, but God . . .

Bending down, she hefted the box up and walked from behind the linen-strewn table. Proceeding out of the dining room through the flap door, she put the box with the other three in the staff hall. Maybe they could return them because the bottles were unopened?

"Every little bit helps," she said to herself.

Figuring that she'd start on the bar out on the terrace, she hesitated at one of the approved staff doors, even though if she used it, she would have to walk all the way around to the other side of the house.

At Easterly, family were allowed to come and go in any fashion at any time. Staff, on the other hand, were regimented.

Then again . . .

"Screw that."

She was not making this effort because she was an employee, but because the man she loved was having a really shitty day and it was killing her to watch it happen and she needed to improve some kind of situation, even if it was just the set-up for an event that had never happened.

Heading through the back rooms, she went out the library's French doors and paused. This was the terrace that faced the river and the big drop down to River Road, and all of the old-fashioned wrought-iron furniture and glass-topped tables had been moved to the periphery to accommodate all the people who had not come.

The bartender who had been stationed out there had left his post, and she went over and lifted the bar's linen skirting. Underneath, empty crates for the stemware and boxes for the bourbon and wine were lined up neatly, and she dragged a couple of them out.

It was right when she was about to get packing, literally, when she noticed the person sitting still and quiet right by one of the windows, their focus into the house, not at the view.

"Gary?"

As she spoke, the head groundskeeper jumped up so fast, the metal chair he'd been in squeaked across the flagstone.

"Oh, jeez, I'm sorry." She laughed. "I think everyone's on edge today."

Gary was in a fresh pair of overalls and his workboots had been hosed off, no dirt or debris on them. His old beat-up Momma's Mustard, Pickles & BBQ baseball cap was in his hand, and he quickly shoved it back on his head.

"You don't have to leave," she said as she began transferring rocks glasses into a crate upside down.

"I wasn't gonna come. Just when I seen . . ."

"No cars, right. When you saw no one was coming."

"Rich people got a weird sense of priority."

"Amen to that."

"Well, back to work. Lest you be needin' anything?"

"No, I'm just giving myself something to do. And if you help me, I might finish faster."

"So it's like that, huh."

"Yes, I'm sorry."

He grunted and went off the far lip of the terrace, taking the path that led down around the base of the stone bulwark that kept the mansion's house lot from falling off its lofty perch.

Later, much later, Lizzie would wonder why she felt compelled to step out from behind the bar and walk across to where the man had been sitting and staring so intently. But for some reason, the urge was undeniable. Then again, Gary was rarely still, and he'd been looking curiously deflated.

Leaning into the old glass . . . she saw Lane's mother perched, as beautiful as a queen, on that silk sofa.

THIRTY

*L*ane got to his feet and walked forward to his brother Maxwell. He wanted to hug the guy, but he had no idea what kind of reception he was going to get.

Max's pale gray eyes narrowed. "Hey, brother."

Still taller and broader than he or Edward, but now even more so. And there was a beard covering the lower half of that face. Jeans were so well washed they hung like a breeze, and the jacket had been made of leather at some point, but most of the hide had been worn off. The hand that extended was callused and the fingernails had dirt or oil underneath them. A tattoo emerged from the cuff on the back of the wrist.

The formal gesture of greeting was a throwback, Lane supposed, to the way they had grown up.

"Welcome back," Lane heard himself say as they shook.

His eyes couldn't stop roaming as he tried to divine from physical clues where his brother had been and what he had been doing these past few years. Car mechanic? Garbageman? Road crew? Something involving physical labor for sure, given how big he was.

The physical contact between their palms lasted only a moment and then Max stepped back and looked to their mother.

She was smiling in that vacant way of hers, her eyes softly focused. "And who might you be?"

Even though she'd just seemed to recognize the man?

"Ah, it's Maxwell, Mother," Lane said before he could stop himself. "This is Maxwell."

As he put his hand on that heavy shoulder, like he was a QVC host highlighting a toaster for sale, Little V.E. blinked a couple of times. "But of course. However are you, Maxwell? Are you here for long?"

Now, she didn't seem to recognize that Maxwell was her son—and not only because he had gone lumber-sexual with the facial hair, but because even the name didn't seem to register as significant.

Max seemed to take a deep breath. And then he went over. "I am well. Thank you."

"Perhaps a shower for you, yes? And a shave. We dress for dinner here at Easterly. Are you a close friend of Edward's then?"

"Ah, yes," he said remotely. "I am."

"That's a good boy."

As Max looked back like he was searching for a life raft, Lane cleared his throat and nodded to the archway. "Let me show you to your room."

Even though the guy no doubt hadn't forgotten where it was.

Lane nodded to the nurse who was hovering in the corner to take over, and then he drew Max into the foyer. "Surprise, surprise, brother."

"I read about it in the newspaper."

"I didn't think we announced the visitation in the *CCJ.*"

"No, the death."

"Ah."

And then there was only silence. Max was looking around, and Lane gave him a second to soak it all in, thinking back to when he himself had returned here after two years. Nothing had changed at Easterly, and maybe that was part of what was so disarming when you returned after an exile: The memories were too sharp because the stage sets had remained unaltered. And, too, except for Edward, the actors were also exactly as you had left them.

"So are you staying?" Lane asked.

"I don't know." Max glanced over at the stairwell. Then nodded to the ratty duffel bag he'd obviously just dropped by the open door. "If I do, it won't be here."

"I can get you a hotel."

"Is it true we're going bankrupt?"

"We're out of money. The bankruptcy depends on what happens next."

"So he jumped off a bridge?"

"Maybe. There are some extenuating circumstances."

"Oh."

Now Max was once again staring into the parlor, at their mother who was smiling pleasantly up at her nurse as the woman delivered her a seltzer water.

"Is she dying, too?" Max asked.

"Might as well be."

"And, ah, when does the event start?"

"I'm closing it down." Lane smoothed his tie. "A reversal of fortune is a social disease with no inoculation. Nobody came."

"Pity—"

"Where the *hell* have you been, Max?" Lane interjected. "We tried to find you."

Max's eyes swung around, and he seemed to notice Lane for the first time. "You know, you look older."

"No, shit, Max. It's been three years."

"You look a decade older."

"Maybe it's because I'm finally growing up. Meanwhile, clearly your goal of turning into a hedge is proceeding apace."

At that moment, a car pulled up to the front of the mansion, and at first, Lane was too busy thinking of throat punching his brother for disappearing to notice who it was. But as an elegant African-American man got out, Lane had to smile a little.

"Well, well, well, timing is everything."

Max squinted into the fading sunlight. Instant recollection had his eyes peeling wide, and he actually stepped back as if from a physical blow.

There was nowhere to run, though.

The Reverend Nyce had seen the man who had broken his daughter's heart into a thousand pieces. And the preacher might have been a godly man, but even Lane, as a disinterested third party, wanted to get out of the way as the guy focused on the degenerate drifter who had come home to roost.

"I'll leave you two to catch up," Lane murmured as he headed back for the parlor.

*A*s Edward arrived at the visitation, he didn't go in the front door. No, he took Shelby's truck up the back way and parked behind the kitchen wing just as he had the day before. Getting out, he tucked his T-shirt into his khakis, smoothed his hair and was glad he'd bothered to shave. But his bad ankle made him feel like he had an iron ball tethered to his leg, and his heart was beating funny. The good news, though, was that the two draws off a gin bottle before he'd left the Red & Black had evened out his DTs nicely, and although he had a hip flask full of the stuff, he hadn't needed to hit it yet.

His heart slowed into a more productive rhythm as he approached Easterly's rear kitchen door, and as the screen creaked when he opened the thing, he caught a whiff of the telltale sweet/bready/spicy smell that took him right back to childhood. Inside, Miss Aurora was sitting at the counter, her heels wedged into the bottom rung of a stool, her apron pulled up to her thighs. She looked old and tired, and he hated her disease with a passion at that moment.

Glancing away so he didn't get emotional, he saw stacks upon stacks of one-use aluminum pans with fitted tops, the packed-up food evidently ready to be taken to St. Vincent de Paul to feed the homeless and sheltered.

"A lot of no-shows?" he said, going over and taking a peak under one of the lids.

His stomach growled at the scent of her lamb *empanadas.*

"Is that the way you say hello," she snapped. "Where are your manners, boy."

"I'm sorry." He turned and bowed to her. "How are you?"

When she just grunted, he straightened and looked at her properly. Yes, he thought, she knew why he'd come.

Then again, he might not have been her favorite—Lane held that spot in the woman's heart—but she had always been one of the few people to read him like a book.

"You want tea?" she said. "It's over there."

He limped across to the glass pitcher she pointed at. It was the same one he'd used as a child, the square-bottomed, thin-necked one with the yellow-and-orange flower pattern from the seventies that was getting worn off.

"You leave this glass out special for me?" he said as he poured himself some.

"I don't want you involved in my business."

"Too late."

He added ice from the plain bucket next to her pitcher using the plastic tongs. Taking a test sip, he closed his eyes.

"Still tastes the same."

"Why wouldn't it?"

He hobbled over and took the stool next to her. "Where are all your waiters?"

"Your brother told 'em to go home, and he was right to."

Edward frowned and looked to the flap doors. "So truly, no one came."

"Nope."

He had to laugh. "I hope there is a heaven and my father sees this. Or that there's a telescope in hell."

"I don't have the energy to tell you to not speak ill of the dead."

"So how much longer do you have?" he said without any preamble. "And I won't tell Lane, I promise."

Miss Aurora's eyes narrowed on him. To the point where he could feel his butt twitch. "You watch yourself, Edward. I still got my spoon, and I may have the cancer, but you are not as fast as you used to be, either."

"True enough. Now answer the question, and know if you lie to me, I'll find out."

Miss Aurora splayed her strong hands out over the counter. The dark skin was still beautiful and smooth, the clipped nails and lack of rings a constant because of her job.

In the silence that followed, he knew she was trying out a scenario where she did lie to him. He also knew, ultimately, she wasn't going to fudge it. She was going to want someone to prepare Lane, and she was going to assume the truth: that for all of Edward's withdrawal from the family, there were at least two things that he would not pull out of.

"I stopped the treatment," she said eventually. "Too many side effects, and it wasn't working anyway. And that's why I mean it when I say you shouldn't get involved in this."

"Time. How much time?"

"Does it matter?"

So it was that little, he thought. "No, I guess it doesn't, actually."

"I'm not afraid, you know. My Savior will carry me in the palm of his hand."

"Are you sure? Even now?"

Miss Aurora nodded and brought a hand up to her short weave of tight curls. "Especially now. I am ready for what is coming for me. I am prepared."

Edward slowly shook his head back and forth—and then figured if she could be honest, so could he. In a voice that didn't sound like his own, he heard himself say, "I really don't want to get sucked into this family again. It nearly killed me once."

"You're free."

"By a baptism of torture in that jungle." He cursed. "But as you know . . . I can't bear to see my brother in pain. You and I suffer from a similar weakness when it comes to Lane, just for different reasons."

"No, it's the same reason. Love is love. It is that simple."

It was a while before he could look at her. "My life is ruined, you know. Everything that I'd planned . . . it's all gone."

"You will create a new path. And as for this?" She indicated all around herself. "Don't save what doesn't need saving."

"Lane will not recover from your loss."

"He is stronger than you know, and he has his Lizzie."

"The love of a good woman." Edward took another drink of the tea. "Did that sound as bitter as I think it did?"

"You don't have to be no hero anymore, Edward. Let this take its proper course, and trust that the outcome is pre-determined and as it should be. But I do expect you to take care of your brother. In that, you shall not fail me."

"I thought you said I don't have to be a hero."

"Don't sass me. You know the difference."

"Well, I will say that your faith has never failed to astound me."

"And your self-determination has worked out so well?"

Edward toasted her. "Touché."

"How did you find out?" Miss Aurora asked after a moment. "How did you know?"

"I have my ways, ma'am. I may be down, as they say, but I'm not out." He frowned and looked around. "Wait a minute, where did that old clock go? The one that used to be on the icebox you had before this place was renovated?"

"The one that clicked?"

"Remember that sound?" They both laughed. "I hated it."

"Me, too. But I'm getting it fixed right now. It broke a while ago, and I miss it. It's funny how you can be lost without something you despise."

He nursed his iced tea until it was gone. "That is not the case with my father."

Miss Aurora smoothed the edges of her apron. "I don't think there are many that miss him. Things happen for a reason."

Edward got up and took his empty glass over to the sink. Putting it down, he looked out the window. The garages were across the way, and then to the left, extending out from the house, the business center was a wing bigger than most good-sized mansions.

"Edward, you let this go. What will be, will be."

Probably good advice, but that wasn't in his nature. Or at least, it had never been before.

And it looked like some parts of his old self weren't dead yet.

THIRTY-ONE

As Sutton's limousine came up to Easterly's main gates and stopped, she frowned and leaned forward to address her driver. "I guess we go right up?"

"Yes, ma'am, I think so. The way is open."

Usually, for large affairs such as William Baldwine's visitation, the Bradfords ran a system of buses up and down the hill with invitees leaving their cars off to be valet'd on the flats. But there were no uniformed parkers. No boxy, twelve-seater vehicles on the ascend or descend. Nobody else pulling in.

But at least the press was nowhere to be found. Undoubtedly, those vultures had been camping out from the moment the story had broken. Clearly, though, they had been shooed away in deference to a property owner's right to use their own grass as a parking lot.

"I can't believe no one is here," she murmured.

Oh, wait, Samuel Theodore Lodge was behind her in his convertible.

She put her window down and leaned out. "Samuel T.?"

He waved. "Why, Miss Smythe. How do you do?"

Samuel T. was a fashion plate as always, a straw boater with a blue-and-maroon band on his head, aviators shading his eyes, the seersucker suit and bow tie making it look like he was going to the track or had already been.

"All the better for seeing you," she replied. "Where is everyone? Is this the right time?"

"As far as I know."

They stared at each other for a moment, asking and answering questions for themselves about the front-page story.

Then Samuel T. said, "Lead the way and I'll follow."

Sutton eased back into her Mercedes and nodded. "Let's go up."

The limousine started forward, and Sutton rubbed her palms together. They were a little sweaty, and she gave in to the impulse to take a compact out of her purse and check her lipstick. Her hair.

Stop it, she told herself.

As they came around the turn at the top, Easterly was revealed in all its majesty. Funny, even though she had just been to the estate for the Bradfords' Derby Brunch, she was still impressed. No wonder they put the great white house on their bourbon bottles. It looked like the King of America, if there had been one, lived there.

"Would you like me to wait?" the driver asked.

"That would be lovely. Thank you—no, don't get out. I'll open my own door."

As Don squirmed behind the wheel, she did the duty herself and smiled at Samuel T. and his vintage Jaguar. "Nice car you've got there, Solicitor."

Samuel T. cut his engine and pulled his emergency brake. "I'm rather fond of her. Most consistent woman I've had in my life short of my dearest mother."

"Well, you better put the top up." She nodded to the thickening cloud cover overhead. "Storms are coming."

"I thought they were kidding."

Sutton shook her head. "I don't think so."

The man got out and secured the car's little fabric cover with a couple of tugs and then a clip on each side of the windshield. Then he put the windows up and came around to her, dropping a kiss on her cheek.

"By the way," he intoned, "you look very well, Madam President—or shall I say CEO. Congratulations on the promotion."

"Thank you. I'm getting up to speed." She linked her arm through his as he offered her his elbow. "And you? How's business?"

"Thriving. There are always people getting into trouble in this town, which is the good news and the bad news."

Approaching the mansion's open door, she wondered if Edward would be inside. Surely he wouldn't miss his own father's visitation?

Not that she was here to see him.

"Reverend Nyce," she said as she entered. "How are you—Max! Is that you?"

The two men were standing close together, and Max broke away from what seemed to be a tense conversation with obvious relief. "Sutton, it's good to see you."

Boy, had he changed. That beard was a thing. And were those tattoos showing underneath his battered jacket?

Then again, he'd always been the wild one.

Samuel T. stepped up and did his greeting, hands being shaken, pleasantries exchanged . . . and then the reverend looked back at Max.

"I think you and I are clear on this, aren't we?" The Reverend Nyce paused for effect. And then he smiled at her. "And you and I have a meeting later next week."

"That's right. I'm looking forward to it."

After the reverend took his leave, there was more conversation between her and Samuel T. and Maxwell—during which she tried not to be obvious as she searched the empty rooms. Where was everyone? The visitation ran until seven. The house should be filled to overflowing.

Looking around the archway into the parlor, she nearly gasped. "Is that Mrs. Bradford? Sitting by Lane?"

"Or what's left of her," Max said tightly.

Sutton excused herself and entered the beautifully appointed room— and as soon as Edward's mother saw her, the woman smiled and reached out. "Sutton. Darling one."

So frail, yet still so regal and elegant, Sutton thought as she bent down and kissed a powdered cheek.

"Come, sit and chat with me," Edward's mother insisted.

Sutton smiled at Lane as she lowered herself onto the silk cushions. "You're looking well, Mrs. Bradford."

"Thank you, darling. Tell me, are you married yet?"

From out of nowhere, a strange sort of heat went through her—and Sutton glanced across the way. Edward had come into the periphery of the parlor from the study, his eyes locking on her as he leaned against the doorway for support.

Sutton cleared her throat and tried to remember what she had been asked. "No, ma'am. I'm not married."

"Oh, how can that be? A nice young lady such as yourself. You should be having children soon before it's too late."

Actually, I'm a little busy running a multi-billion-dollar corporation at the moment. But thank you kindly for the advice.

"And how are you, Mrs. Bradford?"

"Oh, I am very well, thank you. Edward is taking good care of me, aren't you?"

As Mrs. Bradford indicated Lane with her heavily diamond'ed hand, the man nodded and smiled as if he had been going with the misnomer for a while. Covering her surprise, Sutton glanced across the room to that archway again.

The real Edward wasn't looking very Edward at all, at least not by the standard that Mrs. Bradford clearly recalled of her oldest son.

For some reason, the discrepancy made Sutton tear up.

"I'm sure he's doing a fine job of seeing to you," she said hoarsely. "Edward always knows how to handle everything."

*L*adies were supposed to wear panty hose beneath their skirts. As Gin sat on the edge of the pool in the back garden, she moved her bare feet in lazy circles through the warm water—and was glad she never wore hose. Or slips. Or gloves.

Although the latter two were passé now. Well, arguably the L'eggs stuff was, too, what with Spanx having come along—although women like her mother certainly wouldn't ever go out without nylons.

She wasn't her mother, however. Names notwithstanding.

And yes, it was hot here on the tiled edge, no wind reaching this part of the garden thanks to the high brick wall that encircled the geometric layout of flower beds and pathways. Birds chirped from the blooming fruit trees, and up above, on the currents of what appeared to be a gathering storm, a hawk sailed around, no doubt looking for a spot of dinner.

Amelia was at Chesterfield Markum's house . . . or so Mr. Harris had informed Gin prior to the visitation. And that was fine enough. There was no one here to see, really, and Field and Amelia had been friends since they had been in diapers. Nothing romantic or sexual there.

A professor. God, Gin found the expulsion debacle at once wholly believable and totally inconceivable. Then again, she didn't really know her daughter very well at all—which was probably the why of the liaison, wasn't it. Or maybe she gave herself and her absenteeism too much credit: her own parents might not have been big players in her life day to day, but she'd had Miss Aurora.

And yet look at how well she had turned out.

Feeling faint, Gin removed her cropped jacket, but left her Hermès scarf in place. She was of half a mind to jump in the pool with her clothes on—and in an earlier incarnation of her rebellious self, she would have. Now, she simply didn't have the energy. Besides . . . no audience—

"So is the wedding off or just the reception?"

Gin closed her eyes briefly at the sound of that too familiar voice. "Samuel T. I thought you weren't coming."

As his footsteps approached from behind her, she refused to look at him or welcome him.

"How could I not pay respects to your family," he drawled. "Oh, were you speaking of your nuptials?"

There was a *shhhhcht* sound and then she caught the fragrant scent of tobacco.

"Still with the Cubans," she muttered as she focused on her feet moving around in the aquamarine water.

"So which is it? The e-mail you sent a mere half hour ago was not specific. It also had two spelling mistakes in it. Do you need me to show you where spell-check is in Outlook?"

"I'm marrying him. But there won't be a reception." She waved a hand over her shoulder, indicating the house. "As you see, people have a rather dim view of us at the moment. What's the saying? Oh, how the mighty have fallen?"

"Ah. Well, I'm sure you'll find a way to repurpose the funds. Perhaps into some clothes? A little bauble to match your ring—oh, no, that's Richard's job, isn't it, and he's certainly starting off on the right foot. How much does that sparkler weigh? A pound? Three?"

"Do fuck off, Samuel."

When he didn't say anything, she twisted around. He hadn't left, though. Quite the contrary, he was standing over her, his brows down under his aviators, a straw boater in one of his hands, that cigar in the other.

"What?" she snapped as all he did was continue to stare at her.

He indicated her with the cigar. "What's that on your arm?"

Turning back to the water, she shook her head. "It's nothing."

"That's a bruise."

"No, it isn't."

"Yes, it is."

Next thing she knew, he crouched down beside her and took her wrist in his grip.

"Let go of me!"

"That's a bruise. What the hell, Gin?"

She yanked herself free and put her jacket back on. "I had a little too much to drink. I bumped into something."

"Did you. Then why does it look like a man's handprint?"

"You're seeing things. It was a doorway."

"Bullshit." He pulled her around to him and then looked lower than her face. "What's under the scarf, Gin."

"Excuse me?"

"Take off the scarf, Gin. Or I'll do it for you."

"You're finished removing my clothes, Samuel T." She got to her feet. "And you can leave now. Or I will. Either way, this conversation is—"

"You never wore scarves when I was with you." He got right up in her face. "What's going on, Gin?"

"Nothing—"

"I'll kill him if he lays a hand on you. I'll fucking kill that bastard."

Abruptly, Samuel T.'s face became a mask of rage, and in that moment, she saw him for the hunter he was: He might have been in one of his patented seersucker suits, and yes, he was handsome as F. Scott Fitzgerald . . . but there was no doubt in her mind that he was capable of putting Richard Pford, or any other living thing, in an early grave.

But he wouldn't marry her. She'd already asked him and he'd told her no.

Gin crossed her arms. "He was just trying to keep me from falling."

"I thought you said it was a doorway."

"I hit the doorjamb first and then Richard kept me on my feet." She rolled her eyes. "Do you honestly think I would ever marry someone who was rough with me—when I didn't deliberately ask him to be?"

In response, Samuel T. just took a puff on that cigar, exhaling off to the side so the smoke didn't get in her face.

"What," she snapped. "I hate when you look at me like that. Just say it, whatever it is."

He took his damn sweet time, and when he finally spoke, his voice seemed falsely level. "Gin, you're not in as desperate a situation as you think. This financial stuff—it'll work itself out. People will keep buying that bourbon, and your family will rebound. Don't do anything stupid."

"Richard can afford me." She shrugged. "And that makes him valuable whether my family has money or not."

Samuel T. shook his head like the thing hurt. "At least you're not even trying to pretend you love him."

"Marriages have been built on far less. In fact, there is a grand tradition of marrying well in my family. And not to doctors . . . or lawyers. To real money."

"I should have known that was coming." With a curse, he smiled coldly. "And you never disappoint me. Have fun with your man, especially when you're lying back and thinking of England. Or is it Bergdorf's?"

She lifted her chin. "He treats me beautifully, you know."

"You've clearly picked a winner." He muttered something under his breath. "Well, I'll leave you to it. My condolences on the loss of your father."

"It was no loss."

"Just like your scruples, right?"

"Be careful, Samuel T. Your bitchiness suggests a hidden weakness. Are you sure you're not jealous of a man you consider beneath you?"

"No, I feel sorry for him. It's the biggest curse in a man's life that he loves a woman like you. That sad sack has no idea what he's in for."

As he turned away, a rush of emotion hit her. "*Samuel.*"

He pivoted back around slowly. "Yes."

If only you hadn't said no, she thought. If only you were the one I could turn to.

"Don't go back through the house with that cigar. My mother's downstairs, and she doesn't abide them indoors."

Samuel T. glanced at the smoldering length. "Right. Of course."

And then . . . he was gone.

For some reason, Gin's legs started to shake and she barely made it to one of the Brown Jordan recliners that were lined up down the long sides of the pool. As she all but fell into the chair, she had to peel off her jacket again.

When she couldn't breathe, she took off the goddamn scarf. Underneath, her neck was sore, particularly on the right side where the worst of the bruising was.

Yoga breaths . . . three part . . . just . . . she needed to take a deep breath . . .

"Gin?"

She looked up at Lane's girlfriend—fiancée . . . whatever. "Yes," she said roughly.

"Are you okay?"

"Of course I am," she snapped. But then she couldn't keep up the anger. "I am . . . just fine."

"All right. But listen, bad weather's coming."

"Is it?" God, she felt as though she had fallen into the pool and was drowning. "I thought it was sunny . . . or something."

"I'm going to go get you some water. Stay right there."

Gin was of half a mind to argue, but her tongue felt like it had swollen in her mouth and then her head started to spin in earnest.

When Lizzie came back, it was with a long/tall of lemonade. "Drink this."

Gin put her hand out, but it was shaking so badly, there was no hope of holding anything.

"Here . . . let me."

Lizzie brought the glass to Gin's lip, and Gin took a sip. And then another. And then a third.

"Don't worry," Lane's fiancée said. "I'm not going to ask."

"Thank you," Gin mumbled. "I greatly appreciate that."

THIRTY-TWO

$\mathcal{E}$dward could have spent the rest of the visitation just watching Sutton and his mother sit together on that silk sofa. Contrary to Lane's chilly relationship with the woman who had birthed them, Edward entertained little bitterness to their dam—mostly because, having worked so closely with their father, he had a healthy respect for all Little V. E. had been forced to endure.

Why wouldn't one find relief at the bottom of a pill bottle?

Especially if you'd been cheated on, ridiculed, and relegated to all but a Tiffany vase in your own home.

And now it appeared as though his sister, Gin, was falling into the same trap with Pford.

Sutton, on the other hand . . . Sutton would never do something like that, never conscribe herself to a marriage of convenience just so she could live a given lifestyle. In fact, she didn't need a man to define her at all. No, her life plan? She was going to run a multi-national corporation like a boss—

As if she knew he was thinking something about her, her eyes flicked over in his direction, and then refocused on his mother.

His own stare stayed put on Sutton, lingering on her hair and the way it had been swept up off her neck and away from her face. Her earrings were fat pearls anchored by brilliant diamonds, and in a truly uncharitable moment, he wondered if the Shit Dagney had bought those for her. They did compliment the pale blue of her suit, but such placid gems didn't do her justice.

She was better in rubies.

His rubies.

But whether treasures from the Orient or from Burma, from a good suitor or a bad footnote in her love life, she was still arrestingly beautiful: Behold, the new CEO of the Sutton Distillery Corporation. And yet she still had the grace and class to take time to speak gently to an addled lost soul like his mother. When she was done here, however? She would get back in her limo in her moonlight-on-a-snowfield blue suit and her hopefully-not-the-governor's pearls, and promptly reconnect with her senior executives, her sales force leaders, maybe a Japanese investor whose kind offer to buy out the company would be rejected with a charming, but totally unequivocal, *no*.

Yes, he had heard on the radio on the way in that she was taking over her family's business. And it couldn't be in better hands—

A man entered the parlor, took one look at Edward and came on over—and in spite of the scruffy beard and battered clothes, Edward would have recognized his brother Maxwell anywhere. Then again, he had reason to.

"Edward," the guy said remotely.

"Max, you're looking well, as usual," Edward replied dryly. "But you must forgive me, I must be going."

"Tell Moe I said hello."

"Of course."

Moving around his brother, he limped forward into the parlor proper. It seemed unbearably rude, even for an asshole such as himself, to not at least greet his mother as he left.

He had no idea what to say, however.

Approaching the sofa, Sutton looked up at him first. And then his mother did the same.

As he searched for proper words, Little V.E. smiled at him as beautifully as a Thomas Sully portrait. "How lovely that the grounds staff have come to pay their respects. What is your name, son?"

As Sutton blanched, Edward bowed his head. "Ed, ma'am. That's my name."

"Ed? Oh, I have a son named Edward." Her hand swung toward Lane in indication, and God, the poor bastard looked like he'd rather have been swallowed by a hellhole. "And where do you work on the estate?"

"The stables, ma'am."

Her eyes were the exact blue of his, and as beautiful as a morning glory in the July sunshine. They were also as clouded as window glass on a frosted morning. "My father loved his horses. When he goes to heaven, there will be thoroughbreds a'plenty for him to race."

"There certainly will be. My condolences, ma'am."

Turning away, he began what seemed like a very long trip out of the parlor, only to hear her say, "Oh, and that poor man is crippled. My father always had a soft spot for the poor and unfortunate."

It was a while before Edward's consciousness returned from wherever it had momentarily evaporated to—and he discovered that he had walked himself out the grand front door instead of back to the kitchen and where he'd parked Shelby's truck.

In fact, he was standing on Easterly's steps, the astoundingly beautiful river view down below something that he had managed to disregard the entire time he had lived at the mansion, both as a child and as a young adult, and, later, as the business leader he had become.

And yet as his eyes took it all in now, he wasn't awestruck by nature's beauty or inspired by the landscape's breadth or even sad for what he had lost and was currently missing. No, what occurred to him . . . was that his mother, believing he was a mere stablehand, would not have approved of his exit. Staff were only allowed to use certain prescribed entrances, all of which were in the rear of the house.

He had gone out the formal door.

His legs were weak as he took a step down. And then another. And then a final one to the cobblestones of the circular drive and parking area.

Dragging himself forth, he set a path around to the back of the great white mansion, to a stranger's truck that had been loaned to him with the generosity of a family member.

Or at least how you wished a family member would—

"Edward—Edward!"

Of course, he thought as he continued on. But of course his escape could not have gone unencumbered.

Sutton had no problem catching up to him. And as she touched his arm, he wanted to keep going, but his feet stopped: As always, his flesh listened to her over anything and anyone, including himself. And oh, she was flushed with upset, her breath too quick for the short distance she had traveled, her eyes so wide.

"She didn't recognize you," Sutton said. "She just . . . didn't recognize you."

God, she was beautiful. Those red lips. That dark hair. That tall, perfectly proportioned body. He had known her for so long, fantasized about her for so long, one would think when he saw her there would be no further revelations. But no, that was not the case.

His fantasies of her were going to have to keep him going, however. The way things were headed, with what was happening on the estate . . . they were all he was going to have for quite some time.

"Edward . . ." As her voice cracked, he felt the pain she was feeling sure as if it were his own. "Edward, I'm sorry."

Closing his eyes, he laughed harshly at himself. "Do you have any idea how much I love that sound? The sound of my name on your lips? It's rather sad, really."

When he reopened his lids, she was staring at him in shock.

"I am not of my right mind," he heard himself say. "Not at this moment."

In fact, he felt like things were falling off shelves up there, great weights tumbling and hitting the floor of his skull, their contents spilling out and getting broken into shards.

"I'm sorry?" she whispered. "What?"

Taking her hand, he said, "Come with me."

*W*ith a pounding heart, Sutton followed Edward as he led her off. She wanted to ask where they were going, but the haunted expression on his face kept her quiet. And besides, she didn't care. The garage. The fields. The river.

Anywhere. Even though it was crazy.

He was just . . . undeniable.

As usual.

As they came around to the back of the house, there were a number of waiters loitering by the kitchen screen door, their bow ties hanging loose around their necks, a cigarette lit here and there, a number of por-table ice coolers, all in U of C red, waiting to get loaded into a Ford truck.

Edward bypassed them and continued on to the business center.

There were no fancy sedans parked along its flank. No lights in the windows—although that might have been because the drapes were drawn. No one coming and going.

And there was no problem for him to get inside, the code he entered on the pad freeing up the lock.

Inside, the air was cool and dry, and the darkness, coupled with the relatively low ceilings, made her feel like she was entering a cave . . . a very nice cave with deep pile carpeting and oil paintings on the walls and a full-service kitchen she had heard about but never personally sam-pled the wares of.

"What are we doing?" she asked his back as he kept on limping along.

He did not reply. He just led her into a conference room . . . and closed the door.

And locked it.

There was nothing but dim security lighting on in the corners of the room, the royal blue drapes closed as tightly as if they were zippered shut, the glossy table clear of anything save a flower arrangement in the center that appeared to be a few days old.

There were twelve leather chairs.

He pushed the one at the head of the table out of the way and then he turned to her. Came up to her. Lowered his eyes at her body.

As her lungs began to sting from a sweet suffocation, she knew exactly why they were here . . . and she also knew she wasn't going to deny them this.

It made no sense. But she was desperate and so was he, and sometimes the primordial overrode all logic and self-protection.

"I want you," he said as his eyes roamed over her, hot and greedy. "And I'd tell you I need you, but that truth scares me too much to say it out loud. Oops."

She reached for him. Or maybe it was the other way around.

And oh, God, the way he kissed her, hungry and demanding as one of his hands locked on at the back of her neck—and the other circled her waist. With a lurch, he walked her backward until she felt the table bump against her hamstrings.

"Can you get up on this?" he groaned against her mouth. "I can't lift you."

Typical of the Bradfords, everything was the best of the best, and even though she was a healthy weight, the table didn't care in the slightest as she hopped up on it.

Edward's hands pushed her skirt higher and higher as he kissed her even more deeply. And then he worked his way between her thighs, his fingers trailing up her blouse and stripping off the Armani jacket she had on. She was the one who took her hair out of its chignon.

Buttons came loose under his deft fingers, and then her breasts were exposed, the lace cups of her bra getting pushed aside as he bent down and got her even hotter. Letting herself go, she fell back on the slick conference table and he followed, staying with her, covering her with his body.

His hands swept up and cupped her breasts as his hips rolled against her, stroking her with an erection that was so hard, so distinct, she didn't know whether he'd taken his pants off. Her skirt didn't last long, Edward taking advantage as she arched up to his mouth to release the back fastening and do away with it.

Her stockings followed suit.

And then her panties.

And then his mouth left her breasts . . . and went other places.

The orgasm was so strong, her head knocked into the hard table, but she didn't care. Throwing her palms out, they squeaked against polished wood as she called his name freely.

There was no one to know.

Nobody to hear.

And after stitching herself up at corporate headquarters all day long, after resolutely shutting down the worried daughter she was for the professional she wanted and needed to be at the office . . . after denying her feelings for Edward for so long . . . she wasn't going to hold anything back.

"Oh, God . . . look at you . . ."

As she heard him talk, she lifted her head. He was staring at her, his eyes full of lust, his hands locking on her breasts.

And then, as if he knew exactly what she wanted, he reared up and went for the fly of his khakis.

Reaching out, she went for his shirt, her hands fumbling with—

"No, no, that has to stay on."

She wanted to argue. But then she felt the blunt head of his stroking at her . . . and then penetrating.

Sutton cried out again and then Edward was on her, the sex fast and furious, the driving thrusts threatening to slide her down the table. Locking her legs around his lower body, she held them together.

She hated the shirt he'd left on. Hated the reason for it. Wanted him to be as free as she was.

But she would take what he gave her. And knew better than to ask for any more.

Soon, Edward's orgasm was as loud as hers had been, the harsh sounds of his breath in her ear, his curses, the gritted way he said her name, helping her find another release.

It seemed like forever and not nearly long enough before he was still.

And it was then she was reminded for the first time since he took her hand and brought her to the business center . . . that he wasn't as strong as he had once been.

As he collapsed against her, he did not weigh very much, and his breath was ragged for quite some time.

Unlatching her legs, she wrapped her arms around him and held him as she closed her eyes.

And it felt like the most natural thing in the world to open her heart even as she kept her mouth shut: As good as this had been, there was an unmistakable stolen quality to it, and sooner or later, she was going to have to put her defenses back on along with her clothes—

He whispered something in her ear that she didn't catch.

"What?" she said.

"Nothing."

Edward stopped her from asking again by kissing her some more. And then he was moving inside of her, his erection still hard, his hips still strong, his need still for her.

For some reason, her eyes watered. "Why does this feel like you're saying good-bye?"

"Shhhh . . ." he said before kissing her again.

THIRTY-THREE

"**M**y car has never broken down like this. Like, ever."

As Beth spoke to Mack, the rain started to fall, the drops hitting the back of his suit jacket as he popped the hood and looked into the hissing engine.

"It's all right," he said. "These things happen. So listen, make my day . . . and tell me that you have some bottled water with you."

"I think so—hold on."

Waving his arms, he cleared away the clouds of hot, oil-smelling vapor while, overhead, thunder rolled through the sky like a bowling ball.

"Here," Beth said. "Got it."

Taking off his jacket, he covered his hand with a sleeve and bent down to the radiator. "Stand back."

"No, wait! You'll ruin your—"

As he loosened the cap, the pressure exploded and he got nailed with a razor-sharp burn on the bottom of his arm. "Sonofabitch!"

"Mack, are you crazy?"

Trying to be a man about having been stupid, he dropped the damn jacket and flapped things around. "Give me the water," he gritted when he wasn't seeing double anymore.

A flash of lightning provided him with a first-class view under the hood, and the clap of thunder that immediately followed meant the storm was coming in fast and had good aim.

"Get back in the car, okay?"

"What about your arm?"

"We'll look at it when this thing isn't overheating. G'on."

A deluge of rain cut the argument off, and Beth ran around and got behind the wheel again. The wet rush was cool, which helped on a lot of levels, especially as a stiff gust threw a wash of the stuff onto the engine. And what do you know, filling up the radiator went better than the cap-tastrophe—and then he was shutting the hood and heading back for shotgun.

"Well, that was fun." He yanked his door shut and pushed his wet hair back. "You want to give the ignition a shot?"

"How's your arm?"

"Still attached. Let's see if we can get going."

Beth was muttering and shaking her head as she cranked the key. "I don't know anything about cars, and after this, I'm really looking to keeping things that way."

But the engine started up like a champ, and as she looked over with a smile, Mack almost forgot the pain in his arm.

"Don't be too impressed," he robin-breasted. "All men with names like Mack or Joe are constitutionally required to be able to fix situations like this."

Unfortunately, the respite didn't last. As rain pelted the front wind-shield and more lightning disco-balled the sky, the pain from the burn got back to business and he found himself cursing and not wanting to look at the damage.

Grinding his teeth, he started to take off his tie because of the nausea.

"I think we should go to the emergency room," she said.

"Let me see how bad it is."

When all he could do was fumble, Beth pushed his hands out of the way. "I'll do it."

The tie knot she had done for him dissolved under her deft finger-tips, and then he tilted his head back so she could get at the top button of his collar.

From his vantage point, he could see her in the rearview mirror, her brows down in concentration, her lips parted.

He got hard.

He didn't mean to. He didn't want to. And he sure as hell wasn't going to do anything about it. But here it was—the adult equivalent of a high school boy's come-up-and-solve-this-math-problem nightmare.

Man, this trip kept getting any better, the pair of them were going to be struck by a bajillion joules of wake-up juice.

With a jerk, he made sure his blazer was covering his lap, and then Beth was working her way down his shirt and pulling the tails out as she went. Which meant a whole lot of him was getting airtime.

Well, at least he wasn't as preoccupied with his Freddy Krueger.

"I'll take it from here," he said gruffly.

"You're not going to manage. Lean toward me."

Mack slowly shifted off the back of the seat, bringing them close together. She was talking about something, God only knew what, going on and on as if nothing particularly notable was happening . . . while she stripped his chest and shoulders.

". . . butter, you know? Right from the fridge. I don't know if it worked on my neck burn necessarily, but I smelled like I had breakfast for perfume when I went to the dance. The boys were crazy for me."

Laugh, you idiot, he told himself.

"That's funny," he said.

"Oh . . . Mack."

As she looked down and shook her head, he thought for a cringing moment she had noticed his erection, but no, his wet blazer was still covering up everything.

Actually, she had managed to get the shirt completely off where he'd been burned, the thing now hanging damply from his "good" arm. Like it was depressed it wasn't going to get to go to a party.

"You're going to need a doctor," she said at the horrible red bomb burst in his skin.

"It's fine."

"You'd say that if you had an arterial bleed, wouldn't you?"

That was when she looked at him.

And instantly she went still . . . as if she knew exactly where his brain had gone—and it certainly was not on her radiator, his arm, or any kind of medical intervention.

Not unless she was playing nurse to his patient and was half naked at the time.

Damn it, he was a pig.

"I'm fine," he said again as he focused on her lips—and wondered what they felt like. Tasted like.

Her eyes drifted down to his pecs and his abs—and man, he was glad that he had never been afraid of physical labor. And that he was in a basketball league that played hard twice a week. And that he could bench-press twice his weight, easy.

Clearing her throat, she eased out of reach. "Ah . . . so, the hospital?"

"I'm fine." His voice was so low it was all gravel. And where the hell had the rest of his grown-up words gone? "Don't worry about it."

She put her hands on the wheel and stared out the front windshield, as though for the life of her she couldn't remember where they'd ended up stopping. Or why. Or what they were doing in the car.

"No," she said as she put the engine in drive. "I'm taking you to the emergency room. Text whoever you need to, but we're not going to make it to the visitation."

"Stay at one of the cottages, then."

As Lane spoke to Max, he removed his bow tie and folded the thing into the side pocket of his jacket. The foyer was empty of people, but that had been the case all afternoon, hadn't it?

When his brother didn't respond, Lane took that as a "fuck no." "Come on, how about it? I think I heard from Lizzie that the second cottage from the end is open. Key's under the front mat and it's furnished."

He wasn't sure whether Max heard him or not. The guy was staring through the archway into the parlor, at that portrait of Elijah Bradford.

In the background, thunder and lightning did a rumble-tumble through the sky, the open front door seeming to invite the storm inside. Then again, the tornado was already in the house. Had been for the past few weeks.

"Max?" Lane prompted.

"Sorry. Yeah, I'll stay down there." His brother glanced over. "Edward looks . . ."

"I know."

"I'd read the papers . . . but the articles hadn't had a lot of pictures with them."

"It's also different in person."

"I'm not used to it yet."

As Lane's phone went off in his breast pocket, he took the thing out and wasn't surprised at the text indicating that John Lenghe's plane had been rerouted due to bad weather. Just as well. He was exhausted and not up for an epic game of poker right now.

Before he could put it away, a second text came through, almost as if the storms had caused a cellular tower to briefly blink out before starting to function again. Mack couldn't make it either. Something about car trouble.

Not missing much, Lane typed to his old buddy.

"You need some food?" he asked Max.

"I ate before I came."

"How long are you here for?"

"I don't know. Long as I can stand it."

"In that case, we might as well say our good-byes now," Lane said dryly.

Funny, his brother's roughneck exterior belied the fact that Max had a Yale education behind that scruff. Proof positive you shouldn't judge books by covers, et cetera . . . although maybe the guy had done so many drugs that he'd rusted all that higher learning out of his brain cells.

"You know . . ." Max cleared his throat. "I have no idea why I came back."

"Well, a piece of advice. Find that out before you leave. It's more efficient. Oh, but make sure you say hello to Miss Aurora, okay? She's going to want to see you."

"Yeah. And yes, I know she's ill."

For a split second, a flag got raised, but Lane lost track of the warning or instinct or whatever it was. And then a flash of silver blue outside in the circular drive caught his eye. It was Sutton Smythe out in the rain, her hairdo ruined, her fancy suit soaked, her high heels splashing through puddles. She wasn't running, though. She was walking as slowly as if it were just the gloaming on a summer night.

"Sutton!" Lane called out as he rushed for the doorway. "Do you want an umbrella?"

Dumbass question. It was way too late for that.

She turned to him on a startle, and seemed to recognize where she was for the first time. "Oh, ah, no, thank you. I appreciate it, though. My condolences."

Her chauffeur jumped out from behind the wheel of the C63 she'd come in. Then doubled back and fumbled for an umbrella. "Miss Smythe!"

"I'm fine," she said as he ran over to her. "Don, I'm fine."

As the man got her into the backseat of the car and then the Mercedes took off down Easterly's hill, Lane stayed in the mansion's entrance, the breath of the storm hitting him with a wet kiss. When he finally eased back around, Max was gone and so was the duffel he'd brought with him.

No doubt he'd proceeded down to the kitchen.

Putting his hands in the pockets of his slacks, Lane looked around at the empty rooms. The waitstaff had removed the bars and returned the furniture to its proper place. His mother had retired upstairs once again, and he had to wonder when, if ever, she would come down once more. Lizzie was off somewhere, likely organizing the rented table-cloths, napkins, and glasses for pick-up to keep herself from jumping out of her skin.

And Edward? He must have left.

All around him, the mansion was quiet as the wind battered the highest point in Charlemont, as the streaks of deadly lightning lashed out, as the thunder cursed and swore.

Taking his cue from Sutton, he walked out of the door and lifted his face to all the fury. The rain was cold against his skin and spiked with hail. The gusts battered his body. The threat of a strike increased as the core of the storm rolled ever closer.

His clothes slapped and flapped against him, reminding him of the fall from the bridge. The sting in his eyes made him blink, and a sense that he was plummeting made the drop down to the river below seem as close as his own hand.

But there was a truism that kept him upright, a strength that he tapped into, a power that came from within.

As Easterly withstood the onslaught . . . so would he.

THIRTY-FOUR

When Edward returned to the Red & Black, he parked Shelby's truck in front of the caretaker's cottage, killed the engine and shucked the key from the ignition. But he didn't immediately get out. Not because of the storm, though.

As raindrops pelted the windshield like God was angry at him but couldn't get His hands on anything better to throw, images of Sutton lying back on that conference table, her body so gloriously naked as she gasped and moaned, replaced even the overwhelming storm that was rushing over the land.

Looking through the deluge to the cottage, he knew Shelby was waiting for him there. With dinner. And a bottle of alcohol. And after he finished eating and drinking, they would go back to that bedroom and lie together side by side in the darkness, him sleeping and her . . . well, he didn't know if she slept or not.

He had never asked.

Tucking the key into the visor, he disembarked and was pushed against the wet flank of the truck bed by the wind. Throwing wide a steadying arm, he didn't want to go inside. But staying out here—

Promptly, all was forgotten.

There was some kind of chaos going on at Barn B. All the lights in the place were on, for one thing, which was rare. But even more alarming, there were a dozen people swarming around the open doors at the rear.

Pushing himself off the truck, Edward limped across the grass toward the drama, and soon enough, even over the wind, he heard the shrieks from the horses.

Or, rather, one particular stallion.

When he got to the nearest door, he hobbled inside as fast as he could, passing through the tack and supply room, pushing out into the stalls area and going down the aisle—

"What the *hell* are you doing?" he hollered over the screaming and the yelling.

Nebekanzer was spooked wild in his berth, the stallion bucking and thrashing, his back hooves having splintered the bottom door to the stall. And Shelby—like a complete raving lunatic—had climbed over the top of the bars that were still in place and was trying to catch his bridle.

Stable hands and also Moe and Joey, were right there with her, but the bars were separating them, and oh, God, she was right in range of the stallion's gnashing teeth and thrashing head, the one who was most likely to get thrown to the ground and have her head cracked open like a melon on the cement if she went one way—or trampled under those hooves if she went the other.

Edward moved before he was conscious of making the decision to get all up in there, even though Joey was closer, stronger and younger than he was. But by the time he got all the way down to . . .

Shelby caught the stallion's bridle.

And somehow, as she made eye contact with the beast, she managed to hold her body in place upside down by squeezing her thighs on the top of the bars, and simultaneously arch down and start blowing directly into the horse's nostrils. This gave the stable hands just enough time to open the ruined door and get it out of the way so that the wood splinters didn't cut Neb any further and replace it with a sturdy nylon webbing. At the same moment, Shelby threw her hand out through the bars and one of the men put a head mask in it.

It took her a split second to get the contraption over Neb's eyes and secured under his throat.

Then she kept blowing into those flaring nostrils, the stallion settling down, his panicked, blood-streaked flanks falling into a twitching display of partially leashed power, his belly pumping in and out . . . even as his steel-shod hooves became still in the sawdust.

Shelby righted herself with the grace of a gymnast. Climbed down. Ducked into the stall.

And Edward realized for the first time since he'd been kidnapped that he was terrified about something.

One of the few rules he'd given Jeb Landis's daughter when she'd started to work here was the same across-the-board that applied to everybody at the Red & Black: No one got close to Neb but Edward.

Yet there she was, a hundred pounds of five foot five, in an enclosed space with that killer.

Edward hung back and watched her smooth her palms down the stallion's neck as she spoke to him. She wasn't stupid, though. She nodded to one of the hands, who unhooked the netting on the side closest to her. If Neb started going at it again, she could get to safety in the blink of an eye.

As if sensing his regard, Shelby looked over at Edward. There was nothing apologetic in her stare. Nothing boastful, either.

She had saved the horse from seriously injuring—or even killing— himself in a professional, expert fashion, without putting herself at undue risk. After all, Neb could have punctured an artery on that shredded, knife-sharp ruined door, and she could very easily have been terribly hurt as well.

It was beautiful to see, actually.

And he wasn't the only one who had noticed.

Joey, Moe's son, was standing on the periphery and staring at Shelby with an expression on his face that suggested the twenty-something man had regressed to being a sixteen-year-old boy again . . . and Shelby was the prom queen he wanted to dance with.

Which was proof that we were always every age we had ever been.

And also not something Edward particularly appreciated. With a frown, he was struck by a nearly irresistible urge to put himself right between the pair of them. He wanted to be a billboard with HANDS OFF on it. A living, breathing caution tape. A foghorn of warning.

But the protective instinct was rooted in the concern of a big brother watching out for his little sister.

Sutton had reminded him, in the most basic of ways, that she would forever be the only woman for him.

*U*pstairs in whoever-the-hell-Bradford-ancestor's bedroom, Jeff hit print and put his hand out in front of the Brother machine. The ink-jet made a rhythmic whirring sound, and moments later, a perfect line-up of numbers came out. And then another. And a final one.

There were tiny words on the three pages, too, explanations for line items, notations he had spent the last two hours typing out on a laptop.

The most significant thing on the sheet, however, was the title.

BRADFORD BOURBON COMPANY
OPERATIONAL DEFICIT SUMMARY

Jeff put the document down on the desk, right on the keyboard of the open laptop. Then he looked over the snow pile of papers, notes, account reports, tables, and charts on the antique desk.

He was done.

Finished.

At least with the part where he traced the rerouting of accounts receivable payments and operating capital.

On second thought . . . he picked up the report, and made sure he was logged out of the laptop. He'd changed his password. Encoded all his work. And only sent his private e-mail account an electronic copy.

Pulling out the flash drive he'd used from the USB port, he put the thing in the pocket of his slacks. Then he went over and sat at the foot of the messy bed. As he stared at the desk, he thought . . . yup, just like his office in Manhattan.

Where he worked for a corporation. Along with a thousand other human calculators, as Lane put it.

Across the way, his packed luggage was lined up by the door. He'd been fishing through it all for whatever he needed, knowing he wasn't staying.

The damn things looked like they were mortally wounded and bleeding his clothes and toiletries.

At the knock on the door, he said, "Yup."

Tiphanii walked in, and wow, her jeans were as tight as skin and her loose top was as low cut as a string bikini. With her hair down and her make-up done, she was youth and sex and excitement all in a naughty little package that she was happy to have on display for him.

"Congratulations," she said as she shut the door and locked it. "And I'm glad you texted for me to come celebrate."

"I'm glad you're here." He moved back on the bed and nodded at the report. "I've been working non-stop. Feels weird not to have it hanging over me."

"I snuck up the back stairs," she said as she put her purse down.

"Is that a new Louis?" he drawled as he nodded to the thing.

"This?" She picked the printed LV satchel back up. "It is, actually. You have good taste. I love men from the city."

"That is my home."

Tiphanii's lips went into a pout. "Does that mean you're going to be leaving soon?"

"You going to miss me?"

She came over and stretched out on the bed next to him, rolling over onto her side and flashing her breasts. No bra. And she was clearly aroused already.

"Yes, I will miss you," she said. "But maybe you can bring me up there to see you?"

"Maybe."

Jeff started kissing her, and then he was getting her naked . . . and then he was getting naked. They had done this enough now so that he knew what she liked. Knew exactly what to do to get her off quickly. And he was turned on. It was hard not to be. Even though his eyes were wide open as to why she was here, what she wanted, and how exactly she was going to use him—he was good with currency exchanges and rates.

He was a banker, after all.

And after she spent the night? After she snuck out in the morning early to go put her uniform on and pretend that she hadn't been in bed with him? After that, he was going to sit down with Lane and make his full report. And then he had a piece of business he needed to take care of.

As he mounted Tiphanii and she purred into his ear, he was still not sure what he was going to do about the equity offer. Lane had seemed serious, and Jeff knew the company inside and out now. There was risk involved, though. A possible federal investigation. And he'd never really managed anyone before.

It was a The Clash problem. Straight up.

Should I Stay or Should I Go . . .

THIRTY-FIVE

The Metro Police homicide detective showed up at nine a.m. the following morning. Lane was coming downstairs when he heard the brass knocker, and when he didn't see Mr. Harris butlering along to answer the banging echo, he did the duty himself.

"Detective Merrimack. What can I do for you?"

"Mr. Baldwine. Do you have a moment?"

Merrimack was in the same uniform he'd been wearing the other day: dark slacks, white polo with the police crest, professional smile in place. He'd had his hair trimmed even tighter, and the aftershave was nice. Not too much.

Lane stepped aside and indicated the way in. "I was getting coffee. You want to join me?"

"I'm working."

"I thought that was an issue for alcohol, not caffeine?"

Smile. "Is there somewhere we can go?"

"Here is fine. Considering you've turned down the Starbucks Morning Blend in my kitchen. So what do you need? My sister, Gin, is not an early bird, so if you want to talk with her, you better come back after noontime."

Merrimack smiled. Again. "Actually, I was interested in your security cameras." He nodded up at the discreet pods on the ceiling by the molding. "There are a lot of them around, aren't there."

"Yes, this is a big house."

"And they're both on the outside and the inside of your home, right?"

"Yes." Lane put his hands in the pockets of his slacks so he didn't worry the watch band of his Piaget. Or the collar of his button down. "Is there something specific you're looking for?"

Duh.

"What happens with the footage? Where is it recorded and stored?"

"Are you asking if you can view it?"

"You know, I am." Smile. "It would be helpful."

When Lane didn't immediately answer, the detective smiled some more. "Listen, Mr. Baldwine, I know you want to be helpful. You and your family have been very open during the course of this investigation, and my colleagues and I have appreciated it."

Lane frowned. "Actually, I'm not sure where it's kept."

"How can that be? Don't you live here?"

"And I don't know how to get access to it."

"Show me where the computers are and I'll handle it." There was another pause. "Mr. Baldwine? Is there a reason why you don't want me to see the footage from your estate's security cameras?"

"I need to talk to my lawyer first."

"You're not a suspect. You're not even a person of interest, Mr. Baldwine. You were down at the police station when your father was killed." Merrimack shrugged. "So you have nothing to hide."

"I'll get back to you." Lane returned to the door and opened it wide. "Now, if you don't mind, I'm going to go have breakfast."

Merrimack took his sweet time walking over to the exit. "I'll just go and get a warrant. I'll still get access."

"Then this doesn't present you with a problem, does it."

The detective stepped over the threshold. "Who are you protecting, Mr. Baldwine?"

Something about the look in the man's face suggested Merrimack knew exactly who Lane was worried about.

"Have a wonderful day," Lane said as he shut Easterly's door on that knowing smile.

*A*s Gin inspected her throat in her dressing room's mirror, she decided the bruises were faded enough such that, with a little make-up, no one was going to notice them.

"Marls." She sat down in the padded chair she used when she was getting done up. "Where is Tammy? I'm waiting in here."

Her suite of rooms was done in shades of white. White silk drapes hanging from white-sashed antique windows. White wall-to-wall carpet thick as frosting on a cupcake in the bedroom and white marble with gold veining in the bath. She had an all-white bed that was like sleeping on a cloud and this walk-in dressing/closet enclave was nothing but mirrors and more of that carpeting. Lighting was provided by crystal chandeliers and crystal sconces that dangled like Harry Winston earrings from key vantage points—but the fixtures were the new ones, not that old, distorted Baccarat stuff downstairs and elsewhere.

She had beyond had it with stodgy Orientals and oil paintings that were like dark stains on the walls.

"Marls!"

This dressing area was a connector between her bathing space and where her clothes hung, and she had long used it, even before the quarter-of-a-million-dollar overhaul, as her prep area. There was a professional hairdressers' set-up for the cutting, coloring, and washing of her hair, a make-up station to rival the Chanel counter at Saks in Manhattan, and enough perfume bottles, lotions and potions to put goop.com in the shade.

There was even a long window overlooking the back gardens in case they wanted to see anything in natural light. Or look at some flowers. Whatever.

Tapping her manicured fingertips on the chrome arm, she twisted the chair around with her bare foot. "Marls! We're leaving in a half hour for the courthouse. Come on! Call her!"

"Yes, ma'am," her maid flustered from the suite proper.

Tammy was *the* make-up artist in town, and she always booked Gin ahead of her other clients for several reasons: One, Gin tipped well; two, the woman got to say that she did Gin's make-up; and three, Gin allowed Tammy to attend the parties at Easterly and elsewhere as if she were actually a guest.

While Gin waited, she inspected her make-up collection, the lot of it fanning out in a professionally mounted display, the complete compliment of MAC eye shadows and blushes a child's playground of colorful trouble, the rolling tables of foundations, beauty treatments, and brushes looking like something you might need a PhD to operate. In front of her, a twin set of theater lights went down both sides of the mirror, and overhead, there was a set of track lighting you could change the hue of, depending on whether you wanted to see the reds, yellows, or blues of a given hair color or make-up look.

Directly behind her, hanging on a chrome hook, her "wedding dress" such as it was, looked terribly plain. Nothing but an Armani suit with an asymmetrical collar—and the thing was white, because yes, she was the damn bride.

Nude Stuart Weitzman slingbacks were lined up underneath it.

And on a pullout shelf, a dark blue velvet Tiffany's box that was worn on all four of its corners sheltered the massive Art Deco pin that her grandmother had received upon her marriage to E. Curtinious Bradford in 1926.

The debate was whether she was going to take the two halves off its pin backing and do a Bette Davis, or if she was going to put it off to one side as a whole piece on that dramatic collar.

"Marls—"

In the mirror, her maid appeared in the doorway looking as twitchy as a mouse about to make a bad move with a trap, her cell phone in her palm. "She's not coming."

Gin slowly turned the chair around even further. "I beg your pardon."

Marls put up the phone as if that proved anything. "I just spoke to her. She said . . . she's not coming."

"Did she indicate exactly why?" Even though with a cold rush, Gin knew. "What was her reason?"

"She didn't say."

That little bitch.

"Fine, I'll do it my damn self. You may go."

Gin hit the make-up like a pro, a hypothetical conversation with Tammy lighting up her temper as she imagined telling that—what was the word . . . feckless—that feckless little whore who Gin had been nothing but good to for all these years . . . all those galas Tammy had been comped on . . . that fucking cruise through the Mediterranean last year where the only thing the woman had had to do for her luxury fucking berth was slap some mascara on Gin every day—oh, and then what about those ski trips to Aspen? And now that woman doesn't show up . . .

Thirty minutes of barely coherent internal monologue'ing later, Gin had her face, her suit and that pin on, her hair cascading over her shoulders, those slingbacks giving her that extra bit of height. The make-up counter had not fared nearly as well as she had. There were brushes, tubes of mascara, and false eyelashes scattered everywhere. A pick-up-sticks mess of eye pencils. And she'd broken one of her powder compacts, the flesh-colored cake cracked and disintegrated all over the rolling table.

Marls would clean it up.

Gin walked out into the bedroom, picked up the pale, quilted Chanel shoulder bag from her bureau, and opened her bedroom door.

Richard was waiting in the hallway. "You're six minutes late."

"And you can tell time. Congratulations."

As she kicked up her chin, she started by him and was not surprised when he grabbed her arm and yanked her about.

"Do *not* keep me waiting."

"You know, I've heard they have effective drug therapies for OCD. You could try cyanide, for instance. Or hemlock—I believe we have some on the property? Rosalinda solved that mystery for us quite readily—"

Two doors down, Lizzie came out of Lane's suite. The woman was dressed for work, in khaki shorts and a black polo with Easterly's crest on it. With her hair pulled back in another of her rubber bands and no make-up on, she looked enviously young.

"Good morning," she said as she approached.

Her eyes stayed forward, as if she were walking the streets of New York City, determined not to make trouble or seek it out.

"Are you still on the payroll," Richard said, "or is he no longer cutting checks to you now that you're not just bringing flowers to his bedroom?"

Lizzie showed no reaction to that. "Gin, you look beautiful as always."

And she just kept going.

In her wake, Gin narrowed her eyes at Richard. "Don't speak to her like that."

"Why? She's neither staff nor family, is she. And given your money situation, cutting costs is very appropriate."

"She is *not* up for discussion or dissection. You leave her alone. Now, let's get this over with."

THIRTY-SIX

$\mathscr{A}$s Lizzie descended the main staircase, she was shaking her head. Gin . . . defending her. Who would have thought that would ever happen?

And no, she wasn't going down to the mall to get BFFL bracelets for the pair of them. But the not-so-subtle back-up was a lot easier to handle than the condescension and not-at-all-subtle ridicule that had gone on before.

Down in the foyer, she headed around to the back of the house. It was time to do fresh bouquets—with so many late-spring flowers blooming, there was no florist cost, and creating something beautiful was going to make her feel like she was doing work to improve things.

Even if she was the only one who noticed.

Entering the staff hallway, she went down toward Rosalinda's old office and Mr. Harris's suite of rooms—

She didn't make it through to the kitchen.

Outside the butler's residence, there was a line-up of suitcases. Some photographs and books in a box. A rolling rack that suspended a bunch of suit bags.

Putting her head through the open door, she frowned. "Mr. Harris?"

The butler came out of the bedroom beyond. Even in the midst of his apparent move, he was dressed in one of his suits, his hair gelled into place, his clean-shaven face looking as if he had put a light layer of make-up on it.

"Good day," he clipped.

"Are you going somewhere?"

"I've taken another position."

"What?"

"I'm moving on. I am being picked up in approximately twenty minutes."

"Wait, and you're not giving notice?"

"My check bounced at the bank this morning. Your boyfriend, or whomever he is to you, and his family owe me two thousand nine hundred eighty-seven dollars and twenty-two cents. I believe failure of payment is grounds for me to redact the clause in my contract requiring me to give notice."

Lizzie shook her head. "You can't just leave like this."

"Can't I? I would suggest you follow my example, but you seem to be inclined to get further involved, not less so, with this family. At least one can guess that you are emotionally vested at a proper level. Otherwise, your self-destruction would be laughable."

As Lizzie turned away, Mr. Harris said, "Do tell Lane I'm leaving my resignation letter here on the butler's desk. And try not to depart on a snit, will you."

Out in the hall, Lizzie smiled at the man as she picked up his box of things. "Oh, I'm not in a snit—or whatever you call it. I'm going to help you get out of this house. And I'm more than happy to tell him where to find your letter. I hope it has your new address on it, or at the very least a phone number. You're still on the Charlemont Metro Police Department's interviewee list."

*F*ine, I'll come to you, Lane thought as he pulled the Porsche in between the gates of Samuel T.'s farm.

The lane proceeded down an allée of trees, which had been planted seventy-five years ago by Samuel T.'s great-grandparents. The thick, rough-barked trunks supported broad branches of spectacular green leaves, and a dappling shade was thrown across the pale little pebbles of the driveway. Off in the distance, centered among the fields that rolled with grace, the Lodges' farmhouse was not rustic in the slightest. Elegant, of perfect proportion, and almost as old as Easterly, the clapboard box had a hip roof and a wraparound porch to end all porches.

After Lane parked next to the old Jaguar, he got out and went to the front door, which was wide open. Knocking on its screen, he called out, "Samuel T.?"

The interior of the house was dark, and as he helped himself and walked in, he liked the smell of the place. Lemon. Old wood. Something sweet like fresh cinnamon buns that have been homemade in the kitchen.

"Samuel T.?"

Some kind of rustling got his attention, and he tracked the sound, walking into the library—

"Oh, shit!"

Pulling a fast pivot from the doorway, he turned away from the image of a very naked woman sitting on Samuel T. on a leather sofa.

"I knocked," Lane called out.

"It's okay, old man."

Samuel T. didn't seem bothered in the slightest, and the blond was solidly in that camp, too: From what Lane could tell in his very, very peripheral vision, she didn't bother to even get dressed. Then again, maybe her clothes were in another part of the house. Out on the lawn. Hanging from a tree.

"Wait for me upstairs," Samuel T. ordered.

The woman murmured something, and there was the sound of a kiss. Then the model—because she was that good-looking and that tall—sauntered by in one of Samuel T.'s business shirts.

"Hi," she said in a voice that was like whiskey, smooth and probably heady to a lot of guys.

"Yup, good-bye," Lane said as he ignored her and went in to join his friend.

Samuel T. was pulling a black silk robe closed and sitting up with a blurry expression. As he rubbed his messy hair and yawned, he looked outside. "So it's morning, I see. Where has the night gone."

"On a scale of one to ten, where one is Sunday church and ten is the last frat party you were at, how drunk are you currently?"

"Actually, I was typically drunk in church on Sundays, too. But I'd give me a six. Unless I have to take a field sobriety test. Then maybe a seven and a half."

Lane sat down and picked up an empty bottle of Bradford Family Reserve off the floor. "At least you're drinking the good stuff and remaining loyal."

"Always. Now, what can I do you for? And bear in mind, I am over the legal limit, so please don't make the request too difficult."

Rolling the bottle back and forth in his hands, Lane eased back in the chair. "Detective Merrimack showed up first thing this morning. I called you right away."

"I am sorry." Samuel T. pointed to the ceiling. "I think I was with her sister at that time."

Lane rolled his eyes but didn't judge. He'd gone through that man-whore phase in his own life, and though it had seemed fun at the time . . . he wouldn't trade any of it for what he had with Lizzie.

"They want access to the security tapes from the estate."

"Not a surprise." Samuel T. rubbed the stubble on his jaw. "Did you allow them? Where is the security room, by the way?"

"There are two of them. A monitoring room in the staff hallway at Easterly, and then the real nuts and bolts of the system in the business center. And no, I didn't. I told them to get a warrant."

Abruptly, Samuel T. seemed stone-cold sober. "Any particular reason? And I'd like to remind you that I am your attorney. It may technically be for your divorce, but unless you're actively planning to commit a crime, I can't be subpoenaed to testify against you, so please speak freely."

Lane focused on the label on the bourbon bottle, tracing the famous ink drawing of Easterly's front expanse.

"Lane, what's on the footage?"

"I don't know."

"What do you fear is on it?"

"My brother. And maybe someone else. Taking my father alive."

Samuel T. just blinked once. Which was a sign that he'd thought the same thing. Or maybe an indication of that blood alcohol level of his. "You talk to Edward about this?"

"No." Lane shook his head. "I'm currently pretending that I'm just being paranoid."

"How's that workin' for ya?"

"Well enough." Lane exhaled a curse. "So can I do anything else to keep them away?"

"They're absolutely going to come back at you with a warrant." Samuel T. shrugged. "They have enough probable cause with what you found in the dirt. If you'd wanted to keep them away, my advice would have been to not call them in the first place."

"Obstruction of justice much, Counselor? And believe me, don't think I haven't wished I'd kept quiet. Oh, and get this. They found that my father had terminal lung cancer. He was going to die anyway—which is just one more reason to support the suicide theory. Provided you forget about the piece of him that got buried under my mother's window."

The pitter-patter of sexy bare feet got louder and then stopped in the entryway to the room.

But Samuel T. shook his head at yet another woman. "I'm not done here."

"Oh, my God," she said, "is that—"

"A friend of mine? Yes, he is. Now, please excuse us."

As the lady disappeared, Lane said, "How many are in this house?"

"Five? Maybe six? There was a cheerleading thing at the Kentucky Convention Center downtown. All of them are coaches, don't worry."

"Only you, Samuel T."

"Untrue. You've had your moments as well."

"So how's the self-medicating going? Is it distracting you from what my sister is doing right now?"

The attorney looked away. Fast.

When there was only silence, Lane cursed. "I wasn't being an ass-hole, I swear. I was just talking."

"I know." That stare swung back around. "Is she really marrying him? Wait, isn't that a song? Is she really goin' ouuuuuut with him . . ."

"Yes, they're down at the courthouse now."

"So it's done," Samuel T. said absently.

"You know Gin, though. Her version of marriage is going to be a revolving door, and not because she's going shopping. Although with Richard and his money, she'll be going shopping, too."

Samuel T. nodded. "Yes. Too true."

"But, man, do they argue."

"I'm sorry?"

"The pair of them go at it. You can hear them through the walls, and Easterly was built to last, if you get what I mean."

Samuel T. frowned. After a moment, he said, "You know what the real problem with your sister is?"

"She has a number of them. You want to give me some direction as to which sector of life you're focusing on?"

"The problem with your sister . . ." Samuel T. tapped his temple. "Is that as flawed as she is, no one ever compares to her."

That's how I feel about my Lizzie, Lane thought.

Well, except his Lizzie had no flaws.

"Samuel," he whispered sadly.

"Oh, I can hear the pity in your voice."

"Gin is a tough case."

"As am I, my dear friend. As am I." The attorney sat forward. "Annnnnd we're going to chalk this little interchange"—Samuel T. motioned between the pair of them—"to my being seriously drunk off my ass. If you ever bring it up again, I will deny it. I also may well not remember us talking about this at all. And that would be a blessing."

"Wow, hardcore for a six on the drunk scale."

"I may be underestimating things." On that note, Samuel T. reached over to a side table and poured more bourbon into a rocks glass. "Back to your security camera issue. They're going to get in and see what's there, and moreover, they will notice if anything is missing or altered with. I advise you not to try to tamper with any of the footage."

"And yet you suggested I keep quiet about what was in that ivy bed?"

"But the difference is that if you hadn't called them in at that time, they would never have known. If you try to splice anything on those recordings, however, or shadow the footage, change or delete it, they will be able to tell. It's one thing to pretend something was never found. It's an entirely different prospect altogether to try to fool their IT department when you're a layman and they have a geek squad full of people who are members of Anonymous in their spare time."

Lane got up and went to the windows. The glass in the panes was the same as Easterly's, the beautiful farmland beyond wavy and spotted thanks to the bubbles in the antique squares.

"You know," he said, "when Edward was down in South America, in the hands of those bastards? I didn't sleep for a week. It was from the time between when the ransom demand came in and when he was finally rescued and brought back to the States." Memories from the past became like the panes of the old glass, obscuring what was in front of him. "When we were growing up in that house, Edward protected us from Father. Edward was always in charge. He always knew what to do. If I had been kidnapped down there? He would have come and saved me if the roles had been reversed. He would have flown down to that jungle and machete'ed his own way in if he'd had to."

"Your brother was—*is*, excuse me—your brother is a quality man."

"I couldn't sleep because I couldn't do the same for him. And it ate me alive."

It was a while before Samuel T. spoke.

"You can't save him now, Lane. If he did what you think he did . . . and there's video evidence of it? You're not going to be able to save him."

Lane turned around and cursed. "My father deserved it, okay? My father fucking deserved what came to him. He should have been thrown off a fucking bridge years ago."

Samuel T. put his palms up. "Don't think that hasn't occurred to me as well. And yes, your brother had all the justification in the world—in a *Game of Thrones* scenario. Kentucky homicide law begs to differ, however, and it is going to win in this situation. Self-defense only counts if you currently have a knife to your throat or a gun to your head."

"I wish I'd found that fucking finger. I would have just piled the earth right back on top of the goddamn thing."

But he couldn't have put Lizzie and Greta in the position of lying to the authorities. Especially not with Richard Pford having come out of the house with Gin as he had. That bastard would use his own mother if it got him somewhere.

"You know . . ." Samuel T.'s face assumed a philosophical expression. "What your brother should have done was invite your father out to the Red & Black. And then shoot him just as he stepped over the threshold."

"I'm sorry?"

"That's the way to kill someone in Kentucky. We've got a homesteader law that says if someone is trespassing, whether or not they are threatening you with a weapon, you have the right to defend your property against them provided they have entered the premises without your permission. Only two caveats. You have to kill them. And they must not be facing the way out or trying to make it to an exit." Samuel T. wagged his index finger. "But that's the way to do it. As long as no one knew your father had been asked to meet him out there? Edward would have gotten away with it."

As Lane stared across at his attorney, Samuel T. waved his hand like he was clearing the air of the words he'd just spoken. "But I'm not advocating that course of action, however. And I'm drunk, as you know."

After a moment, Lane murmured, "Remind me never to come here without a written invitation, Counselor."

THIRTY-SEVEN

*I*n the back of the Phantom Drophead, which had its top up in deference to her hair, Gin sat beside her future husband and looked
out the window. The river was muddy and swollen from the storms of the
afternoon and night before, the waters rising so much, it looked like they
were trying to consume parts of Indiana.

Downtown was up ahead, the skyscrapers glinting in the sunshine, the
asphalt necklaces of highway lanes encircling their steel and glass throats.
There was a little construction to deal with, her father's chauffeur hitting
the brakes every now and again, but the delay wasn't going to cost them
much time.

As they approached the Big Five Bridge, she stared at the span's five
arches, at the cables that suspended the pavement over the water . . . and
remembered the fight she and her father had had over her marrying Richard. She had refused—only to find that she was cut off financially, marooned
on a deserted island of insolvency.

And so she had caved.

And now she was here.

Closing her eyes, she pictured Samuel T. out by the pool during the visitation that had had so few visitors.

"Sign this, would you."

Opening her lids, she glanced across the cream leather seats. Richard was holding out about twenty pages of some kind of document along with one of his black and gold monogrammed Montblanc pens.

"I beg your pardon."

"It's a prenuptial agreement." He jogged both at her. "Sign it."

Gin laughed and looked up at the chauffeur. The uniformed man with his jaunty little cap was about to get a helluva show.

"I'll do no such thing."

"Yes, you will," Richard said.

Staring back out the window, she shrugged. "So turn the car around. Call this off. Do whatever you need to, but I'm not signing away my rights as your wife."

"May I remind you of the distribution help I bring to your company. Given how it's struggling, you're going to need those favorable contracts. And they can disappear fast if I want them to."

"Given how we're struggling, there may not be a Bradford Bourbon Company next year. So your personal fortune is a better bet for me."

He recoiled at that, his thin neck flexing in a way that reminded her of a horse who had been starved. "Have you no shame?"

"Nope."

"Virginia Elizabeth—"

"Even my father never called me that." A Porsche sped by in the breakdown lane, and as it shot past all the stagnating traffic, she realized it was her brother. "Not that I would have found it persuasive if he had."

"This is boilerplate, you know. And if you're not familiar with the term, that means it's very simple. You keep everything that is yours going into the marriage. I keep everything that is mine. And never the twain shall meet or mix."

"Simple, really? Is that why it's the size of *War and Peace*?" She glanced over at him. "And if it was so simple, why didn't you give me a chance to read it and review it with a lawyer first?"

Like Samuel T., for instance. Although she could guess how that would go.

"You don't need to concern yourself with legal jargon."

"Don't I? You might be interested to discover that I've already researched divorce law, and you want to know what I learned?"

"Gin, seriously—"

"I learned that I'm going to be very faithful to you." As he recoiled again, she muttered, "You know, I really should be offended by your surprise. But before you get too excited that I'm respecting you in some way, I've learned that whereas Kentucky is a no-fault state for divorce grounds, evidence of infidelity can be used to reduce spousal support. So those two pilots I fucked the other night are my last forays into infidelity. I will be an honorable wife to you and I encourage you to have me trailed and photographed. Bug my bedroom, my cars, my closet, my underwear. I will give you no opportunity to find fault with me."

She leaned in. "How's that for legal jargon? And you're not going to turn this car around because here's the truth—I'm not signing it, and we're still getting married. Your entire life, you've created nothing. You've done nothing that's your own. You have no respect given to you on your merits, only on your inheritance. You're going to marry me because then you can hold your head up high at cocktail parties and galas. After all, you are still that kid no one picked for teams in elementary school, but you can be the one to tame the great Gin Baldwine. And that will be worth more to your ego than anything I can ever take from your bank account." She smiled sweetly. "So you can take your twelve-pound boilerplate and blow it out your ass, darling."

As his eyes flared with pure murder, she resumed her perusal of the Ohio River. She knew damn well what was coming in her direction when he got home from work later tonight, but in her own way, she was itching to fight it out.

And she was also right.

"Oh, and something else to consider," she murmured as there was the sound of the paperwork getting put back in his briefcase. "Spousal abuse isn't going to play well in divorce court, any more than being a whore does.

You know, all things considered, it's a wonder the pair of us don't get along better."

*L*ane sped along, passing by the line-up of traffic that had bottlenecked going into town on spaghetti junction. At one point, out of the corner of his eyes, he was sure he saw the family Drophead.

No doubt Gin and Richard on the nuptial express.

She was crazy to be marrying that fool, but good luck trying to talk her out of anything. With his sister, criticism merely put a bull's-eye on whatever it was you were suggesting wasn't such a hot idea. Besides, as usual, he had other things to worry about.

The parking garage he was looking for was on the corner of Mohammad Ali and Second Street, and he ditched the 911 in the first spot that wasn't whittled down on both sides by idiots in SUVs who couldn't park straight.

Funny, usually he did the defensive parking thing because he wanted to protect his paint job on principle. Now? He didn't want to have to pay to repair any chips and dents.

Or make any insurance claims that might raise his rates.

And speaking of insurance . . .

Back during the night, when he hadn't been able to sleep, he'd gone downstairs and over to the business center where he'd let his fingers do the walking in the file room. And there, nestled in between senior management's employment contracts—all of which he'd pulled—and the original corporate bylaws—all of which he'd read, with subsequent amendments—as well as a top secret HR file that contained some shocking nuggets of bad behavior . . . there was his father's corporate life insurance policy.

After he'd read through it three times, he'd called the office who had sold the policy and scheduled this happy little confab.

Some things you wanted to do in person.

The Englishman, Battle & Castelson Insurance Company was located on the thirty-second floor of the old National Charlemont Building, and as he stepped out of the elevator at its lofty perch, he found he had an entirely new appreciation for the view.

Considering that he now knew what free falling was actually like.

Ten minutes later, he was in a conference room with a Coke, waiting for—

"I'm sorry to keep you waiting." Robert Englishman, of the Englishman part of the name, came in with a legal pad, a smile, and an air of professionalism. "It's been a crazy morning."

Tell me about it, Lane thought.

Shaking hands. And then there was some conversation of the condolences, catch-up variety. Lane didn't know Englishman very well, but they were the same age, and Lane had always liked him whenever they'd run across each other's paths socially. Robert was the kind of guy who wore golf shorts with whales stitched on them and pink seersucker suits for Derby and perfectly pressed Brooks Brothers navy-and-club-tie get-ups to work—and, no matter what he had on, always seem poised to ride off in a Hacker Craft from the thirties. To a party where Hemingway was stopping. And Fitzgerald was getting drunk in the corner with Zelda.

He was old school meets new school, WASPy without the condescension and prejudice, classically handsome as a Polo Ralph Lauren ad yet down to earth as a sitcom father.

As the pleasantries died off, Lane pushed the glass of fizz to the side and took the folded documents out of the breast pocket of his linen jacket. "I thought I might come down here and talk to you about this."

Robert took the pages. "Which policy is it?"

"My father's through the Bradford Bourbon Company. I'm a beneficiary along with my brother and sister."

With a frown, the man started to review the terms.

"Contrary to news reports," Lane interrupted, "we believe he may have been murdered. I know that there is a clause excluding payment in the event of suicide by the policyholder, but it's my understanding that provided any beneficiary is not found to be the—"

"I'm so sorry, Lane." Robert closed the documents and put his hand on them. "But this policy was canceled for nonpayment about six months ago. We tried repeatedly to get in touch with your father, but he never returned our calls or responded to our inquiries. MassMutual let it go—and it was a key man term policy. There was no equity building up in it."

As Lane's phone went off, he thought, well, there was seventy-five million down the drain.

"Is there something else we can help you with?"

"Were there any other policies? Personal ones, maybe? I only found this because I went through the corporate files. My father was fairly closemouthed about his affairs."

Personal and professional.

"There were two personal ones. One was a term life, much smaller than this one." Robert tapped the documents again. "But he didn't act on the renewal when it came up a couple of months ago."

Of course, Lane thought. Because he couldn't have passed the physical, and he'd known that.

"And the other?" he prompted.

Robert cleared his throat. "Well, the other one was to benefit a third party. And that third party has come forward. I'm afraid I can't disclose to you their identity or any information about the policy because you are not incidental to it."

Lane's phone rang again. And for a split second, he wanted to throw the thing at the bank of glass windows across the table.

"I totally understand," he said as he took the document, refolded it, and put it back in his inner pocket. "Thank you for your time."

"I really wish I could be more helpful." Robert got to his feet. "I swear, I tried to get your father to act, but he just wouldn't. Even though he knew it would have been to the benefit of his family."

The story of the guy's life.

Oh, Father, Lane thought. If you weren't already dead . . .

THIRTY-EIGHT

*W*hile Lane was downtown checking into the insurance policy issue, trying to drum up some money, Jeff was waiting for the guy's hopefully triumphant return out front at Easterly, the sun on his face, the stone steps under his ass functioning very nicely as bun warmers. Just as he was beginning to think about the merits of Coppertone, he heard the Porsche's engine at the base of the hill. Moments later, Lane tooled to a stop and got out.

Jeff didn't bother asking. He could read that face. "So it's a no-go."

"Nothing."

"Damn it." Jeff rose to his feet and brushed at the seat of his pants. "Listen, we need to talk."

"Can you give me one minute?" When Jeff nodded, the guy said, "Wait here. I'll be right back."

A minute and a half later, Lane re-emerged from the mansion. "Come with me."

Jeff frowned. "Is that a hammer?"

"Yup, and a nail."

"You're going to fix something? No offense, but you're not exactly the handyman type. I should know. I'm not, either, and I've also lived with you for how long?"

Lane went back to his car and leaned over the passenger-side door. Springing the glove box, he—

"Wait, is that a gun?" Jeff demanded.

"Yup. Boy, you're observant. Come on."

"Where are we going? And will I be walking on my own at the end of this?"

Lane headed across the courtyard, but not in any direction that made sense. Unless you were going out into the woods. To shoot an old roommate of yours.

"Lane, I asked you a question." But Jeff followed before he got an answer. "Lane."

"Of course you'll be walking."

"I'm really not interested in becoming your Big Pussy."

"That makes two of us."

As Lane breached the tree line and continued on, going deeper into the maples and oaks, Jeff stayed with the guy because he just wanted to know what the fuck he was doing.

Another fifty yards or so in, Lane finally stopped and looked around. "This'll do."

"If you turn on me and ask me to start digging my own grave with my hands? Then our relationship really is over."

But Lane just went over to a tree that was dead, its skeletal branches and partially hollow trunk at odds with the verdant everything-else-that-was-around. Putting the handgun in the outer pocket of his linen suit jacket, he took out a sheaf of papers . . . and nailed them to the rotting bark.

Then he walked back to where Jeff had come to a halt, put two fingers in his mouth and blew a whistle so shrill, Jeff's third-great-grandmother heard it in her grave. Up in New Jersey.

"Fore!" the guy yelled.

"Isn't that for golf—"

Pop! Pop! Poppoppoppoppopop!

Lane was an excellent shot, the bullets shredding the paperwork into a flurry of white pieces that fell to the decaying leaves and bright green undergrowth.

When that gun muzzle was finally lowered, Jeff looked over. "Man, you Southern fruit loops with your NRA. Just out of curiosity, what was that?"

"My father's seventy-five-million-dollar key man term life insurance policy through MassMutual. Turns out he stopped paying the premiums so it woke up dead."

"Okay. Good to know. FYI, most people would merely throw the thing out. Just sayin'."

"Yeah, but this was so much more satisfying, and I've about had it with bad news." Lane turned around. "So you wanted to tell me something?"

"You got any more bullets in that thing?"

"Nope. Emptied the clip."

Lane pulled some fancy moves with the gun and produced some kind of slide-thingy that, yup, appeared to be empty. Not that Jeff would know what any of it was.

"So?" Lane prompted.

"I've decided to accept your little job offer, John Wayne."

*A*s his old college roommate said the magic words, Lane's sense of relief was so great, he closed his eyes and sagged. "Thank you, sweet Jesus—"

"And I found you two point five million dollars—"

Lane pulled a snatch and grab on his old friend, dragging Jeff in for a hard embrace. Then he shoved the guy back. "I knew if I waited long enough, there had to be some good news coming. I *knew* it."

"Well, don't get too excited." Jeff stepped back. "There are conditions."

"Name them. Whatever they are."

"Number one, I've fixed the news leak."

Lane blinked. "What?"

"Tomorrow morning you'll be reading in the paper that what looked like improperly diverted funds were actually part of a diversification project sanctioned by the chief executive officer, William Baldwine. The projects have failed, but poor business decisions are not illegal in a privately held corporation."

Lane ran the words back and forth in his head a couple of times just to make sure he had them right. "How are you managing that?"

Jeff checked his watch. "If you really want to know, get me a car at five o'clock. And not your kind of car—a nothing special. I'll show you."

"Deal. But yeah, wow."

"And I've decided I want to invest in your little bourbon company." The guy shrugged. "If there's a federal investigation, with all that negative press? It's going to slow sales in this moralistic, judge-everyone-and-everything Facebook and Twitter era. And what I need, if I'm going to turn the organization around, is time. Income from operations gives me time. An investigation takes away my time. And you're right. Your family are the only shareholders. If the company is in debt, goes into bankruptcy, fails? Your father fucked you all, no one else."

"I'm so glad you're seeing things my way. But what about the two and a half million for the board members?"

Jeff put his hand in his pocket and held out a small, folded check. "Here it is."

Lane took the thing and opened it up. Looked at his friend. "This is your account."

"I told you, I'm investing in your business. Those are live funds, and I made it out directly to you so you can keep this incentive thing off the corporate books for now. Pay them privately."

"I don't know how to thank you for this."

"Wait for it. That part's coming. I've finished my analysis and I've accounted for all the money—and the total diverted, including that loan from Prospect Trust to your personal household account, is one hundred seventy-three million, eight hundred and seventy-nine thousand, five hundred and eleven dollars. And eighty-two cents. The eighty-two cents is the real kicker, of course."

Shit. And that was in addition to the hundred million missing from his mother's trust.

The magnitude of it all was so great, Lane's body felt the impact even though the losses were a mental concept. But at least the final bottom had been found. "I was hoping . . . well, it is what it is."

"I am prepared to come on board on an interim basis and sort everything out. I'm going to want to get rid of your senior management, all of them—"

"I read through their employment contracts last night. There's a gag clause in every one of them. So we can fire them for not catching the improper diversion of funds, which is cause, and even if the news reports say something else is going on, there's nothing they can say otherwise. Not unless they want some back-breaking penalties, and they won't. Those bastards will be looking for jobs, and no one hires snitches."

"They could go off the record."

"I'd find that out. I promise you."

Jeff nodded briefly. "Fair enough. My goal is to keep the trains running on time, keep the money coming in, steady the ship. 'Cuz right now, you might as well be in a hostile takeover for what morale has got to be like. And we don't have the wiggle room for delays in shipments, account collections, product order processing. The employees are going to need positive motivation."

"Amen to that."

Lane turned away and started walking through the woods to the house.

"Where are you going?" Jeff called out.

"Back to my car." Lane just kept going, some paranoia that Jeff would change his mind making him antsy. "You and I are going down to headquarters right now—"

"And in return, I want an annual salary of two point five million dollars—and one percent of the entire company."

The words were spoken like they were bombs being dropped, but Lane just swept the air with his hand as he continued to march out of the woods.

"Done," he said over his shoulder.

Jeff grabbed ahold of Lane's arm and spun him back around. "Did you hear what I said? One percent of the company."

"Did you hear what I said? Done."

Jeff shook his head and pushed his glasses up higher on his nose. "Lane. Your company, even in its dire straits, is probably worth three to four billion dollars if it were up for acquisition. I'm asking for between thirty and forty million here, depending on valuation. For an initial investment of two point five."

"Jeff." He echoed that strident tone. "Your money's all I've got in this cesspool of debt and I don't know how to run a company. You want one percent to be interim CEO? Fine. Dandy. Have fucking at it."

When Lane started walking again, Jeff fell in step. "You know, if I'd had any idea you were going to be such a pushover, I'd have asked for three percent."

"And I'd have paid you five."

"Are we doing a scene from *Pretty Woman*?"

"I don't want to think like that, if you don't mind. Hostile work environment. You could sue me. Oh, and there's one more thing on our side." They stepped out of the tree line and onto the manicured grass. "I'm having the board appoint me as chairman. That way it'll be easier for the both of us to get the work done."

"I like your style, Bradford." Jeff nodded at the gun. "But I think we should leave that in the glove compartment. As your new CEO, I'd like to come in on a conciliatory note, if you don't mind. The second amendment's great and all, but there are some fundamental management techniques I'd like to try first."

"No problem, boss. No problem at all."

THIRTY-NINE

With a relieved sigh, Lizzie splashed cool water on her hot face. She was so glad to be out of the sun and up in the suite she was sharing with Lane, the dry AC'ed air wicking the sweat from her overheated body. It had been a long day working in the gardens, she and Greta attacking the beds around the pool with a stress-related gusto that was warranted, but ultimately useless except as it related to removing weeds. Neither of them had said anything about the visitation, nor had the subject of the engagement gotten much coverage.

Greta remained suspicious of Lane and nothing except time was going to change that.

Reaching blindly for a towel, she pushed the soft fibers into her forehead, cheeks and chin, and when she looked up, Lane was standing behind her.

Man, he looked good in that linen jacket and open-collared shirt, his aviators tucked into the breast pocket, his hair ruffled in a way that meant he'd been driving around with the top down. And he smelled of his cologne. Yummy.

"You are a sight for sore eyes," he said with a smile. "Come here."

"I'm stinky."

"Never."

Putting the towel aside, she went into his arms. "You actually look happy."

"I've got some good news. But I also have an adventure for you."

"Tell me, tell me—"

"How'd you like to go spying with me and Jeff?"

Lizzie laughed and stepped back. "Okay, not what I was expecting. But heck yeah. I'm down with espionage."

Lane shrugged out of his jacket and disappeared into the closet. When he came back out, he had a golf visor, a U of C baseball cap, and a ski hat with earflaps.

"I'll take what's behind door number two," she said, going for the cap.

Lane slapped that godforsaken ski-mare on his head. "We need to go in your truck, though."

"No problem. As long as I'm not the one who has to look like Sasquatch."

"That bad?"

"Worse."

Lane struck a pose, one hand on his hip, the other up in the air. "Maybe I can borrow one of my sister's Derby hats?"

"Perfect, that's *so* much less noticeable."

She went into the closet and came back out. "There was this other Eagles hat right there."

"Yeah, but I wanted you to think I was cute."

Lizzie put her arms around his neck and leaned in to him. "I always think you're cute. And sexy."

As his hands moved down onto her waist, he growled. "Nowisnotthetime. Nowisnotthetime . . ."

"What?"

He kissed her deeply, holding her against his body even with the hats in his hands. And then he cursed and stepped back. "Jeff's waiting."

"Well, come on, then! Let's go."

It felt good to laugh, to be free, to see him look for once like the whole weight of the world wasn't on his shoulders. And yes, okay, maybe now he was sexually frustrated, but even that was kind of cheerful in a way.

"So what's going on?" she asked as they went out into the corridor.

"Well, I'm just back from corporate headquarters, and . . ."

By the time they bottomed out in the foyer, she was doing a jaw drop. "So you're making some progress. And you're chairman of the board?"

"You're with a man who actually has a job. For the first time in his life."

As he put his palms up for high fives, she smacked 'em a good one. "You know, I loved you even when you were just a poker player."

"The technical term is card shark. And yes, I realize it isn't a paying gig"—he held a finger up—"but it's going to involve a lot of work. And I even have an office downtown. Or here. Or whatever."

"And now you're a spy, too."

"Double-oh Baldwine." They walked over to his old roommate who was waiting by the door. "And here is the Jeff to my Mutt in crime. Or, well, not crime, exactly. Fiscal responsibility."

Lizzie gave Jeff a quick hug. "So what are we doing, boys?"

Minutes later, they were crammed into the front seat of her Toyota truck, heading down Easterly's hill on the staff road, all with the hats on. She was behind the wheel with Lane stuck in the middle on the hump, his head almost hitting the ceiling.

"Go to the bottom and hide around the last greenhouse facing out," Lane said. "And hurry. It's quarter of five already."

"Who are we waiting for?"

Jeff spoke up from the far side. "If I'm right, the upstairs maid. Tiphanii."

"What?" She twisted around. "You guys think she's stealing the Charmin or something?"

"Not even close—"

"Wait, that's her car!" Lizzie nodded to the rearview. "Behind us."

"She's leaving early," Lane said with a curse. "Can I dock her fourteen minutes of pay?"

"As someone who knows your financial situation?" Jeff nodded. "Yes, you really should."

Lizzie shook her head. "Let me get this straight. You're going to all this trouble just to see if she's working till five?"

"Keep going," Lane said. "And we'll see which way she turns. We need to follow her."

"Any idea where she's going?" Lizzie came up to River Road. "Wait, I know what to do."

Heading to the right, she took her sweet time accelerating—which with four hundred extra pounds of man in the cab was not just a strategy.

Lizzie whistled under her breath. "Perfect, she's going to the left! Hold on, gentlemen."

As the boys braced themselves, she sped up as quickly as she could, shot down a dirt lane and pulled a road cartwheel, the rear of the truck skidding around as she punched the brakes and wrenched the wheel. Someone got nailed a good one and cursed, but she was too busy shooting back out to River Road—so that Tiphanii's little Saturn was now in the lead.

By the time they hit the light by the Shell station at Dorn Avenue, two cars had come between them. Tiphanii took a left and headed up the four-laner . . . and then stayed on it across Broadsboro Lane to Hilltop, the Halloween road, where the houses went all out during October. Over the railroad tracks and a right on Franklin, which was home to all kinds of little shops and cafés that were locally owned.

When Tiphanii parallel-parked four blocks up, Lizzie went by her, the three of them staring out the front windshield like absolutely nothing was doing—with their hats down low.

A trio of bobbleheads without the bobbling.

At the next light, she pitched an abrupt left through an orange signal and hurried down the alley behind the restaurants and shops. When she thought she'd gone far enough, she punched the brakes and lucked out by finding a spot right there.

"Let's do this," she clipped as she canned the engine and popped her door. "And get ready to say hi to the dogs."

"What?" Jeff asked as he got out. "Dogs?"

Lane gave her a salute when he was free of the cab. "Whatever she says, we're gonna do."

Lizzie led the way through an alley that was barely bigger than her shoulders. Just before she got to the end, she stopped short. "Oh, my God, there she is."

Across Franklin Ave., Tiphanii got out of her beater and jogged through the traffic. In the shadows, Lizzie leaned forward a little so she could see where the woman was heading.

"Knew it. She's going into Blue Dog. Come on."

Lizzie jumped out into the pedestrians who were chilling their way down the sidewalk, and a mere fifteen feet later, she bent over an English bulldog who, she learned by the collar's tag, was named Bicks. Meanwhile, Tiphanii was just inside the café, right in front of its plate-glass window.

She was shaking hands with a tall African-American woman.

"That's the reporter I met with," Lane said as he and Jeff clustered around Bicks. All three of them waved back at Bicks's apparent owner, who was smiling and nodding at them from inside the consignment shop next door. "And yup, she's giving her something. Some papers."

Jeff nodded. "Bingo."

"What's the paperwork?" Lizzie asked.

Jeff spoke in hushed tones as he shifted over to pet a mutt named Jolene. "It's a false report I left out for her last night. There's a copier down the hall in the second-story study. All she had to do was sneak out, make the xeroxes, and put the document back where she found it. Work of two minutes."

"She spent the night?" Lizzie said. "With you?"

"Ah . . ."

Lizzie laughed. "I'm asking as part of our assignment here, not because I'm judging."

As the guy blushed, she was reminded of how much she liked him.

"Okay, yes, she did," he said, pushing up his glasses. "That was the plan. And we need that information to hit the airways, thank you very much."

Lane leaned in and kissed her. "Good work getting us here, and now if you'll excuse me for a minute."

"Where are you going?"

"I'm going to go say hi to that reporter. LaKeesha and I are old friends after she grilled me for two hours. And listen, she hasn't done anything wrong. It's not her fault that a source has come to her with information they found somewhere—and what better way to further develop our relationship than to tell her about all the shake-ups and our promotions. Jeff, I'm going to set up a meeting between the two of you for seven o'clock tonight. I don't want her first impression of you to be when you look like a hobo. You need a shave and a fresh suit before you represent my company to the press. Oh, and it's time to fire Tiphanii with two *i*'s at the end. Just not in front of my good buddy the reporter."

"Let me take care of that," Lizzie said.

"That would be a huge help."

After he kissed her again, he straightened to his full height and walked into the café.

Through the big glass window, Lizzie watched the two women turn to him and Tiphanii stumble back. But Lane was all smiles, shaking hands, talking. The reporter looked at him intently—and then Lane turned to the young woman.

He was totally in control of himself, and she could just imagine his level voice, excusing the maid, leaving her on the hot seat.

He's doing it, Lizzie thought with pride.

Her future husband was . . . becoming a leader. A family head. A man, instead of a playboy.

A moment later, Tiphanii came out, but she didn't get far as Jeff stepped in her path. Lizzie thought she might better give them privacy, but as Bicks the bulldog and Jolene stared at the drama, she figured what the heck, so would she.

"Ah . . ." The maid was as red as a tomato. "Jeff. So, um, this is not what it looks like—"

"Oh, come on." The guy shook his head. "Stop. I'll have more respect for you if you don't try to pretend."

"And I'm sorry, Tiphanii," Lizzie said, "but your services are no longer required at Easterly. I'm terminating you effective immediately, and if you're smart, you'll just walk away."

The woman's face changed, growing ugly. "I know things. And not just about the finances. I know a lot of things about what goes on in that house. I'm not the kind of enemy that family needs right now."

"There's a nondisclosure clause in your contract," Lizzie snapped. "I'm aware of this because there's one in mine, too."

"You think I care about that." Tiphanii moved a very expensive bag up onto her shoulder. "You haven't heard the last from me."

As she strode off into traffic, Lizzie shook her head. "That went well."

"Maybe she'll get run over as she crosses—nope, made it. Pity." When Lizzie shot him a look, the guy put up a palm. "I'm from New York. What do you want from me."

FORTY

Half an hour later, Lane was feeling pretty damn good about things as he and Lizzie and Jeff headed back to Easterly in her truck. LaKeesha was dying to meet the new CEO, and the fact that Lizzie had handled Tiphanii? Fantastic.

The bliss didn't last, though. As they crested the rise to the mansion's front door, there was an unmarked police car and a CMP SUV parked in the courtyard.

Merrimack got out of the former before Lizzie even stopped her truck.

"Shit," Lane muttered. "I've got to deal with this."

"I love you," Lizzie said as Jeff got out so Lane could do the same.

"I love you, too." He leaned back in. "I was hoping we could go to Indiana tonight."

"I'm happy to be here or there. Whatever works."

For a moment, he stared into her eyes, drawing strength from her support. And then he kissed her, closed the door and jacked his slacks up.

When he turned around, he had his poker face on. "I am so happy to see you again, Detective."

Merrimack smiled in that way he did and offered his palm as he approached. "Are you?"

"You here for dinner? And who's your friend?"

A plainclothes guy who had pencil neck written all over him shuffled up. "Pete Childe. I'm an investigator."

"And I've got some paperwork for you, Mr. Baldwine," Merrimack said.

"You know Jeff Stern." Lane stepped back for the introduction. "Now, let's check out your grocery list. You remember the eggs and butter?"

As Jeff walked back into the house, Lane passed his eyes over the warrant, even though he didn't know what one was supposed to look like. But come on, it was essentially a coupon for legally trespassing, and there were seals and signatures.

And the thing stated expressly that it was limited to security footage for a period covering the day before through the day after his father's death.

"So I'm not sure you're aware of this," Merrimack said as Lane got to the last page. "But your front door was wide open. I knocked and knocked. Eventually, a maid came down. I also called you a number of times."

"Phone's in the car." Lane walked over to the Porsche and got the thing out of the console. "So, let's get this done, shall we?"

"Lead on."

Lane took the detective and Pete around the side of the mansion and out to the back—and it was the longest walk of his life. Under his poker face, beneath his composure, he was screaming like he was standing at the side of the road as two cars came tearing toward each other on black ice—and yet no matter how loud he yelled, the drivers couldn't, or wouldn't, heed his warning.

But in the back of his mind, since the moment he'd sent Merrimack away, he'd known this reckoning had been coming.

At the business center's rear door, he entered the code and escorted them inside.

"The security for the whole estate is run out of the computers here." He went left down the corridor to where the utilities rooms were. "This is where the motherboard, or whatever you call it, is."

Stopping in front of a steel door that had no signage on it, he entered another code, and after a clunking sound indicated the dead bolt was free, he opened the heavy panel wide.

As the automatic overhead lights came on, he meant to keep talking. Keep moving. But a sudden mental connection shorted him out.

"Mr. Baldwine?"

He shook himself and looked back at the detective. "I'm sorry, what?"

"Is something wrong?"

"Ah, no." He stepped to the side, getting out of the way and indicating the workstation with its bank of monitors and keyboards and rolling chairs. "Have at it."

Pete went Captain Kirk at the set-up, sitting behind the collection of technology like he knew what any of it meant. "So I'll need access to the footage. Can you get me in?"

Lane shook his head to clear it. "I'm sorry?"

"I need a log-in and a password to the network."

"I don't have that."

Merrimack smiled like he'd expected this. "You better get us one. Now."

"Give me a moment, will you?"

Stepping back out into the hall, he went a distance away and palmed his phone. As he stared at the glossy screen, all he could do was shake his head.

Because now he knew what his brother had been doing during the visitation. Damn it.

Taking a deep breath, Lane dialed the Red & Black caretaker's cottage. One ring . . . two rings . . . three rings . . .

"Hello?"

As Edward's voice came over the line, Lane closed his eyes. "Edward."

"Little brother, how are you?"

"I've been better. The police are here with me at the business center.

They have a warrant for the security footage." When there was only silence, he muttered, "Did you hear what I said?"

"Yes. And?"

For a split second, he wanted to tell Edward to grab as much cash as he could, find a car, and get the fuck out of town. He wanted to yell. He wanted to curse.

And he wanted the truth.

But he also needed the lie that everything was okay and his brother hadn't traded a figural prison for a literal one, all in the name of revenge.

Lane cleared his throat. "They need to get into the network so they can copy the files."

"Give them my sign-on details."

What the fuck did you do, Edward? Edward, they're going to find out if you tampered with—

"Having any luck, Mr. Baldwine?"

As Merrimack leaned out of the security room, Lane said into his phone, "Text them to me, okay?"

"You called me on a rotary phone, remember?" Edward's voice was as smooth as always as he recited the details. "You got that?"

"Yes."

"They know where to find me if they have any questions. Is that Merrimack with you? He came out and paid me a visit the other day."

"Yes, he's the detective."

There was a short pause. "It's all going to be okay, little brother. Stop worrying."

And then the call was ended on Edward's side.

Lane lowered his phone. "I have what you need."

Merrimack smiled once again. "I had every faith you'd comply with the order. Was that your brother Edward?"

"Yes."

Merrimack nodded. "Nice guy. Sorry to see him in that condition. Did he tell you I've been out to see him?"

"He did."

"You know, he doesn't really look like you."

Lane stepped around the detective to enter the security monitoring room. "He used to."

Out in Ogden County, at the Red & Black, Edward hung up the receiver on the wall by the kitchen just as Shelby came through the cottage's main door. She was freshly showered, her hair drying across her shoulders, her jeans clean, her short-sleeved shirt blue and white checked.

"What?" she said as she saw his face.

"I'm sorry?"

"Why are you looking at me like that?"

He shook his head. "I'm not. But listen, I want to go out for dinner. And I want you to come with me."

When she just blinked at him, he rolled his eyes. "Fine. I'll be more polite. Please. Come eat with me. I would greatly appreciate your company."

"No, it's not that." She patted her shirt. "I'm not dressed for anything fancy."

"Neither am I, and I'm in the mood for good chicken. So we should go to Joella's."

Limping over to the door, he opened the panels wide. "Are you up for it? Six levels of spice, and each one is a taste of heaven—and that isn't blasphemy."

"Do you want to be asking Moe?"

"Nah, I just want you. To come eat with me, that is."

As he indicated the great outdoors, there was a pause . . . and then Shelby went out first. When she passed by him, he breathed in deep and had to smile a little. She smelled like old-fashioned Prell shampoo, and he wondered where she had gotten the stuff. Did they even make it anymore? Maybe it was a leftover of her father's, or perhaps it had been abandoned by the previous occupant of that apartment she stayed in over at Barn B.

Before Edward followed her out, he snagged the cash he'd left on the corner of the bureau the night Sutton had come and he'd mistaken her for—

Stopping that little cascade of memories, he closed the cottage door and looked up to the sky. For a moment, he paused to measure the wide expanse and the gradation of color from the banked ember glow of the sunset at the west to the velvet blue of early night in the east. Inhaling deeply once again, he smelled the sweet grass and the good earth and something vaguely charcoal-y as if Moe and Joey were grilling burgers out behind a barn.

The feel of the still air on his skin was a kind of benediction.

Strange that he hadn't appreciated it all. And that had been true even when he had been out in the world.

Back then, he had been so focused on work, the company, the competition.

And afterward, he had been mired in too much pain and too much bitterness.

So many missed opportunities.

"Edward?" Shelby said.

"Coming."

Approaching her truck, he went around and opened her door, and though she seemed unfamiliar with the gesture or the idea she would be driven somewhere, she hopped up into the passenger seat. Then he limped in a circle and got behind the wheel.

Starting the engine, he backed out and headed toward town. At first, there were only a few other vehicles on the road with them and he even had to go around a tractor that was putting along at the shoulder. But soon there were proper cars and even some stoplights.

As they came into the suburbs proper, he found himself looking all around, noting changes to storefronts. Neighborhoods. He recognized new styles of cars. Billboards. Plantings on the medians and—

"Oh, my God, they got rid of the White Castle."

"What you say?"

He pointed to a perfectly anonymous new building that housed a bank. "There used to be a White Castle right there. Forever. I went there when I was young on my bike. I'd save up my allowance and buy sliders for my brothers and me. I had to sneak them into the house because I never wanted Miss Aurora to feel like we didn't love her food. Which we did. But I enjoyed, you know, getting them something that made 'em happy. Gin never ate even one of them. She started worrying about getting fat when she was three."

Edward kept quiet about the fact that the trips usually came after their father had gotten the belt out. Nine times out of ten, Max was the one who got that ball rolling, whether it was setting fireworks off from the roof of the garage, or riding a horse in through Easterly's front door, or taking one of the family cars and going four-by-fouring in the corn-fields down below the hill.

He smiled a little to himself. Certainly, in other households, that last one might not have been that big a deal. Rolls-Royces, however, though superior automobiles all the way around, were engineered to go to opera openings and polo matches. Not to try to harvest August corn.

God, he could still picture that brand-new 1995 Corniche IV with a snaggle-toothed grille full of husks and stalks. William Baldwine had been far less than amused to find his new toy ruined—and Max hadn't been able to sit down for a week afterward.

To clear that part of the memory out of the way, he said, "I was pretty impressed with what you did last night."

Shelby looked over. Looked away. "Neb's not so bad. He wants to be in charge and he'll prove it if he has to. Your best bet is to work with him, not to try to get him to do what you want."

Edward laughed—and Shelby's head snapped back around. As she just stared at him, he said, "What?"

"I've never heard you . . . well, anyway."

"Laugh? Yes, you're probably right. But tonight is different. I feel like a weight is off my shoulders."

"Because Neb's going to be okay? Those were just superficial cuts, and them front legs'll be all right. It could've been worse."

"Thanks to you."

"Don't mean nothing."

"You know . . . I love that stallion. I can remember when I bought him. It was right after I got out of the rehab hospital here. I was in so much pain." Edward stopped at a light by a big white church with a brass steeple. "My right leg felt like it was breaking over and over again, every time I put weight on it. And I'd been on so many opiates, my digestive tract had completely shut down." As things went green, he hit the gas and glanced over. "TMI, but opiate-induced constipation is nearly as bad as whatever you're taking the drugs for. God, I had never before appreciated basic bodily functions. No one does. You walk around in these bags of flesh that are vehicles for our gray matter, taking it all for granted when nothing is wrong, bitching about work and how hard it is, or—"

Edward did a double take on his passenger: Shelby was still staring across the seat at him, and so help her God, her jaw was totally lax.

She'd looked less surprised when she'd been dealing with that stallion.

"What?" he asked.

"Are you drunk? Should you be driving?"

"No. Last drink I had was . . . last night? Or before that. I've lost track. Why?"

"You're talkin' a spell."

"Do you want me to stop?"

"No, not at all. It's just . . . a nice change."

Edward came up to an intersection. And had to reach deep to remember which way to go. "I think it's down here on the left."

They went by a strip mall with a jeweler's, a hair salon, a Pilates studio and a lamp store in it. And then there was a stretch of apartment buildings that were three stories high and made of brick, with fleets of cars parked in slots by the doorways.

So much life, he thought. Teeming on the planet.

Funny, when his sole way of relating to the world had been from his lofty Bradford status, he had ignored all these people who were busy living their lives. It wasn't that he had outwardly disdained or disrespected them, but he had certainly felt so much more important because of the number of zeros to the left of his decimal points.

Pain and his various physical issues had sure cured him of that arrogance.

"Here it is," he said with triumph. "I knew it was here."

Parallel parking across from the low-slung, homey little restaurant, he tried to get around to get Shelby's door, but with his ankle and his bad leg, there was no moving fast enough—and she didn't wait for him, disembarking on her own. Together, they paused for a break in traffic and then they were crossing over and he was holding the way inside open for her.

As he took a deep breath of the spices and the hot chicken, his stomach let out a roar.

"I learned about this place," he said as he surveyed the crowded interior, "from Moe. He started talking it up a couple of years ago and finally he brought takeout home with him. It was before I . . . it was before South America."

They were shown over to a table in the back, which suited him fine. He looked a lot different and he wasn't from this neighborhood, but he didn't want any attention. Tonight? He just wanted to be as everyone else in the place was: part of humanity, no better, no worse, no richer, no poorer.

Popping open the menu, he was so ready for half the things on it.

"How long have you and Moe known each other?" Shelby asked over the din of other customers.

"Years. He started working at the Red & Black when he was fourteen or fifteen, hauling hay and cleaning stalls. He's a smart guy."

"He speaks about you with a lotta respect."

Edward folded his menu back up. "The feeling is entirely mutual. Moe's like a brother in a lot of ways. And Joey, his son? Known the kid his whole life."

In fact, Joey was the reason they were here.

Edward had been thinking about that expression the guy had had as he'd watched Shelby handle Neb's little freak out.

Ordinarily, Edward wouldn't be meddling in other people's business like this. But he found himself wanting to do right by Shelby.

Before things changed.

Their waitress came by, and after they ordered, he sipped his water. "So about Joey."

"Yes?" Shelby's eyes were open and guileless. "What?"

Edward played with his fork. "What do you think about him?"

"I think he's real good with the horses. He never loses his temper. He gets it."

"Do you think he's . . ."

"You're not gonna fire him for what happened last night, are ya? It wasn't his fault. That weren't nobody's fault and—"

"What? God, no." Edward shook his head. "Joey's a good boy. I was just wondering what you thought of him, you know."

Shelby shrugged. "He's a good man. But if you're asking me whether I'm fixin' to get with him, the answer would be no."

When she fell silent, Edward thought . . . of course, you're not interested in him. He's not a hot mess of self-destruction.

"Shelby, I need to 'fess up to something."

"What's that?"

He took a deep breath. "You're right. I am in love with someone."

FORTY-ONE

$\mathcal{T}$he Charlemont Presbyterian Theological Seminary took up
about forty manicured acres right next to one of Olmstead's
gorgeous city parks. With distinguished brick buildings and lamp posts
that glowed orange in the gathering darkness, Gin imagined the pictur-
esque campus as a place where no one drank, safe sex was not an issue
because everyone was still a virgin, and the closest thing there was to a
fraternity party was the raucous chess club, which was known to serve
the occasional Red Bull.

It was therefore rather ironic to her that she was pulling into its
entrance . . . considering who she had come to meet.

The students had all been flushed out for the summer, no doubt finding worthwhile internships for the warm months doing Good Work.
Likewise, there were no administrators and no academicians strolling
around, either. The lovely, winding lanes, which reminded her of the kind
one saw in a cemetery, were, like the dorms and the classrooms, empty.

Pulling the Drophead into a parking space, she got out and smelled
freshly cut grass. With a shove, she closed the heavy door and checked
what she looked like in the window's reflection. Then she locked the car

and watched the Spirit of Ecstasy sink into its little safe haven inside the front grille.

The seminary's reflecting garden was a well-photographed and quite famous Charlemont institution, and although it wasn't exactly open to the public, it was not exactly private, either. With one gate on each of its four sides, it was the centerpiece of the school, the place where commencements and convocations were staged and alumni were sometimes married and people went to . . . well, reflect.

Her palms were sweating as she proceeded over to one of its round-topped, Hobbit-ish entries, and when she toggled the old-fashioned latch and pushed her way inside, she felt light-headed.

For a moment, the beauty and the tranquillity were so resplendent, she actually took a deep breath. Even though it was only May, there were blooming flowers everywhere, and verdant leaves, and brick walkways that all led to the square of lawn in the middle. Fountains along the ivy-covered brick walls offered a symphony of calming sounds, and as the last of the light drained from the sky, peach-colored sodium lanterns on tall wrought-iron stands made everything seem like Victorian London.

Without Jack the Ripper.

"Over here."

At the sound of the male voice, she looked to the right.

Samuel T. was sitting on one of the stone benches, and he was staring off at the lawn, his elbows on his knees, his face as serious as she had ever seen it.

In her stilettos, she had to be careful over the brick walkway or risk shucking the silk covering of her heels—or, worse, tripping, falling, and making an ass of herself.

As she approached him, he got to his feet because he was first and foremost a gentleman, and it would be unthinkable for a man not to greet a lady properly.

After a quick, stiff embrace, he indicated the vacant space beside where he had been. "Please."

"So formal."

But her voice lacked the normal venom. And as she lowered herself onto the cool stone, she felt compelled to pull her skirt down to her knees and sit properly with her legs tucked under and her ankles crossed.

He was quiet for a while. So was she.

Together, they stared off at the ghostly shadows thrown by the flowers. The breeze was as soft as a caress and fragrant as bathwater.

"Did you do it?" he asked without looking at her. "Did you marry him?"

"Yes."

"Congratulations."

In any other circumstance, she would have offered a snappy comeback, but his tone was so grave, it provided no target to trigger any aggression on her part.

In the silence that followed, Gin fingered both her engagement ring and the thin band of platinum that had been added beneath it.

"God, why did you do it, Gin?" Samuel T. rubbed his face. "You don't love him."

Even though she had the sense he was speaking to himself, she whispered, "If love were a requirement for marriage, the human race would have no need for the institution."

After another long period of quiet, he muttered, "Well, I have something to say to you."

"Yes, I gather," she intoned.

"And I don't anticipate this going over well."

"So why bother."

"Because you, my darling, are like poison ivy to me. Even though I know that it will only make things worse, I can't help but scratch."

"Oh, the compliments." She smiled sadly. "You are as debonair as always."

When he fell silent once again, she swung her eyes around to him and studied his profile. He really was a beautiful man, all the angles of his face straight and even, his lips full, his jaw prominent without being heavy. His hair was thick and parted on the side. With his aviators hooked on the V made by his fine, handmade and initialed button-down shirt, he looked like a polo player, a yachtsman, an old soul in a young body.

"You're never this quiet," she promoted, even as she began to worry about what he was going to say. "Not for this long."

"That's because . . . shit, I don't know, Gin. I don't know what I'm doing here."

She wasn't sure what made her do it—no, that was a lie: When she reached out and put her hand on his shoulder, it was because she recognized that they were both suffering. And she was tired of being so proud. Tired of fighting a battle where neither of them won. Tired . . . of everything.

And instead of pushing her away, either literally or figuratively, Samuel T. turned to her . . . and then she was holding him as he curled in close, all but laying out in her lap.

It felt so good to rub his back in slow circles, comforting herself as she comforted him. And oh, his body. She had been with him many times, in many places, and in many ways, and she knew every square inch of his muscular form.

Yet it felt like forever since they had been together.

"What has gotten you so upset?" she murmured. "Tell me."

Eventually, he straightened, and as he ran his palms over his eyes, she became alarmed. "Samuel T.—what is going on?"

His chest expanded, and as he exhaled, he said, "I need you to just let me get this out, okay? For once in your life—and I'm not fixing to argue here—for once in your life, please just listen. Don't respond off the cuff. In fact, if you don't respond at all, it's probably better. I just . . . I need you to hear what I'm saying, all right?"

He glanced over at her. "Gin, okay?"

Abruptly, she became aware that her heart was beating in a crazy way and her body had broken out in a sweat.

"Gin?"

"Fine." She put her arms around her stomach. "Okay."

He nodded and splayed out his hands. "I think Richard hits you." He put a palm up. "Don't respond, remember. I've already decided he does, and you know me better than anyone. As you've so often told me, once I make up my mind, it takes an act of Congress to get me to change it—so there is nothing you can do to alter this conclusion."

Gin refocused on the beautiful flowers . . . as she tried to ignore the fact that she felt like she couldn't breathe.

"I think those bruises came from him, and that you're wearing scarves to cover them up." His chest rose and fell. "And although I can quite confidently say that you have driven me to the brink of madness many, many times, it never once occurred to me to lay a hand on you. Or any other woman."

She closed her eyes briefly. And then heard herself say bleakly, "You're more of a man than that."

"The thing is, I just . . . I need to tell you that the idea of anyone, and I don't care who the fuck it is, striking you or yanking you or . . . oh, God, I can't bear to think of what else . . ."

She had never heard him trail off before. Never heard this cocksure, maddening, contrary man seem so completely defeated.

Samuel T. cleared his throat. "I know you married him because you think your family's out of money and that scares you. At the end of the day, you don't know how to be anything other than rich. You're not trained to do anything. You almost dropped out of school because of that child you had. You've flitted around creating drama for a living. So yes, the idea of having to rely on yourself, without a safety net of incredible wealth, is going to be really terrifying, to the point where you can't even comprehend it."

She opened her mouth.

And then closed it.

"What I really want to say is two things," he continued. "First, I want you to know you're better than that, and not because you're a Bradford. The truth is, no matter what happens to the money, you're a strong, smart, capable woman, Gin—and up until now you've used those virtues in bad ways, dumb-ass ways, because quite frankly, you haven't had any real challenges put in front of you. You've been a warrior without a field of battle, Gin. A fighter without a foe, and you've been lashing out at everything and everyone around you for years now, trying to burn off the energy." His voice grew unbearably hoarse. "Well, I want you to channel all that in a different way now. I want you to be strong for the right reasons. I want you to take care of yourself now. Protect yourself now. You have people who . . . you have people who love you. Who want to help you. But you're going to need to take the first step."

As he fell silent, Gin found her own eyes pricking with tears, and then her throat began to hurt from her trying to swallow without making a gulping sound.

"You can call me," he said roughly. "Anytime. I know you and I haven't made sense. We're bad for each other in all the ways that count, but you can call me. Day or night. No matter where you are, I'll come for you. I won't ask for any explanations. I won't yell at you or berate you. I won't judge you—and if you insist, I won't tell Lane or anybody else."

Samuel T. moved to the side and took his cell phone out of the pocket of his slacks. "I'm going to start sleeping with this left on from now on. No questions asked, no explanations demanded, no talking during or afterward. You call me, you text me, you say my name in the middle of a party, and I'm there for you. Are we clear?"

As a tear escaped down her cheek, he brushed it away, and his voice cracked. "You're better than this. You deserve better than this. Your family's glorious past is not worth a man hitting you in the present just because you're afraid you won't be anything without the money. You're priceless, Gin, no matter what's in your bank account."

Now he was the one pulling her in and holding her to his chest.

Beneath her ear, the beating of his heart just made her cry more.

"Take care of yourself, Gin. Do whatever you need to do to make yourself safe . . ."

He just kept saying those words in an endless stream, as if he were hoping the repetition might get through to her.

When she finally sat up, he took his handkerchief out of his back pocket and pressed it to her cheeks. And as he stared at her with sad eyes, she found it was hard to believe that after everything they'd been through, he was there for her like this.

Then again, maybe everything they'd been through was the explanation.

"So what's the second thing you wanted to say," she murmured looking down at their feet.

When he didn't immediately respond, she glanced back over at him—and recoiled.

His eyes had grown cold and his body seemed to change even as he didn't shift at all.

"The second is . . ." Samuel T. cursed and let his head fall back. "No, I think I'll keep that to myself. It's not going to help this situation."

But she could guess what it was. "I love you, too, Samuel."

"Just think about how strong you are. Please, Gin."

After a moment, he reached out and moved that big diamond around so it was hidden. Then he brought her wrist up and pressed a kiss to the back of her hand. "And remember what I said."

Getting to his feet, he showed her his phone again. "Always on. No questions asked."

With a last look at her, he put his hands in his pockets and walked away, a solemn figure bathed in the peachy light of the lampposts.

And then he was gone.

Gin stayed where they had sat together for so long, the night air turned cold enough to raise goose bumps on her forearms.

Yet she found it impossible to go home.

FORTY-TWO

As Edward said the words in the middle of the busy restaurant, he was amazed at how good they felt. It was a simple chain of syllables, nothing too fancy vocabulary-wise, but the admission was a tremendous one.

I'm in love with somebody.

And actually, he'd already told Sutton the truth of it all. At the business center after they'd made love. He'd just done it so softly, she hadn't heard the words.

In response, Shelby looked around at the other diners. The waitress. The people behind the counter and the ones cooking in the back. "Is she the reason you wouldn't . . . you know, get with me?"

"Yes." He thought of those nights they'd spent side by side in that bed. "But there was another reason, too."

"What's that?"

"I know what you're doing with me. I remember what your father was like. Sometimes we do things over, you know? When we feel like we didn't get them right the first time."

Hell, it was the story of him and his brothers and their father. If

Edward was brutally honest with himself, he had always wanted to save his siblings from the man, but the damage had been done anyway. Their father had had that much power, at once absent, and at the same time, totally controlling.

And violent in a cold way that was somehow scarier than outbursts of yelling and throwing things.

"I've done that myself," he said quietly. "Actually, I'm still doing it—so you and I are the same, really. We're both saviors looking for a cause."

Shelby was quiet for so long, he started to wonder if she was going to walk out or something.

But then she spoke up. "I took care of my father not because I loved him, but because if he killed himself, what was I going to do? I had no mother. I had nowhere to go. Living with his drinking was easier than facing the streets at twelve or thirteen."

Edward winced as he tried to imagine her as a little girl with no one to care for her, desperately attempting to fix an adult's addiction as a survival mechanism for herself.

"I'm sorry," Edward blurted.

"For what? You had nothing to do with his drinkin'."

"No, but I had everything to do with being drunk around you. And putting you in a position you're too goddamn good at—"

"Don't you take—"

"Sorry, darn—"

"—my Lord's name in vain."

"—good at."

There was a pause. And then they both laughed.

Shelby grew serious again. "I don't know what else to do with you. And I also hate the suffering."

"That's because you're a good person. You're a really, really GD good person."

She smiled. "You caught yourself."

"I'm learning."

Their food arrived, the chicken nestled in baskets lined with red and white paper, the French fries thin and hot, the waitress asking if they needed more soda.

"I am starving," Edward remarked after they were alone with their food.

"Me too."

As they set to eating, they fell into silence, but it was the good kind. And he found himself feeling so glad they hadn't ever had sex.

"Have you told her?" Shelby asked.

Edward wiped his mouth with a paper napkin. "What? Oh . . . yeah. No. She leads a totally different life than I do. She's where I used to be, and I'm never going back there again."

For more reasons than one.

"You should probably tell her," Shelby said between bites. "If you were in love with me . . . I'd want to know."

As she spoke, there was a wistful tone in her voice, but her eyes were not glassy from some kind of fantasy or sad from some sort of loss. And when she didn't pursue the issue, he thought about what she'd said before, about her accepting people exactly where they were, just like she did the horses.

"I want you to know something." Edward smacked the bottom of a bottle of ketchup to add more to the side of his fries. "And I want you to do something."

"Do I get to pick which one you tell me first?"

"Sure."

"What do you want me to do? If it's about Neb, I've already scheduled the vet's check-up for tomorrow afternoon."

He laughed. "You read my mind. But no, that's not it." He wiped his mouth again. "I want you to go out with Joey."

As she looked up sharply, he put his palm up. "Just a dinner date. Nothing fancy. And no, he hasn't asked me to talk to you, and frankly, if he knew I was, he'd leave me limping worse than I already do. But I think you should give the poor guy a chance. He's got a bad crush on you."

Shelby stared across the table in complete confusion. "He does?"

"Oh, come on. You're spectacular around horses, and you're a damn good-looking woman." He put his finger up. "I did not say God."

"I just never noticed him much, other than the workin'."

"Well, you should."

She sat back and shook her head. "You know . . . I really can't believe this."

"That someone might actually be attracted to you? Well, someone who isn't trying to suck you down into their own black hole of self-destruction, that is?"

"Well, that, too. But I just never would have guessed that you'd be openin' up like this."

He picked up his Coke and considered the fizzy goodness. "Guess sobriety affects me like alcohol does most people. Makes me chatty."

"It's kinda . . ."

"What? And be honest."

"It's real nice." Her voice got soft and she looked away. "It's real good."

Edward found himself clearing his throat. "Miracles do happen."

"And I've never seen you eat this much before."

"It's been a while."

"So do you just hate my cooking?"

He laughed and pushed his fries away. One more and he was going to burst. On that note, he said, "I want ice cream now. Come on."

"I don't think she left a bill."

Edward leaned to the side and took out the thousand dollars. Peeling off two hundred-dollar bills, he said, "This should cover it."

As Shelby's eyes bugged, he got to his feet and held out his hand. "Come on. I'm stuffed, so I need that ice cream now."

"That makes no sense."

"Oh, it does." He started limping for the door, going around the other diners at their tables. "Cold and sweet settles the stomach. It's what my momma, Miss Aurora, has always said, and she's always right. And no, I don't hate your cooking at all. You're very good at it."

Outside, he took a moment to appreciate the night air again, and it felt good to have a certain lightness in his chest for once, a singing sensation that would have been optimism in someone else, but in his case, was relief.

"Except you don't want to go heavy with the ice cream," he informed her as he walked forward, checking to see if there were any cars coming. "Keep it light. Vanilla only. Maybe with chocolate chips, but nothing with nuts and nothing too gooey. Graeter's is best."

With a clear shot across the two lanes to her truck, Shelby fell in step beside him, shortening her stride to accommodate his lack of speed.

"Sir! Oh, sir?"

Edward looked back as they got to the other side of the road. Their waitress had come out of the restaurant with the money he'd left.

"Your bill's only twenty-four and some change," the woman said across the street. "This is way too much—"

"You keep the change." He smiled as her eyes grew wide, and then she looked at the money like she didn't know what it was. "I'll bet being on those feet all shift makes your back ache like hell. I should know from the aching. Treat yourself to a night off or something."

She focused on him—only to frown. "Wait a minute . . . are you—"

"Nobody. I'm nobody." He waved good-bye and turned to the truck. "Just another customer."

"Well, thank you!" she called out. "It's the biggest tip I've ever gotten!"

"You deserve it," he said over his shoulder.

Heading around the cab, he opened Shelby's door and helped her in even though she didn't need the help.

"That was a really nice thing to do," she said.

"Well, it's probably the best meal I've had since—no offense."

"None taken." She put her hand on his arm before he could shut her in. "What's the thing you want me to know?"

Before he replied, Edward leaned against the door, removing the weight from his bad ankle. "You're always going to have a job at the Red & Black. For however long you want it, you will always have the work and

the apartment. Hell, I can see you and Moe running the thing together—
whether or not you let his son take you out on a date, whether or not you
like Joey back."

Shelby glanced away in that manner she seemed to when she was
emotional. And as Edward studied her face, he thought, *Huh, this must be
what it's like to have a proper little sister.*

Gin was more like having a banshee in your house.

Or a tornado.

After all, much as he loved that woman, he had never felt particularly close to her. He wasn't sure anyone ever got close to Gin.

And so yes, it was nice to feel protective, but not possessive, over
someone. Nice to do a good thing or two. Nice to send something other
than acid anger out into the world.

Abruptly, she looked at him.

"Why do I get the impression you're leaving?" she asked grimly.

*I*n the end, Gin returned to Easterly because there was nowhere
else for her to go. Parking the Drophead in its berth in the
garages, she walked over to the kitchen entrance and went in through
the screen door.

As usual, everything was neat and in order, no pans in the sink, the
dishwasher quietly running, the countertops gleaming. There was a
lingering sweetness in the air, that old-fashioned soap Miss Aurora used.

Gin's heart was beating as she proceeded to the door to the woman's
private quarters. Curling up a fist, she hesitated before knocking.

"Come on in, girl," came the demand from the other side. "Don't just
stand there."

Opening the way in, Gin hung her head because she didn't want the
tears in her eyes to show. "How did you know it was me?"

"Your perfume. And I've been waiting for you. Also saw the car
come in."

Miss Aurora's living space was set up in exactly the same way it
always had been, two big stuffed chairs set against long windows,

shelves full of pictures of kids and grown-ups, a galley kitchen that was as spotless and orderly as the women's big, professionally appointed one. Gin had never been in the bedroom and bath; nor would it ever have occured to her to ask to see them.

Eventually, Gin looked up. Miss Aurora was in the chair she always used, and she indicated the vacant one. "Sit."

Gin went across and did as she was told. As she smoothed her skirt, she thought of doing so when she'd been in the reflecting garden with Samuel T.

"It's called an annulment," Miss Aurora said abruptly. "And you should do it immediately. I'm a Christian woman, but I will tell you plainly that you married a bad man. Then again, you act before you think, you are rebellious even when no one is doin' you wrong, and your version of freedom is being out of control, it's not about making choices."

Gin had to laugh. "You know, you're the second person who's torn me apart tonight."

"Well, that's 'cuz the good Lord clearly thinks you need to hear the message twice."

Gin thought about her whole out-of-control thing. Remembered her and Richard fighting in her room just the other night, and her going for that Imari lamp. "My mood's been all over the place lately."

"That's because the sand's shifting under your feet. You don't know what you're standing on, and that makes a body dizzy."

Putting her face in her hands, she shook her head. "I don't know how much more of this I can take."

During the trip back from the seminary, she had vacillated between that emotionally difficult, but clear-sighted, conversation with Samuel T. . . . and her urge to re-embrace the calculated mania of her old way of doing things.

"There is nothing that cannot be undone," Miss Aurora said. "And your true family will not desert you, even if the money does."

Gin thought of the great house they were in. "I failed at being a mother."

"No, you didn't try."

"It's too late."

"If I'd said that when I came into this house and met the four of you, where would you all be?"

Gin remembered back to all those nights the five of them had eaten together in the kitchen. Even as a fleet of nannies had cycled through the household, mostly because they were tortured and way out-gunned, Miss Aurora had been the one person who could corral her and her brothers.

Searching the photographs on the shelves, Gin became teary again as she saw several of her—and she pointed to a picture of her in pigtails. "That was on the way to summer camp."

"You were ten."

"I hated the food."

"I know. I had to feed you for a month after you got home—and you'd only been away for two weeks."

"That one's Amelia, isn't it."

Miss Aurora grunted as she turned in her chair. "Which one? The pink?"

"Yes."

"She was seven and a half."

"You were there for her, too."

"Yes, I was. She's the closest thing to a true granddaughter I have because you're the closest thing to a daughter I have."

Gin brushed under her eyes. "I'm glad she has you. She got kicked out of Hotchkiss, you know."

"That's what she told me."

"I'm so glad she comes to talk to you—"

"You know I'm not going to be here forever, right?" As Gin looked over, Miss Aurora's dark eyes were steady. "When I'm gone, you need to pick up the slack with her. No one else will, and she's got one foot in childhood, one in adulthood. It's a precarious time. You step up, Virginia Elizabeth, or I swear I will haunt you. Do you hear me, girl? I will come back as your conscience and I will *not* let you rest."

For the first time, Gin properly focused on Miss Aurora. Under her housecoat, she was thinner than she had ever been, her face drawn with bags under her eyes.

"You can't die," Gin heard herself say. "You just can't."

Miss Aurora laughed. "That's up to God. Not you or me."

FORTY-THREE

$\mathcal{L}$ane was not leaving the business center until the detectives were finished. As a result, therefore, he found himself walking in and out of the offices, killing time until eventually, he found himself opening the way into his father's space and taking a seat in the chair his dear old dad had always sat in.

And that was when he had an aha! moment.

Pushing himself around on the leather throne, he shook his head and wondered why it hadn't dawned on him sooner.

There were shelves behind the desk, shelves that were filled with your standard-issue, leather-bound volumes and framed diplomas and manly effects of a life lived to impress other people with money: sailing trophies, horse pictures, bourbon bottles that were unusual or special. But none of that was what interested him.

No, what he had suddenly noticed and cared about were the built-in, hand-tooled, wood-faced cabinets that were underneath the ego display.

Leaning down, he tried a couple, but they were all locked—and yet there didn't seem to be any obvious places to put keys or enter codes—

One of the French doors to the terrace opened, and Lizzie came in, a pair of sweet teas in her hands and something that looked like a sleeve of Fig Newtons in the pocket of her shorts.

"I'm hungry," she said. "And I feel like sharing the wealth."

As she headed around and dropped a kiss on his lips, he pulled her into his lap and helped her take out the cookies. "Sounds good to me."

"How are things going in there?"

"I have no idea. I keep expecting them to say that they've copied the files and are off, but not yet."

"It's been a while." She opened the plastic wrapping and offered him one. When he shook his head, she put a cookie in her mouth. "But they haven't asked for anything else?"

"No." Taking a sip of what she'd brought, he sighed. "Oh, yeah. This is good."

"So guess what?"

"Tell me."

"I'm giving myself a promotion." As he laughed, she nodded. "I'm appointing myself house manager."

The instant she said it, he thought, *Oh, thank God.* Because yes, the bills were piling up, and staff had to be handled, and the endless details of the estate had to be dealt with even if there was a freeze on spending. But . . .

"Wait, you have so much work already. The gardens, and—"

"Here's the thing. Mr. Harris has quit."

Lane shook his head. "You know, I'm actually relieved."

"Yeah, me, too. I helped him move out today. I didn't want to go into it with you at the time because he'd made up his mind and there's been so much else going on. But his check bounced, and it made me think about what's going on with your household accounts—this place is expensive to run with a lot of moving parts. I mean, like, we need to pay all those waiters. We can't just leave them hanging. The groundsmen all have checks that go out automatically, I just don't know when? And if there weren't enough funds for Mr. Harris? Then there aren't enough for the other people."

"Shit, I didn't even think about that."

"I know that you're going to want to do right by everyone. So we've got to get money into the household account, and we need to make staffing plans. If cuts have to be made, we've got to give people notice. We can't have the folks who work here in good faith get hurt."

"I agree." He kissed her again. "One hundred percent."

"But I'll figure it out. I'll go through everything and then let you know where we are. I don't know where we can find the cash—"

"Actually, I do. I'll take care of it first thing in the morning before Lenghe comes."

"Lenghe?"

"Yeah. I'm playing some high stakes poker tomorrow night. And before you say that's crazy, I'll remind you that I have to work with what I got—and it ain't much."

"Who's Lenghe—how do you say it?"

"Lang-ee. And we call him the Grain God—and that's self-explanatory. You're really going to like him. He's right up your alley, a good soul who loves the land. And remember, I played poker in college and afterward. It's my only skill."

She put her arms around his neck. "I think you've got a couple of others—"

"Am I interrupting anything?"

Lane pivoted the chair toward the door, and thought it was so damned appropriate that Merrimack picked that moment to make an appearance. "You guys finished in there, Detective?"

Annnnnd there was the smile. "Getting there. Ma'am, it's nice to see you again."

Lizzie got to her feet, but stayed by Lane. "You, too."

"Well, I thought you'd like to know that I'm removing the seal on the controller's office." Merrimack smiled. "We have everything we need from there."

"Good," Lane said.

"We were wondering about that," Lizzie murmured.

"Were you? What a coincidence." The detective got a little pad out.

"Now, I'd like a list of people who have access to the security sector of the computer network. Do you know who has that information?"

"Not a clue." Lane shrugged. "I'm happy to ask the IT department at corporate. Maybe they know."

"Or maybe your brother Edward knows."

"Perhaps."

"Tell me something, did he play a role in installation of the security programs?"

"I don't know." Okay, that was a lie. "Why?"

"You don't know whether he did or he didn't?"

"I haven't been much involved with this household or the business until recently. So I can't really tell you."

"Okay." The detective clapped the pad against his open palm. "I think I'll just call your brother directly, then."

"He doesn't have a cell phone. But I can give him a message to get in touch with you."

"No need. I know where he lives." The detective looked around. "Sure is impressive in here."

"It is."

"You must miss your father."

Anyone who was fooled by this casual, Columbo-esque routine was an idiot, Lane thought.

"Oh, of course. I miss him to distraction."

"Father and son. It's a special bond."

"Yes."

There was a pause, and when Lane didn't take things paternal any further than that, Merrimack smiled again. "I heard your brother Max is home again. That's kind of a surprise. It's been a while since he's been to Easterly, hasn't it."

"Yes."

"But he's been in Charlemont for a number of days." As Lane frowned, the detective lifted a brow. "You didn't know that? Really? Well, I've got a couple of witnesses who say he and Edward were together. The afternoon of the day your father died. Did you know about the two of them meeting up?"

Lane felt a curse shoot up his throat, but he kept it to himself by force of will. "That's putting me on the spot, you realize."

"Is it? It's just a simple question."

"No offense, Detective, but you're conducting a homicide investigation. There are no simple questions coming from you."

"Not as long as you're telling the truth and not trying to protect someone. Are you protecting someone, Mr. Baldwine? Or do you have something yourself that you're hiding? Because we've got a lot of information that's working for me. I strongly encourage you to be as open and honest as possible."

"Are you saying I'm a suspect?"

"If you were, I'd be talking to you downtown. And we're not there yet, are we." Smile. "I am curious, though, as to whether you were aware that your two brothers met up."

Lane breathed deep in his belly, refusing to give in to the urge to leap up, run down to the cottage where Max was camping out, and beat the shit out of the guy until he found out what the hell was going on.

The detective smiled again. "Well, I guess it's pretty clear you didn't know about that. The witnesses say it was just the two of them alone. They were spotted on the Indiana side of the river. Below the falls. Right by where your father's body was found, actually."

Lane smiled back. "Maybe they were just enjoying the view of the river."

"Or maybe they were talking about what might happen to a body if it got dropped off the Big Five Bridge." Merrimack shrugged. "Or perhaps it could have been the view. You're right."

"Where have you been?"

As Gin entered her bedroom suite, she was not surprised to find Richard sitting in one of her white silk chairs, his face twisted in a rage, his lanky arms and legs twitching as if her being out on her own at night was a personal affront to him.

Like someone slashing his tires. Spray-painting graffiti all over his office. Lighting a Bible on fire in front of him.

Closing the door, she waited for the usual mania she felt around him to put gas in her veins. She braced herself for the high-octane rush of crazy, the one that helped her through these situations. She got ready for the cutting words that came to her mind from out of nowhere, and that sly, bitchy smile to hit her face.

None of it materialized.

Instead, she experienced a crushing weight settling all over her body, to the point that, even as he burst up from the chair and came across the white rug at her, she couldn't move. It wasn't because she was scared of him—at least, she didn't think that was what was happening. Rather, her body had turned into a numb block . . . while her consciousness sailed above the immovable stone of her flesh.

She watched from somewhere over her right shoulder as he ranted and raved, grabbed her arm, shook her, threw her onto the bed.

Hovering over herself, she played witness to what happened next, feeling nothing, doing nothing . . . even seeing the back of his head, his shoulders, and his legs from her lofty vantage point as he tore at her clothes and pulled at her limbs.

Underneath her body, the duvet was getting so messy, the former order ruined, the fine Egyptian cotton wrinkling up as he sweated on top of her.

Gin focused mostly on her own face. The features were quite beautiful. The eyes, however, were totally vacant, with all the inner light and life as a pair of cobblestones. The composure was admirable, she supposed. Lying back and thinking of England, or something.

Bergdorf's, was it Samuel had said?

When Richard was done, he sagged and then removed himself. And Gin's body just lay there as he said some more things. Then he turned on his heel and left with his chin up, like a boy who had successfully defended his sandbox from the older kids and now was content to leave it be as the dominance had been the thing for him, not the particular possession.

After a while, Floating Gin came down from above the bed and sat beside Real Gin. She didn't want to go back in her body yet, though. It was better to be apart from it all. Easier . . .

As she had a passing thought that she should cover up, Real Gin's arm moved and pulled the duvet over their lower body.

In the stillness, Gin reflected that maybe she deserved what she got. She had treated everyone around her with derision, deliberately and knowingly flaunted every rule there was, been judgmental and cruel for sport, led the mean girls' club in every grade, camp and school she'd ever been in—and now that all the classrooms and gathering of degrees was in the rearview mirror, she was at the forefront of the catty women of leisure.

Well, at least that had been the case.

Given the crushing numbers of people who had not showed up at her father's visitation? And the fact that Tammy wouldn't come anymore? She had clearly been demoted.

So maybe this was karma.

Maybe this was what happened when you threw bad energy out into the world. Maybe this was the tsunami of what she'd done to others coming back to crash on her shoreline.

Then again . . . maybe she had simply married an asshole for all the wrong reasons and Richard was a sadistic rapist and victims were never to blame—and it was up to her to be clear-eyed and courageous and end this before he killed her.

Because that was where they were headed: She had seen Richard's eyes get excited like a hunter's did. He wasn't going to be satisfied over time with the level of violence they were currently at. He was going to keep pushing it because he got off on the hurting and the subjugation— but only if it had a fresh edge to make things really sizzle for him.

He'd learned to bully at the feet of masters. And now he was getting off on being the one doing the intimidation.

Maybe she should just kill him first?

That was her last thought as sleep claimed both parts of her, her body and her soul, the blanket of unconsciousness easing the traffic jam in her head: Yes, maybe the way out was just to get rid of him.

And not in an annulment kind of way.

FORTY-FOUR

$\mathcal{T}$he following morning, Lane left Lizzie asleep in their big bed at Easterly as he took a quick shower and got dressed. Before he left, he spent a moment watching her in her slumber and thinking that he'd so picked the right woman.

And then he was on his way, striding down the corridor, descending the front stairs, leaving out the main entrance.

The Porsche came awake at the turn of the key, and he sped down to the bottom of the hill, taking a left and going to the Shell station. A large coffee and a cardboard breakfast sandwich later and he was heading to the local branch of the bank, going around bicyclists, getting stuck behind a school bus, cursing as a minivan full of kids nearly wiped him out.

Then again, that might have been his fault. He hadn't slept well and the coffee hadn't properly kicked in yet.

What the hell had his two brothers been doing on that shoreline? And why had that shit not come up in conversation?

Because they had something to hide. Duh.

After Detective Merrimack and Pete the Geek had finally left the business center, Lane had had the impulse to drive out to the Red & Black, but he wasn't sure whether Team CMP was going to head that way themselves. After all, Edward rarely answered that phone for anybody, and the detective had the focus and follow-through of a bloodhound on a scent.

The last thing Lane wanted was to appear confrontational in front of a peanut gallery of police—and he was sure as hell ready to do some hot stepping all over both of his brothers.

In the end, he and Lizzie had stayed on the estate, making love in the pool house again and then upstairs in the tub . . . and in the bed.

Great stress relief. Even if it didn't change what was going on.

Pulling into the bank's parking lot, he found an empty space and realized he'd picked the same one he'd used before when he'd first found out there were problems.

He almost backed up to leave the car somewhere else.

Recognizing that magical thinking wasn't going to help, he got out and left the top down even though the sky was heavy with rain not yet fallen and the weatherman was calling for a tornado watch. That was the thing with Kentucky. There was no seasonal weather: You could start the morning off in shorts and a T-shirt, need your torrential rain gear at noon, and end the afternoon with a parka and snow boots.

As his phone rang, he took it out of the pocket of the linen jacket he'd worn the day before. When he saw who it was, he almost let it go into voice mail.

With a curse, he accepted the call and said, "I'm getting you the money."

Even though he had no clue how.

Ricardo Monteverdi's panties were back in a wad, the ten-million-dollar cash injection thanks to Sutton having bought fewer days of peace than Lane remembered bargaining for. The man was once again pulling the whole we're-out-of-time, save-my-ass-before-I-ruin-your-family thing, and as he droned on, Lane measured the sky once more.

Lenghe's jet was due to arrive in forty-five minutes—and if it wasn't on time, it was going to get delayed for hours and hours.

"Gotta go," Lane said. "I'll be in touch."

Hanging up, he waited for an SUV to pass and then strode over to the double doors. The local branch of PNC was your standard-issue glass-fronted, single-story box, and as he walked in, that attractive blond manager came forward to greet him.

"Mr. Baldwine, how nice to see you again."

He shook her hand and smiled. "Mind if we talk for a minute?"

"But of course. Come inside."

He went into her office and sat down in the chair for customers. "So my father has died."

"I know," she said as she took a seat on the other side of her desk. "I'm so sorry."

"I'm not going to mess around with—thank you, thank you for that. Anyway, I'm not going to mess around with trying to shift signatories on the household account. I want to open a new one, and I'm going to wire three hundred thousand dollars into it ASAP. We're going to have to transfer the automatic payments for all Easterly employees over to the new account effective immediately, and I need a list of anyone whose salaries pinged the old one and bounced. It's a big mess, but I want to take care of everything today, even if the funds aren't live until Monday."

Lizzie was going to work with Greta to get a handle on the staffing this morning, and hopefully they could sort everything out and get people transitioning off the payroll immediately. The faster they could cut employees, the fewer expenses they were going to need to cover.

"But of course, Mr. Baldwine." The manager began typing on her keyboard. "I'll need some identification, and tell me, where are the funds coming from?"

From out of nowhere, he heard Jeff's voice in his head: *I'm investing in your little bourbon company.*

Hell, if his friend could write a check, so could he. And there were more funds he could pull from his trust if he had to, but he was going to have to start selling stock after this. The key was making sure he kept Easterly's roof over his mother's head, the skeleton crew they were going to retain on the estate paid, food in the pantry, and the electricity and the running water on. Oh, and Sutton Smythe's mortgage payments needed to be covered, too.

After that? Everything was nonessential until they got this all worked out.

As he handed over his driver's license and his account number at J. P. Morgan, she smiled. "Very well, Mr. Baldwine. I'll be happy to take care of this for you right away."

Lane left the bank about twenty minutes later. He'd signed everything he had to, initiated the transfer, and called Lizzie to give her the update. Sorting through the direct deposits was going to be a thing, and Lizzie was going to let the bank manager know who was staying on and who was getting let go—

Lane stopped in the middle of the parking lot.

Standing right next to his car, with a mountain bike by his side and a way-too-old look on his face . . . was Rosalinda Freeland's son.

*L*izzie ended her call with Lane and took a seat in the first chair in the controller's office that caught her eye. It wasn't until she put her hands on the padded arms and leaned back . . . that she realized it was the armchair Rosalinda Freeland had been found dead in.

Bursting back up to her feet, she brushed at the seat of her pants even though the slipcover had been removed and the pillows cleaned.

"So what do you think?" she asked Greta.

The German looked up from the laptop on Rosalinda's old desk. Like the rest of the office, which was as cheerful and light-filled as a gopher hole, the desk was free of non-functionals, nothing but a lamp, a pen holder full of blue Bics, and an in-box on the blotter.

Likewise, there had been no personal effects to remove after the passing. And not because the woman had emptied the place of them prior to the tragedy.

"She kept very good records, *ja*." Behind a set of bright pink, round-as-bubbles reading glasses, pale blue eyes were alert and focused. "Come see. Iz all the goods."

Lizzie went around and peered over her partner's shoulder. There was a chart on the laptop screen of names, contact information, hourly rates, and bonuses. Scrolling to the left, Greta was able to show everything that had been paid out to anyone for the previous five years, month by month.

"Very good. This is very good." Greta removed her glasses and sat back. "I call out names, you tell me what we do vis them."

"How many people are there?"

Greta reached out to the mouse and scrolled. Scrolled. Scrolled. Annnnnnnd scrolled.

And still with the scrolling.

"Seventy-sree. No. Seventy-two."

"Wow. Okay, let's go through them one by one." Lizzie grabbed a white pad that had EASTERLY embossed across the top and then snagged one of the Bics. "I'll take notes."

Greta held up her hand. "I will stop. Taking salary, that is. Put me down, top of zee list."

"Greta, listen—"

"No, Jack and I have no need for me to work. My kids, they're gone, they're on their own. I had the salary because I deserved it and I still do. But right now?" Greta pointed to the screen. "These are in need of money more. I still work, though. What else would I do?"

Lizzie took a deep breath. With her having paid off her farm, she had decided to stop accepting money for the short term as well, but that felt different.

This was her family now.

"We'll pay you," she said, "in arrears when we can."

"If that makes you feel better."

Lizzie put out her palm to shake on it. "It's the only way I'll agree."

When Greta reached forward, her large diamond ring flashed, and Lizzie shook her head. Her partner was probably the only horticulturist in the country who was almost as wealthy as the estates she "worked" for. But the woman was constitutionally incapable of not being busy at something.

She was also, aside from Lane, Lizzie's source of sanity.

"I don't know how long it's going to take," Lizzie said as they clasped hands. "It could be—"

"Where's your butler?"

At the sound of an all-too-familiar female voice, Lizzie looked up.

And promptly let out a string of curses in her head: Standing in the doorway, looking like she owned the place, was Lane's ex-wife. Make that almost ex-wife.

Chantal Baldwine was still every bit as blond as she'd been when Lane had kicked her out—which was to say she was tastefully highlighted. And she'd retained her delicate tan and her short, perfect manicure, and her dress code of Rich, Young, and Socially Superior.

Today's shift, for example, was peach and pink, floaty as a breeze, and fitted like it had been made for her. Which meant it was just ever so tight around her pregnant lower belly.

"May I help you?" Lizzie said evenly.

At the same time, she put her hand on Greta's shoulder and pressed down. The woman had started to get out of the chair, but it was hard to tell whether it was to give Lizzie and Chantal some privacy—or to throat punch the other woman on principle.

"Where's Lane?" Chantal snapped. "I've called him twice. My lawyer has repeatedly asked him to grant me access to my private property, but he has refused to respond. So I'm here now to get my things."

Lizzie gave Greta a sit-stay stare and went over to Chantal. "I'd be happy to escort you upstairs, but I can't leave you unattended on the premises."

"So now you're security, too? Busy, busy. I heard no one came to Mr. Baldwine's visitation, by the way. Such a shame."

Lizzie walked by the woman, giving Chantal no option but to follow. "Do you have moving men? Boxes? A truck?"

Chantal stopped in the middle of the staff hallway. "What are you talking about?"

"You said you were here for your things. How do you intend to move them?"

Okaaaaaaaay. It was like watching a first grader try to do advanced physics.

"Mr. Harris handles all that," was the eventual answer to the question.

"Well, he's not here. So what's your plan?"

When that vacant, calculator-with-no-batteries look returned to that beautiful face, Lizzie was tempted to let the woman just stand there for the next twelve hours and enjoy the brain cramp. But there was too much work to be done, and frankly, having Chantal around was uncomfortable.

"What car did you come in?" Lizzie asked.

"A limousine." As if anything else would be unthinkable.

"Greta?" Lizzie called out. "Would you be able to get some—"

The German came out and headed for the cellar stairs. "—Rubber-maid bins. *Ja.* Coming."

Clearly, she had been listening, and it had nearly killed her not to solve the problem. With maybe a shotgun.

"Let's go," Lizzie said. "I'll take you upstairs. We'll get this done somehow."

She'd already moved one blowhard out of the house with Mr. Harris's departure. She kept this up, and it was going to become a core competency.

"*R*andolph." Lane started walking toward his car—and his half brother. "How are you?"

"It's Damion, actually." The kid pulled at his open jacket, but given his lanky frame and the fact that it wasn't zippered shut, the thing was not too tight. "And I wasn't following your car. I didn't follow you— well, I was going by on the way to school."

"Which school are you in?" Even though, considering the khaki pants, white shirt, and blue and green tie, Lane knew.

"Charlemont Country Day."

Lane frowned. "Isn't that out of the way?"

The kid looked away. Looked back. "I go the long route because I wanted—I want . . . to see what it's like. You know, the house . . . where he lives. Lived."

"That's totally understandable."

Damion stared at the pavement. "I thought you'd be angry at me or something."

"Why? None of it is your fault. You didn't ask for this, and just because I don't want to deal with some of what my father did, doesn't mean I'm going to be hard on you."

"My grandmother told me you all would hate me."

"I don't know her and I'm not going to disrespect her, but that won't happen. I meant what I said. You come anytime—I'd take you there right now, but I'm meeting someone at the airport."

As Damion glanced up at Easterly's hill, Lane reflected that yes, it was going to be hard to bring the kid into the house with his mother still alive and upstairs. But she couldn't even recognize her own children at this point, and she never really left her room.

"I'm late for a school event, anyway."

After an awkward pause, Lane said, "We're going to be burying him. We were supposed to do it today, but with the weather, and some other things, it's been delayed. How can I reach you? I'll let you know—and you can bring your grandmother, too. Whatever you like."

"I don't have a phone. And I don't know. I don't think I'd want to go. It's too weird. You know . . . I didn't see him much. He didn't really come around at all. You know."

Annnnd here it was again. Another son living in pain thanks to that man.

Lane cursed in his head. "I'm really sorry. He was . . . a very complicated man."

Read: asshole and a half.

"I might want to go later though."

"How about this." Lane leaned into the car and got the wrapper from his sausage and biscuit. "You got a pen?"

"Yeah." The kid brought his backpack around and pulled out a Charlemont Country Day pencil. "Here."

Lane wrote down his number. "Call me when you're ready. And I'll tell you exactly where he's interred. Also, let me know when you want to come to the house."

Yes, Easterly was his mother's legacy, but William Baldwine had lived there for decades upon decades. If Lane were in the kid's position, and barely knew his sire, he would want to see where the guy had worked and where he had slept, even if it was only after the man was dead.

"Okay." Damion looked at the wrapper. Then he put it in his back-pack. "I'm sorry."

Lane frowned again. "About what?"

"I don't know. I guess because you've got a mom, too. And she . . . he . . ."

"A piece of advice that you can take for what it's worth." Lane gave the boy's shoulder a squeeze. "Don't try to own problems or faults that aren't yours. It's not a good long-term strategy."

Damion nodded. "I'll call you."

"Do that."

Lane watched the kid mount up and pedal off. And for some reason, when it dawned on Lane that there wasn't a helmet on that head, he wanted to call Damion back and drive him safely to school.

But maybe he should follow his own advice. Damion had a guardian, and he had, hypothetically, ten million dollars, depending on how things turned out. Lane's plate, on the other hand, was full to breaking, no more space left on the porcelain of his attention span and capabilities.

Getting behind the wheel, he cranked the engine and sped out onto Dorn, taking the surface road to the airport so he avoided spaghetti junction. When he finally pulled through the gate to the private jet tarmac, John Lenghe was just disembarking. Wow. The golf shorts this time were made from fabric with a pattern of grass on it. Bright green blades on a black background. Like a thousand of them.

It was a look that only someone with his net worth could carry off.

The man waved with his free hand, the other locked on the handle of a beaten-up old suitcase.

"Figured I might get stuck here," the guy said as he came over to the Porsche and indicated his luggage. "Best to pack a toothbrush given the weather."

"We've got plenty of bedrooms. And my momma cooks the best soul food anywhere. Do you like soul food?"

Lenghe put his case in the six-inch-sized backseat. "Is Jesus my Lord and Savior?"

"I like your style."

As the man got in, he looked at Lane's linen jacket and pressed slacks. "Really? You sure about that, son?"

Lane put the car in gear and hit the gas. "I'm not saying I could wear your wardrobe. But on you? It works."

"You're a smooth one, you know that?" Lenghe winked. "You well rested? Ready to play some poker?"

"Always, old man, always."

Lenghe barked out a laugh, and as Lane took them back to Easterly, the conversation was surprisingly relaxed. As they waited at the bottom of the hill for the gates to open, Lenghe sat forward and looked up at Easterly's white expanse.

"Just like what's on the bottles." He shook his head. "I have to give you guys credit. This is quite a spread."

Especially if we manage to keep it in the family, Lane thought wryly.

The rain started to fall just as they crested the top—but Lane forgot about the weather as he saw a long black limousine parked right across the front entrance.

"Who the hell is that?" he said aloud.

After John got out with his piece of luggage, Lane put the top up and went over to the uniformed driver.

As the window went down, Lane didn't recognize the chauffeur. "May I help you?"

"Hello, sir. I'm here with Chantal Baldwine. She's picking up her things."

Sonofabitch.

FORTY-FIVE

"No, I'm not using tissue paper."

As Lizzie opened drawer after drawer of clothes, she thought to herself, *Not only am I not wrapping your stuff in frickin' tissue paper, but you're lucky that I don't just open a window and start pitching things on top of your limo.*

"But the wrinkles."

Lizzie cranked her head in Chantal's direction. "Are the least of your problems. Now, come on, get working. I'm not doing this on my own."

Chantal looked affronted as she stood over the five Rubbermaid containers Greta had brought into the walk-in wardrobe. "I don't usually do things like this, you know."

"You don't say."

Grabbing one of the bins, Lizzie began to transfer folded things—pants, jeans, yoga gear—in a steady stream. Then she moved on to the next drawer. Underwear. Jeez, she remembered going through these before, when she'd snuck in to match the lingerie she'd found under William Baldwine's bed to something that Chantal owned.

Surreptitiously, she glanced over to the make-up table.

The blood on the cracked mirror had been cleaned up. But the glass was still broken.

She could only imagine the fight William and Chantal had had. But that was not her business. What was her biz? Getting this woman as far away from Lane and Easterly as she could get her.

It was kind of like weeding an ivy bed, she decided. Get out the bad, keep the good.

"Start on the hanging things," she ordered the woman. "Or I'll strip them off that rod on a oner."

That got Chantal moving, her manicured hands opening the glass doors and taking garments out hanger by hanger. But at least she made a pile to be carried from the suite.

Lizzie was on the third bin when Lane strode into the dressing room.

Chantal turned, looked at him . . . and put her hand on her lower abdomen.

Yeah, yeah, we all know you're pregnant, sweetie, Lizzie thought to herself. *Like we would forget?*

"These are my things," Chantal said with self-importance. "And I shall remove them."

Like she was Maggie-frickin'-Smith—

Okaaaay, maybe someone needed a Snickers bar, Lizzie decided. And it wasn't yonder beauty queen.

After all, there was no reason to get bitchy. It wasn't going to improve the situation and God knew there was enough of that under this roof already.

"Yup," Lane said, coming in. "You really should get them out of my house."

He walked over to one of the glass-fronted closets, threw the doors open, and put his entire upper body into the line-up of hangered clothes. When he reemerged, his strong arms were full of colorful, expensive swaths of silk, taffeta and organza.

"John!" he called out. "We need an extra pair of hands in here!"

"What are you doing!" Chantal rushed forward. "What are you—"

A stocky older man came in wearing . . . wow, an absolutely amazing set of golf shorts there. Who knew you could make clothes out of grass?

"Hey, there," the guy said with a flat Midwestern accent and a wide-open smile. "How can I help?"

"Grab some and carry it down to the limo."

"Sure thing, son."

"You can't! You won't! I can't—"

"Oh, and this is my fiancée, Lizzie." Lane smiled in her direction. "I don't think you've met her before."

"Fiancée!" Chantal stamped her stiletto. *"Fiancée?"*

As she stamped her actual foot again, Lizzie thought, Wow, she'd always assumed that move was reserved for *Friends* episodes.

"This is my friend John," Lane said to Lizzie. "You remember, the Grain God?"

"Hi." She offered the man a wave. "Thanks for helping."

"I'm a farmer, ma'am. I'm not afraid of work!"

The guy looked at Chantal, who was still going firecracker, and then he stepped around her, opened the next compartment, and strong-armed about two dozen full-length gowns.

It was like he was hugging a rainbow.

As the two men left with the clothes, Chantal followed after them, tripping over the padded hangers that fell to the floor in their wakes, a trail of sartorial bread crumbs.

Lizzie smiled to herself and went back to her packing.

Man, it felt good to clean house.

*O*utside of Gin's bedroom, some kind of commotion was making its way down the corridor.

She was too busy trying to find her cell phone to care, however. Last time she had used it . . . the pilots. She had used it when she'd been in the cockpit of Richard's jet. Had she lost the thing?

It wasn't on the bed stand. Nor under the bed. Nor on top of the decorative bureau.

And it wasn't in her purse.

Distantly aware of a rising panic, she went into her dressing room. The mess she'd made at the make-up station was tidied up—and for a moment, she stopped to think of what might have been involved in the cleaning of it all. There had been powder everywhere on the rolling table, streaks of eye pencil, tubes of lipstick and liner left out. So, in addition to putting everything that was still usable back in its place, Marls must have had to get glass cleaner or something, paper towels . . . who knew what.

Even the carpet underneath, the white carpet, was pristine.

"Thank you," she whispered, even though she was alone.

Walking over to the open shelves where she kept her collection of Gucci, Vuitton, Prada, and Hermès bags, she tried to remember what she'd taken with her—

The sound of ringing snapped her head around.

Tracing the ding-a-ling-a-ling across to the hanging sections of the room, she opened the panel closest to the noise . . . and pulled out a pink, white, and cream Akris silk coat.

She found the phone in the pocket and answered the call even though whoever it was didn't register in her contacts.

Maybe it was God, letting her know what to do next.

After all, it was entirely conceivable that Miss Aurora might have that kind of pull.

"Hello?"

"Ms. Baldwine?" a female voice said.

"Yes?"

"Hi, I'm Jules Antle. I'm the house parent on your daughter's floor at her dorm?"

"Oh. Yes. Yes, of course." This explained the 860 area code. "Are you looking for me to make arrangements to pick up Amelia's things?"

Shit, Mr. Harris had left. Who could handle—

"I'm sorry? Pick up her things?"

"Yes, I shall have someone collect her things immediately. Which dorm is she in again?"

"The semester's not over with."

"So you would prefer us to wait until the other students leave?"

"I'm—please forgive me, but I'm not following. I called to see when she was coming back. I took the liberty of speaking with her professors, and if she needs to take her finals from home after the study break, she's more than welcome to."

Gin frowned. "Exams?"

Ms. Antle, or Jules, or Mrs. House Parent, slowed her speech down, like maybe she thought Gin had cognitive difficulties. "Yes, the tests before summer break. They're going to be taken soon."

"But why would she . . . I'm sorry, it was my understanding that Amelia was asked to leave school."

"Amelia? No. Why would she have been? In fact, she's one of our favorites here. I could see her being a proctor when she's a senior. She's always helping people out, generous with tutoring, always there for anybody. But that's probably why she was elected class president."

Gin blinked and became aware that she'd turned such that she could see her own reflection in one of the mirrors by the hairdressing chair. Dear Lord, she looked awful. But then she'd fallen asleep with all her make-up on, so that although her hair wasn't that much of a tangle, her face looked like an evil clown with haunted eyes.

Rather ironic that she appeared such a mess while finding out her daughter's life was actually going quite well.

"Hello?" Miss Antlers or Anteater or whatever her name was prompted. "Ms. Baldwine?"

There was no reason to go into the lie with the woman. "I'm sorry. There's a lot going on here."

"I know, and we're so sorry. When Amelia learned that her grandfather had died, she really wanted to go home for the funeral. And again, if she would like to stay and be with family, we understand and are willing to make accommodations. We will need to know what she's going to do, however."

"I'll speak with her," Gin heard herself say. "And call you back directly."

"That would be great. Again, we think the world of her. You're raising a wonderful young woman who's going to do a lot of good in the world."

As Gin ended the call, she continued to stare at her reflection. Then she went over to the hair and make-up chair and sat down.

How she wished there was a guru you could go to and have everything put to rights in your life. One could try different styles of fixes: Caring Mother; Charismatic Professional; Sultry, But Not Morally Corrupt Thirty-Three-Year-Old.

There was no Chanel counter to go to for what ailed her, however.

And, yes, she supposed she could follow through on her first impulse, which was to go to Lane and have him firstly find out why Amelia had thought it was a great idea to lie about leaving school and then leave him to deal with getting the girl back to Hotchkiss to finish her finals . . . but abruptly that lacked appeal.

God, she didn't even know where the school was really, just its area code.

She certainly didn't know where her daughter was.

Going into her contacts, she found Amelia and initiated a connection. When she got voice mail, she hung up without leaving a message.

Where was the girl?

Getting to her stocking feet, Gin padded out into her bedroom and opened the door to the main upstairs corridor. Whatever drama had been going on had found a resolution or a different location, so she was alone as she went down and knocked on Amelia's door.

When there was no answer, she cracked the panels and looked inside. The girl was in her bed, fast asleep—or at least pretending to be asleep—and she wasn't in lingerie. She was wearing a Hotchkiss T-shirt and was on her side facing the door, those eyelashes of hers, which were every bit as long as Samuel T.'s, down hard on her cheeks.

Amelia frowned and twitched her brows, and then she rolled over onto her back. And then continued onto her other side.

With a deep sigh, she appeared to sink back into her rest.

Gin backed out of the room.

Probably better to get herself cleaned up before she tried to talk sense into anyone.

Back in her own suite, she proceeded into the bathroom and took off the dress she'd slept in. Wadding it up, she threw the thing away and then got into the shower.

She was running a monogrammed washcloth up her arm when the giant diamond on her left hand winked in the overhead light.

From out of nowhere, she heard Samuel T.'s voice in her head:

You've got to take care of yourself.

FORTY-SIX

"You're engaged?" Chantal demanded as Lane shut the trunk of the limousine.

"Yes," Lane answered. For what was it, the hundredth time?

The whole engagement thing had been the woman's theme song as she had played fruit fly from hell while everyone else had packed as much of her clothes, make-up, and costume jewelry as would fit in the limo's big extended body. And now she and Lane were alone but for the driver—who was in the vehicle with the doors all shut and his face buried in his cell phone. Like he didn't want to catch shrapnel.

Good luck getting a tip out of her, Lane thought.

"Really, Lane," Chantal said as raindrops started to fall yet again. "You couldn't wait until the ink was dry even on our separation papers—"

"I should have married her in the first place," Lane cut in. "And you are not in a position to be indignant about anything."

As he pointedly looked down at her lower belly, Chantal smiled with as much sweetness as a nine-millimeter pistol had. "When is the will going to be read?"

"My father's?"

"No, the pope's. Of course your damn father's!"

"It already was. There was no provision in it for you or your child. If you want to contest it, go ahead, but that's going to be about as lucrative as your professional career—oh, wait. You don't have one, do you. Not one that's legal, at any rate."

She jabbed a finger in his face. "I'm keeping this baby."

"Unlike mine, right?" He ignored the pain in his chest. "Or are you going to make that trip to the clinic in Cinci again when you find out there's no money in it."

"Maybe I only wanted your *father's* child."

"Probably. Actually, I don't doubt that that's true." He opened the limo's rear door. "The executor of the will is Babcock Jefferson. Look him up, give him a call, get in line—and sue the estate or not. Whatever works for you."

As she got in, she said, "You'll be hearing from my attorney."

"Boy, those words roll right off your tongue, don't they. And I look forward to the call—as long as it'll keep you off my property. Bye now."

He shut the door on whatever she was going to say next and took the time to give the driver a wave. Then Lane went back into the house. As he closed Easterly's heavy panels, he had no idea what time it was.

It felt like one a.m.

Heading deeper into the mansion, he found John Lenghe and his grass shorts in the game room. But the guy wasn't flexing his fingers over the two decks of cards on the felt poker table. He wasn't racking balls on the antique pool table. He wasn't playing chess against himself at the marble top with the hard-carved pieces nor was he fiddling with the backgammon board.

Lenghe was over at the far wall, staring at the painting that had been hung dead center in the middle of the incredible oak paneling.

Spotlit from above, the depiction of the face of Jesus Christ was done in tones of ivory and deep brown, the downcast eyes of the Savior so realistic, you could practically feel the divine sacrifice he was about to make.

"Not bad, huh," Lane said softly.

Lenghe wheeled around and clutched his heart. "I'm sorry. I didn't mean to wander. Well, I did. But I figured you and that lady could use some privacy."

Lane came into the room and paused at the pool table. The balls were in the rack and ready to go, but he couldn't remember the last time anyone had put a cue stick to them.

"I appreciate that," he said. "And your help. You cut the time that debacle would have taken in half."

"Well, without meaning any disrespect to the lady, I can kind of see why you might encourage her to find happier lodging somewhere else."

Lane laughed. "You Midwesterners have the nicest way of putting down someone."

"Can I ask you something?" Lenghe pivoted back to the painting. "This nameplate here . . . it says . . ."

"Yes, it is a Rembrandt. And it's been authenticated by multiple sources. All the paperwork on it is somewhere in this house. In fact, last year a private collector who came to the Derby Brunch offered my father forty-five million for it—or so I heard."

Lenghe put his hands in his pockets as if he were worried that they might make contact with the oil painting's surface.

"Why is it hidden all the way in here?" The man glanced around. "Not that this isn't a grand room or anything. I just don't understand why a masterpiece like this wouldn't be displayed more prominently, maybe in that pretty parlor up front."

"Oh, there's a good reason for it. My grandmother, Big V.E. as she was called, didn't approve of gambling, drinking, or smoking. She bought the painting overseas back in the nineteen fifties and installed it here so that anytime my grandfather and his good ol' boys had a hankering to be sinful, they had a reminder of exactly who they were letting down."

Lenghe laughed. "Smart woman."

"She and my grandfather collected Old Masters paintings. They're all over the house—but this one is probably among the most valuable even though it's on the small side."

"I wish my wife could see this. I'd take a picture on my phone, but it wouldn't do it justice. You have to stand in front of it in person. It's the eyes, you know?"

"She's welcome here anytime."

"Well, my wife, she doesn't like to travel. It's not that she's worried about flying or anything. She just hates to leave her cows and her chickens. She doesn't trust anyone with them or the dogs. Not even me. Those animals and those birds are her babies, you know."

As Lenghe refocused on the masterpiece with a wistful expression on his face, Lane frowned and put a hip on the pool table.

"You really like it, don't you," Lane said.

"Oh, yes."

Lane palmed the white cue ball and threw the thing up in the air a couple of times, catching it as he thought.

"You know," he said, "there have been some changes at the Bradford Bourbon Company since you and I saw each other last."

Lenghe looked over his shoulder. "I read about them in the paper. New interim CEO, an outsider. Smart move—and you want a numbers cruncher if you're going to exert control over the finances. And I should have congratulated you right away, Chairman of the Board."

Lane bowed his head. "Thank you. And yes, we are developing a plan that optimizes cash flow. I think I see a path out of our black hole, thanks to Jeff."

As thunder rattled the French doors, Lenghe nodded. "I have faith in you, son."

"My point is, I think I can safely say that if you give us only two months of grain on account, we should be okay. We'll give you favorable terms, of course. But really, after what Jeff is proposing to do, that should keep us going."

"So are you saying you don't want to throw cards with me, son?"

"Not at all." Lane narrowed his eyes. "Actually, I have something else you might be interested in playing for."

• • •

*T*hanks to the thunderstorms that were bubbling up over the flat stretches of the Plains states and drifting over Indiana and Kentucky, the heat of the afternoon was mercifully sapped.

And that meant Edward was enjoying the work he was doing out at the Red & Black.

No broom on the end of a stick, though. Not this time.

As rain began to fall once again from the purple and gray sky, and lightning made more shows of strength, he lowered the hammer in his hand and wiped his brow with his free arm. It had been . . . years . . . since he'd tended fences, and he already knew, going by the aches in his shoulders, that he was going to pay for this folly for days afterward. But as he looked down the five-rail, brown-painted track that cut through this pasture, and as he counted the number of nails he'd added and loose boards he'd secured, a flush of simple pride went through him.

Yes, he'd been at it for only an hour and he was about ready to quit. And indeed, a real man would have been working the fields for eight or ten at a clip.

But it was a start.

Right before the ending.

As he limped back to the Red & Black pick-up with his bag of supplies, he thought about the vodka he'd brought with him but had left in the cab.

He was going to need just a little more. But not much.

Getting behind the wheel, he shut himself in and took out his flask. One sip. Two sips. Then he washed it down with Gatorade like it was medicine. If he had another two days, given the way the DTs were easing, he was probably going to be fine. He wasn't sure things were going to hold until then, however.

Starting the engine, he began the trek back to the cottage, bumping along the cropped bluegrass, catching the attention of a hawk that was up in one of the shade trees by the water trough, flushing a couple of sparrows from a nest on a low-hanging branch.

Edward was careful to memorize everything about the gentle rolling land . . . and the way the fences cut man-made lines into the fragrant green expanse . . . and how the looming majesty of the red and gray slate-roofed barns made him think of his grandfather. As sweat rolled down between his shoulder blades, he still didn't put the air-conditioning on in the cab. Anyone who had ever done physical labor knew that once hot, stay hot. Short-term relief in your truck was just going to make your body temperature problems worse when you had to get back out into the heat.

Plus, it felt good to perspire.

As he came up to Barn B, he parked the pick-up in the rear and got out with the sack of nails and his hammer. Both seemed to have gained about fifty pounds of weight since he'd started. Hell, since he'd put 'em in the cab for the ride home.

Entering through the rear bay, he heard voices, a man's and a woman's, and he paused.

Shelby and Joey were standing in front of Neb's stall side by side. Shelby was talking about the stallion, clearly—likely about how they were going to handle the newest wave of bad weather with him. And Joey was agreeing with whatever she was saying, probably about how it had been a good idea to put the hood back on Neb's head and keep it there.

Smart move. Exactly what Edward had been of a mind to do as well.

Joey said something. She said something back.

Shelby looked at Joey. Looked away.

Joey looked at Shelby. Looked away.

Leaning against the barn's sturdy beams, Edward put the sack down, crossed his arms over his chest . . . and smiled.

Only to abruptly straighten.

While he was watching the two of them . . . there was a figure all the way down at the open bays of the front end of the barn.

Watching him.

"Wait. What did you say?"

Back in Easterly's game room, John Lenghe had turned around from the Rembrandt, and going by the expression on the man's face, Lane probably could have dropped a smoke bomb in the center of the pool table and the guy wouldn't have noticed.

Lane nodded at his grandmother's painting. "Let's play for that."

"You can't be serious."

"Why? Because it's worth at least forty-five million dollars and that's too much at stake."

"Not at all. Because why would you want to ever part with it."

Yeah, only a billionaire could say that with a straight face. And mean every word.

You really just had to smile at stuff like that, Lane thought.

"So you would be interested." He held up a palm. "Provided, of course, that I give you a chance to review the documentation, the insurance policy we have for it, and talk to your wife. And yes, I know that you're going to want to check with her, but keep in mind, if you beat me, you get to bring it home to her."

Lenghe rubbed his strong jaw, his huge biceps curling up thick. "Let me get this straight. I put up forty-five million. You put up the painting."

"It has to be forty-five million plus whatever capital gains I'd have to pay. I need to clear the forty-five. I can call a tax person right now and give you the exact figure. And that painting is not part of my father's estate. It is an asset owned by my mother, gifted to her by her mother when Big V.E. moved out and my mother became the mistress of Easterly. So I can get you clean title."

"Won't your mother—"

"She's never been attached to it. She's a Maxfield Parrish person. Her mother's taste has always been too heavy, in her opinion."

Yes, there might be an issue of capacity on his mother's side, but that really wasn't going to be a problem: All he needed was for Samuel T. to back date a power of attorney for her, in favor of Lane—something his old friend would do in a heart beat.

Lane summed it all up just so they were clear with each other. "Forty-five million plus long-term-capital-gains cost against that painting. Five-card, Texas Hold 'em. Same number of chips. We play mano a mano until one of us is out. I give you all the documentation we have—and if for any reason you get it valuated and it's worth less than what I need, I'll throw in as many other paintings as I have to to make up the difference." Lane pointed at the painting. "I will tell you this, though. The MFA's curator of Old Masters was at that Derby Brunch last year. My father asked the guy whether he should sell for forty-five and the answer was no, because it was worth about sixty."

John turned to the painting again.

"It will never be of less value," Lane said. "Your money couldn't be in a safer place. Or a more beautiful one. Assuming you win against me."

It was a while before the man pivoted back toward Lane.

In a grim voice, like he really wished his answer could be different, the Grain God said, "I better call the wife. And you better get me that paperwork."

FORTY-SEVEN

*S*utton had been between meetings.

Really.

She had been between meetings and had just, you know, decided to drive from the Sutton Distillery Corporation headquarters in downtown Charlemont, all the way out into Ogden County.

Where her Mercedes had, of its own volition, taken a left-hand turn onto a perfectly paved lane that happened to be the entrance to the venerable Red & Black Stables. After which the sedan had followed the way through the fields, past the perfectly appointed barns . . . and onward still to the little caretaker's cottage where Edward had been staying.

After she had pulled into the shallow parking space she had used before, she had gotten out with the intention of . . . well, hell, she hadn't gotten that far. But she'd walked up to the door, knocked, and when there had been no answer after a couple of tries, she had pushed her way in.

As she had looked to the chair in the center of the room, she had half expected to find Edward upright and unconscious, dead from so much: the injuries, the alcohol, the bitterness.

But no.

Feeling like she had been saved from making a fool of herself, she had backed out, shut the place up, and decided that if she got right back in her car and hit the gas, she could still catch a workout before the dinner meeting she was having with Richard Pford about new distribution contracts for Sutton products. Which was not something she was looking forward to. The man was about as charismatic as an abacus, but there were millions of dollars on the table and there were going to be at least four lawyers and three members of her senior management with them.

So, yes, a workout was exactly what she needed—

The sight of a Red & Black truck pulling up behind the nearest barn had caught her eye. And when Edward had gotten out and gone inside without seeing her, she'd been torn.

In the end, she had walked over to the front bay in spite of the rain.

With the light coming in from behind her, she had seen a woman standing by a stall down farther than halfway, talking with somebody . . . and Edward had stopped and was staring at her, his arms linked over his chest, his body leaning against the opening's supports.

The expression on his face . . .

Well, it was nothing Sutton had ever seen before. Warm. Tender. Slightly wistful.

And all of that made her refocus on the female. She was short and built very strong, her thighs tightening her jeans, her boots worn, her blondish hair pulled back in a practical ponytail. It was hard to judge the features from just a profile, but her skin had been kissed by the sun and she positively radiated youth and health and competence in her environment.

From time to time, she turned to the man next to her.

She didn't seem to notice Edward.

Edward certainly didn't notice Sutton—

As if he had read her mind, his eyes shifted and he straightened. And at the same moment, the woman and the man she was with discovered they were no longer alone and got all startled.

Sutton ducked out the open bay so fast she nearly lost her footing, thanks to her stilettos—and wasn't that a reminder that whereas the woman in front of that stall was clearly in her element, Sutton was lost out here, no more capable of riding a horse in her current Chanel suit than mucking out after one in her Louboutins.

And this was Edward's new life. He'd always had an interest in horses, but now he was breeding and racing his stock in earnest.

That woman, that naturally beautiful, physically fit woman, was perfect for the farm. Perfect for the new him.

Sutton, with the Mercedes she was heading to, and her board appointments and her corporate strategies, was everything about his old existence.

She shouldn't have come.

"Sutton!"

As he called her name, she was tempted to go even faster for her car, but she was worried he'd try to follow her and hurt himself.

Stopping in the rain, she almost couldn't bear to turn around: She had been thinking about him non-stop since they had been together, but meanwhile, he had been out here, with that woman—and even if he wasn't currently "with" her? Going by that look on his face? He was going to be.

Squaring her shoulders, Sutton pivoted on the grass. And for a moment, she was taken aback.

Edward's coloring was good, his skin not the gray cast it had been, but flushed with—

Well, hell, maybe he was just embarrassed that he'd been caught. Except he hadn't been doing anything wrong, had he. She had only discovered him in a private moment, and they were certainly not in a relationship.

"I'm sorry," she said. "I shouldn't have come."

He stopped in front of her. "It's raining."

"Is it?" As he looked at her strangely, she waved a hand. "I mean, of course it is. Yes."

"Come on inside."

As he took her elbow, she shook her head. "No, honestly, it's fine—"

"I know. But come inside. There's lightning—"

The flash and violent *CRACK!* of a bolt of electricity hitting something made of wood made her feel like God was determined to teach her a lesson. For the life of her, though, she didn't know what it was.

Oh, who was she kidding. She needed to let this whole Edward thing go. That was what she had to get through her thick skull.

"Come on," he prompted. "Before we get killed out here."

Heading over to the cottage, she remembered the Governor of the Commonwealth volunteering to be her rebound date, and you know, that didn't seem like such a bad idea, after all.

Once inside, Edward turned on the lights, and the wall of silver trophies gleamed.

"Let me get you a towel."

"I'm fine." Really? Was she really fine? "Honestly, I shouldn't have come."

Guess that was her refrain, wasn't it.

Ignoring her protest, he passed her something that was the color of raspberries. Or had been before it had been washed a hundred times. The terry cloth was as soft as chamois, though, and as she pressed it to her face so she didn't smudge her eye make-up, she decided her expensive Matouk towels weren't as good.

Also decided that his little girlfriend out in that stable would just rub and go. Or maybe not dry off at all so she looked as dewy as she was.

Twenty. Twenty-two at the most. And Sutton, at thirty-eight, felt like a hundred in comparison.

"I was going to call you," Edward said as he went into the galley kitchen.

The sounds of cupboards opening and closing seemed as loud as jet engines taking off.

"I don't need anything to drink—"

As he came back and presented her with a glass, she frowned as she caught a telltale whiff of— "Is this my lemonade?"

"Yeah. Or at least, it should be close to it." He limped over to his chair and let out a curse as he sat down. "I remembered the recipe. Your grand-mother's."

She took a test sip. "Oh, you got it right."

"Took me forever to squeeze the lemons."

"They have to be fresh."

"Makes a difference." He glanced up at her, his eyes tracing over her features. "You look . . . so good."

"Come on, my hair's wet, and I—"

"No, you are as beautiful as you always are."

Sutton stared into the lemonade as she felt him stare at her. "Why are you looking at me like that?"

"I'm re-memorizing everything about you."

"And why are you doing that?"

"I need something to keep me warm at night."

She thought of that woman out in that barn and almost asked him what was up. But she didn't have that right. Or . . . more likely, she didn't want to know.

"Sutton, I really . . ."

"What?"

He cursed softly. "I wish I could give you what you deserve. I truly do. You are . . . one of the most amazing people I've ever met. And I should have told you that sooner. I wish had. I wish I had . . . well, done a lot of things. But it's just . . . life has changed for me, as you know. I'm never going to be what I once was. The things I used to do, the person I used to be, the company I kept . . . hell, the company I worked for? That's all gone for me and it's never coming back."

Sutton closed her eyes. And as a silence bloomed, like he was waiting for her to respond, all she could do was nod: She was afraid if she tried to speak, the sobs she was holding in would escape.

"What you need in a man is nothing I can provide you with. I'm not going to be good for your public profile—"

"I don't care what people think."

"You have to. You're head of that whole company. You *are* the Sutton Distillery Corporation. I mean, maybe it wouldn't be quite so bad if you weren't selling your own name, if you were an arm's length businessperson, but you're not. Plus you need stability in your life. You deserve someone who's going to hold you at night and be there on holidays and stand by your side at your civic things. Don't lie to yourself, Sutton. You know I'm right."

She took another sip of the lemonade. "Why did you make love to me the day before yesterday?"

"Because I'm a weak asshole. And sometimes we do things we feel like we need to even if they're not really right."

"Ah."

"I won't ever forget you, Sutton. Ever."

"You make it sound like Ogden County is on the other side of the world."

Then again, it wasn't geographical distance that was the problem.

"If you want to hate me," he said roughly, "I won't blame you."

"I don't want to do that." She went across and focused on the trophies because she didn't want him to see her eyes. "Tell me something."

"What?"

"When I see you, you know, out and about—"

"You won't."

Abruptly, she imagined him avoiding her at the Derby by running and jumping behind support columns and bathroom doors.

"You won't see me, Sutton."

"So you're really closing me off, huh." She turned back around and indicated her glass. "Do you mind if I put this down somewhere? I'm not really thirsty."

"I'll take it."

Lifting her chin, she walked over and put the glass in his hand. It seemed appropriate that thunder shook the cottage as she stepped back.

"Do me a favor?" she said hoarsely.

"What?"

"Don't try to walk me to my car, or suggest I stay in here a minute longer. Let me leave with some pride, okay?"

His eyes, those fucking eyes, stared up at her with such intensity that she felt like he was taking a long-exposure photograph.

He nodded once.

Blinking hard, she whispered, "Good-bye, Edward."

"Good-bye, Sutton."

Out of the cottage. Into the storm.

The dumping rain was cold, and she lifted her face to the sky as she went for her Mercedes, thinking it was the third damned time she'd gone through the rain because of him. And after she got behind the wheel and slammed the door, she gripped the steering wheel as hail marched over the metal and glass that sheltered her like a tiny army that had countless little boots.

Unlike the first time she'd taken the C63 out here alone, she now knew how to work the gearshift. No more hunting for reverse . . . so that a prostitute who looked just like her had to tell her what to do.

As she headed out to the rural route that would take her back where she belonged, she took so many deep breaths that she got to be light-headed.

Goddamn it, she could still taste that lemonade in her mouth.

As Edward heard Sutton's car pull out and speed off, he exhaled long and slow. Then he looked at the two glasses in his hands.

Pouring all of his into what had been hers, he put the empty glass aside and drank what her grandmother had taught her to make on hot Kentucky afternoons: One dozen lemons. Cut in half on a wood board with a stout knife. Fresh Kentucky water that carried the kiss of limestone in it.

Sugar. Whole cane sugar. But not too much.

You put the ice in the glasses, not the pitcher. You kept the pitcher in the refrigerator with a tinfoil seal on it so whatever you also had in there didn't season it by exposure.

You shared it with the people you loved.

Closing his eyes, he saw images of her from the past, like back when she was twelve and he had chased her at Charlemont Country Day because she was one of the first class of girls they'd let in. Or when she was sixteen and that asshole had stood her up for prom . . . and he'd punched the SOB in the face. And then even later, at twenty-one, as she'd graduated and come back for the summer, looking like a full-blown woman for the first time.

And then he remembered the stories about Sutton's grandmother, a woman who hadn't been "classy." In fact, her grandfather had gone out West as a young buck and cattle ranched against his fancy family's wishes—and there he had met a beautiful young woman who rode better than he did, shot better than he did, and wrangled better than he did.

When he'd brought her home, she had made that fancy family bend to her will. It hadn't been the other way around. And it had been, as Sutton had always said, a grand romance for the ages.

The love remained alive in the lemonade he was drinking now.

When the door to the cottage opened, he knew it wasn't Sutton. She wasn't coming back now, or ever, and though his heart hurt, that was the right answer to their equation.

Shelby shut the heavy weight and brushed wet tendrils of hair out of her face.

He cleared his throat. "Neb okay?"

"Yeah, he's doing good. Joey's with him."

"Thanks for coming to tell me."

"That's not why I'm here." There was a pause. "That your woman?"

When he didn't answer, Shelby whistled softly. "She sure is beautiful. I mean, she almost didn't look real. I don't see people like her very often. Outside of magazines maybe."

"Oh, she's real."

"Where'd she go?"

"Home."

"Why? Why you let her go?"

Edward took a sip from Sutton's glass. "Because it's the right thing to do."

"Is that the lemonade you spent all morning makin'? You make it for her?"

"No, I didn't know she was coming." He looked at it. "I made it because I had to have it."

One last time.

"You letting Joey take you out?" he asked without glancing up.

There was a pause. "Yeah."

Edward smiled. "I can hear the blush in your voice."

"I ain't blushin'."

"Bullshit."

As she huffed up, he winked at her. "Come on, I needed to make sure you were paying attention. And there wasn't a 'God' in that one anywhere."

Shelby glared at him for a minute. Then she started to smile back. "Ah, but He's everywhere. And you know what?"

"What's that?"

"I'm glad He brought you and me together."

Edward shook his head. "That was your father, remember."

"Maybe it was Father with a capital 'F.'"

"You say tomato, I say tah-mato."

"Well . . ." She looked around. "I'm going to head back over to the apartment. Unless you need anything? I left lunch leftovers in your fridge for your dinner."

"That was good of you, thank you. And nope, I'm good. But again, thanks."

With her hand on the door latch, Shelby looked over her shoulder. "You going to be here in the morning?"

"Of course I will." He let his head fall back and took a mental picture of her. "Where else would I be?"

He gave her ample time to measure his expression, read his energy, assess his intent with all of her horse sense—and he must have passed the test because she nodded and scooted out and into the storm.

To Joey.

It was good to be where you belong, Edward thought as he stared at all the trophies. And best to do the things you can live with.

Even if it killed you in the short run.

FORTY-EIGHT

*B*erkley Sedgwick Jewelers was the third-oldest jewelry story in all of the United States. Nestled in a neighborhood that mixed residential housing with commercial endeavors, the establishment was ensconced in a charming old Victorian home . . . which had bars on every window, security cameras on all the eaves, and an ex–Army Ranger who patrolled the premises.

Gin had been a faithful customer for years—and had also enjoyed learning more about that particular man in uniform.

As well as out of it.

But all of those fun and games seemed like a million years in the past, however, as she parked the Drophead in the back lot. It was eight o'clock, so the other spaces were empty—except for a huge black-on-black SUV that had, quite tragically, a Kentucky University plate on its tail.

It was really the only thing she didn't like about Ryan Berkley, the owner.

The business was closed to regular customers, but it wasn't the first time she had come in after hours, and before she could even knock on the bolted, metal rear door, Ryan opened it for her.

"I'm so glad you called me," he said as she came over.

Ryan was a direct descendant of one side of the founders, and sharing that in regard to her own family's business, she had always felt a kinship with him. That was the extent of their affiliation, however, apart from her buying things from time to time: Even though Ryan was tall and muscular, still fit as the Division I basketball player he'd been in college—for Kentucky University, pity—and in spite of the fact that he had a handsome face, a great haircut, and blue eyes that matched his school colors, there had never been anything between them.

Ryan was a good man, married to a former Miss Kentucky, and interested only in his wife, his four children, and his store.

"As if I would trust anyone else," Gin said as she entered.

After locking them in, Ryan hustled her through the office and storage space, as if he hated any customer seeing the less formal parts of his establishment. Past all that, the store proper was done in royal blue with thick carpet and heavy drapes that were closed for privacy. Glass cases extended down both sides of the long, thin, high-ceiling'ed space, and vintage chandeliers and discreet track lighting made the incredible gems sparkle and wink for attention.

Ryan clapped his big hands together. "So tell me, what may I do for you?"

"Do you have any champagne?"

"For you? Always. DP Rosé?"

"You know what I like."

As he disappeared into the back again, she strolled along, pausing at the estate cases. Millions of dollars were for sale in the forms of tutti-frutti bracelets by Cartier, bar pins by Tiffany, rings that had center stones as big as thumbnails.

There was even a particularly stunning Schlumberger necklace of pink and yellow sapphires with turquoise and diamonds accents. Late sixties. Had to be.

"You always know the best," Ryan said as he came up to her with a flute. "And I just got that in."

"Is this the one from the Christie's sale last month?"

"It is."

"You paid nine hundred eighty thousand and change with the buyer's premium. What's the mark-up? Because I think you overpaid for it."

He laughed. "You know, if being a socialite ever bores you, you can always come consult for me."

"It's just a hobby."

Although he was right, jewelry was an obsession of hers, and throughout the year, she poured over all the Christie's and Sotheby's catalogues for the houses' New York, Geneva, and Hong Kong sales. Often, in the past, she had been a buyer.

No more, though.

Gin looked up at him. "I need you to handle something discreetly for me."

"Always." He indicated a pair of chairs that had been pulled up by the diamond case. "Come, tell me what you require."

Following him over, she sat down and put the flute on the glass case. Taking off her engagement ring, she held the thing out.

"I want you to remove this stone and replace it with a cubic zirconia."

Ryan took the diamond but didn't look at it. "Why don't we just make you a travel copy? I can have one ready for you tomorrow by ten a.m.—"

"I want you to buy the stone from me. Tonight. For gold."

Ryan sat back, shifting the ring onto the tip of his forefinger. And yet he still didn't look at the thing. "Gin, you and I have done a lot of business together, but I'm not sure—"

"I believe it's an H color. VVS2. Harry Winston on the shank, and I think he got it new. Carat weight has to be high teens, low twenties. The value is around a million and a half, retail, a million at auction. I'm asking five hundred thousand—which is slightly higher than wholesale, I know, but I'm a loyal customer of yours, number one, and number two, I know you've read the newspapers. I may be in a position of having to liquidate some of my mother's collection, and if you don't want me going up to New York to the auction houses, you have to do right by me on this deal."

Again, he didn't examine the ring, just kept looking at her. "You know I want to help you, but it's not as simple as you're making it out to be. There are tax implications—"

"For me, not you. And the ring is mine. It was given to me in contemplation of marriage, and I married Richard Pford yesterday. Even if we divorce tomorrow, it stays with me legally."

"You're asking me to be complicit in insurance fraud, though. This must be insured—there's no way this asset isn't scheduled."

"Again, my problem, not yours. And to make things easier, I'm telling you right now that I'll cancel the policy, whatever and wherever it is. You have no reason to think I won't follow through on this, and no way to know if I don't."

Finally, he looked at the stone, holding it up to his naked eye.

"This is a good deal for the both of us," she said.

Ryan got to his feet. "Let me look at it under the microscope. But I have to take it out of the setting."

"Do whatever you need to."

Leaving the champagne behind, she followed him into an anteroom that was used for private consultations during business hours, typically by men buying diamonds for their girlfriends.

Richard, you cheap bastard, she thought. *That stone better be real.*

*B*ack at Easterly, Lane entered the kitchen and followed the sound of chopping to where Miss Aurora was making quick work of a bag of carrots, reducing the lengths to perfectly even, quarter-inch-thick orange disks.

"Okay," he said, "so we're you, Lizzie, me, John, and Jeff for dinner. I don't think Max is coming, and I have no idea where Gin or Amelia are."

To kill time while Lenghe was looking over all the documentation on the Rembrandt, Lane had gone down to the row of cottages to try to talk to Max. When he'd found the guy sound asleep, he'd tried Edward, but had gotten no answer—and as Lane didn't know when he was going to get a response from his potential poker opponent, he didn't want to leave the estate.

"Dinner's ready and holding," Miss Aurora said as she reached for another carrot out of the mesh net. "I did us a roast beef with mashed potatoes and stewed beans. This here's for Gary. My puree is the only vegetable he'll eat, and he's likewise joining us for dinner."

"You got any cobbler left?"

"Made a fresh one. Figured you boys will be hungry."

Bracing his palms on the granite, Lane leaned into his arms and watched Miss Aurora work that blade like a metronome on a piano top, the rhythm always the same.

He cleared his throat. "So Lizzie and Greta made up a list of the staff who are going to have to go."

"Oh, yeah?"

"A lot of people are being laid off."

"Who's staying?"

"You, Lizzie, Reginald, Greta, and Gary. Gary'll wanna keep Timbo, and that makes sense. Everyone else goes. Turns out Greta loves paper-work—she'll become the new controller for accounts half time. Lizzie says she'll take over cleaning the house and helping Gary and Timbo with the mowing."

"Atta girl." Miss Aurora paused in the chopping and looked up. "And that's a good crew. We can handle it all."

Lane exhaled in relief. "That's what I think. Mother will retain her nurses, of course."

"I wouldn't rattle her cage too much. Keep things the same up there."

"We're going to be saving . . . almost a hundred thousand dollars each month. But I feel bad, you know? I'm going to talk to each one of them myself."

"You'll hire 'em back. Not to worry."

"I don't know about that, Miss Aurora."

"You'll see."

As she resumed chopping, she frowned and moved her shoulder around as if it was stiff. And then Miss Aurora paused, put down the knife and seemed like she was having to catch her balance with the help of the countertop.

"Miss Aurora? Are you okay—"

"I'm fine, boy. Just fine."

Shaking her head as if she were clearing it, she picked up the knife and took a deep breath. "Now, go get your friend from out of town. That roast is drying in my holding oven, and I don't want to be wasting all that meat."

Lane searched her face. God, he felt like she lost more weight every time he laid eyes on her. "Miss Aurora—"

"The out-of-towner is here," Lenghe said as he came into the kitchen. "And he is hungry—and ready to play poker."

Turning around, Lane made a mental note to follow up with Miss Aurora. Maybe she needed more help in the kitchen?

"So," Lane said as he clapped his palms. "We going to do this?"

"The documentation could not be more impressive." Lenghe took a seat at the counter after greeting Miss Aurora with a "ma'am." "And the value is there."

"I also checked with my tax guy." Who had been a buddy of Jeff's up in New York. "At our tax rate, which is the highest, long-term capital gains on a collectible is twenty-eight percent. My grandmother, as you know from the paperwork, paid a million dollars for the painting when she bought it. Accordingly, the tax man is going to be looking for ten million, nine hundred and twenty thousand from me."

"So fifty million, nine hundred twenty is the magic number."

"Looks that way."

Lenghe put his hand out. "You put up the painting, and I'm prepared to wire that sum to the account of your choice Monday morning if I lose. Or, if you'd feel more comfortable doing an escrow overseas, where there's a market open right now, we can do that, too."

Lane shook the older man's palm. "Deal. No escrow necessary, I trust you."

As they shook, Lenghe looked over at Miss Aurora. "You're our witness, ma'am."

"Yes." Then she nodded at Lane. "And as much as I enjoy catering to our guests here at Easterly, you'll be understandin' that when y'all play, I'll be prayin' for my boy."

Lenghe bowed his head. "I would expect nothing different."

"Wash up for dinner," she commanded as she put the knife down and turned to the stove. "I'm serving family style tonight in the small dining room."

Lane headed for the sink across the way and Lenghe fell into step right with him. As he turned on the water, soaped up his hands, and passed the bar to the Grain God, he had to smile. Only Miss Aurora wouldn't blink an eye at a poker game with over fifty million at stake—and just as blithely order a billionaire to wash his hands before sitting at her table.

Indeed, he loved his momma so.

FORTY-NINE

As Ryan Berkley took his time at the microscope, Gin went back for her flute and returned to sip at the Dom Pérignon as she waited. From time to time, she glanced into the cases there in the private area, where the diamonds were even larger than the ones displayed out in the open. Still, they were but chips compared to what Richard had gotten for her.

Assuming it wasn't a CZ.

When Ryan finally straightened from the equipment, she said, "Well?"

"You're right. VVS1. H—or maybe an I with medium blue fluorescents kicking the color up a grade."

He went to another machine, an infrared light flashed, and he nodded. "No, it's an H. You've got a hell of an eye, Gin."

"Thank you."

Ryan took a deep breath. "Okay. You have yourself a deal."

To hide her relief, she took another draw from the champagne. "Good. That's good."

"You realize that five hundred thousand in gold is going to weigh just over twenty-five pounds?"

"Two bags. Twelve and a half in each. I can carry them just fine."

Her jeweler frowned. "That's a lot of money just to walk out of here with. Are you going to be okay? Where are you going to put it?"

"It's all taken care of. Not to worry."

Ryan inclined his head. "All right. I'm going to have to split it between bars and coins. I don't have enough of one or the other. And according to APMEX, the current price per kilo is forty thousand, one hundred eighty-eight dollars, and forty cents. Do you want to see the report?"

"No. And I'm not going to nickel-and-dime you."

"Fair enough."

It took him a good forty-five minutes to get everything organized, and then he brought her into the cellar where he did the weighing and measuring of the gold in front of her at a long worktable. The kilo bars clocked in at just over two pounds apiece, and she liked the feel of them in her hand. Stamped with EMIRATES GOLD in a crest and engraved with 1 KILO, GOLD, and serial numbers, the thin blocks were about the size of her iPhone and he had seven of them to give her.

The rest of the price was made up of South African Krugerrands, which were one troy ounce of twenty-two-karat gold, even though, Ryan explained, they weighed a little more because of the almost three grams of copper alloy added to make the coins harder and therefore more durable.

Lots of coins. A pirate's booty of coins.

The sacks were of a heavy nylon, and under the caged lights over the worktable, the glow of the pile gradually decreased as the gold was shifted into the bags.

When it was all apportioned, she signed the paperwork and stood up to leave.

"Wait," he said. "We need to put the CZ in the setting."

Gin closed her eyes as she imagined Richard's reaction to her showing up with an empty ring. "But of course."

Ryan made fast work of it, finding a suitable fake emerald-cut "diamond" and securing it in the platinum cage. Then he steam-cleaned the thing and gave it back to her.

As she slid the ring back onto her finger on top of her wedding band, she fanned out her hand. "Perfect."

"You're going to have to keep that really clean if you want it to look real. The CZs are great, but any oil from the skin or soap residue and they dull immediately."

She nodded and went for the bags. With a grunt, she lifted them. "Heavy—"

"Will you please let me take them to your car for you?"

"Actually, I think I will. Thank you."

She followed him out of the cellar and back into the fancy part of the store. And they almost made it to the rear door.

But Ryan stopped. "I can't . . . Gin, this really isn't safe. I know that St. Michael's is a relatively safe area of town, but please, let me see you home with these. Or call a security detail you. Please."

"I'm not going home."

His blue eyes were grave. "I'm licensed to carry. I have a gun on me at all times and two in my car. Let me get you wherever you're going in one piece—I will never forgive myself otherwise, especially if something happens."

She looked at the two bags and thought of how much value was in them.

Funny, she had spent her whole life around huge amounts of money . . . but it had been mostly represented by numbers in bank accounts, charge cards that fit in her wallet, and wads of cash that hadn't come anywhere close to equaling half a million dollars. Even the value in the artwork, antiques, and silver in the house, or the jewels in the vault seemed different, more statements of style, decor, and grand living than worth.

There was something very nuts-and-bolts about bags of gold.

"I can drive you in my SUV," Ryan pushed, "which is retrofitted for security. And then bring you back here for your car."

"Are you sure?"

He rolled his eyes. "I'm a good Catholic boy whose father is about to turn in his grave if I let you walk out of this store by yourself. So yes, I'm sure."

"All right. Thank you. Thank you very much."

Minutes later, he had backed the SUV right up to the rear door, got her settled in the passenger seat . . . and put the two bags in her lap.

"We're just going up to the bank," she told him as he reversed.

"Thank you, Jesus," he muttered.

The local PNC branch was just up the road a little, and as soon as they pulled up, the manager, who was an attractive blond woman, opened the delivery door in the back.

She was in yoga-wear and had her hair in a ponytail, looking far younger than she did in her business suits.

"Hi there," she said as they got out with him, lugging the weight once again. "Ryan, this is a pleasant surprise. I left your Stacy in class about twenty minutes ago."

"Can I just tell you how happy I am to see you?" he said as he dropped a kiss on the woman's cheek.

"That's nice to hear."

After they entered a shallow, dim space that was not ordinarily for customers, the woman closed things up, cranking a circular wheel until there was a *clank!* As they moved further in, passing into the regular part of the bank, the lights were down low, everything quiet and orderly.

"The paperwork is right over here."

Gin felt in a bit of a daze as she went across and signed some things at a countertop. And yes, the pen was attached to a date block with a little metal leash of tiny silver links. The thing hissed like a snake as she scribbled her name here . . . here . . . and . . . right here, thank you.

"This is your key," the woman said. "And I'll take you to the box now."

Ryan spoke up. "Do you want to go in alone, Gin?"

"No, if you can carry that?"

"Absolutely."

The three of them entered the vault that had been opened just for her, and she was escorted to a safe-deposit box down by the floor that seemed like the size of a kitchen trash bin. Taking back the key, the manager leaned in and put it into the slot, added one of her own and then the hatch was opened.

The woman extracted a square metal container out of the compartment with a grunt. "This is our biggest size."

"Please don't hurt yourself." Gin turned to Ryan. "May I?"

She wanted to be the one to put the gold in there—and as soon as she did, she stared at the two of them.

"I want you to be my witnesses. This is for my daughter. In case anything happens to me, this is all hers. I'm giving it to Amelia."

Gin took a sealed envelope out of her purse. "I put it in this letter. This is for Amelia."

And the provisions for who got the gold weren't the only things she'd written down. Samuel T. was in there as well.

He would no doubt be a fantastic father. Once he got over the shock . . . and the surge of hatred for Gin.

Laying the letter on top of the nylon sacks, she could feel the pair of them looking at her funny, and she couldn't say she blamed them. After all, her father had just killed himself—or maybe hadn't, who knew.

They were probably wondering if she was next.

"And if I'm found dead, I want you to know that Richard Pford did it." She looked them both in the eye, ignoring the alarm she caused. "That's also in the letter. If I'm killed, he murdered me."

*L*izzie could hardly eat.

It wasn't that the company was bad. It wasn't that the small dining room, with its collection of Imari platters mounted on its cream silk walls and its Aubusson rug, wasn't elegant. And there certainly wasn't anything wrong with Miss Aurora's food.

It was more the fact that her man was about to play poker for a pot totaling over fifty thousand—

Million, she corrected herself. Fifty *million* dollars.

God, she couldn't get her mind around the sum.

"—good idea at the time," Lane was saying as he sat back from his second helping and wiped his mouth. "The river was at its high point, and come on, Land Rovers are hearty vehicles. I wanted the challenge. So I took Ernie—"

"Wait," she said, plugging into the story. "Who's Ernie?"

Lane leaned over and kissed her on the mouth. "My first car. Ernie."

Jeff spoke up from across the table. "Why do I think this doesn't end well for Ernie?"

"It didn't." Lane took a sip of his ginger ale. "Anyway, I went down to River Road, broke through the police tape—"

Miss Aurora shook her head, even as she was trying to hide her grin. "I'm so glad I didn't know about this before now or I woulda had words with you, young man."

"You may still get your chance," John said with a laugh as he reached for his Coke. "The night is young."

"Anyway," Lane interjected, "I learned that as long as you keep moving forward, you got it. That water came all the way up until it was lapping over the hood."

"This was without a snorkel?" Lizzie said. "Or with?"

"Without. And that was kind of the problem. See, there was this tree floating under the surface—"

"Oh, God," Lizzie muttered.

"—and it caught me right at the grille. My velocity slowed . . . and yeah, that was when Ernie died. He was stuck there until the river went down, and you want to talk about silt? The inside of that car looked like it had spent a fortnight out in the desert during a sandstorm."

As people laughed, Lizzie had to ask, "Wait, so what happened next? What did you tell your father?"

Lane grew serious, the smile leaving his face. "Oh, you know . . . Edward came in and saved the day. He had a bunch of money that he'd been investing—it wasn't family cash, it was from summer jobs and birthday presents. He bought me a used one that looked just like Ernie, same interior, same exterior. A few more miles, but like Father was going to check the speedometer? Without Edward . . . man, that wouldn't have gone well."

"To big brothers," John said as he raised his glass.

"To big brothers," everyone answered.

"So," Lane murmured as everybody lowered their drinks back to the table. "You ready to do this?"

John got to his feet and picked up his plate. "Soon as we help clear. I can't wait. I'm feeling lucky tonight, son. I'm feeling lucky!"

As Jeff and Miss Aurora got up as well, Lizzie stayed where she was, and Lane, as if sensing her mood, didn't move either as everyone else filed out.

"You sure this is a good idea?" she whispered as she took his hands in hers. "Not that I don't trust you. It's just . . . that's so much money."

"If I win, Ricardo Monteverdi and that loan at Prospect Trust largely goes away—and then we've got half a chance because Jeff is going to turn the company around. God, you should have seen him down at headquarters. He's . . . amazing. Just incredible. We'll have some lean months, but by the end of the year? We'll be up to date on accounts payable and Mack won't have to worry about where the grains for his mash are coming from anymore."

"I can't believe you're so calm." She laughed. Or cursed. It was hard to know what that sound coming out of her was. "I feel like I'm a nervous wreck and I'm just on the sidelines."

"I know what I'm doing. The only thing I'm worried about is luck— and that you can't control. You can make up for it with skill, though. And I've got that in spades."

She reached up to his face. "I'm so proud of you."

"I haven't won yet."

"I don't care about the outcome—well, I do. I just . . . you're doing what you said you were going to do. You're saving your family. You're taking care of your business. You're . . . you're really amazing, you know that?"

As she went in to kiss him, he laughed deep in his chest. "Not a recalcitrant playboy anymore, am I. See what the love of a good woman will do for a guy?"

They kissed for a moment, and then he pulled her into his lap. Putting her arms around his neck, she smiled.

"Absolutely." Lizzie smoothed the hair at the base of his neck. "And guess what?"

"What?"

Lizzie put her mouth to his ear. "Win or lose . . . you're getting lucky tonight."

Lane let out a growl, his hands tightening on her waist, his hips rolling underneath her. As he went to kiss her again, she stopped him. "We better head for the game room now before distraction sets in."

"It's already set in," he said dryly. "Trust me."

"Just remember," she murmured as she got off of him. "The sooner you're done . . . the sooner we can go—"

Lane burst out of his chair, nearly knocking the thing over. Grabbing her hand, he started dragging her out of the room at a dead run.

"Will you quit wasting time, woman!" he said as she laughed out loud. "Jeez, I got poker to play . . . !"

FIFTY

About half an hour later, Lane sat at the circular poker table in the game room about three chairs away from Lenghe. The spectators, by mutual agreement of the players, had taken a line-up of chairs on the far side of where the cards were being thrown so no one could see over anyone's shoulders. Lizzie and Miss Aurora were together, with Jeff and Gary, the head groundskeeper, sitting next to them.

There was no way of pretending that this wasn't one of those moments that was inevitably going to become Bradford lore, just like when one of Lane's ancestors had lent money to Abraham Lincoln or another had had to fight a fire at the Old Site with water from the aquifer, or when Bradford horses had come in one, two, and three in the 1956 Derby.

That trifecta had won his grandfather enough to pay for one whole new barn out at the Red & Black—

"Are we too late?"

Lane looked over to the doorway. "Mack, you came."

"Like I'd miss this?"

Lane's Master Distiller walked in with a very nice-looking young woman—oh, the assistant, Lane thought. That's right.

"Mr. Lenghe," Mack said as he went over. "Good to see you again."

"Well, if it isn't my favorite distiller."

After the two clapped palms, Mack said, "This is a friend of mine, and my assistant, Beth Lewis."

Introductions and greetings were made all around, and Lane couldn't resist pumping his eyebrows at the guy behind Beth's back. Which got him flipped off in return.

"Anyone else coming?" John asked as the group resettled.

"This is it," Lane said.

"Heads or tails?"

"You're the guest, you choose."

"Heads."

John flipped a coin in the center of the table. "Heads it is. I deal first. Big blind is one hundred, little blind fifty."

Lane nodded and watched the guy shuffle the cards. They'd mutually agreed on arbitrary values for the stacks of red, blue, and yellow chips, with both of them having the same number of each. There were going to be no buy-ins—which meant when you were out of chips or couldn't make blind, you were done.

Lane put in a red chip as big blind, John a blue, and then John was dealing them two cards each. There would be a round of betting based on what they had in their hands, and then the dealer would "burn" a card by putting it aside and lay the next card face-up. More betting. Another "burn" and face-up card. More betting, et cetera, until there was a line-up of five cards that each of them was free to use to complete sequences with the help of whatever they personally had and kept private.

High card beat fruit salad if nobody had anything. Two pair beat one pair. Three of a kind beat two pair. A flush, which was five cards of one suit, beat a straight, which was five cards in numerical order, regardless of suit. A full house, which was three of a kind and two of a kind, beat a flush. And a straight flush, which was five cards in order of the same suit, beat four of a kind, which beat a full house.

A royal flush, which was ace, king, queen, jack, and ten, all of one suit, beat everything.

And probably signified that Miss Aurora did in fact have a direct line to God.

Assuming Lane held those cards and not Lenghe.

If John pulled something like that? Well, then his wife was back in Kansas was praying harder than Miss Aurora was here in Kentucky.

Lane picked up his first hand. Six of diamonds. Two of clubs.

In short . . . nothing.

Not even a card high enough to get excited about.

The flop, which was what the first three face-up cards were called, was his only hope.

Across the way, John was studying his pair, his eyebrows together, his heavy shoulders curled in like he was getting ready for a tackle. He chewed on his lip a little. Rubbed the bottom of his nose. Shifted in his chair.

He was more juiced than nervous, though: With so much playing time ahead of them, no pot developed yet, and five cards yet to come, it was too soon on a lot of fronts for the guy to be exhibiting anxiety.

Lane, on the other hand, was utterly calm, more interested in what was happening in his opponent's chair than even his own cards.

The key was remembering the ticks and twitches of his opponent. Some of them would fall by the wayside as playing wore on and they got into a groove. One or two the guy would keep, though—or fight not to show.

Or maybe something else would be revealed.

But as Lane had learned long ago, there were three things that mattered at the table even more than how much money you or your opponent had at your disposal: the math of the cards in play, which going mano a mano was going to be hard to apply with any specificity because there were no other players making bets; the cards you had and those on the flop; and your opponent's facial and bodily reactions around their betting patterns.

John might well have been feeling lucky.

They'd have to see if it was enough.

. . .

A mere ten minutes after Ryan Berkley dropped Gin back at her Rolls behind his store, she pulled the convertible into its bay in the garage and checked her watch.

Perfect timing. Nine-thirty.

Richard had told her he had a very important business meeting that was going to go late, and that meant she was home before he knew anything.

Proceeding around to the front of the house, she passed by the windows of the old game room that wasn't used very much. Through the half-pulled drapes, she saw her brother and an older, gray-haired man she didn't recognize at the poker table, pairs of cards in their hands, stacks of multi-colored chips on the green felt beside them.

There was a gallery of people lined up watching them, and everyone was so serious. Her brother seemed to have more chips than the other guy, but then . . . no, it looked like Lane's opponent won that one, the man flashing his cards and then dragging the pile in the center toward himself.

Gin continued on, going around to the grand entrance and looking up to the second floor.

No light on in Amelia's room.

Entering the mansion, Gin went into the parlor and sat on the sofa that allowed her to see out into the foyer through the archway.

She waited.

And waited.

And waited some more.

The sounds of the poker game bubbled through Easterly's silent rooms. There were occasional shouts, a cheer, a curse. Laughter that sounded strange, although only because it seemed like a while since there had been any in the house.

Dimly, she wondered who Lane was playing.

She would not go down there, however . . . she had to be here.

Amelia finally came through the door after God only knew how long. The girl was in blue jeans, pencil ones yet again, and a blousy Stella

McCartney top that had blocks of color all over the front and groups of hashtags in the back.

As she crossed the black-and-white marble floor, heading for the stairs, Gin called out, "A moment, if you don't mind."

Amelia froze with one flat on the lowest step. "What?'

"I've been waiting for you. Please come in here."

"I'm going to bed—"

"I spoke to your proctor."

That got the girl's attention and she turned. "What?"

"Your proctor, Ms. Antler."

"Okay, that's my dorm parent, Ms. Antle. A proctor is a senior who's like a residential adviser. Which you would know if you'd ever been to my school."

"Why did you lie about getting kicked out?" Gin put up a hand and idly noted that the fake diamond was looking good. "And I'm not confronting you about it. I'm certain you had your reasons, and I'm curious what they are."

Amelia marched into the parlor, clearly ready to fight. "I'm not going back there."

"That wasn't the question I asked."

"I don't owe you any explanation for anything."

"True." This seemed to surprise the girl. "But I would like to know why—"

"Fine." Amelia crossed her arms over her chest and kicked up her chin. "No one called me to let me know Grandfather died. I read about it on the Internet and had to get myself home—and I'm not going back to school. I refuse to. I figured if I told you I quit, you'd make me go back, but if you thought I was kicked out, you'd let me stay."

"Are you unhappy at Hotchkiss?"

Amelia frowned. "No."

"Is there something wrong with the academics? The dorms? Another classmate?"

"No."

"Is there another school you'd like to be at?"

"Yes."

"And which school is that—"

"What's wrong with you?" Amelia demanded—and not in a hostile way. More like she was wondering who had kidnapped her actual mother and replaced her with this facsimile. "What's going on?"

Gin held the girl's eyes even though it was hard. "I have not been a mother to you. And I'm sorry about that. I'm very . . . sorry about that. I was so young when I had you, and although you have been doing your job of growing up . . . I can't say the same has been true for myself with respect to maturation. And honestly, when the dorm parent called me, my first thought was to go get Lane and have him deal with you. But the thing is this . . . my father is dead. My mother might as well be. Edward's gone for all intents and purposes. Lane is busy trying to do right by all of us. And Miss Aurora isn't feeling . . . well, anyway, at the end of the day, you and I have each other, and that's it. There isn't anyone else to turn to."

"What about your new husband?" Amelia said bitterly. "What about him?"

"He's my problem, not yours. In fact, he's the best example of everything that I've always done wrong, and I need to deal with him."

Gin looked around at the familiar, elegant room and then refocused. "We *literally* have no one but each other. And you can hate me all you want—I deserve it. I'll take it. I won't question it, and I won't get angry in return. That emotion, though . . . however justifiable it is . . . won't change the fact that if you don't want to be at Hotchkiss, you and I are the only ones who can address that. And if you change your mind and want to stay there? You and I will need to get you back to campus. And if you want to drop out . . . well, I'm not going to let you do that. Because whether or not you respect me, you're a minor and I'm your mother in the eyes of the law if in no other. And you're going to at least get your high school degree. After that? In two more years? I have no right over your life except that which you freely grant me."

Amelia blinked a couple of times.

And it was funny; she seemed to grow younger before Gin's eyes, even as nothing particularly changed about her, the largely intangible regression the result of some feelings or thoughts or . . . Gin didn't know what.

"Talk to me," Gin said after a moment. "Tell me what you're thinking."

"I'm afraid if I'm up there . . ." The girl looked away. "I'm afraid if I stay up there everyone will disappear here and I'll have nowhere to go. I mean, I know about the money stuff. Will Easterly even stay ours? What about the company? Like, is the power going to be cut off here?"

"Honestly? I don't know. And I hate that I can't give you an answer. But I promise you it's going to be all right for you."

"How?"

Gin reached into her purse and took out the safe-deposit key. "I'm going to give this to you right now. You won't be able to get into the box as long as I'm alive, and if I die, you need to go to your Uncle Lane and tell him that I gave this to you. He's the executor of the will I signed this afternoon. This key goes to a box down at the PNC branch by Taylor's Drugstore. I'm not going to tell you what's in there, and as I said, you won't be able to access it until I'm gone. But what's inside will keep you safe regardless of what happens here."

When Amelia didn't come over, Gin held it out farther. "Take it. Put it wherever you want, but don't lose it. Go on."

Amelia approached cautiously, and as she came over, Gin found herself blinking back tears. In all her negligence and selfishness, she had missed the suffering she had caused this innocent child—and the wariness being shown now was such a painful reckoning that Gin could not breathe.

"I'm sorry," Gin rasped as the key changed hands. "I can't apologize enough, and I won't blame you if you never let me in. But let's . . . for the next two years, let's try and do right for you. Now tell me, what school do you want to go to?"

Amelia stared at the key for the longest time. "Charlemont Country Day. Field is there. I know a lot of the kids. I like it there."

"Okay. So here's what I'd like to suggest. I think your Uncle Lane plans on burying Grandfather tomorrow or the day after. Your dorm parent said you can take your exams here or back at school. What do you want to do?"

"Umm . . ."

"If you decide you want to take them at school, I'll drive you up after the funeral, or we can fly. If you want to stay home and do them here, I'll get your things and bring them back myself."

Amelia rolled her eyes. "You would have no idea how to get my stuff organized."

"Boxes and bags. How hard can it be?"

"You'd do that? You'd go allllll the way to Connecticut and get my stuff?"

"Yes."

"With Uncle Lane, of course—"

"No, I would do it alone. I can figure it out. So what do you want to do?"

Amelia went across and sat on the other sofa. As she tucked her legs up under herself, she kept looking at the key. "What's in the safe-deposit box?"

"I'm not going to tell you. You'll find out when you're supposed to."

"I think I want to go up and take my exams there. It'll be easier. And I can say good-bye to people in less of a rush."

"Okay. Then we'll depart together after the funeral. How long do you think the tests will take?"

"Oh, God, like ten days."

"All right. I'll come back here and then make another trip up to get you and your things. After that, we'll get you registered at Charlemont Country Day for the fall semester."

Amelia's eyes were narrowed when she finally looked up again. "What's the catch?"

"There isn't one. There's no catch at all. And I have no expectations for our relationship, either. Other than making sure you stay in school."

The girl took a deep breath . . . and tucked the little odd key into her jeans pocket. "Okay. All right. That's . . . our plan."

Gin closed her eyes in relief . . . as down the hall, a bunch of hollering rolled out from the game room.

"Good," she whispered to her daughter. "This is good."

FIFTY-ONE

*I*t was the most expensive game of seesaw Lane had ever been
associated with.

And John was a hell of a poker player, amazingly composed, especially as he settled in. He was smart, decisive, never lost his temper—and
one hundred percent a rule abider.

Gave you a good idea of why he was so successful at his business.

In the end, after hours of playing, they were neck and neck. Lane was
making no mistakes, but neither was John. There had been straights and
flushes, a three of a kind, two pairs, full houses . . . the tide rolling in one
direction before self-correcting and changing course.

Over in the line-up of witnesses, Lizzie was clearly exhausted. And
Miss Aurora was even holding on to Lizzie's forearm as things appeared
like they were going to go on forever.

But the end did come—and seemingly from out of nowhere.

"My deal," the Grain God said as he gathered the cards from his
latest winning hand. "You ready for me?"

"Always."

John dealt the cards, and Lane looked at what he got.

He had . . . the two of hearts. And . . . the ace of spades.

Okay, so maybe he was working a flush here. At the very least, he had a high card.

He put in his big blind. John did the same with the little blind. And then there was a knock from John. Lane held tight and knocked as well.

First of the flop was a ten of diamonds.

Second of the flop was the eight of diamonds.

Fuck.

Then the ace of diamonds landed—which was good news. Kind of.

And yup, John liked that card, too, or at least seemed to, going by his nod. "Okay. I'm going to . . ."

Lane's heart started beating. And he knew it before the guy even said the words.

"I'm going all in."

So he had a flush. Which beat a pair of aces every day of the week and twice on Sunday. Also beat three of a kind. Lane's only chance was a full house.

As the people in the room gasped, Lane was dimly aware of Gin and Amelia coming in and finding seats. They both seemed surprised as there was some whispering as people brought them up to speed—and then the two of them looked downright shocked as they clearly got the full story.

"I'll see you," Lane said as he pushed his chips forward. "Let's get the turn and the river and let God decide."

"Amen to that."

John put his two cards down, and yup, his king and two of diamonds were a powerful twosome. In response, Lane shared his ace and two of diamonds.

"Not bad," John murmured.

"That's 'cuz you're winning," Lane said with a wink.

Next card up was . . .

An ace of clubs.

"Oh, lookey-lookey." John sat back, bracing the hand that wasn't holding the deck on the table. "That's a big one."

"Depending on what the last one is, yessir."

Lane was aware of his heart beginning to skip behind his sternum. There was no reason to hide any reaction on his part because the bets were in and the outcome predetermined at this point: there would be a card burned, and then whatever was up next was going to be the decider. End of story, no need to try and poker face this one.

And yet he didn't want to let anything out, not the dread nor the excitement, superstition locking him in place as if his emotions might tip luck in a bad way for him.

Glancing over at Lizzie, he found that she was focused on him, not the cards—like maybe she'd been waiting for him to look her way. And when she mouthed, *I love you*, all he could do was smile at her and marvel that for a man who had grown up with great wealth . . . that woman he had picked was one who reminded him over and over again that money didn't matter. Possessions weren't the thing. The car you drove and the house you lived in and the clothes you wore . . . were nothing but vocabulary. They weren't the true communication that mattered, they weren't the connections that were important.

He thought of that moment when he'd fallen off the bridge. Funny, he'd been braced for the hard impact of the water below, tucking into himself to withstand, to survive, the hit that he'd been convinced would kill him.

In reality, the fall was what was dangerous, though. Not the river.

The river had saved him.

I love you, too, he mouthed back.

And then he heard himself say, "Next one?"

The Grain God burned a card . . .

Everyone gasped.

The ace of hearts.

"Sonofa . . ." Lenghe didn't finish the curse, though, as was his way.

And Lane? He looked at Miss Aurora. The woman wasn't focused on the game. Her eyes were closed and her head was back and her lips were moving.

And later, much later . . . that was the image that would come back to him, both her hands gripping Lizzie's, her whole body locked in a strained rope of devotion and prayer, her belief in her God and Savior so strong, Lane could have sworn that yes, she was capable of calling a miracle right down from heaven.

He glanced over at the Rembrandt. The fact that Jesus Christ seemed to be staring at his momma felt right. "Guess you're staying in the family," he murmured to the painting.

The cheer that erupted was loud as it echoed around, and Lenghe was a total gentleman about it all, coming over not for a handshake, but for a hard embrace. And then Lane was vaguely conscious of Mack and Jeff rushing to him and shaking him until his teeth rattled, and Lizzie jumping up and down, and even Gin and Amelia getting into the buzz.

Lenghe was obviously a little shaken. Then again, when you suddenly owed someone over fifty million dollars? Your world went a little wonky.

Lane knew that one firsthand.

"You know," Lenghe said as Lane came back over, "if I hadn't seen it myself . . ."

"Me, too."

"And you know something, you're a good boy. You're a fighter and you're gonna make it. You're going to do just fine, son."

As Lenghe smiled up at him with such honest regard, Lane didn't really know how to handle it.

"Get some champagne," the Grain God announced to the crowd. "You Bradfords have something to celebrate!"

As another round of cheering let out, the man shook his head. "I, on the other hand, need to go make a really tough phone call. Man, I'm going to be sleeping on the couch for . . . months after this."

Lane laughed, and then Lizzie was in his arms, and they were kissing.

"I'm calling Monteverdi right now," Lane said. "Then we're going to have some champagne."

She leaned her body in to his. "And then . . . ?"

"I'm going to start feeling really, really tired—and I'm going to have to go to bed," he said as he kissed her deep. "With the love of my life."

"I can't wait," she whispered against his mouth.

FIFTY-TWO

*T*he next morning, Lane took John Lenghe back to the airport in the Porsche before breakfast. As he slowed down at the check-in and waved at the guard, Lenghe looked over.

"You know, that was a helluva game."

Lane hit the gas again and took them past the concierge building. "It was. It truly was."

"I still can't believe it. Well, that's the way Lady Luck went, and there's no arguing with it."

Slowing down again, Lane proceeded through the open gate in the chain link fence and then idled over to Lenghe's jet, which was gassed up and waiting. "Frankly, I'm still not over it. I didn't sleep at all afterward."

"Me, neither, just for a different reason." Lenghe laughed. "But at least the wife is still speaking to me. She ain't pleased, but she loves me more than she should."

Lane stopped the sports car a couple of yards from the set of metal stairs that extended out of the jet like a shiny tongue. "She really going to make you sleep on the sofa?"

"Nah." Lenghe got out and reached for his small suitcase in the nonexistent backseat. "Truth is, her feet get cold and she needs me around so she has something to warm them against."

Lane engaged the emergency brake and got out, too. As Lenghe came around to the front grille, Lane said, "I'm never going to forget this."

Lenghe clapped a meaty hand on Lane's shoulder. "I meant what I said last night, son. You're going to do well. I'm not saying it's not going to be a struggle, but you're going to right your ship. I'm proud of you."

Lane closed his eyes. "Do you have any idea . . ." He cleared his throat and laughed awkwardly. "You know, I would have loved to have had my father say that to me just once."

Lenghe laughed, but his version of the sound was natural and relaxed. "Why do you think I'm bothering to tell you? Just because he didn't speak the words doesn't mean they aren't true."

With a final clap on Lane's shoulder, Lenghe turned away. "I'll see you soon, son. You can always call me—"

"Wait," Lane called out. "I have something for you. You know, to remind you of the game."

Lenghe pivoted back around with a laugh. "If it's those four aces for framing? You can keep 'em."

Lane smiled and ducked back under the dash on the driver's side. "No, those puppies are mine."

As the Porsche's hood popped, Lane went over, lifted the panel and exposed a brown-wrapped square that was about three feet long and two and a half feet wide. The thing had barely fit inside.

With a grunt, he lifted the package out. "Here."

John put down his case. "What is this—"

But the man knew the minute the painting changed hands.

Before Lenghe could say anything, Lane put his palm out. "Take it home to your wife. Let her hang it wherever she wants, and every time you look at it, remember . . . you're a father figure to a guy who's wanted one all his life, okay? And before you remind me that you lost, let's just look at it like you bought your wife a great present for a very fair price—and you and I got to play one helluva game of cards."

Lenghe held the thing for the longest time. Then he cleared his throat. "Well. Now."

"The documentation's in there. On the back side of the painting. Not the front."

Lenghe cleared his throat again and looked off into the distance. After a moment, he said, "Did your father tell you?"

"About what? And before you answer, he and I didn't talk about much."

"My, ah . . . my wife and I never could have children, you know." More with the throat clearing. "So. There you go."

Guess it was kind of perfect, Lane decided. A man who had no sons being a father to a guy with no parents.

Without conscious thought, Lane went in for the clinch, holding those strong shoulders.

When he stepped back, John Lenghe's face was florid with emotion, so red it was like he'd gotten a sunburn mowing those acres of his.

"You're going to come out West and stay with us in Kansas," John announced. "With that nice girl of yours. The wife's gonna wanna thank you in person, and she does that stuff with food. So come hungry."

"You got it."

With a final handshake, the Grain God tucked his Rembrandt under one arm and picked up his suitcase with his free hand. Then he walked up the stairs and disappeared into his plane.

Lane leaned back against the Porsche and saw through the oval windows as the guy sat down and put his cell phone to his ear.

And then, with a final wave and a big fat smile that suggested "the wife" was over the moon, the jet was taxiing out . . . and taking off.

Just as the early sunlight winked off its fuselage, and Lane started thinking about his father's impending funeral that afternoon, his phone rang. He answered without looking. "Hello?"

"Lane, it's Mitch Ramsey. Get out to the Red & Black. They're going to arrest your brother for the murder. Hurry—*hurry!*"

. . .

*L*izzie was heading back down to the kitchen with her work clothes on as she heard the purr of Lane's Porsche disappear down the hill. What a night. What a miracle.

And what a nice thing Lane had decided to do.

She had found the roll of brown paper and had helped him carefully remove the painting from the wall and get it covered safely. Then they'd had the fun of seeing whether or not it fit in the Porsche's extremely limited truck space under the front hood. In the end, though, just as with the card game, luck had been on their side—and she could only imagine how pleased the man was going to be to bring the masterpiece home to his wife.

God, she wanted to meet Mrs. Lenghe at some point, she really did. Dollars to doughnuts, as the saying went, the woman was going to be as down to earth and kind as that billionaire was.

And now, it was time to get back to work.

The plan for the morning, after she ate whatever ambrosia Miss Aurora was serving, was for her to go for a check-the-grounds tour and try to find something to mow: Making neat on a John Deere outside in the fresh air just seemed like her idea of heaven.

After all, the interment of William Baldwine was scheduled for that afternoon, and watching Lane put his father to rest was not going to be easy.

Pushing her way into the kitchen, she said, "Miss Aurora, what's cooking—"

Except the woman wasn't at the stove. And there was no coffee brewing. No fruit out. No sweet smell of cinnamon bread.

"Miss Aurora?"

Lizzie went in further, checking the mudroom and the pantry. Even poking her head out the back door to see if the red Mercedes Lane had given the woman was still there—and it was.

It had been a late night, true, and their out-of-town guest had also left early, but there were still people in the house to feed, and even if the woman had worked the Fourth of July until one a.m., she was always on breakfast—besides, it was pushing eight a.m.

That was almost the middle of the day for the woman.

Going over to Miss Aurora's private quarters, Lizzie knocked. "You in there, Miss Aurora?"

When there was no answer, fear curled a fist in her gut.

Knocking louder, she said, "Miss Aurora . . . ? Miss Aurora, if you don't answer, I'm coming in."

Lizzie gave every opportunity for there to be a reply, and when none came, she turned the knob and pushed. "Hello?"

Taking a couple of steps inside, she saw nothing out of place. Nothing that was—

"Miss Aurora!"

Running into the bedroom, she crouched down by the woman, who was sprawled on the floor as if she had fainted.

"Miss Aurora!"

FIFTY-THREE

*L*ane made it to the Red & Black in record time, and as he skid-ded to a halt next to the three police cars parked in front of the caretaker's cottage, dust and gravel kicked up all over the place.

He didn't know whether or not he turned off the engine. And he didn't care.

Taking the shallow steps on a oner, he burst in on a tableau that was a never-forget: Three uniformed police officers were standing with their backs against the wall of trophies while Deputy Ramsey loomed in the opposite corner, looking like he wanted to hit someone.

And in the center of the room, Detective Merrimack was standing over Edward, who was sitting in that chair.

"—for the murder of William Baldwine. Anything you say can and will be used against you—"

"Edward!" Lane rushed forward, but Ramsey caught him and held him back. "Edward, what the hell is going on!"

Even though he knew. Goddamn it, he *knew*.

"You can stop with the Miranda rights," Edward said impatiently. "I did it. I killed him. Take me down, book me, and don't bother getting me a defense attorney. I'm pleading guilty right now."

Annnnnnd that was how you turned the volume of the entire universe down: Lane literally went deaf as Merrimack said something further, and Edward replied, and there was more conversation—

A blond woman entered the cottage in the same way Lane had, in a panic.

But unlike him, no one had to drag her back. She stopped on her own and, after she got a gander at everyone, she crossed her arms over her chest and kept silent.

"Edward . . ." Lane was not consciously aware of speaking. "Edward, no."

"I'll tell you how I did it," his brother said as he looked over. "So you can have your peace about this. But after I'm finished speaking . . . Lane, you don't come to see me down there. You keep going about your life. You marry that good woman of yours. You take care of the family. You do *not* look back."

Merrimack opened his mouth, and Edward turned on the guy. "And you just shut up, okay. Get your pad out. Take notes. Or wait for me to do this again a hundred times down at the station, I don't care. But he deserves to hear the story."

Edward refocused on Lane. "I acted alone. They're going to try to say I had help. I didn't. You know what Father did to me. You know that he had me kidnapped and tortured." Edward indicated his body. "These scars . . . this pain . . . it's all because of him. He arranged for it all and then didn't pay the ransom so he'd look like the victim. I have hated him all my life . . . and then this happened and . . . let's just say I had a lot of time to think about ways to kill him as I lay in agony, unable to sleep or eat, because I'm ruined."

"Edward," Lane whispered.

"I snapped the night I killed him. I went to our house to confront him because I just couldn't take it anymore. I parked in the back and waited for him to come out of the business center from his having worked late as usual. I didn't think I was going to murder him at the time, but then, just as I was getting out of the truck, he lurched, fell down to the ground, and rolled over onto his back like something was wrong." Edward's face assumed a faraway expression. "I approached him and stood over him. I know the signs of a stroke, the symptoms, and he was having one. He was wincing and motioning to his head . . . and then his left side didn't seem to work, his arm and leg flopping as if he couldn't move them."

"The autopsy did show evidence of a stroke," the detective broke in. "Because of the brain tumor."

Edward nodded. "I watched him suffer. I don't have a cell phone, and I thought about going into the house and calling nine-one-one, but you know what? I decided not to. It was funny . . . the way he contorted up like he did?" Edward curled one of his hands into a claw. "It was like what I do. When I'm really hurting and the pain meds haven't kicked in yet . . . it felt good to see him like that. Fair. Right. And I can't tell you when exactly I came to the decision that I really was going to kill him—I guess when it became apparent he wasn't going to die right then and there."

Edward shrugged. "Anyway, I went over to the Red & Black truck I'd driven in—it's the one that's parked behind Barn B right now. The keys are in it, and I figure you boys in blue are going to want to take the thing with you. So . . . yes, I went over and backed the truck up. There's a winch attached to the outside of the cab. There was some rope, and I hog-tied him, attached the hook, and dragged him into the bed because I knew I wasn't going to be strong enough to lift him myself. Then I drove down to the shores of the Ohio. That was the hard part. I got him out of the truck, but pulling him along the ground? I hurt my ankle badly—to the point where a couple of days later, she"—Edward pointed to the blonde—"had to call Dr. Qalbi out to see about it."

Lane frowned as the blonde seemed to recoil, but then he refocused on his brother.

"But wait," Lane interjected. "He fell off the bridge."

"No," Merrimack said. "He didn't. Or at least, there is no footage indicating whether he did or he didn't. The security cameras that were supposed to be operational weren't on that night—part of a number of glitches the city has had since the thing newly opened. So we have no footage—and given the poor condition of the body, extended time in the river would account for the extent of the damage to the extremities and torso."

Edward nodded. "So I got him over to the edge of the water. We'd had so much rain, the current was strong. I found a big stick and started to push him in . . . but then I went back to the truck, got a hunting knife, and cut off his finger. I wanted the ring. He screamed when I did it, so he was clearly alive, but he could barely move so he couldn't fight me. Then one last shove with the stick and he was gone. I threw the knife in after him, kept hold of the finger, and drove back. I buried it underneath my mother's bedroom window because he had treated her with disrespect their entire marriage— he'd had at least one child out of wedlock that we know about, and he fucked your soon-to-be-ex-wife and got her pregnant! I just . . . so yes, I did that thing in the ivy bed, and then came back here. I live alone, so no one knew I'd even been gone, and no one knew I'd waited for him, either."

"But then the finger was found," Merrimack said.

"That was when I knew I had to do something. I came to the visitation hours and snuck away to the business center. I went to the security room, signed into the system, erased the footage from that night, and waited to see if you guys would figure it out."

"And we did." Merrimack looked around at the other officers and nodded. "We got you."

"So take me down and let's get this over with."

There was a lull, and Lane couldn't believe it, but he thought he heard his phone ringing out in the car—no, wait, it was in his pocket. He silenced the thing without looking at it.

"Come on," Edward said impatiently. "Let's go."

All at once, the officers got organized and Edward rose to his feet. Merrimack insisted on handcuffs, which was ridiculous, and then Edward was being led out the door.

But he stopped in front of Lane. "Let this be, Lane. Don't fight this. You know what he was like. He got what he deserved, and I don't regret it in the slightest. You need to take care of Gin, Amelia, Miss Aurora, and Mother, do you hear me? Don't let me down."

"Why did you have to do it?" Lane said hoarsely. "You didn't have—"

"I take care of my own. I always have. You know that about me. My life's over, you know that as well. I've got nothing left, and he was the one who took it all away. I love you, little brother. I always have and I always will."

And then they were leading Edward down the shallow steps, across the grass, over to one of the squad cars. He was helped into the rear, his balance bad with his hands behind his back, and Merrimack got behind the wheel and started the engine.

In the wake of the departure, Lane just stood there, staring at the dust that rose up in their wake.

As his phone began to ring again, he looked over at the blond woman. "What did you say your name was?"

Even though she hadn't spoken.

"Shelby Landis. I'm one of the hands here."

"Nice to meet you. I'm his brother Lane. I think I saw you here before?"

"Yes. You did."

He looked over at Ramsey. "What do we do now?"

The tall man ran a hand down his face. "That was a helluva confession, and it fits. The whole damn thing . . . makes sense. And all things considered? I think your brother's going to jail for the rest of his life."

Lane looked back out the open door.

When his phone started ringing a third time, he took it out and almost threw the fucking thing on the ground.

But then he saw who it was. "Lizzie, listen, I—"

The unmistakable sound of sirens was not all that muffled, and Lizzie had to speak up. "Miss Aurora's being taken to University Hospital downtown. I found her collapsed and barely breathing next to her bed about fifteen minutes ago. Oh, God, Lane, I don't think she's going to make it. You have to come to the ER. I'm in the ambulance with her now—where are you?"

He closed his eyes and felt that sensation of falling all over again. "I'll be right there."

FIFTY-FOUR

*E*asily the longest day of his life.

Then again, Lane thought, as he and Lizzie finally dragged themselves over to Easterly's kitchen door at around seven o'clock that evening, it wasn't often that his brother got arrested for murdering his father or his momma went into a coma.

And yes, once again, they'd had to enter the estate through the back way because there were too many news crews at the main entrance.

"I'm starving, but I don't want to eat," he said, even though complaining hardly seemed fair.

Lizzie had been through as much as he had. Even more so, considering she had been the one to find Miss Aurora.

"I'm exhausted," Lizzie said, "but I don't think I'm going to sleep much—"

As they walked into the kitchen, they both stopped.

A totally amazing smell was coming from the stove, and though it was unfamiliar, if Lane hadn't personally witnessed Miss Aurora lying unresponsive in an ICU bed, he might have thought she was up and about, back where she belonged.

But no. The person in front of the platters of food was . . .

"Jeff?" he said.

The guy wheeled around. "Oh, thank fuck. I didn't think you were going to make it in time."

"For what?" Lane took Lizzie's hand and realized, "Gin? Wait, are you cooking? Amelia? What's going on?"

Amelia spoke up. "It's *Seudah Shlishit.*"

"The third meal of the Sabbath," Jeff explained. "Which I've cooked even though it's Sunday, because I'm feeling religious and this is the way I'm choosing to express it. We're just about to sit down so nice timing."

"My roommate at Hotchkiss is Orthodox," Amelia explained. "So I've done this before."

"She's been a great help."

"And I'm learning," Gin said. "Slowly and surely. By the way, Jeff, I set the dining room table—"

"*You* set the table?" Lane blurted.

Okay, that was another shocker.

His sister shrugged like the idea an alien had taken over her body and mind wasn't actually that big a deal. "Like I said, I'm learning. Oh, Gary told me he was going to do one more sweep of the grounds for any more of those cameramen. I took the shotgun away from him. We already have one of us up on murder charges, let's not add to that." When everyone looked over at her, she rolled her eyes. "Come on, people, we better start the gallows humor now or this group is not going to make it—"

Maxwell walked in from the front of the house, some napkins in his hand. "Amen to that, sister. Amen to that."

Jeff started carrying in food. "Now, traditionally this is supposed to be a light meal, but we're bending the rules a little. No one's eaten anything all day, and let's face it, my mother isn't here—although she was willing to fly down. Which was kind of scary, actually . . ."

It turned out to be exactly what Lane needed.

As they all sat around the formal dining room table, which Gin had miraculously set to perfection, it was not Lane's tradition, either spiritually or familially speaking, but it was warm, and it was real: It was shelter that had no roof, and sustenance that had no weight, and air that didn't need lungs for the breathing.

And it was *exactly* what he needed. His heart was mangled, his spirit deflated, his optimism terminated. He had had that one cresting moment at the airport . . . and then once again, he was sunk beneath a crushing burden.

But as he looked around the table, as he reached out and took Lizzie's hand, as he saw his sister and her daughter actually speak without yelling at each other, as he stared at his old friend who was still by his side, and looked at his long-lost brother . . . he knew that he was going to eat this lovingly prepared Jewish food, and he was going to pass out upstairs with his woman . . .

And he was going to get up tomorrow . . .

And fight for his momma to live. And fight for his brother to get treated fairly in prison. And fight to keep the company going. And fight to keep the house and the land of his ancestors.

And fight for his family.

He was a warrior.

He had learned that the hard way.

He had *earned* that title the hard way.

As Lane accepted the loaf of bread and tore off a piece, he thought of Edward and had to grit his teeth not to tear up all over again. Edward, in making a final sacrifice that was too great to comprehend, too tragic to contemplate, too horrific to ignore, had actually paved the way for all this.

If William Baldwine had still been alive?

None of this would be happening.

It was hard not to be grateful. Even as this miracle had come at too high a price and with a compromise of morality that almost tarnished the love.

Almost.

At the end of the day, though, a cancer had been rid from the family, and yes, they were all better for it. But, God, the way it had happened.

Lane knew he, personally, was forever changed by all this but, ultimately, as difficult as it was, and was going to get, he was improved. No matter the ins and outs, and the drama and the pain, he knew he was better off as a man, a brother, a husband . . . and if God so provided, as a father to his and Lizzie's children if they were granted that gift.

The nature of the aging process was brutal, though, and yes, he felt like he had lost parts of himself along the way.

The angels had to have their share, however, as was their right and their due.

And at least those parts of his soul would be in good hands, forevermore.

Looking at his Lizzie, he waited to catch her eye. After he mouthed "I love you" to her . . . he started to eat.

With the rest of his family.

ACKNOWLEDGMENTS

There are far too many people to thank, as always, and that makes me a very lucky person. But I do want to extend my gratitude to Steven Axelrod, Kara Welsh, and Kerry Donovan, and also Craig Burke and Erin Galloway along with everyone else at New American Library. Further, I need to acknowledge my wonderful Team Waud, my immediate family, and my wonderful friends. And also Nomers, my WriterAssistant. Oh, and Go Cards!